Pearl Cove

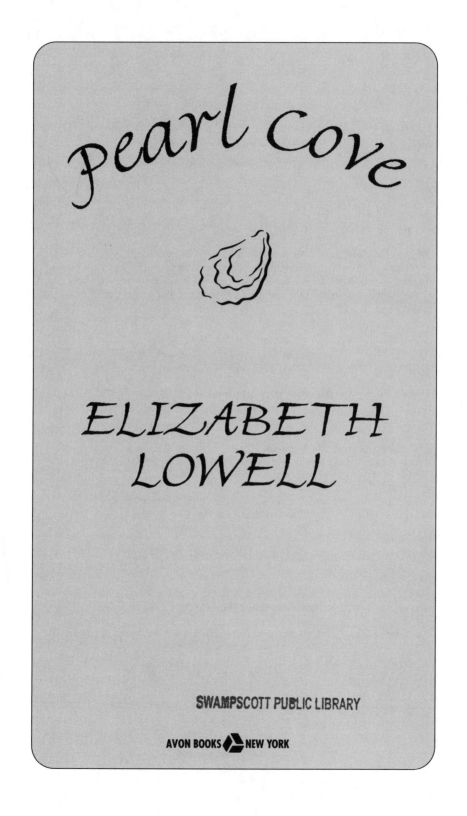

Pearl Cove

ELIZABETH LOWELL

AVON BOOKS ◆ NEW YORK

This is a work of fiction. Names, characters, places, and incidents either are the product of the author's imagination or are used fictitiously. Any resemblance to actual events, locales, organizations, or persons, living or dead, is entirely coincidental and beyond the intent of either the author or the publisher.

Avon Books, Inc.
1350 Avenue of the Americas
New York, New York 10019

Copyright © 1999 by Two of a Kind, Inc.
Interior design by Kellan Peck
ISBN: 0-380-97404-5

Library of Congress Cataloging in Publication Data:
Lowell, Elizabeth, 1944–
Pearl Cove / Elizabeth Lowell.
p.   cm.
I. Title.
PS3562.08847P43   1999   99-21639
813'.54—dc21   CIP

First Avon Books Printing: June 1999

AVON TRADEMARK REG. U.S. PAT. OFF. AND IN OTHER COUNTRIES, MARCA REGISTRADA,
HECHO EN U.S.A.

Printed in the U.S.A.

FIRST EDITION

QPM   10 9 8 7 6 5 4 3 2 1

www.avonbooks.com

For my sister
Susan Mills

always there for me
always a pleasure

Errors, like straws, upon the surface flow;
He who would search for pearls must dive below.

DRYDEN

Prologue

Those are pearls that were his eyes.
SHAKESPEARE

BROOME, AUSTRALIA
November

The sky was violent over the southern sea. There was no horizon, no center, no boundary to the onrushing storm. Heat lay over the land like an invisible, burning shadow of the sun.

Humidity stuck to the man's naked chest as he unlocked the door to the pearl sorting shed, entered, punched a code into the security panel, and relocked the steel door behind him. Even though he had just tossed out the sorters on the pretext of a random security check, it would quickly become murderously hot inside. In a metal-roofed building, air-conditioning didn't last long after the switch was thrown to Off, but that was the first thing he did after entering his security code.

He didn't enjoy sweating. It was simply that when the air-conditioning was running, he couldn't hear the sound of the door opening or footsteps sneaking up behind his back. So he flipped a different switch and settled for the small comfort of ceiling fans. Overhead, metal sliced like slow mixing blades through the sullen air. He could have opened steel-shuttered windows to let light and air flow through the shed, but he didn't. The last thing he wanted was to be spied on by any of the eager employees.

Everybody was dying to know where he hid his hoard of magnificent pearls.

Automatically he wiped sweat off his face and arms and hands with a cotton towel. Only then did he approach the sorting tables. Beneath full-spectrum lights, gleaming sea gems lay in tidy rows and inviting mounds. The pearls begged to be touched, stroked, savored, caressed.

Worshiped.

But not by sweaty hands. Pearls were the most delicate of all gems. The oils and acids of human sweat ate away the thin, smooth layers the captive oyster had so patiently, mindlessly, created to mask an internal wound. Careless handling dulled the fabled orient of pearls, dimmed the subtle ribbons of dawn dancing just beneath the satin surface, just out of reach. Like a dream. Like a miracle.

Just out of reach. Always.

But man reached. Always.

Four thousand years before Christ, man collected, treasured, revered, and wondered about the gleaming miracles from the sea. Born of thunder, conceived in mist, impregnated by moonlight, tears of the gods . . . all explanations for the pearl's origin shimmered with the transcendent mystery of the pearl itself.

Barbarous or civilized, savage or aesthetic, few cultures had been proof against the pearl's allure. It was the most perfect of all gems, for it needed no cutting, no polishing, nothing but man's recognition. And greed. Believed to embody both the carnal and the sublime, pearls adorned the altars of Venus and the reliquaries of saints. Dissolved in wine, pearls cured diseases of the flesh. Buried with the dead, pearls celebrated the wealth of the living. Worn by kings, priests, emperors, sultans, and sorcerers, pearls were a signal of absolute power.

Whoever owned pearls owned magic.

Magic lay all around him, trays and mounds of miracles gleaming, pregnant with all possibilities. The gap between modern rationality and Stone Age awe was as thin as a layer of nacre spread over the glowing ocean gems.

Surely in the midst of all these miracles, another one was possible. . . .

Slowly he went past the virginal white, shimmering gold, and peacock black of the South Sea pearls that keen-eyed sorters had been matching for size, color, and degrees of perfection. None of the pearls on the tables interested him. He had been the one to do the first sort, at harvest, when he creamed two years of work, taking only the best. When a man made offerings to gods or devils, only the best would do.

As he moved toward the twin steel doors that went from floor to ceiling at the end of the shed, the whisper of hard rubber gliding over the tile floor followed him wherever he went. He no more noticed it than a walking man would notice the soft sound of his shoes on a floor.

Though this second set of doors led nowhere, another combination lock guarded them; behind their steel lay a treasure like no other on earth. He released the lock and pushed the doors wide. The lockers inside the vault were deep, protecting tray after tray of pearls, the riches of other seasons, other harvests. Each locker had a hefty steel handle and a tumbler lock of the type popular on low-tech personal safes. The tropical climate was hell on fancy electronics. Behind the locker doors lay tray after tray of pearls, enough wealth to make a saint covetous.

Even though he knew he was alone, he couldn't help looking over his shoulder again. Again, nothing was there but the long shadow of his own suspicions. He turned back to the vault.

Now came the difficult part. Everybody knew that he could no longer come to his feet without help; therefore, he couldn't reach higher than a sitting man's head. No one would believe that he could get to the top lockers by himself.

When they searched in darkness for his cache of pearls, they always looked low, not high.

With a grim smile he wiped his hands again, reached up, and grabbed the highest handle he could. His legs might be pipestems, but his arms and shoulders were heavily muscled. He dragged himself up the ten-foot-high wall of lockers in a series of one-armed chin-ups. Once his hand slipped on its own sweat. Before he caught himself, the odd stainless steel ring he wore on his right index finger clanged and scraped steel. The fine scratches blended with many others, silent testimony to the number of times he had climbed this very personal mountain.

Breathing hard, he grabbed the handle of the top center locker with one hand and worked its combination with the other. A latch gave way somewhere at the back, toward the wall. *Click. Click.* Then, slowly, a final *click.*

Quickly he let himself down the cabinet until he could take the weight off his arms. Then he grabbed two handles at random and gave them simultaneous yanks.

The front of the bank of lockers shifted. Slowly, with elephantine grace, a thick steel panel swung open on concealed pivots. The lower lockers weren't quite as deep as they seemed from the front. Behind them, cut into the vault itself, lay a series of narrow, shallow, locked drawers. He fitted the spiky steel edges of his oyster ring into the holes at the front of the left-hand drawer, turned, and pulled gently.

The drawer slid out.

For the first time he hesitated. Looking quickly over his shoulder to assure himself that he was still alone, he pulled a long, flat jeweler's case from the drawer. With the reverence of a priest taking communion, he opened the case.

The Black Trinity glowed against velvet the color of dawn.

Though he had seen it many times, the unstrung triple necklace made his heart squeeze and his breathing quicken. Undrilled, untouched, as natural as the day he had eased them gently from their cool, slippery wombs, the pearls were like no other on earth.

Each pearl came from a genetically singular strain of Pearl Cove oysters. The result was a black pearl with unique orient, utterly distinct from the familiar Tahitian gems. The harvest from Pearl Cove's special oysters resembled a black opal as much as a pearl.

That difference alone would have made the triple necklace recklessly valuable. But the Black Trinity was value piled on value, rarity on rarity. Each strand was made up of a single size of pearl. The shortest necklace held twelve-millimeter pearls. The second, longer necklace, had fourteen-millimeter pearls. The third and longest strand was made up of incomparable sixteen-millimeter gems. Each pearl was round. None had any obvious imperfections. The color match between pearls in each strand was very, very close, which added immeasurably to the worth of the necklace as a whole.

Yet it wasn't wealth that had urged the man to claw hand over hand up a steel wall. Nor did beauty goad him. Like a medieval alchemist or a bloody penitent, he was driven by the hope of transcendence. A miracle. Something unspeakably valuable replacing the ordinary dross of life.

He opened drawer after drawer, scanned the oddly radiant black pearls within, compared them to the Black Trinity, and moved on to the next drawer and then the next and the next until none remained.

Frowning, he glanced from the shimmering Black Trinity to the last drawer of Pearl Cove's unique midnight-and-rainbow gems. No matter how closely he looked, none of the new harvest offered a better match or a more perfect pearl for the triple strands than any of the gems already chosen.

A chill went through him, a panic darker than the blackest pearl. The Black Trinity was complete.

But he was not.

No! It needs better eyes, that's all. Her eyes, damn her. Damn her to hell for her strong legs and unnatural eyes.

For seven years he had needed her almost as much as he hated her. He would have to take the new harvest to her and watch in seething impotence while her profane fingers handled his most sacred prayers.

Outside, the storm struck with the casual savagery of a beast whose womb had been a cauldron of warm water as big as an ocean. Lights dimmed and brightened, then dimmed again. It was early for the monsoon's battering storms, but the graveyard in Broome was filled with men who had drowned out of season in their quest for saltwater miracles.

Finally fuses melted and darkness fell inside the shed. Slowly the fans stopped turning. There was no lag time for the alarms on the front door. They died as the lights had, instantly.

The electronic lock on the outside door froze. Unless he used the interior manual release, no one could get into the shed.

Just before rain battered on the metal roof like buckshot, drowning out the ground-shaking thunder, he heard the sounds of metal gnawing at metal. He knew it was a chisel against the hinges of the front door; he knew, because it was what he would have done.

Someone was out there, gnawing away at the barriers to the Black Trinity.

Quickly, working by touch alone, he replaced the jeweler's case and closed up the trays of less worthy but still priceless rainbow pearls. In his haste, he wrenched one tray free of its tracks. Exquisite black rainbows flew in every direction. There was no time to go after them, for he would have to drag himself over the floor like a snake. Swearing viciously, he jammed the empty tray back in, swung the heavy panel into place, and closed up the highest tier of lockers, the ones he wasn't supposed to be able to reach.

He didn't close up the rest of the vault. Instead, he began flinging pearls from the lower locker trays onto the floor of the shed. When the middle tier of lockers was empty, he went on to the lowest tier. He emptied those trays, too, scattering pearls like ball bearings in all directions.

After he emptied the lockers, he left them open, like square tongues sticking out of the smooth face of the vault. Nor did he close the vault itself. He wanted whoever was hacking his way into the shed to believe that Pearl Cove's treasure lay undefended at his feet.

When he was finished, he grabbed a piece of discarded oyster shell, went into the deepest pool of darkness he could find, and worked on the shell until he had a pointed fragment as long as his hand. Then he did the only thing left for a man in a wheelchair to do.

He waited.

one

> Like grains of sand grinding inside the oyster,
> Like pearls being formed from the grains;
> Still waiting, though in unbearable patience
> Still believing, though almost in disbelief.
>
> ZHOU LIANGPEI

SEATTLE, WASHINGTON
November

Archer Donovan wasn't easily surprised. It was a hangover
from his previous line of work when surprised men often ended
up dead. Yet the unique, peacock-and-rainbow radiance of the
teardrop black pearl Teddy Yamagata was holding out did more
than surprise Archer. It shocked him. He hadn't seen a black
pearl with such color for seven years.

That particular pearl had been clutched in a dead man's
hand. Or nearly dead. Archer had fought his way through the
riot in time to pull his half brother out of the mess and get
him to a hospital in another, safer place.

Long ago, far away, in another country.

Thank God.

Archer had done everything in his power to bury that part
of his past. Years later he still was shoveling. But he had
learned the hard way that no matter how determined he was,

his previous undercover life had a nasty habit of popping up and casting shadows on his present civilian life. The proof of it was gleaming on the palm of Hawaii's foremost pearl collector and trader.

Teddy wasn't in Hawaii now. He had flown to Seattle with a case full of special pearls to show Archer. The extraordinary black pearl was one of them.

"Unusual color," Archer said neutrally.

Peering through the thick, blended lenses of his glasses, Teddy measured the expression of the man who was a sometime competitor in the pearl trade, an occasional client, and an invariably reliable appraiser. If Archer was particularly interested in the tear-shaped black pearl, nothing showed on his face. He could have been looking at a picture of Teddy's grandchildren.

"You must be a helluva poker player," Teddy said.

"Are we playing poker?"

"You've got your game face on. At least I think you do. Hard to tell under all that fur."

Absently Archer rubbed his hand against his cheek. He had given up shaving several months ago. He still wasn't quite certain why. One morning he just had picked up his razor, looked at it as though it was a remnant of the Spanish Inquisition, and dropped the blade in the trash. The fact that it was six years to the day since he had quit working for Uncle Sam might have had something to do with it. Whatever, his beard had grown into a short black continuation of his short black hair.

And if there were a few gray hairs among the black, tough. The dead didn't age. Only the living did.

"Must be hot when you go to Tahiti," Teddy said.

"It's always hot there."

"I meant the beard."

"I never sent it to Tahiti."

Teddy abandoned subtlety and tried the in-your-face approach. "What do you think of the pearl?"

"South Sea, maybe fourteen millimeters, teardrop, unblemished surface, fine orient."

"Fine?" Teddy hooted. His black eyes nearly vanished into

lines of laughter. "It's goddamn spectacular and you know it! It's like . . . like . . ."

"Molten rainbows under black ice."

Teddy's thin black eyebrows shot up and he pounced. "You *do* like it."

Archer shrugged. "I like a lot of pearls. It's a weakness of mine."

"In my dreams you're weak. What's the pearl worth?"

"Whatever you can get for it." Archer's cool, gray-green glance stopped Teddy's immediate protest. "What do you really want to know?"

"What the damn thing's worth," he said, exasperated. "You're the best, most honest judge of pearls that I know."

"Where did you get it?"

"From a man who got it from a woman who got it from a man in Kowloon, who supposedly got it from someone in Tahiti. I've looked for that man for six months." Teddy shook his head emphatically. "He's not there. But if you buy the pearl, I'll give you the names."

"Are there more?"

"I was hoping you could tell me."

"I'll bet you were."

Archer looked at the stainless steel space-age clock his father had brought back from Germany and placed in the front room of the series of suites that were the Donovan family residence in downtown Seattle.

Two o'clock in Seattle. Wednesday afternoon. Autumn closing in on winter.

Where the black pearl had come from, it was early morning. Thursday. Spring closing in on summer.

What went wrong, Len? Archer asked silently. *Why, after seven years, are you selling your unique Pearl Cove gems?*

He looked at the radiant black gem, but it had no answers for him except the one he already knew—seven years ago, his half brother, Len McGarry, had mixed the undercover life with one too many shady deals. It had nearly killed him. It had certainly maimed him.

Archer was one of three people on earth who knew that Len had discovered the secret of how to culture extraordinary black pearls from Australia's South Sea oysters. But Len had refused to sell even one of the thousands upon thousands of black gems Pearl Cove must have produced in seven years.

Yet here was one of those gems: beautiful black ghost of the past.

Part of Archer, the part that stubbornly refused to bow to bleak reality, whispered that maybe Teddy's pearl was a sign that something had gone right, not wrong. Maybe Len was finally healing in his mind, if not his body. Maybe he was beginning to understand that no matter how many glorious South Sea pearls he hoarded, he was still the same man.

Linked with the thought of Len came unwelcome memories of Hannah McGarry, Len's once innocent, always alluring wife. Alluring to Archer, at least. Too much so. He had seen her only twice in ten years. He could recall each moment with brutal clarity.

She was like the black pearl, unique. And like the pearl, she hadn't the least idea of her own beauty, her own worth.

When he had showed up with her broken, bleeding husband in his arms and told her she had two minutes to pack, she didn't faint or argue. She simply grabbed blankets, medicine, and her purse. It had taken less than ninety seconds. Their flight out of hell had taken a lot longer. He was bleeding over the controls of the small plane he flew and seeing double from the concussion he got fighting his way through to Len.

Hannah hadn't said a word the whole time. She sat in the copilot seat and mopped blood out of his eyes, ignoring the blood that welled from her lower lip where she had bitten through skin to keep from screaming her own fear.

Automatically Archer shoved Hannah McGarry from his mind. He wasn't the kind to yearn for what he would never have. Hannah was married. For Archer, marriage—family—was one of the few things left in the modern world that had meaning. Old-fashioned of him, even mulish, but there it was. The twenty-first century was big enough to have room for everyone, even unfashionable throwbacks.

"So you don't think this is a Tahitian pearl?" Archer asked almost idly.

"What makes you say that?"

"You're asking questions in Seattle, not Tahiti. Either you ran into a dead end there, or you already know where the pearl came from and want to know if I know, too."

Teddy sighed. "If I knew where it came from and how to get more, I wouldn't be wasting time talking to you. I'm here because I'm tired of banging my head into walls. As for Tahiti, none of the suppliers and farmers I've talked with admit to seeing this pearl or one like it before. Ever. And it's not the type of gem a man would forget."

Unique, fascinating, never the same twice. Like Hannah McGarry. The thought came and went from Archer's mind with the quickness of the colors sliding just beneath the surface of Teddy's amazing black pearl.

"What are you asking for it?" Archer said, surprising both of them.

"What'll you give me?"

"Not as much as you want. You can't match the pearl's color, so the usual kinds of jewelry won't work. Maybe one of my sisters—Faith, most likely—could design an interesting setting for it as a brooch or a pendant, but then the artistry and workmanship rather than the pearl would become the true value. I'd be paying Faith, not you."

Teddy didn't argue the point. Though cultured by man, pearls weren't mechanically produced: it still took an oyster to make a pearl. Being a natural, organic product, relatively few pearls matched well enough to be combined in jewelry. Lining up pearls for a necklace was like lining up a thousand redheads to match nineteen. Once you got past the superficial similarity, the differences came screaming through.

"It could be a ring," Teddy said after a moment.

"It could, but not many people would spend thousands of dollars on a ring whose irreplaceable centerpiece could be ruined by a careless motion of a woman's hand. Or a man's."

The Hawaiian grumbled.

"Your pearl is big," Archer continued, "but not nearly big enough to interest high-end collectors or museums. They already have black pearls twice that size. *Round* black pearls."

"But the luster," Teddy protested. "And have you ever seen a pearl with half the color? It's like a black opal!"

Archer had seen one pearl that put Teddy's in the shade, but all he said was, "Yes, the orient is lovely. To someone who collects unusual pearls—"

"Like you," Teddy cut in.

"—this one would be worth perhaps three thousand American."

"Three? Try twenty!"

"You try it. I wouldn't pay more than five."

"Bad joke. It's worth at least fifteen and you know it."

Archer looked at his watch. He had a few hours before he had to help his sister Faith close her little shop in Pioneer Square. Though it didn't look like much from the outside, his sister's store carried a multimillion-dollar inventory of international gems and one-of-a-kind jewelry. Normally one of the guards from Donovan International escorted Faith and her stock to and from the Donovan vaults. Today it was Archer's job. In the past her useless live-in boyfriend, Tony, had guarded her, but to the great relief of the Donovans, Faith recently had rubbed the fairy dust out of her eyes and dumped him.

"What else do you have to show me?" Archer asked.

Teddy looked at the tall American, measured the steely green of his eyes, and put the pearl back into its small velvet box with a sigh. "I keep hoping for a free lunch."

Archer smiled. "It's part of your charm, Teddy. That and your relative honesty."

"Relative!" he yelped. "Relative to what?"

"If I knew the answer, you would be, in effect, completely honest."

The short, thickset man frowned. It wasn't the first time he hadn't been able to follow the other man's baroque mental twists.

"Hungry?" Archer asked.

Teddy smacked his stomach with a broad palm. Though hefty, his belly was more muscle than flab. "I'm always hungry."

"Bring your case to the kitchen. I'll scrape up a sandwich for you. While you eat, I'll look over the rest of the goods."

"Thanks."

"No problem. I'll take lunch off the price of whatever I buy. *If* I buy."

Laughing, Teddy followed Archer through the living room into the condo's large, lemon-yellow kitchen. A view of Seattle's muscular waterfront filled the corner windows of the room. Out in Elliot Bay, huge container ships from all over the Pacific Rim waited at anchor for their turn to be unloaded by cranes that crouched like immense orange insects along the docks. Ferries churned among the mammoth commercial ships, leaving white wakes. Herded by a brisk southeast wind, low clouds trailed veils of rain over the dark gray water.

"Nice view," Teddy said. "But don't you get tired of the rain?"

"Think of it as a moat protecting the city."

Teddy blinked, opened his mouth, and closed it again. Then he shook his head and laughed.

Archer waited until Teddy was wedged into the breakfast alcove with a beer in one hand and a thick cheese sandwich in the other before he angled the conversation back to the pearl dealer's recent travels.

Because somewhere along the way, Teddy had found one of Len's black beauties.

"Did Sam Chang have any special pearls to sell?" Archer asked.

Teddy made a muffled sound, swallowed, and said, "That son of a bitch. Owns two thirds of the Tahitian pearl farms and acts like he's selling off his first son at every harvest. Prices the goods like it, too."

"Golden Rule," Archer said, popping the cap off one of the local microbrews. "He has the gold, he makes the rules."

"Japan is going to bust his ass. He's crowding their sales monopoly too hard. Great cheese—what is it?"

"Gorgonzola with pesto. What about the smaller pearl farmers?"

Eyebrows raised, Teddy looked at the sandwich. "Nothing's changed. They still line up like milk cows."

"Surprising. Aussies are even more contrary than Americans."

"Oh, there are some holdouts," Teddy said, waving the ragged remnant of his sandwich. "But they're being squeezed down to the bone by the consortium. Their shelling licenses are being cut, they're not given the results of the latest government research until long after their competitors have it, their pearls end up in the doggy lots at the auctions. That sort of thing."

"Who's their leader?" Archer asked, though he knew very well. Just as he knew more than Teddy did about who was doing what and with which and to whom in the international pearl trade. But a man who stopped asking questions never learned anything new.

"Len McGarry," Teddy said, downing the last bite of his sandwich. "I gotta tell you, that is one mean bastard. Whatever put him in that wheelchair might have cut off his balls, but it didn't soften him up one bit."

For an instant Archer saw again the terrible image of Len covered in blood, broken, lying utterly motionless in the aisle of the small plane. The memory was one that could still awaken Archer from a deep sleep, covered in sweat and hearing whimpers of pain echoing in the silence. Some of the sounds were his own.

"Rumor is that he's sitting on at least five years worth of the best pearls," Teddy said. "His own, some other farms, and maybe a few of the Tahitian farmers on the sly."

Archer had heard about that, too. He believed at least part of it. For the past five years, Pearl Cove's balance sheets had been sinking like a stone in still water. Either the oysters had stopped producing pearls reliably or Len was holding out. As half owner, Archer should have cared. He didn't. Whatever Len squeezed out of the ruins of his dreams was fine with his silent partner. Money was the least of Archer's problems with his half brother.

"You always hear rumors about under-the-table alliances among pearl farmers," Archer said.

"Sometimes they're true."

"Sometimes." He opened Teddy's case and gave the contents a quick, comprehensive glance. No more Pearl Cove gems. But he wouldn't let Teddy go away empty-handed. The Hawaiian was too good a source of gossip. Even outright misinformation—intelligently processed—could be as revealing as a sworn version of the truth.

In any event, Archer planned on buying that black rainbow pearl. He just didn't plan on making Teddy rich in the process.

"You've been busy," Archer said.

The interest in his voice was a balm to Teddy's pearl-trading soul. He smiled and leaned forward over the table. "So, what do you see that you like?"

"That orange pearl. The one from a Vietnamese conch."

Teddy looked surprised, then laughed ruefully. "Damn. I was hoping to stump you on that one, too."

"Too?"

"Like the black pearl."

Archer looked at the pearl, night-dark, yet brooding in all the colors of the rainbow. "Nothing is like that pearl."

It was the type of gem men killed for.

Two

BROOME, AUSTRALIA
November

Sunlight hammered down on the land. Even the Indian Ocean lay flattened beneath the weight of the summer sun. The water was a shimmering turquoise stillness unmarked by any wind, any breeze, any stirring of air. Nothing moved but sweat sliding over flesh in oily silence.

Hannah McGarry didn't notice the brutal heat or the slickness of sweat on her own skin or the weight of the Chinese child she held in her arms. *Len McGarry was dead. Victim of a cyclone.*

No one else from Pearl Cove had been killed, though a few other men had been hurt by flying debris and such. Qing Lu Yin had the worst of it: deep bruises, a nasty gash on his chin, a black eye. But he insisted on working anyway. So did the rest of the men. They knew that Pearl Cove was their living.

Despite the ruin of the rafts and sorting sheds, only a few

cottages had been damaged. No children had been so much as scratched. For that she was greatful.

Shifting the child's weight on her hip, she ignored the vague ache in her lungs and the lukewarm salt water leaking out of her short hair, residue of her most recent dive to the bottom of the shallow cove. Diving was hard work, but she loved it. Suspended in the shimmering, translucent water, she was free.

She wasn't diving now. She wasn't free. She was trapped in sunlight, struggling to keep her face from giving away her thoughts. She couldn't afford to show any fear, any anxiety, any of the violent emotions seething just beneath the fragile lid of her self-control.

"Sad-sad?" the four-year-old asked.

Terrified was the word that leaped into Hannah's mind, but she smiled down into the child's beautiful, innocent face as though nothing was wrong. "Just thinking, darling."

"Think-ing," he repeated carefully.

"Good," Hannah said automatically. Of the seven workers' children she gave English lessons to, Sun Hui was the quickest. "The storm damaged—hurt—many things."

Hui nodded solemnly.

From the direction of the workers' cottages came a spate of Chinese. Hui turned, looked, and said, "Ma-ma."

"Okay, darling." She kissed his golden cheek and was kissed in turn. Reluctantly she released his vital, eager weight. Of all the disappointments her marriage had brought, the lack of children was the most painful. "Off you go. Careful! There's a lot of debris—junk—left by the storm."

"Junk. Storm. Yes!"

Dark blue eyes narrowed, Hannah watched until Hui vanished into a cottage. Only then did she turn back and concentrate on the wreckage that had once been Pearl Cove. Broken things were hopeful; they could be fixed. There was a lot that needed fixing right here, right now.

A ruined dock jutted out from the sand like broken teeth. Rafts that had once supported thousands upon thousands of pearl oysters in various stages of growth lay washed up on distant beaches or sunk where no eye could see. Boats for harvesting and seeding sat on the watery bottom of the cove.

The damage wasn't limited to Pearl's Cove's floating equipment. Flung by a savage wind, the main sorting shed's door lay drunkenly alongside the path to the house. The metal roof gapped and curled around the edges. Wrenched, crumpled, useless, the windows' remaining steel shutters guarded a gutted building. The shed itself sagged where footings had been undermined by the furious waves.

Even Len's "cyclone-proof" pearl vault hadn't stood against the violence of the storm. The wind's greedy fists had battered the metal until something exploded, strewing pearls everywhere. And everywhere, someone had been there to scoop them up. Or maybe many hands had grabbed the iridescent wealth. Hannah didn't know. It was important that she not know. Or at least, not appear to know.

Len was dead. But it wasn't an accident.

Whoever had killed her husband could just as easily murder her. More easily, probably. Even in a wheelchair, Len would have been dangerous. He knew too many ways to kill. It was what he was best at. Destruction.

But that didn't mean he deserved to die.

Deserve.

Fair.

Hannah's mouth twisted in a bitter smile. She hadn't known that much of the missionary child still survived in her twenty-nine-year-old mind. The world was what it was. She was what she was: a woman who could die if she trusted the wrong person.

Or even if she didn't.

Fair had nothing to do with it. Survival was the only thing that mattered. To be or not to be wasn't the question for Hannah. How to keep on being was.

Len had played his power games with too many dangerous people. He had won millions of dollars. Then he had lost his life.

"Chérie?"

Coco's soft, husky voice slid through Hannah's concentration. As always, the beautiful Tahitian woman was just on the edges of whatever happened, watching and listening and waiting for whatever it was she waited for. Hannah didn't know.

She didn't care. Len valued Coco's eerie skill in seeding oysters. When it was Coco's delicate hands working on the oysters, the pea crab that lived within each shell survived. Without that pea crab, the oyster died.

"Yes?" Hannah said. She turned toward the sound, confident that none of her bleak reverie showed on her face. Living with Len had taught her how to hide everything, especially fear. It was a simple matter of survival. Not easy. Just brutally simple.

"You come inside, yes?" Coco said lazily. "You not born to stand under this sun at noon."

"Was anyone?"

"My mama is." Coco's smile flashed whiter than any pearl against the rich brown of her skin, legacy of her half-Polynesian mother. "My papa isn't. Sun finally burned him down." She stretched her hands toward the sun. "Sun won't hurt me. I am born for it. My half sister is same."

Hannah would have smiled at Coco's confidence, but she was afraid that her smiles had become more and more like Len's, a feral warning to the world to keep its distance. Not that she would, or could, hurt Colette Dupres of the smooth skin and cat-graceful body. Even Len in his blackest moods hadn't ruffled the Tahitian. She simply had laughed and walked away, giving him an eye-level view of the best ass in Western Australia.

"Ian come soon," Coco said, watching the other woman closely for a response at the mention of Ian Chang's name. There was none. She gestured to the dive fins, mask, and snorkel piled at Hannah's feet. "Shower and dress nice for him, yes? You look like a diver after twelve hours down."

"Only one in my case, and I wasn't really diving."

"Find anything?"

"What's to find?" Hannah answered, turning aside the question. "More wrack and ruin?"

"Is bad, but not as bad as it looks."

It's worse. But Hannah didn't say it aloud. She wanted to trust Coco, wanted to believe that her beautiful tan hands hadn't been among those scrambling after stolen pearls.

Hannah's mouth thinned into a savage smile when she listened to her own foolish thoughts. So much of the child still surviving. Still hoping. Still stupid.

It could be the death of her.

"Even if bad," Coco added with a casual, Gallic shrug, "Ian fix ever'thing for you."

"Why would he do that?"

Coco's laughter was as sexy as her voice. "Know why."

"He got over wanting me years ago."

"Small white child," Coco said, smiling and sounding much older than thirty-seven, "men never get over woman they no have. Now your husband dead. You no married."

"Ian is."

"What?"

"Married," Hannah said succinctly.

"His wife, she no care."

"I do. I was raised by Christian missionaries. Marriage matters."

"*Oui.* Len talk sometimes when he drink," Coco said, yawning and stretching to her full height, which put her almost at eye level with Hannah's five feet nine inches. "Your . . . How you say? honor?"

Hannah grimaced.

"*Oui,* honor," Coco said. "He smile at that. Sometime he even laugh."

"I know."

The thought of the innocent, sexually ripe teenager she had been no longer made Hannah wince with shame. She had wanted out of the rain forests of Brazil. She had gotten out. End of one life. Beginning of another. It hadn't been the life she expected. No surprise there; she had been painfully naive when she formed her expectations. Life went on anyway, and the living went on with it.

A boil of red dust from the road leading to Pearl Cove announced Ian Chang's arrival. The cyclone's twenty-three inches of rain had long since run back to the sea. Western Australia's relentless summer sun quickly sucked all moisture from the ground, leaving behind the paradox of red dust in a humid desert.

Chang's car vanished into the scrubby mangroves that lined the sparkling white sands of one of the tidal creeks. The creeks held fresh water during the monsoon and filled with salt water at every high tide year-round. Given the flatness of the land, the tidal creeks ran miles inland. So did salt water. Even without help from storms, Broome's tides went through a thirty-five-foot swing at their peak. It was great for feeding the oysters and hell on anything that tried to occupy the shoreline. Rock, mud, and sand were the rule. Only palm trees and the improbably hardy mangroves survived the tides of abuse.

And man, of course; that clever, adaptable, lethal primate.

Broome and its outlying areas were home to a racially varied population that was as tough as mangroves. They were survivors who relished their own survival. They were the gently crazed and the fully mad. Drunks and teetotalers, celibates and satyrs, saints and Satan worshipers. Broome was at peace only with extremes.

Chang fit right in. Extremely intelligent, extremely ambitious, extremely rich. His family was worth more than all but a few Third World nations. He walked up to Hannah with the confidence of a man who is respected by other men and sought by many women. He was wearing the Outback uniform—sunglasses, shorts, and sandals. Since the occasion wasn't formal, he hadn't bothered with a tank top.

"Hannah, darling, even in this sun you're too pale," Chang said.

He took her hands and leaned in to kiss her. She slipped through his grasp with the grace of long practice. It wasn't anything against Chang. In the past seven years, she had simply lost the habit of being touched. If she decided to get back in the habit again, it wouldn't be with a married man.

Because Hannah didn't want to see Chang—didn't want to see anyone, actually—she had to concentrate to smile politely. "G'day, Ian. There was no need for you to drive out from Broome in this heat. You could have called."

"The phone lines are still down."

"Next time use the cellular number. Or the radio. They're battery powered."

"I wanted to check on you," Chang said. "You lost more than power during that cyclone. You lost a husband and most of Pearl Cove."

Fear crawled beneath Hannah's skin, making her feel cold despite the burning sun. Chang didn't know the half of it. "I know what I lost."

"Are you grieving for the man or the pearl farm?"

Silently Hannah watched Chang with eyes so deep a blue they were like a twilight sea, dark and luminous at the same time. The contrast between her indigo eyes and her sun-streaked brown hair fascinated him, as did her slender, oddly voluptuous body. He wanted to believe she had worn the string bikini to entice him, but he knew better. Obviously she had been snorkeling. Probably she hadn't even remembered he was coming out to see her.

Irritation prickled over him like a rash. "Well?"

"Is that what you came all the way out here for?" Hannah asked in a neutral voice. "To find out if I cared more for Pearl Cove than for my husband?"

"Don't try to tell me that you and Len were close. I know better. Len was a snake. The only thing he was close to was his own skin, and he shed it once a year just to prove he could." Chang gave Coco a look. "Leave us."

Coco glanced at him. Then she turned away, moving slowly enough to let him know that she didn't jump for anyone, even one of the richest men in Australia.

"No," Hannah said.

Coco stopped.

"We were just going to the house for some tea," Hannah said to Chang. "You can join us."

"We need to talk privately."

"I have no secrets from Coco or anyone else."

"This is Chang family business."

Hannah's dark brown eyebrows lifted. She knew Chang well enough to understand that family business was entirely separate from whatever personal lusts he might have.

"All right," she said. "Coco, would you call and see if Smithe and Sons can expedite delivery of the building materials? Especially the spat collectors."

"They want money."

"They'll get it," Hannah said with a confidence that was utterly false. *The Black Trinity was gone.*

Chang started to object, but didn't. Hannah would know soon enough that rebuilding Pearl Cove was beyond her means. With Len dead, no one would lend her money. If someone tried to, the Aussies would step in. But the Australian government wouldn't take on the family of Chang. Not yet, anyway. Everyone was still pretending to be partners in the development of Pacific Rim assets.

Automatically Chang reached for Hannah's arm to escort her to the house. His irritation spiked when he realized that she was already walking away from him with the easy, lithe movements that never failed to arouse him.

Coco saw his expression, laughed, and asked in French. "Did you think it would be that easy?"

"Call Smithe." Chang spoke in French even though his voice was too low to carry as far as Hannah. "I'll own Pearl Cove before the bill comes due."

"The Aussies, they will not like that."

"They can get stuffed."

"Mmm, sounds like fun." She stretched again, arching her back and pressing her full breasts against the thin fabric of her bikini top. At the height of her stretch she knew she had Ian's full attention. Smiling, she let her fingertips trail lightly down his bare chest. "You going to get stuffed tonight?"

"No. You are."

"The usual time?"

"I've got a conference call with the States. We won't be done until midnight."

"You will be done two minutes after I put my face in your lap."

"Care to wager on that?"

Anticipation sent a faint curl of heat through Coco. Nothing turned her on like a sexual challenge. Men were usually too easy. One look at her ass and their palms sweated. "When does your call start?"

"Ten o'clock."

"I will be there at five after. What do I get when I win?"

"A black pearl."

"What do I get if I don't win?"

"Fucked."

Coco's teasing, confident laughter drifted up the sand path to the house.

Hearing the sexy, hot-woman sound, Hannah smiled. She often wished she could be more like Coco, utterly comfortable in her body, in her mind, in her sex. But she wasn't. She never had been. She doubted that she ever would be. Some parts of her missionary upbringing went straight to the bone.

Coco had been raised in a culture that was part expatriate French, part Polynesian, and one hundred percent sensual. Hannah's parents would have called Coco a slut. Hannah didn't. Coco was simply a physical female who ate when she was hungry, slept when she was tired, and had sex when she pleased with anyone she pleased. If Coco was also a ruthless tease, well, there weren't all that many saints in Western Australia.

When Hannah came to Chang's car, she didn't hesitate before walking on past it. Even in the unreasonable heat, she didn't mind the half-kilometer path from high tide line to the house. Not that she would set any speed records. She didn't want to. She just wanted to avoid being locked up by four walls. Since Len's death, she had become claustrophobic.

Locked in the shed. Waiting. Trapped.

The weight of the sunlight was almost welcome on her skin. It was hot, bright, burning; everything that death was not.

Chang caught up with Hannah halfway to the house, where the road cut across the path. Dust from the four-wheel-drive Mercedes settled over Hannah like a bad reputation.

"Get in, darling," Chang called through the open passenger window. "Much as I'd love to see your beautiful ass swing all the way to the house, I have appointments in Broome."

Instead of reaching for the door handle, she stood at the side of the road and watched him with remote indigo eyes. "Darling? Beautiful ass?" Her voice was neutral, as emotionless as her eyes. "You told me this was family business."

"You can let go of the nun act now. You're not a married woman anymore. Pleasure and business, the best of both worlds. You'll like it that way. I'll see to it."

The impatience and irritation in his voice angered Hannah, though it didn't show in her body, her eyes, her voice. "Business, Ian. That's all. Just business."

Chang said something rude in Chinese, then leaned over and pushed the passenger door open. "Get in, Sister McGarry."

"I'll get the leather wet."

"There's not enough cloth on your butt to make a difference."

After a long, level look, Hannah slid in and closed the car door.

"There, that didn't hurt, did it?" he asked curtly. "I won't jump you, if that's what you're afraid of."

"You're married." Hannah's voice was flat.

"My wife lives in Kuala Lumpur."

"I don't care if she lives on Jupiter. I'm not in the market for a married lover. Nothing personal, Ian. It's just the way I am. It won't change. I value your friendship, but not enough to have this conversation every time we talk. Change the subject."

"Bloody nun," Chang muttered under his breath.

"Yes."

Neither said another word until they were in the shade of the verandah. The storm had done little damage to the house: broken windows, ripped screens, one corner of the roof torn away, plants snapped off or whipped to rags by the wind. Small things, compared with death.

"Who replaced the windows?" Chang asked.

"Christian's brother-in-law is a glazier. Christian did all the screens. The verandah was a mess."

Chang's full mouth thinned. He didn't like the thought of the sexy, shrewd, young Aussie hanging around Pearl Cove, even if he was living with the type of blonde most men only dreamed of getting their hands on. "Why didn't you call me?" Chang asked. "I would have sent workmen over."

"Thanks, but Christian was here when the storm hit."

"I suppose he fixed the roof, too."

"Tom did. Since he stopped diving, he's made himself invaluable as a handyman."

Chang tried to imagine the bent old Japanese man scrambling up a ladder and nailing tin sheeting in place. He shook his head. "Nakamori is too old for that kind of work."

"He's only sixty." What Hannah didn't say was that Chang was fifty-three. And Len had been forty-five. Too young to die.

"A sixty-year-old former diver is an old man." Chang looked at his watch. "I have ten minutes. Fifteen at most."

"Tea? Beer? Water?"

"Nothing."

Hannah rinsed off her dive gear, dumped it in a basket on the verandah, and waved Chang toward the wicker chairs. She went to her favorite place, a hammock chair suspended from a bolt in the slanting roof. The airy netting of the sling let a breeze swirl around her with every gentle push of her foot against the wooden floor. The verandah's new screening shimmered and rippled in the sun, making the world beyond look dreamy, unreal.

"All right, Ian. What does the Chang family want from me?"

"We're willing to assume Pearl Cove's debts."

"Any particular reason?"

"The usual."

"Which is?"

"Business," Chang said curtly.

"I see. What do I get out of this business?"

"A partner who can rebuild Pearl Cove."

"Partner." Hannah toed the floor and swung gently. If Chang knew she had a partner already, he wasn't letting on. She wondered if that made him more or less likely to be Len's killer.

"I give you fifty percent of Pearl Cove and you assume all debts, is that it?" she asked.

"Seventy-five percent."

The hammock chair paused in its swing. "We give up seventy-five percent?"

"There's no 'we' about it. Len is dead. Pearl Cove is just you, Sister McGarry."

"I'll think about your family's offer."

"Don't think too long."

"Is there a time limit?"

Abruptly Chang stood up. "Mother of God, you can't be that naive!"

For a time there was only the soft squeak of the hammock chair against the ceiling bolt as Hannah swung back and forth, back and forth.

"I guess I am that naive," she said finally. "Explain it to me."

"Do you really think Len died because of that cyclone?"

Every muscle tensed. She wanted to get up, to scream, to run. Since it would be stupid to do any of those things, she did nothing at all.

"I could list Len's friends on one finger," Chang said bluntly. "I don't have enough hands to list his enemies. It's not only his charming personality I'm talking about. It's pearls and double crosses. He buggered one too many big players."

"How?"

"Don't waste my time. You're his wife."

"Yes. His *wife*. Not his business partner. I run the house, keep the payroll, collect rent from the workers who live on site, order equipment for the farming operations, and have the final say on color matching the harvest. That's it."

"What about the black pearls?"

"What about them? The 'big players' you mentioned know how to make silver-lipped oysters produce black-toned pearls or gold-toned or pink or all three in the same oyster. Members of the South Sea Consortium developed the technology. And they kept it to themselves. It has nothing to do with Pearl Cove."

"I'm not talking about the normal run of black pearls. I'm talking about the rainbows."

Stillness crept through Hannah's blood like ice forming on an autumn pond. Though no one was supposed to know about the extraordinary pearls, word had inevitably leaked out. Rumors thrived like termites in the emptiness of Western Australia. Yet no one had actually seen those special pearls, except Len and herself. And his killer. Len had died because he knew the secret of producing extraordinary black pearls. People assumed she knew the secret, too. But she didn't.

Her husband had trusted no one. He always opened the "experimental" oysters himself. And he was careful to have ordinary oysters in among the special ones, just to have some pearly junk to show the curious. He never would have told her about the rainbows at all if he hadn't needed her hyperacute color perception to find the best matches among the iridescent, seductively colorful black gems.

Despite all Len's care, despite his paranoia, in the past few years, some of the special black pearls had been stolen and found their way to the marketplace. Yet Len wouldn't share the secret of producing the black rainbows.

He had been killed for it. As soon as the murderer discovered that she knew nothing about producing them, her life would be worthless. She would be all that stood between the killer and ownership of Pearl Cove, home of the oysters that produced fabulous, unique black pearls.

"Rainbows?" she asked through stiff lips. "We've had some lovely peacock blue—"

"No," Chang cut in. "They're not the same."

"If your family is buying in to Pearl Cove for these so-called rainbows, you'll be disappointed. I don't have any for you." That, at least, was the truth. Most of the special pearls had been destroyed as unworthy. The rest had been kept in the vault.

And the vault lay like a cracked steel egg inside the ruined shed.

Chang watched her with clear black eyes and formidable intelligence. "Think about our offer."

"You don't believe me."

"I believe that the cyclone season is coming."

"Is that a threat?"

"It's a fact. Sell Pearl Cove to the Changs. We're big enough to weather the coming storm. You aren't. Don't follow Len into the grave."

For a breath Hannah wished she owned all of Pearl Cove and could turn it over to the Changs. Then she would run. The Stone Age villages in the rain forests of Brazil had never looked so good to her. So safe.

But that was cowardice whispering seductively in her ear. She couldn't sell, had no money to run, and was damned if she would be again what she had been at nineteen—a runaway stranded in a strange city with night coming on and no assets to sell but her newly unvirginal body.

"I can't sell Pearl Cove," she said evenly.

"You mean you won't."

"No. I mean I can't."

"Why?"

"Half of it belongs to Archer Donovan."

"What?" Chang demanded, too shocked to hide it.

"Archer—Mr. Donovan—was Len's silent partner."

"For how long?"

"Seven years."

"Bloody hell. No wonder Len is dead. He finally buggered the wrong man."

"What are you saying?"

Chang laughed curtly. "They don't come any more ruthless than Archer Donovan."

"I didn't think the Chang family would back up for anyone."

"A man who can tangle with the Red Phoenix Triad and come out on top deserves respect. Archer Donovan has it." Chang turned away. "I've got to make a call. This changes everything."

The screen door swung shut behind Chang. Moments later, red dust boiled, then settled in the wake of his car.

For a long time Hannah sat on the verandah in the hammock chair, unmoving but for the occasional prod of one foot against the floor. Back and forth. Back and forth.

She didn't doubt Chang's appraisal of Archer Donovan; she had been in a position to see just how ruthless he could be. But not with Len. Never with Len. Despite ample provocation, Archer had never acted against Len McGarry. Quite the opposite. He had saved Len's life, paid for his rehabilitation, and made him a partner in Pearl Cove. Then he did what Len had demanded: he got the hell out of Len's life and stayed out.

She didn't know what the bond was between the two men. She only knew that it existed. Perhaps it extended beyond the grave. Perhaps Archer Donovan would care enough to do what no one else would—find Len's murderer.

If revenge wasn't enough to move Archer, there was always money. Even the most ruthless man might be persuaded to search for Pearl Cove's vanished treasure if he was promised half of something that was worth three million dollars wholesale.

The Black Trinity.

Three

*W*ith reflexes left over from the years he couldn't leave behind, Archer came from deep sleep to full wakefulness. Lean fingers snatched the phone from its cradle before he even looked at the clock.

Two A.M.

Visions of all that could have gone wrong with the family sleeted through his brain. Faith was first in his mind. The man she had just broken up with had knocked around his first wife and at least one of his girlfriends. The Donovan brothers had told Tony what to expect if he laid a hand on Faith, but Tony's memory wasn't reliable when he started drinking.

Archer looked at the display on the phone that gave incoming numbers. It was blank. That left out the family, and let in Uncle Sam.

Shit.

"What," he said. It was a statement, not a question.

"Is this Archer Donovan?"

"Yes."

"This is—"

"Hannah McGarry," he interrupted, wondering if he was still asleep. That smoky voice of hers had haunted too many of his dreams.

"How did you know?"

"I have a good memory. What's wrong, Hannah?"

"Len's dead."

Archer didn't try to sort out the boil of emotions those two words brought him: disbelief, relief, guilt, anger, sadness for all that might have been. He didn't say anything about his own feelings. The tension in Hannah's voice told him that she had more to say, none of it good.

"When?" he asked.

"Just . . . days."

Old habits were hard to break. Especially when he could all but taste the fear in Hannah's desperately level voice. The quality of the connection told him that she was using a cellular phone, open to anyone who cared enough to eavesdrop. So he didn't ask her where or how or why Len had died.

"I'm sorry," Archer said softly. "That's not adequate, but in the face of death, no words are. I'll be there no later than noon tomorrow, your time, earlier if at all possible."

Hannah's fingers loosened a bit on the thin, vaguely oblong plastic body of the cellular phone. All she could think of was that Archer understood everything she hadn't said. "I . . . thank you."

Archer knew he shouldn't ask, but the words were out before he could stop them. "Are you all right?"

She shivered, remembering Len's stripped, battered body and sightless eyes, and Chang's warning: *Cyclone season is coming. Don't follow Len into the grave.*

"Hannah?"

"Hurry, Archer. I'm getting . . . sleepy."

The quality of the sound changed, telling him that she had disconnected. He didn't bother cursing the empty line. If someone had a lock on her cellular, she was safer not talking at all.

He punched in one of Donovan International's unlisted numbers, the one Donovan executives called when things started to go from sugar to shit. No matter what time it was, someone would answer this number.

"This is Archer Donovan," he said. "Put me through to someone who can get me to Broome, Australia, no later than noon tomorrow. Shave every minute you can."

"Noon U.S or Australian time?" asked a woman's voice.

"Australian."

"Where are you now?"

"Seattle."

"Thank you. One moment, please."

It was more than one moment, but at least he was spared any canned music. He waited quietly, not showing the urgency riding him or the adrenaline licking in his blood, called by the fear that even Hannah's smoky voice couldn't conceal. He simply held the phone and made a list of things that had to be done before he landed in Australia. Some could be handled from the plane. The important things couldn't.

Kyle Donovan was in for a rude awakening.

"Thank you for waiting," said a man's voice. "None of the Donovan International aircraft can get you from Seattle to Australia in your time frame. We have chartered a jet from Boeing Field to Hawaii. A company jet will meet you there. Our files show that your Australian visa is up-to-date."

Archer's passport was never mentioned. People in Donovan International would sooner take up nude ice-climbing than let their passport lapse.

"Are you at the Donovan family suite in Seattle?" the man asked.

"Yes."

"A car will pick you up in half an hour. A rental car has been reserved in Broome. Will there be anything else?"

"Not at the moment. Good work."

"That's what you pay me for, mate," the man said, allowing his native Australia to color his voice for the first time.

Archer hit the disconnect and headed for the door that led to the family areas of the Donovan suites. Kyle and Lianne were in town to celebrate Donald Donovan's birthday. Jake and Honor were due in this afternoon. Archer regretted missing his sister and her husband, but not as much as he regretted having to tell The Donovan that Len McGarry was dead. *Happy Birthday, Dad. And by the way, the son who hated you is dead.*

Grim-faced, Archer started knocking on the door to Kyle's suite. Moments later, it opened. The person who opened the door wasn't Kyle, who wouldn't get out of bed before nine o'clock for anything but a dawn salmon-fishing raid. His wife, however, didn't need a kick-start to get going. Mussed with sleep, wearing a navy man's T-shirt that came to her knees, six months pregnant with twins, looking like a grumpy Munchkin, Lianne stood in the open door. One look at Archer's face had her wide-awake.

"What's wrong?" she asked quickly. "Is—"

"It's nothing you need to worry about," he cut in quickly. "Everyone you love is just fine. Get your husband's lazy ass out of bed. I need him."

"It's four-fifteen!"

"I know what time it is. Get Kyle or let me do it." With an effort, Archer gentled his voice. "It's all right, Lianne. I just need his computer magic right now. I'll be in the kitchen making coffee. Or do you want me to wrestle him out of bed for you?"

"Any bed-wrestling Kyle does will be with me. Make enough coffee for three."

The door closed before Archer could thank his sister-in-law, or even pat the taut mound of her stomach where another generation of Donovans was doing lazy backflips.

By the time Archer had coffee and Canadian bacon made, Kyle wandered into the kitchen wearing navy shorts and a hairy chest. Archer handed his youngest brother a mug of well-creamed coffee and turned back to the pancakes that were just beginning to firm on the griddle. With Kyle, there was no point in trying to talk until the first cup of coffee—and sometimes the second or third—had burned through the morning fog that passed for his brain.

Lianne was more alert. She was still wearing Kyle's T-shirt, the one that celebrated the hazards of men who went fly-fishing naked. She pushed long, black hair out of her face, poured her own coffee, sugared it, and scooted in next to Kyle in the breakfast nook without saying a word to her husband. Early in their relationship, she had decided that there was only one thing Kyle was good for in the first few minutes after waking up, and she didn't need a witness for that. Sipping coffee, she looked at Seattle's glittering lights spread against the utter black of a November morning.

Kyle took his second cup without cream, drank it down, shuddered, and held out his cup for more without looking at Archer. Halfway into the third cup, he raked his fingers through his blond hair, straightened, and clicked into focus.

"Where's the fire?" he asked irritably.

"If there was a fire, you'd be toast by now," Archer said.

"Yeahyeahyeah. This better be good."

"A half brother you never knew just died." As Archer spoke, he flipped pancakes onto a warm plate.

Kyle's green-and-gold eyes narrowed to slits. It took him less than two heartbeats to realize that his brother was serious. "Jesus."

"I doubt that religion had anything to do with it. Len McGarry wasn't a churchgoing man." Archer put the pancake plate in the oven and poured more batter onto the griddle.

"Half brother. Holy shit." Kyle looked into his coffee and took a slow, deep breath. "Dad or Mom?"

"Dad. Before he met Mom."

"How do you know?"

"Long story. I don't have time for it and it doesn't matter now. Just don't say anything to The Donovan or Susa," Archer added, using his parents' nicknames. "I'll tell Dad when I know more. He can tell Mom whatever he wants."

"Was The Donovan married before?" Lianne asked.

"No."

She winced. "I hope being raised a bastard was easier on your half brother than it was on me."

"Len wouldn't know easy if it walked up and tied a knot in his pecker," Archer said, putting a plate of pancakes and bacon in front of his sister-in-law. "Eat. You're too thin to be carrying that big mutt's children."

"Thin?" she asked, outraged. "Archer, I could barely get into the breakfast nook!"

"We run to twins, sugar," he said, smiling at her. It was one of his rare smiles, the kind that made people want to get closer rather than to look for the nearest exit.

"Who are you calling sugar?" Kyle asked, rubbing Lianne's belly and eyeing her plate of food at the same time.

"Not you, fish breath. There's nothing sweet about you in the morning." Archer pulled a plate out of the oven and shoved food under Kyle's nose. "Feed your nerd cells. I need them."

"Talk to me." Kyle picked up the syrup and began pouring generously. "I can listen and eat at the same time."

"About two this morning, Len's widow, Hannah McGarry, called and told me he was dead. Her voice told me a lot more. She's scared down to the soles of her elegant feet."

Something in Archer's tone made Kyle stop shoveling in food and look at his brother. *Elegant feet?*

Archer didn't notice his brother's glance. His eyes were narrowed, more gray than green, with not a hint of the blue that sunlight and sky could bring out. He was focused on a past only he could see.

"She was calling on an open line," he said, "so I didn't ask questions and she didn't offer answers. I told her I'd be in Broome by noon tomorrow."

"Broome? In Australia?" Lianne asked.

Archer nodded.

"Pearls," Kyle said instantly.

Archer nodded again. "Len and I are—were—partners in a pearl-culturing venture. Pearl Cove Farms."

"I didn't know that," Kyle said.

Archer didn't answer. There was a lot about his past that his family didn't know. He planned on keeping it that way. If he could have wiped some of the memories from his own brain, he would have. But he couldn't, so he lived with them and did whatever it took to make sure that no one else had to.

"Normal spelling on Pearl Cove Farms?" Kyle asked, already organizing the computer search in his mind.

"Yes."

"Is it a registered business?"

"Licensed, taxed to the max, and all but one form duly filed," Archer said.

"Which one?"

"The partnership agreement."

"Why?"

"Len's choice. I didn't care. But the partnership will stand up in court, here or there, if that's what you're worried about."

"What do you want from me?"

"Everything you can get electronically on Hannah McGarry."

Archer slid into the opposite side of the breakfast nook. His knees bumped Kyle's. Archer was older by four years and a timeless amount of experience, but Kyle was every bit as large physically.

"What about Len?" Kyle asked. "You want me to go after him while I'm at it?"

"Sure, get what you can. Pearl Cove, too."

"You got me up before dawn to do what any hacker could do?"

"Yes."

"Why?"

"Because you aren't any hacker. You're my brother and Len's half brother. You won't leave any tracks, you'll keep your mouth shut about what you find, and you won't be tempted by bribes or blackmail. And if it gets really nasty . . ." Archer shrugged. Kyle, for all his blond good looks, could fight for his life. And had.

"Why don't I like the sound of that last bit?" Lianne asked beneath her breath.

"Because you know how nasty family fights can be," Archer said.

"Family?" Kyle asked.

"Len," Archer said curtly. "He's dead, but whatever snowball he pushed off the mountain is still rolling. And I have a nasty feeling that his widow is standing right in the center of the avalanche chute."

"So you're flying halfway around the world to stand there with her?"

"I'd do the same for Lianne."

Kyle blinked, then sighed. "Sorry. I'm just not used to having another brother, much less a sister-in-law to worry about. You're right. She's family." He gave Lianne a sideways glance. "Will the Tang family give me a rain check on—"

"No," Archer said instantly. "You're staying here."

"Wrong. I'm going to Australia. As you pointed out, Len was my brother, too."

"You didn't know him. I did."

Lianne's tilted, cognac eyes went from brother to brother. Though one man was dark and one was light, both were stubborn to the core.

"If you go, I go," she said to Kyle.

"No," the brothers said as one.

"Why is it," she asked sweetly, "that every time you two agree on something, I'm the loser? Like hell I'm staying here."

"You're both staying here," Archer said. "If I need anyone, you'll be the first to know."

"Damn it—" Kyle began.

"No." Archer's voice was cold and deadly. Like his eyes. It was the very part of himself he had tried to keep from his family. "Don't push me on this, Kyle. Neither one of us will like what happens. But it will happen just the same."

Beneath the table Lianne's small hand settled on her husband's thigh and squeezed with surprising strength, silently asking him to use his head on this one instead of his balls. Slowly the tension seeped out of Kyle's clenched muscles.

"We'll try it your way first," Kyle said finally. "If that doesn't work—"

"You'll do whatever it takes," Archer finished, hearing his own words from the past, seeing some of his own dark shadows in his brother's eyes. Silently Archer held his hand across the table, but he held it as someone looking for contact rather than a handshake.

Kyle took his brother's hand. They both gripped hard.

"Thank you," Archer said simply. He slid out of the booth, turned to Lianne, and brushed his fingertips over her cheek. "You're good for him, little sister. For us."

Kyle watched his brother walk out of the warm yellow light of the kitchen. When he turned to Lianne, he was surprised to find tears in her eyes.

"Hey, it's all right," he said. "Donovans fight and then it's over. Not like the Tang family, where no one fights and everything festers."

Lianne thought of her father's family and shook her head.

The difference between Chinese and American families wasn't what was bothering her. "It's not that."

"Then what?"

"Archer's eyes," she whispered. "What happened before I knew him?"

"He worked for Uncle Sam in a lot of ugly places. Then he quit. Now he's Donovan International's troubleshooter."

"I think . . ." Her voice died.

Kyle bent down, licked a faint shadow of syrup from one corner of her mouth, and settled his big hand over their children. "What do you think, sweetheart?"

"I think Archer has shot enough trouble in his life."

Hannah was staring at the computer when she heard a car pull up in front of the house. Fear and anger battled within her. Anger because it might be Ian Chang, back to press his offer of business partnership and a much more intimate relationship. Fear because she didn't know who was out there.

With tight motions she closed Pearl Cove's accounts and shut down the computer. It was pointless to stare at the screen any more. She was so tired she was seeing double. She hadn't slept in days, hadn't even dozed in the fifteen long hours since she had talked to Archer Donovan. She kept hearing his voice, seeing the past. . . .

She pushed away from the computer and headed for the living room. Before she got there, a knock came from the front door. She froze. She knew the verandah floor near the front door creaked, yet she hadn't heard footsteps. When she looked through one of the gauzy front curtains, she saw the silhouette of a man. A big one. Her heart squeezed in fear.

"Hannah? It's Archer Donovan."

Relief was so great it left her momentarily lightheaded. Until that instant she hadn't realized just how much she was running on sheer nerve. Four days, five. She didn't know how long it had been. She only knew that finally she could look at another human being and trust him not to kill her.

And if Archer's voice also made her cold with memories of the most brutal hours of her life, she would just have to get over it. Swallowing hard, she gathered herself.

"Just a moment," Hannah said.

Her voice was too hoarse, too strained, but it was the best she could do. She felt like a doll stuffed with sand, and now the sand was running out at every seam. She fumbled with the bolt as she opened the door.

And then she could only stare. She had forgotten Archer's dark male beauty, the intelligence in his light, changeable eyes, his height and physical power, the sensual promise of his mouth. Her husband had been a wild blond Viking. Archer was a dark angel who made a woman want . . . everything.

Unnerved, she stepped back and said, "Come in."

When Archer walked forward, other memories knifed through her. The controlled way he moved, the bleak clarity of his gray eyes beneath the sharp black arch of his eyebrows, the quickness of his hands as he shut the door—all of it reminded her too vividly of the night seven years ago when Len had almost died.

And now Len was dead anyway.

Slowly the rest of Archer's appearance registered on Hannah; the fine lines at the corner of his eyes, the shadows brought by lack of sleep, the worn jeans, the slate-gray dress shirt with the cuffs rolled to his elbows, and what looked like coffee splattered across the front and forgotten.

"You must be exhausted," she said. "Coffee? A drink? Food?"

Archer raked his fingers through his hair in a remembered gesture that sent odd echoes through Hannah. The beard was new, as were the scattered strands of brilliant silver that gleamed in his thick black hair. But his mouth was the same, thin and contained, always on guard against . . . everything.

"Coffee sounds good," he said. "Food, too. Whatever you would normally have now."

"But it's not lunchtime where you came from." She tried to think across time zones and the international date line. She couldn't. "Is it?"

White teeth gleamed in something less than a smile. "No, but don't worry. I've learned to live wherever and whenever I am. Lunch is fine."

Hannah walked to the kitchen, aware every step of the way

that a man was following her. A big, quiet-moving man with quick hands and cold eyes. She wondered if Archer ever really smiled. If he did, it never had happened when she was watching. But then, she had seen him only twice before. He hadn't smiled the first time, at her wedding—she wouldn't have, either, if she had known what lay ahead. Nor had he smiled when he had arrived at her door covered in blood and ordered her to pack.

No smiles, yet he had been everything she needed to survive.

Her hands fumbled as she reached into the refrigerator for fresh fruit and cheese and the roast beef Christian Flynn had brought to her. Every movement was an effort. She was caught between the nightmare of the past and the one in the present. But she wasn't terrified anymore. Smiling or not, Archer was here, bringing with him a sense of safety that was dizzying.

A chunk of cheddar banged against one of the metal racks and thumped to the floor. Silently she cursed her clumsiness and reached for the cheese.

It wasn't there. Archer had already picked it up. He had moved so quickly, so silently, she hadn't even suspected he was that close to her. Her fingers shook as she teetered on the edge of her strength and self-control.

"Unless you're planning to eat off the floor," he said, scooping up everything she held in her hands, "I'd better take this stuff."

"I'm all right. Just—"

"Swaying like a tree in a hurricane," he cut in impatiently. "Sit down before you fall down. When was the last time you ate?"

She closed her eyes, then opened them instantly. She didn't like the images that lurked in darkness, waiting to be played on the back of her eyelids: Len's body, wasted legs trailing in the water like ribbons, one fist clenched around the murder weapon.

Yet nobody had mentioned murder. Not when his body was found. Not afterward. They talked about the storm and freak accidents, and they watched her when they thought she wouldn't notice.

Hannah made a low sound and swayed again. Without warning, strong hands closed over her arms, supporting her before she even knew she was falling.

"When was the last time you slept?" Archer asked, remembering what she had said on the phone. *I'm getting . . . sleepy.*

"I'm fine," she said, her jaw clenched.

"And I'm the Easter Bunny. Sit down."

The back of a chair pushed against Hannah's knees. Hard. They buckled and she sat. Archer shifted his hands and held her upright until he was sure that she could do the job herself. Only then did he turn back to the food he had put on the table when she went into her exhausted trance.

"When was the last time you slept?" he asked. "And I mean real sleep, not catnaps."

"I haven't slept, really slept, since I saw the broken oyster shell buried in Len's chest."

Four

 rcher's hands hesitated for an instant before he resumed
making lunch. He had wondered how Len died. Now he knew,
for all the good it would do Len or himself. He wanted to ask
more questions, to know the cause of the shattered darkness
in Hannah's eyes, but he knew better than to bring up the
subject. She was on the edge of falling apart. He needed her
strong.

"What do you usually drink with lunch?" he asked.

"Iced tea."

He went back to the refrigerator, bypassed the bottles of
beer, and grabbed a pitcher of tea. A few minutes of rummaging
in the cupboards produced glasses and plates. Silverware was
in a nearby drawer. Even the butter knives were lethally sharp.
Len's touch, no doubt. Years ago he had never been happy with
less than three weapons strapped to various parts of his body.
If that wasn't enough, he had always had a gift for turning
ordinary things into deadly tools.

Archer wondered if an oyster shell had been one of them.
He didn't ask. A sideways glance told him Hannah was in one

of her waking trances again, hanging on to consciousness by sheer force of will. She had had that same will when he met her ten years ago—a beautiful, innocent teenager determined to escape from a stifling existence of living, working, and sharing cooking pots with the monkey-eating Yanomami of Brazil.

The determination, the smoky-husky voice, and the indigo mystery of her eyes were the only links Archer could see between the teenager of his memories and the shocky, exhausted woman who was sitting at the table, swaying like grass in a long, slow wind.

Silently Archer sliced fruit, cheese, and beef that looked range fed rather than grain pampered. Without asking her preference in mustard, ketchup, chutney, and the like, he assembled sandwiches. As he put a plate in front of her, a corner of his mouth kicked up. Lately it seemed his mission in life was to feed siblings.

Not that he felt brotherly about Hannah McGarry. He never had. Not at first glance. Not now. It had been the final wedge driven between himself and the half brother he had admired and befriended before he discovered the deep fracture lines in Len's soul.

Archer had been a lot younger then, able to give trust and love without understanding the inevitable consequences if he chose wrong. His half brother had been a big part of the painful, inevitable, and nearly lethal experience called growing up.

"Start with this," Archer said, holding out a juicy, deep gold chunk of fresh pineapple to Hannah.

She jerked as something brushed her mouth. "What?"

He slid the piece of fruit along her lower lip as though he was feeding his niece. Automatically Hannah opened her mouth to catch a drop of juice. Before she realized what had happened, the fruit was on her tongue. Her salivary glands squeezed painfully in response to the tart-sweet taste.

"Chew," he said. "Even as sweet as pineapple is, it won't melt if all you do is suck on it."

She chewed. Gooseflesh rippled over her in pure pleasure at the taste.

"Cold?" Archer asked, looking at her tank top. Her nipples

had risen to press hard and tight against the thin cloth. He jerked his eyes back up to her face. "Hannah, are you cold?"

"No."

"You're shivering."

"It tasted like paradise."

Hannah's simple abandonment to her senses brought Archer's sexuality to full alert. Irritated at his unruly body, he sat and tucked his chair underneath the table so that he wouldn't shock her by his outright lust.

He wasn't surprised by the urgency of his body; he had always responded to her this way. But he was angry about it. He didn't want to need her this fast, this hard, this deep. Wanting like that made a man lose control. An out-of-control man was in trouble up to his stiff, stupid cock.

"Eat," Archer said. "We've got a lot of ground to cover. We can't do it in the shape you're in now."

The tone of his voice straightened Hannah's spine. She reached for her fork, only to send it sliding and clattering across the table when her fingers slipped.

He grabbed the wayward silverware. He didn't remember her as being clumsy. He remembered her as having an unconscious, bone-deep grace that made watching her entirely too hot an experience for his comfort.

"Sorry." Hannah drew a bracing breath. "I'm not usually so awkward."

"Your nerves are shot. Your body isn't any better off. You need food and sleep." Archer stabbed a piece of pineapple, slid it over her lower lip, and said, "Try again."

This time when Hannah shivered with pleasure, he kept his eyes on the food.

After a few minutes, she picked up her sandwich and began nibbling on it. When she reached for her glass of tea, he almost stopped her. He was pretty certain it would end up in her lap. Or his. That thought kept him from interfering. A lap full of ice water was exactly what he needed to get his mind off her nipples and quick tongue.

Cautiously Hannah lifted the glass with both hands. Her teeth clicked against the rim and tea sloshed over her hand.

With a quick motion of her head, she sucked liquid off her skin before any could drip onto the table.

Pure lust shot through Archer, increasing the force of his erection until he could count his heartbeats in his own dick. Disgusted with himself, irritated with her for no better reason than that she turned him on and never knew it, he ate his sandwich in savage silence.

The silence stretched even after he was finished eating. He stared through the kitchen window, across the sheltering verandah, out to the hammered-silver brilliance of the sea. He didn't look back at Hannah until his arousal had subsided to an aching memory.

She was watching him with eyes the color of twilight, blue and purple, bruised, edging into night.

"Thank you," she said. "You were right. I needed food. I just didn't think of it."

"Adrenaline."

Her glossy brown eyebrows lifted.

"It kills the appetite," Archer explained.

She looked at his plate. Nothing was left of the two sandwiches he had made for himself. Ditto for the fruit and cheese. He had eaten everything but the pineapple spines and the plate itself. She watched him slice more beef and cheese, slap mustard on bread, and throw in some mango chutney for good measure.

"Guess you're not on an adrenaline jag," she said.

"Guess not." He took a big bite out of the third sandwich. The bread was white, stale, and tasteless, but he didn't stop eating. He needed fuel. "You ready to talk about it?"

Hannah didn't want to. It showed in her face, in her eyes, a withdrawal like shutters closing and bolts slamming home against the coming storm. She hugged herself, running her hands restlessly up and down arms tanned golden by the sun.

"I don't know where to begin," she said finally.

"Who found Len?"

"I did. After the storm."

"Where?"

"At the beach."

"Was he still alive?"

"No. Dead. Very, very dead. Cold. Like an oyster."

"Was he stiff?"

Hannah bit down hard on her lip, forcing all blood from it, leaving bright red marks behind when she opened her mouth again to speak. "No. His legs were like ribbons. On the water. Floating and swaying . . ."

Archer saw the nerves quivering just beneath Hannah's skin and wanted to pull her into his lap, rock her, hold her, just hold her until the horror went away. But that would be stupid. There was a time and a place for sympathy. This wasn't it. A kind word would make her collapse like a puppet with cut strings. That wouldn't help anyone.

He stood up, shoved his hands in the pockets of his jeans, and turned away from the table. The house was airy, modest, and, like most things in Western Australia, slightly Asian in flavor. Rattan furniture, colorful cushions, low tables. A hammock hung to catch the cross breeze. The only unexpected touch was a wood sculpture the size of a violin. The sculpture had the sinuous, sensual power of a wave on the point of breaking. Within the wave was a shape that suggested a woman; the breaking of the wave would free her or destroy her. Archer didn't know which. He only knew that the tension and sensuality of the piece were riveting.

It was the last thing he needed to look at.

He turned his eyes to the filmy curtains and beyond, to the beautiful, brutal tropic world that surrounded the house. Sky and land, heaven and hell combined, waiting just beyond the verandah's silvery screens.

And silence behind him.

"Were you alone when you found him?" Archer asked curtly.

Hannah jumped, licked her dry lips, and took another drink of tea. "Coco was with me. The others were searching the mangrove side of the headland."

"Coco?"

"Colette Dupres. She's worked here for years."

"Doing what?"

"She's our best technician. The oysters she seeds have a

seventy percent better survival rate and more spherical pearls than anyone's except Tom Nakamori."

"A great asset."

"Great ass, period," Hannah said without thinking.

Archer's left eyebrow rose in surprise or amusement, Hannah couldn't tell which. Then she replayed her own words in her mind, hearing them as he must have. She would have laughed if she had the energy. But she didn't. Archer was going to get the truth from her, without any frills or civilized flourishes. She simply didn't have the strength to be polite, much less coy.

"What did Coco think when she saw the oyster shell in Len's chest?" Archer asked.

"She flinched. Then she laughed."

"Nerves?" He knew that violent death affected people in many ways. Hysterical laughter was one of them. Throwing up your toenails was another.

"I don't know," Hannah said. "She kept on saying, 'Perfect. So fucking perfect. Done off by the shell he worships.' "

"Done off?"

"French is Coco's native language. She still has trouble with English, especially when she's upset. She meant done in. Killed."

"Killed or murdered? There's a difference."

"The police say Len was killed."

"But you don't."

"No, I don't." She tensed, waiting for him to ask why. He didn't, which surprised her into relaxing just a bit.

"How long had Len been dead when you found him?" Archer asked, keeping his opinion on murder to himself. He would have to examine Len's body before he decided whether Hannah was smart or paranoid.

"I don't know."

"Who does?"

"You could try the Territorial Police in Broome, but it's a waste of time. They're understaffed, overworked, and had their own cyclone problems to deal with."

"Where is Len's body?"

Hannah drew a shaky breath. "In Broome. The cremation is set for tomorrow. Early."

Archer glanced at his watch. He would have to move quickly if he wanted to see Len. "Do you miss him?"

He shouldn't have asked. He had no right to the answer. But it was too late to call back the words.

Abruptly Hannah laughed, then pressed her hands over her mouth to push the laughter back down. It was impossible. The thought of missing what Len had become was so horrifyingly absurd it was hysterical.

Archer watched Hannah struggle with her composure, watched her lose, and felt a chill in his gut as her laughter rose and rose, only to crash into sudden silence. *Len, what did you do to your innocent, missionary-raised wife?*

But that was the one question Archer wouldn't ask Hannah. He had no right to the answer. He was part of whatever had happened to her.

"I mourn the man I thought I married," she managed finally, breath breaking. "I mourn the man who could laugh. But that man died seven years ago. I'm through mourning him. The man who took his place, I can't mourn. He taught me too well."

"What do you mean?"

"Len came to hate me as much as he loved pearls, and he loved pearls more than my parents loved God. Len taught me not to love him, not to like him, not to care about him at all." She looked up at Archer with eyes that were as bleak as his own. "If that shocks you, I'm sorry."

"It doesn't. I knew Len better than you did." Archer wanted to ask why Hannah had stayed with Len, but he had no right to that answer, either. It had nothing to do with Len's death. And that was the only reason Archer was here: his half brother's death.

If he told himself that often enough, maybe the message would sink through his skull all the way to his crotch.

"Why do you think someone killed Len?" Archer asked.

"Pearls," she said simply.

"Greed?"

"Greed. Money. Power." Hannah closed her eyes. "Maybe he was killed because someone could, so someone did."

"Who do you think killed him?"

Hannah went still. It was a question she had asked herself over and over again. She had no answer but the one she gave Archer. "I'm only sure of two things. I didn't kill him. You didn't kill him. After that, there's a whole bloody world of people who hated Len."

"What makes you think I didn't kill him?"

"You had no reason."

Archer looked at her short, sun-streaked hair, spiked by careless combing and shining like a dream. Her lashes were long, thick, the color of bittersweet chocolate, and her eyes were an indescribable color from the dark end of the rainbow. Her lips were too pale, too tight, yet nothing could hide the promise of sensuality in their full curves. As for the rest . . . she was long, slender but for her breasts, even more elegant than his memories.

If he had known how it was going to turn out, he would have fought Len McGarry ten years ago and let hell take the leftovers. But Hannah had watched Len with worshipful eyes, and Archer had told himself that she was what Len needed, that her lush, sweet innocence would heal the breaks in his half brother's soul.

Remembering his own naïveté, Archer smiled. The curve of his lips was about as comforting as a scythe. *No reason to kill Len?* "You have no idea how wrong you are, Hannah."

Her breath stuck in her throat at what she saw in his face. At that moment he reminded her chillingly of Len. Dangerous. Distant. Ruthless.

"But in one thing you're right," Archer said. "I didn't kill Len. Where were *you* when he died, Mrs. McGarry?"

She met his eyes straight on, as controlled and remote as he was. "I didn't kill Len."

"You had a better motive than most."

"If I wanted his death on my conscience, all I had to do was walk out on him."

"What does that mean?"

"Hating me kept him alive. Loving pearls almost kept him sane."

"Almost," Archer repeated softly, understanding much of what Hannah didn't say. Even ten years ago, Len had gone off on rages of laughter or drinking or screwing. Or mayhem. "Yet you stayed with him. You're either very brave or very stupid, Hannah."

"I'm neither. Life happens one day at a time, like water dripping on stone. You don't notice the change except over years." She rubbed her aching eyes. "As for the rest, no one deserves all the good or the bad that comes their way. You just take it the way it comes, one day at a time."

"Echoes of a missionary upbringing?"

She shrugged and stuffed a slippery piece of hair behind her ear. "I no longer thank God for the good that happens or blame my inborn evil for the bad. I just . . ." Her voice faded.

"Survive," Archer finished.

"Yes. What else is there?"

"Everything."

"For some people, perhaps. Not for me."

There was no self-pity in Hannah's voice, no anger. She accepted, and from that acceptance she drew the strength to survive. It hadn't always been that way. Len had very nearly destroyed her.

"What do you want from life?" Archer asked before he could think better of it.

"What I've earned: the Black Trinity. But to find it, I—we— will have to find Len's murderer. Whoever killed him took the pearls. If you help me find what has been lost, I'll give you half of whatever we get for it."

Hearing all that Hannah hadn't said in the tension of her voice, Archer wondered who else knew about the pearls, who had killed to take them, and who would kill again to keep them.

She rose, gathered plates, and took them to the sink. When she turned, he was watching her, waiting.

"What's the Black Trinity?" he asked.

"An unstrung triple-strand necklace of black pearls. The whole necklace is worth three million American, wholesale."

Archer whistled softly through his teeth. "Three million?

That would be some necklace. Especially since the Aussies took the steam out of the Tahitian black pearl market when they learned how to make Australia's huge silver-lipped oysters produce big black pearls."

"The Black Trinity is worth at least three million," Hannah said evenly. "The smallest strand is twenty inches long, with twelve-millimeter pearls. The middle strand is twenty-two inches, with fourteen-millimeter pearls. The longest strand is twenty-four inches, with sixteen-millimeter pearls. All of the black pearls are round and color-matched within and across their strand."

"Luster?"

"Superb. The pearls have a surface that is as close to flawless as nature gets. If nature doesn't provide it, I try."

"You're a pearl doctor?" he asked, surprised. Softly, softly, sanding a pearl down through layer after layer of nacre in the hope of finding a less flawed surface was like rolling dice with the devil. When you lost, you lost it all. It took guts and confidence to peel a pearl as patiently as the oyster had created it in the first place.

"If the stakes are high enough, I doctor pearls," Hannah said. "It's rather like sculpting. You remove whatever gets in the way of the vision. Sometimes your vision is clear and you end up with something beautiful. Sometimes you end up with a pile of sawdust."

Soapy sponge in hand, she began washing the lunch dishes. The food had helped her physically. Her hands were much more sure. Not that it mattered. Her dishes were the high-tech kind that could be shot from a canon without taking a scratch.

Archer watched, thinking about Len and pearls, greed and obsession, cruelty and accident. Len had loved pearls, but only one kind of pearl had obsessed him enough to make him take crazy risks. "What shade of black?"

For the first time Hannah hesitated. Once she told him, she wasn't certain she would be able to trust him. But she didn't really have any choice. If she went after the murderer alone, she would end up like Len, facedown in the warm, pitiless sea.

"The Black Trinity's pearls are every color of the rainbow, all at once," she said flatly. "Red, green, blue, gold, all of it gleaming under a clear black surface, like liquid gemstones under black ice."

"So he *did* succeed. I assumed he had, but I never saw the proof of it."

Swiftly Hannah turned toward Archer. Her eyes were wary. She was very much afraid that she had just invited the wolf to dine with, and possibly on, the lamb. "You knew about the black rainbows?"

"I knew Len found an extraordinary pearl in Kowloon. I knew he was determined to discover where it came from, no matter who got hurt. I assumed he had found what he wanted, put it to work, and kept the results to himself. It would be like him."

Breath trickled out of her lungs in a hidden sigh. "Len found out where that first black rainbow came from. Then he found out how to culture more."

"No surprise there," Archer said. "Len could have pried secrets out of the Sphinx."

The casual tone of Archer's voice disarmed Hannah. "Do you want to know the secret?" she asked, curious.

"What will it cost me?"

Oddly, his answer reassured her. She had seen enough envy, enough obsession to possess, enough plain greed, to recognize their presence at a glance. Archer was interested, but he wasn't avid.

Even so, she hesitated. It was one thing to know your life was at risk. It was another to simply hand over the means of your own destruction.

"It won't cost you a cent," Hannah said, her voice low. "I don't know the secret of producing the rainbow pearls." She took a broken breath, let it go. "And if the vultures circling around Pearl Cove discover my ignorance, I suspect that my life won't be worth a handful of broken shell."

This time Archer couldn't resist offering some comfort, however small. Gently he put his right hand on her cheek. Her skin was cool, too cool. On some cellular level, Hannah was running on empty. But there was nothing he could do about that right now.

He had an urgent appointment with a dead man.

"Can you stay awake for a few more hours?" he asked.

She shivered and raised her chin. "Of course. The children will help."

"Children?"

"When I have time, I teach English to some of the workers' children."

He almost smiled. For a few hours, kids would be as good as an armed bodyguard protecting Hannah. "I'll leave when the kids get here and I'll be back as soon as I can."

"Where are you going?"

"Broome."

Hannah didn't ask why. She knew.

Len McGarry.

Five

Before Hannah called the children, someone knocked on the front door. Reflexively Archer stepped to the side and stood deep in the shadows, invisible against the brilliance of the light outside.

Uncertain, Hannah looked at him. He jerked his head, silently telling her to answer the door. She went through the front door, crossed the verandah in a few steps, and opened the screen door that offered a thin, useful shield against the blazing light.

"Christian," she said, surprised. She noted the cuts, scrapes, and bruises on his arms. Fighting with sunken oyster cages wasn't easy work. "Is something wrong?"

"Hello, luv." Christian Flynn looked her over thoroughly. Cutoff jeans, a tank top the color of a peach, and full lips to match. Eyes a blue so deep it slid off into purple. Breasts that would just fill a big man's hands. Bare, narrow, arched feet. "Pretty as a pearl. How do you do it?"

"I sleep with oysters."

She retreated across the verandah into the relative coolness of the house. He followed her without waiting to be asked. His sandals made faint slapping sounds just behind her heels. With his tall, athletic body, quick grin, and rugged Outback blond looks, he went through women like a home-grown Australian flu.

Hannah found Flynn almost amusing, as long as he wasn't turning those cobalt blue eyes in her direction. Of course, there could be another, more sinister reason that Flynn was watching her with predatory interest. Two days ago he had offered to find a buyer for Pearl Cove. She had refused.

The thought that she might be in danger from the genial Aussie made Hannah's stomach twist, so she concentrated on doing what she was good at: keeping a man at arm's length without making an enemy of him.

"You want your usual mud tea?" she asked neutrally, leading Flynn away from the front door and toward the kitchen. "Or are you ready for a beer?"

"Tea or beer, whatever is cold."

"Is something wrong?" she asked again. "More injuries?"

"Nothing new. I came to see how you are."

"She's fine," Archer said from behind them. With a smooth, balanced movement, he stepped out of the shadows by the front door. "Anything else on your mind?"

Flynn spun around, half crouched in a fighting stance, weight poised on the balls of his feet. The sight of a big, handsome, confident male in Hannah's house made the Aussie's blue eyes narrow. "Who the devil are you?"

"Hannah's partner," Archer said calmly. He hadn't missed the automatic movements of someone trained in unarmed combat. Beneath that charming grin and shoulder-length, sun-bleached hair lurked a fighter. Archer knew how bad his mood was when the thought of testing the young Aussie's fighting skills appealed to him.

"Partner!" Flynn's head snapped around toward Hannah. "Did you sell to this bloke?"

"No. Mr. Donovan has been a partner in Pearl Cove since it was founded." She looked at Archer. "This is Christian Flynn. He manages the water end of Pearl Cove."

"Len never mentioned a partner," Flynn said. His voice was even less welcoming than his expression.

Archer just stood there, taking in the good-looking, angry Australian. He wondered why Len had put up with having the muscular young stud around Hannah. Len hadn't wanted Archer within seventeen thousand miles of his wife, and had said so in words that still echoed bleakly deep in Archer's mind.

Get the hell out of my life and stay out. All the way out. You think you can have her now that I'm paralyzed, but you're wrong. You come near her and I'll get even. Not with you. With her.

At the time Archer had told himself it was just the drugs, just the fear, just the rage of a newly paralyzed man speaking. He had tried to get through to Len, to reassure him that he had no intention of seducing Hannah. All he wanted to do was help his brother.

Len hadn't listened. The harder Archer tried, the more wild Len become. So Archer did as his brother asked. He got the hell out of Len's life. All the way out.

"There was no reason to talk about having a partner," Hannah said warily, sensing the currents of tension coiling between the two men. "Archer wasn't an active partner."

Something shifted in Flynn's stance. "Archer? Would that be Archer Donovan?"

"Yes," she said.

"Bloody hell," Flynn muttered. Anybody who knew anything about buying pearls had heard of Archer Donovan. The man was a legend. He had a shrewd understanding of pearls, people, and the marketplace. Unhappily Flynn kneaded his neck with his left hand while he thought about how Archer's presence changed an already fluid situation. None of the possibilities made him smile. But he turned to Archer anyway, smiled, and held out his right hand. "Sorry if I was rude, mate. I'm short on sleep. After the big wind, things are a right bitch around here."

Archer smiled from the teeth out and took the other man's hand. "No worries. I'm short on sleep, too."

The ridges of callus on Flynn's hand told Archer a lot about the other man's training. Whether he could put that training to effective use in face-to-face combat remained an open question.

The sudden flare of speculation in Flynn's eyes told Archer that his own calluses had been noted.

"How long before Pearl Cove is up and running?" Archer asked, distracting the other man.

Flynn looked sideways at Hannah. She was watching Archer. It rankled the Aussie.

"I don't know," he said carefully. "We had just moved the newly implanted oysters to the grow-out areas. Some of those rafts broke loose and sank. We repaired the floats and lines and have been stringing up the cages as fast as we find them. We're losing shell, though. Too much jigging around."

"How much of this year's shell is a total loss?"

Again Flynn looked uneasily at Hannah.

"Tell him," she said without looking away from Archer.

"Sixty-five percent. Maybe more."

"How much more?" Archer asked.

"Worst case?" Flynn asked.

Archer smiled like a wolf. "It's the only case that matters, isn't it?"

"Ninety-five percent," Flynn said.

Hannah made a harsh sound. She had been told fifty-five percent loss, sixty percent tops.

"Total loss, in other words," Archer summarized.

Flynn hesitated, looked at Hannah's drawn face, and wished Archer Donovan was the kind of man who could be intimidated into not asking uncomfortable questions.

"It could be a write-off," Flynn admitted finally. "Frankly, we're not recovering as many of the rafts as we hoped."

"Why?"

Archer's cool, neutral question made Flynn wish that Hannah's partner was someone else. Anyone else. He was certain his bosses would feel the same way. The cyclone had seemed like such a perfect solution to a sodding impossible problem.

"Bloody big wind, bloody big mess," Flynn said, his voice clipped. "This one was a destructive bitch." He looked at Hannah. "Sorry, luv. I didn't want to tell you until I was certain."

"What about next year's oysters?" Archer asked. "How did they fare?"

"We haven't finished our recce yet, so we don't know."

"Guess."

The cool command irritated Flynn. He started to push right back in automatic response to another man testing him. Then he looked at Archer's measuring eyes and remembered the ridges of callus on the side of his hand. It might come to a fight with Archer, but before it did, Flynn would have to have permission from his own bosses. The thought grated worse than crushed shell.

"They're probably better off," Flynn said. "The worst hit were the rafts of experimental shell. I told Len we should put them in a less exposed place, but he wanted them close enough to watch. He was a paranoid bastard." He heard his own words and winced. "Sorry, luv. I—"

"Hannah knew her husband better than you did," Archer cut in. "What of the pearls in the sorting shed?"

"There's an American book," Flynn said with a thin smile. *"Gone With the Wind."*

"Pearl Cove isn't Tara. I find it hard to believe that every last pearl vanished in the wind."

"Believe it anyway."

"Oh, I believe the pearls are gone," Archer drawled. "I just don't believe the wind took them."

"What do you think happened?" Flynn asked angrily.

"I think they've been . . . salvaged."

"Are you trying to tell me something, mate?"

Hannah touched Flynn's arm. "Archer isn't accusing anyone."

The Australian looked at Archer with unfriendly eyes. "It doesn't sound that way to me."

"I'll need a written summary of what was lost, what was found, and what you're doing about the missing," Archer said.

"I don't have time for—"

"Make time," Archer cut in.

The command took Flynn right up to the edge of his self-control. Archer watched the process with cool interest. Even eagerness.

"I don't take orders from you," Flynn said. He turned to Hannah.

"Wrong," Archer said. When Hannah would have intervened again, he confronted her. "Changed your mind?"

"What does that mean?" she demanded.

"You made a call. I came. I can leave just as fast."

Anger snapped along nerve endings that were already frayed raw. Hannah started to tell Archer to leave if he wanted, and go to hell while he was at it. Then she glanced at her foreman and saw his barely concealed satisfaction.

Divide and conquer. The oldest game of all.

Because it worked.

Hannah faced Flynn with a smile that would have frozen fire. "The Yank is a bit overbearing, but he has a point. I'll need that report for my own records. By supper should do it."

"By supper?" Flynn said in disbelief. "I can't do a proper job in that short a time!"

"Then do an improper one. You had answers quick enough when Archer asked."

"That was different."

"Because he's a man?" Hannah's smile widened to show lots of teeth. "No worries, *mate*. I wear pants, too. I'll see you before supper."

Flynn made a rough sound and stared down at his employer. Whatever the situation might have been when Len was alive, Hannah was in charge of Pearl Cove now. And she knew it. Flynn hadn't expected things to turn out this way when he dropped by to console the sexy widow.

"Right," he said. "Supper."

The front door and then the verandah door closed behind Flynn. Hard.

Hands on hips, Hannah turned on Archer. "Why were you so rude?"

"Any manager worth his pay would have had a report on your desk within twenty-four hours of that cyclone."

"But—" A knock at the verandah door cut off her protest. She spun around, expecting to see Flynn again. "Oh, Tom. Come in."

Archer watched as Tom Nakamori opened the verandah door and then the front door. He was wearing the uniform of the day: shorts, tank top, sandals. In his case, all of them were a faded navy blue. His hair was thin and white. His eyebrows were a startling midnight black. A thin scar went from his collarbone to his chin. His knuckles were enlarged, but the hands themselves were still flexible. Like most of the workers, he showed the nicks, cuts, and bruises of trying to save Pearl Cove from the cyclone.

Nakamori paused to make certain that the screens closed gently. He moved with the care of a man who had spent too many years dangling from a dive rope being towed over shell beds. If the physical labor itself didn't get you, nitrogen bubbles in the blood would. Sooner or later, the bends crippled most divers. A special few, it killed.

"Forgive the upset," Nakamori said, half bowing. "The *Perfect Pearl* repairs better. With permission, I take divers and search lost shell early tomorrow."

"Of course," she said quickly. "But check with Christian first. He's preparing a report for me, so he might want you to start in a particular area."

Nakamori nodded and tilted slightly forward again.

Archer had two distinct impressions. One was that English wasn't Nakamori's preferred language. The second was that the wiry, barrel-chested Japanese didn't care much for Christian Flynn.

"Is there room for another diver?" Archer asked Nakamori.

He hesitated, then nodded. *"Hai.* Okay."

"When do you leave?"

"After dawn. One hour."

"Is there extra dive gear?"

Nakamori looked at Archer from head to heels. "Mr. McGarry gear fit chest. But bottom . . ." The Japanese shrugged. "Sorry. No fit."

"If I get too cold, I'll sit up top until I'm warm again. Make sure there's room for Hannah, too." Archer looked at her. "I assume you dive."

She smiled, thinking of the hauntingly beautiful ocean beneath the surface, where colors flowed into a thousand shades of blue and all was grace. "I haven't really been diving since the storm. Christian said there wasn't room, and I didn't want to get in the way of salvage work. Then the engine started having problems. It's fixed now?" she asked, turning to Naka-mori again.

"Not now," he corrected. "Tomorrow."

"Right," she said. "Tomorrow."

"If calm," he added.

She looked out at the sky. No huge clouds loomed or gathered in a solid western wall. "It will be fine."

Nakamori went through the front door, paused on the verandah, and looked back. "Mrs. McGarry?"

"Yes?"

"My divers must feed families. They ask if need find more work."

"Everyone who works for Pearl Cove will be paid," Archer said, understanding the question Nakamori was too circumspect to ask outright. "Tell your men."

Nakamori's black eyes scanned Archer with shrewd intelligence. "Flynn say Pearl Cove—*ffft*—no good. Banks not build again."

"If you work, you get paid," Archer repeated.

"How?" Nakamori's voice was polite but insistent.

"By a check drawn on a Hong Kong bank."

"Mr. Donovan," Hannah said quickly, "is a partner in Pearl Cove. He is underwriting what needs to be done."

Surprise flicked like a whip over Nakamori's face, followed by no expression at all. "Pearl Cove okay?"

"Pearl Cove is a mess," Archer said, "but you'll be paid for every hour you work."

"Okay. I tell." Nakamori bowed slightly and went out into the yellow violence of the sun.

"I don't want to leave you alone while I dive," Archer said. "Are you comfortable diving?"

"Is an ama?" she asked, smiling slightly, thinking of the famous female pearl divers of Japan.

A smile split the darkness of Archer's beard. "An ama? Do you wear what the amas wear, too?"

"White blouse and trousers? No."

"They only wear that for the shows put on by the big Japanese pearl growers for tourists and government officials," he said. "The amas of old wore nothing but a G-string. They wanted to slide like fish through the water while they dove for shell."

"Must have been chilly."

"In Japanese waters, it was damned cold," Archer agreed. "But they worked hour after hour anyway. They kept up their energy by taking breaks to grill and eat whatever they found on the sea floor during their dives. And they gave a haunting, whistling cry when they surfaced after a long dive. . . ."

Though he spoke to Hannah, his eyes were on Tom Nakamori, who was walking down the path to the pearling sheds. One more name to give Kyle to run through his computer. The Japanese man might be nearly sixty, with joints that screamed each one of his years as a diver, but he was plenty strong enough to slam an oyster shell between Len's ribs. Especially if he whacked him over the head with a board first.

"Any other players I should know about?" Archer asked, turning back to Hannah.

"What do you mean?"

"Flynn and Nakamori both have the strength and the access to murder Len. Who else benefitted?"

She closed her eyes and fought a sharp battle with her stomach. "I don't see how either Christian or Tom benefitted from Len's death. If Pearl Cove goes under, they both lose their jobs."

"Jobs aren't hard to find along this coast, especially for experienced pearl men." And unless he was badly mistaken, the young Aussie had more than one job in any case. Archer turned away from the verandah and watched Hannah with eyes that showed only a ghost of green and no blue at all. "Who else?"

"Ian Chang wants to buy Pearl Cove. Or seventy-five percent of it, anyway. He wasn't here during the cyclone, so he can hardly be a suspect, but he does know about the special pearls. I don't know how. Maybe Len told him."

"Secrets are hard to keep, especially one like that. Even Len couldn't have done it year after year after year," Archer added absently. He was running through his mental file marked "Chang." Nothing that came back was good news. Maybe Ian belonged to a different branch of the Changs. Maybe . . . but somehow Archer didn't think he would be lucky on this one. Not the good kind of lucky.

"This past year was the worst," Hannah said. "Len told me he was certain someone had stolen some of the experimental oysters just before we started harvesting."

Archer shrugged. "If Len hadn't been so damned clever playing off one group against another, he would have been stolen blind years ago. Ian Chang, for instance. Would that be Sam Chang's Number One Son? The Changs of Chang Enterprises International? The Changs who own a hefty slice of the Pacific Rim pearl trade and are looking to acquire more?"

She looked at Archer warily, sensing the intensity beneath his neutral voice. "Ian's father is called Sam and is a businessman. Otherwise, you seem to know more about the Changs than I do."

"What do you know about Ian Chang?" Archer asked.

"He works for the family business, has interests from mainland China to New Zealand, and single-handedly helped Australia pry the pearling industry's technology away from the Japanese monopoly. From what Christian has said, Ian—with Australia's help—is now working on ending Japan's pearl *sales* monopoly."

"Married?" he asked, surprising Hannah.

"Yes. Five children. And if gossip can be believed, a mistress. Several, actually."

"Sounds like Sam's Number One Son," Archer said dryly. "How much did Chang offer for Pearl Cove?"

"The Changs would assume all debts and rebuild the farm operation."

"Millions, I assume."

She closed her eyes for an instant. The thought of how much Len had allowed Pearl Cove to slide into debt did nothing to settle her nerves. "Yes. Millions."

"Did you turn Chang down?"

"For Pearl Cove?"

It didn't take Archer a heartbeat to figure out what other offer Chang might have made. "Pearl Cove and anything else he might have put on the table."

"I turned down all of his offers."

"Why?"

The calm question startled Hannah. "Because Pearl Cove isn't mine to sell."

"And the rest?"

"Ian is married. End of discussion."

"But not for him."

"His problem, not mine."

"I'm not married, Hannah." Before she could manage a response, Archer asked another question. "Did you tell Chang you had a partner?"

She nodded.

"And?" Archer asked.

"He didn't like it. Said it changed everything." She paused, gave a mental shrug, and decided it would be interesting to see Archer's response. "Ian thinks you killed Len."

"Did he say why?"

If Archer was irritated or surprised by the accusation, nothing showed. Part of the reason was his short, smooth beard, which concealed small shifts of expression. But most of the reason nothing showed was the self-control that Hannah found herself wanting to ruffle, and to hell with all the warnings about still waters and sleeping dogs. The longer she was with Archer, the more she remembered other things from the past, like the way heat had rippled through her the first time she saw him. She had been too innocent then to understand her elemental response to this one man. She wasn't innocent now.

"What Ian said to me was that Len finally buggered the wrong man," she said flatly. "That you were as ruthless as they came."

"He's half right. I didn't kill Len."

"Yes." She let out a breath she hadn't been aware of holding. "And neither did I."

He nodded as though she had said the sun would set later in the day. "I know."

"How? Do you think I'm not capable of murder because I'm a woman?"

He laughed, but it wasn't a humorous sound. "Anyone is capable of murder, given the right incentive."

"Then why are you so certain I'm innocent?"

"Simple. You asked me for help."

She blinked and watched him with eyes darker than indigo. "I could have killed Len and then asked for your help."

"You're not that stupid. You didn't need Chang to tell you that I wasn't a nice guy."

The look in Archer's eyes reminded Hannah of the night he had appeared on her doorstep with Len's beaten, bloody body in his arms. At the time, they had lived on the outskirts of a dirty village on a hidden bay, a place where men made their living smuggling contraband or by outright piracy. Archer had fought their way to the potholed dirt strip that passed for an airport, loaded them aboard a stolen plane, hot-wired it, and kicked it into the sullen tropical sky while fights and fires raged all around and people fled in all directions as the plane pursued them down the runway.

That night Archer had been everything Chang said he was: utterly ruthless.

Abruptly Hannah was glad that all she was guilty of was failing Len as a wife. The bond between the two men was frighteningly strong. Archer had stayed with Len through all the endless rounds of surgery, all the physical and mental agony. Feeding Len, bathing him, giving him water, holding him like a child while he shrieked through drug-enhanced nightmares and cursed men who had lied to him, men he wanted to kill, men he had killed.

Until finally Len had turned on Archer, screaming at him for wanting Hannah. The idea had shocked her, but not as much as the realization that she was drawn to Archer as she had never been to her husband.

"Hannah? What is it?"

For a moment she couldn't speak. Ghostly emotion rippled over her skin as she watched Archer's eyes, their bleak shadows and pitiless clarity, as though he was seeing everything she remembered, everything she had tried to forget.

"I was thinking," she managed.

"About what?"

"The time Len screamed at you to leave. It was wrong," she whispered. "You never would have touched me."

"No. I never would have. But I wanted to, Hannah. I wanted you until I couldn't breathe."

"I . . ." Her voice died. "I can't believe . . ." Yet when she looked at Archer's eyes now, she believed. He had felt the same sensual heat that rippled through her unawakened body. "I didn't know."

"I made sure of it. But Len knew me. He saw what you were too innocent to see." Archer glanced down at his watch. If he drove like a maniac, there was enough time. Since everyone in Western Australia drove like a maniac, he wouldn't stand out. "I'll help you gather our dive gear. I want to look it over—and the boat—before we use it."

Hannah asked the one question she wasn't afraid to ask, and ignored the one she was very much afraid of: *Do you still want me?* "Don't you trust Tom?"

"Haven't you figured it out yet? I don't trust anyone."

"What about me?"

"You're family.

"Family," Hannah said slowly, tasting the word. It was more than she had any right to expect, yet somehow much less than she wanted.

And she hadn't known that until this instant. Ten years ago she had been innocent and infatuated with a handsome mercenary who was fifteen years older than she was. Yet even then, Archer had tugged at her senses just by being alive. If she had met him first, before Len . . .

"You don't feel like family to me," she said.

"Give it time."

"Time." She laughed abruptly.

"Do you keep the diving gear here or on the boat?" Archer asked.

"I keep it here." Then, before she could think better of it, "And I don't feel anything like your sister."

He didn't move, but he changed. She could see it, the flare of intensity in him as vivid as the corona of the sun.

"What do you feel like?" he asked.

Unease and something more pricked through her. She wanted him with a rushing force that made her light-headed. But fear was greater. Just barely. Just enough to bridle her tongue. Years ago she had learned that sexual hunger led straight to bad judgment, which led straight to hell on earth.

Now she was learning her own unexpected weakness for this one man.

It terrified her.

"I don't know what I feel like," she said distinctly.

Archer watched Hannah for the space of a long breath, saw her fear of him, and accepted it. He didn't blame her. She was no longer nineteen, with hope in her eyes and excitement in her smile. She had discovered that life was always unexpected and often cruel. She had learned to pull back, shut down.

To survive.

He wanted to argue that there was more to life than pain and death, that the Donovan family would take her in and accept her. Yet he didn't say a word. He had no right to demand that she step out of her protective shell and share her life, her laughter, her love. He was the one who had left her to heal a man who couldn't be healed.

But Len could hurt whoever tried to help him. And he had. The fear in her eyes was proof of it.

"Wouldn't life be grand if kindness outlived cruelty?" Archer asked with a neutrality that didn't quite hide the weariness in his soul. "But it doesn't."

He turned away, listing what had to be done in his mind. The sooner he found out what had happened to Len and Pearl Cove, the sooner he would be out of her life.

Broome was first on the list.

"So Mad Dog Len had a partner?" the cop asked, watching Archer skeptically. The big Yank with the sweaty dress shirt, faded jeans, and a worn rucksack slung over one shoulder looked hard and much too controlled for a constable's peace of mind.

Archer nodded.

"That's good news for his widow," the cop said, dragging a match across the metal nameplate that said "Dave" and lighting a cigarette. "No one here will lend her a dollar to rebuild."

"Why? Pearl Cove isn't a license to print money, but it looks better than lot of businesses around Broome."

"Hey, Dave," someone called from the back of the hot,

humid, tin-roofed cave that passed for a police station. "Your wife is on the other line."

"Tell her five," the cop called back. Then his faded green eyes focused on Archer with a show-me-something-new weariness. "You want prosperous, mate? Try Cable Beach outside of town. That's where the rich tourists go."

"I'm not a tourist and you haven't answered my question."

"You're not a native, either, or you'd know that people around here wouldn't piss on Len McGarry if he was on fire."

"No worries," Archer said neutrally, using a favorite Aussie response. "He's dead. An accident, I'm told."

"Too right." Dave blew out a stream of smoke that did nothing to improve the thick, close air of the station house. "McGarry drowned when a cyclone tore open a pearl-sorting shed and shucked him out of it like an oyster out of its shell."

"Was there water in his lungs?"

"He was found floating facedown in six inches of ocean."

"With a piece of oyster shell rammed between his ribs. Didn't that strike you as odd?"

Dave looked bored. "You don't have many cyclones in Seattle, do you? I've picked up blokes that had soda straws shoved through their groin or arteries cut by flying palm leaves. At two hundred and fifty kilometers per hour, a lot of normal things turn lethal. Bloody hell, a piece of paper will slit your throat."

"I know. The U.S. might be short on cyclones, but we're long on hurricanes and tornadoes."

The cop grunted. "A bit of oyster shell was the least of McGarry's problems. He looked like he was run over by a road train. If it hadn't been for his wasted legs, even his wife wouldn't have recognized the bastard."

Abruptly Archer was glad that Hannah hadn't come to Broome with him. He had left her teaching English to eager children whose laughter and sparkling black eyes were like a tonic after all the grim memories of Len. Archer wished he could have stayed. He missed his niece's innocence and uninhibited smile. But Summer was half a world away, and Len's body was in the merciless here and now.

"If Len had been your brother, would you be investigating his death any differently?" Archer asked.

Thick, blunt fingers rubbed over the cop's newly shaved face. He sucked on the cigarette and exhaled smoke. "I'd be crying."

Archer almost smiled. "So it was just an accident, is that it?"

"Bloody right. And it couldn't have happened to a nicer bloke." Dave's hand came up suddenly, cutting off any reply. "Look, Yank. I'm not going to pretend that the world isn't a better place without that sorry sod. But if I was inclined to make trouble about his death—and I'm not—I'd be talking to his widow. Is that what you want?"

For a moment Archer didn't trust himself to speak. Jet lag was gnawing at him like a hangover, Hannah had been terrified beneath her brittle calm, and now this short-tempered Outback constable was threatening her.

"Harassing Mrs. McGarry would be stupid. You're not a stupid man," Archer said evenly. "May I see the body now?"

"You flew a long way to look at a dead man."

"Yes."

The cop waved his thick, sunburned hand, trailing a flag of smoke. "Go see him, mate. He won't care. Nobody will."

With wary cop's eyes, Dave watched Archer walk away. He didn't know what was on the Yank's mind. He didn't want to know. Working as a constable out beyond the Black Stump had taught him that there were two kinds of men: bad men, and bad men to cross. Bad men didn't worry him.

Men like Archer did.

The place where Len's body was being stored looked like what it was, a processing plant for the Kimberley shorthorn cattle that ran through Australia's West like a hoofed red plague. But it wasn't the right season for slaughter, so the meat locker was cold and empty except for three cyclone victims. Two were fishermen. One was Len. All three were covered with what looked like old sheets. The unexpectedly powerful storm had overloaded the tiny funeral home. Bodies destined for cremation had been shunted off to less plush surroundings.

"He's the one over there," the teenager said, his voice as

rough as his red hair. He was too young not to be intimidated by death and too old to admit it.

"Thank you," Archer said. "I'd like to be alone with him for a time."

"No worries, mate," the kid said, relieved. "Close the door hard when you leave."

Archer waited for the door to close—hard—before he went to the table where Len lay. Even without the kid's instructions, he would have known it was Len; below the torso, the sheet was nearly flat on the table. He flipped the covering down far enough to see the face and chest.

He grimaced, but not for himself. The thought of Hannah finding this mangled, battered flesh made him want to cry out in protest. She didn't deserve to have that horrifying image sink into her mind, wellspring of future nightmares.

No one deserves all the good or the bad that comes their way. You take it the way it comes, one day at a time.

Hannah's words echoed in the raging silence of Archer's mind. They didn't calm him, but they made it possible to let go of some of the anger and shove the rest of it down with all the other brutal images breeding nightmares in his own darkness.

Silently, fighting for the emotional distance that was necessary for what he must do, Archer studied what had once been his half brother and mentor in the bleak arts of survival. He remembered Len as a Viking—big, brawny, brawling, laughing like a madman one moment and stone silent the next. All of the silence and some of the brawn remained. Across the shoulders and in the arms, he was as powerful as Archer. The thick mane of blond hair had gone white in great, ragged streaks. Whatever marks rage or laughter might have left on Len's face had been erased by the brutal hammering his body had taken before and after he died.

The piece of oyster shell lay beside Len, as though no one had been certain what to do with it. Four inches long, darkly iridescent on one side and sea-roughened cream on the other, broken at both ends, the shell was shaped like a clumsy, ruined knife. Even against its background of battered flesh, the death wound was obvious on Len's ribs: it was a bloody, bruised mouth opened a finger's width in shock. A knife would have left far less evidence.

Archer shrugged off the soft backpack he wore. The sweaty patch of shirt beneath turned cold the instant air touched it. He didn't notice, any more than he had noticed the chill of the room after the first shock. He reached into his backpack, shoved aside the laptop computer, special cellular phone, and fresh underwear until he found the pencil-slim flashlight he was looking for.

Icy white light stabbed out, striking a gleaming darkness and rainbow colors from the oyster shell's smooth inner surface. He picked it up and fitted it to the blunt, ragged, subtly curving wound between broken ribs. With only a slight pressure from his hand, he pushed the shell in; the previous wound was like a road hacked from a wilderness of intact flesh and bone.

When the shell would go no farther without being shoved, Archer bent and lined up the flashlight with the angle of the shell. It was dead on for the heart.

If Hannah was right that Len had been murdered, it hadn't been an overhand shot, but one that had come up from under. Not the easiest way for a standing man to kill someone in a wheelchair. But if the target was lying on his back, it would be a simple enough maneuver, even for a diver with enlarged knuckles and a careful gait. For Flynn it would have been as easy as smiling.

Archer's fingers closed around the shell fragment and rocked it with tiny motions, loosening it from the ribs. Then he examined the chance weapon beneath the unflinching white blade of his flashlight. The shell indeed could have killed Len, if it was long enough.

But it wasn't. Barely an inch of the shell was bloodstained. That wasn't long enough to reach the heart beyond the protective ribs.

After a final look, Archer put the shell back where he had found it, resting against a dead man's hand. He rummaged in the backpack again. This time he drew out what looked like a pair of blunt-nosed pliers. Various tools—screwdrivers, a file, a punch, knives—were tucked into the hollow handles of the pliers like blades into a jackknife.

He tried one of the knife blades first. It went in between the ribs far enough to kill, and it went in without hesitation, without any force, following a path already made by a larger, broader knife.

Hannah was right. Len had been murdered.

Now that Archer had seen Pearl Cove's isolation, he was betting that the murderer was known to Len, probably even worked on the pearl farm. Hannah certainly hadn't mentioned any outsider staying through the cyclone. The murderer could still be there, secure in the general belief that Len's death was accidental rather than deliberate.

Archer looked one last time at what had once been his brother. The big ring Len still wore gleamed coldly in the harsh light. Archer lifted the cold hand and looked more closely. Len hadn't worn a ring at any time in Archer's memory. This ugly rendition of a rough oyster shell wasn't a wedding ring—neither Len nor Hannah wore one. Nor was it valuable. It had the feel of stainless steel rather than silver or gold or platinum. In a fight, the ring could have opened a man's face to the bone.

He wondered if it was a present from Hannah, but rejected the possibility. There was no beauty in this ring, no grace, no value, nothing to recommend it to anyone but Len, who never looked at the world as other people did.

Archer slid the ugly, oversized ring off, and put it on the keyring in his pocket. It wasn't much to remember a murdered brother by, but it was all he had.

He pulled the sheet over Len and left the building with long strides. The more he thought about Pearl Cove's isolation, the less he liked Hannah being there alone. What was once her home had become enemy ground.

Six

Sitting in Hannah's kitchen Archer looked at her computer and waved away a fly that circled lazily around his sweaty forehead. He doubted he would find anything useful on her machine, but she would think it odd if he didn't even try. After all, Pearl Cove's accounts were on the hard drive, and he was supposed to be an interested, if silent, partner in the enterprise. She had even told him her personal code before she gave in and went to bed.

On very quiet feet, he went to Hannah's bedroom and looked in. She was lying on her stomach, one hand under her chin and the other buried under the pillow. Lemony light filled the room. So did heat. Neither one interfered with her deep sleep.

Archer went back to the kitchen, picked up his backpack, and reached for his cell phone. His brother answered on the first ring.

"Took you long enough," Kyle said curtly.

"I had to go back to Broome."

"Why?"

"Len's body was there." Archer stared through the screen and wished that the air whispering through the verandah could wash away the stink of the meat locker. But it couldn't. Nothing could except time.

A lot of it.

The quality of Archer's voice told Kyle that whatever his brother had found in Broome wasn't pretty. "How bad?"

"Bad enough." He closed his eyes, trying to banish the memory of Len laughing, of Len wounded, of Len raging against his useless legs, of Len lying mangled and murdered in a beef locker. He shifted his grip on the cellular that scrambled outgoing calls and decoded incoming ones from other Donovan phones. "What do you have for me?"

"Are you alone?" Kyle asked.

Archer thought of Hannah in the next room and of her deep, exhausted sleep despite the tropical brilliance of the afternoon. Yet even in the bottomless well of sleep, she twitched and moaned as though pursued.

He had told her about Len's knife wound.

He hadn't wanted to add to the horror of the nightmares that undoubtedly stalked her sleep, but he had done it just the same. She had flinched once. Just that. No more. A flickering of the eyelids, a sudden pallor around her lips, the clenching of narrow fingers into a fist. Then she had turned and walked into her bedroom. He had wanted to follow, to comfort her. He hadn't. He didn't trust himself to stop with a brotherly hug.

Nor was his own mind, his own sleep, free of nightmares. Some people weren't affected by naked violence. Many simply got used to it after the first few times. For others, a lifetime wasn't enough. Archer was one of them.

He hoped that Hannah wasn't another.

"For now, it's just me," he said. "If I get elliptical, you'll know what happened."

"Damn, Archer, you sound whipped."

"I am. Hannah is worse off. She's been living on catnaps for five days."

"Ouch. She must be hallucinating."

"Edging right up to it." He glanced toward the open bedroom door and spoke softly. "That's one gutsy, tough lady. She didn't let go until she knew someone was here to stand guard."

"So who's going to guard you while you sleep?"

"The Tooth Fairy." Archer swallowed another yawn and reached for the lethal cup of coffee that was sitting on a small table next to the graceful, sensual sculpture. "Talk to me. What do you have on her?"

"I sent a lot of stuff to your coded e-mail, if you want more details. Otherwise, I'll just hit the high points."

Archer grunted and shifted in the rattan chair, making it creak. The verandah's hammock chair tempted him, but he wasn't certain it was up to his weight.

"Hannah McGarry didn't exist in any files I could find from the time she was five until she married Len McGarry and applied for a passport," Kyle said. "Her parents were U.S. citizens who lived overseas except for five years in Maine, presumably to give birth and get Hannah through the most dangerous years for a kid's survival. Her mother is dead. Her father's passport is still current, so I presume he's alive."

"They were missionaries who lived with the Yanomami in Brazil. Or did ten years ago. He probably still does. It was what he loved more than he loved his daughter. They disowned her when she ran off with Len." Archer swallowed some more bitter coffee. "Before that, Hannah was raised in the Brazilian rain forest in a Yanomami hunting camp."

"That would explain the lack of documentation. Her marriage was recorded in Macao. Civil ceremony. You were the only witness."

No news there for Archer. The memory of that day wasn't one of his favorites. Savage heat, acrid smoke from street vendors' grills hazing the air, the hurry and stink of poverty chasing wealth, the dreams in Hannah's eyes and the emptiness in Len's.

"Archer? You awake?"

"Keep talking," he said, because it was better than saying what he was thinking: he had been a fool for ever thinking that Hannah's sweet innocence could neutralize, much less heal, Len's bitter experience. "I'm here."

"Her passport shows a lot of action in the next three years.

All over Southeast Asia, Malaysia, Philippines, every port I'd ever heard of and some I hadn't. No credit record, though. They must have paid cash for everything, including the ten days she spent in a hospital in Kuching."

"Hospital? When? Why?"

"About four months after she was married, she got real sick. The records just said something about a fever of unknown origin. They came within an ace of losing her, first to fever and then to bleeding. She's A positive, by the way."

"Did she have one of those hemorrhagic fevers?"

"No. She miscarried a seven-month fetus. Stillbirth. A boy. Hard to believe we had a little nephew and never knew it."

Archer didn't answer. He couldn't. He could barely breathe around the vise gripping his gut. Len had never mentioned Hannah's near-fatal illness or the loss of their child.

"Did you know about that?" Kyle asked after a minute.

"No."

Though Archer said nothing more, Kyle knew his brother too well to be fooled by silence.

"It got to me, too," Kyle said simply. "I went and found Lianne and held her, just held her. When I felt our babies move, I didn't know whether to laugh or cry."

The uncertainty of life and the finality of death haunted Kyle's voice as surely as it haunted Archer's mind. He forced himself to breathe, to talk, to reassure his youngest brother that their twins would be the lucky ones, the ones who not only survived but thrived.

"Don't worry about Lianne and your twins," Archer said. "Len dragged Hannah through some of earth's deepest hell-holes. He didn't live fancy, either. What the natives ate, he ate. What they drank, he drank. That didn't change after he got married."

"I know. I rechecked the passport stamps after I found the hospital records. A week here. Two weeks there. Two days at the next place. Sometimes only a few hours. Flying all over the South Pacific with side trips to Japan or Jakarta just for variety. Was it a coincidence that every place Len went grew, traded, or smuggled pearls?"

"No."

Kyle waited, but his brother didn't say anything more. He started to snap at the lack of response; then he remembered that his brother had been up for more than twenty-four hours, had seen his half brother's corpse, and had just found out about the baby nephew they would never get to nuzzle and tease and love.

"I gotta say," Kyle muttered, "our half brother had shitty taste in friends. I ran the names of some of the people he met with. Bad cess. Really bad. Right down there in the toilet with the Red Phoenix Triad. Different names, of course. Same slime."

"When you go looking for secrets, you make your bargains where you have to."

"Was he a spook?"

Archer didn't want to answer, but he did. Len had been Kyle's brother, too. "He began as an officer in a U.S. foreign intelligence agency. He finished as a mercenary. Sometimes he worked for us. Sometimes for them. And always he worked for himself."

"I'm not sure I like the sound of that."

"You have good instincts. But remember—Len didn't start out where he ended up. What else did you find out about Hannah?"

"She keeps the books for Pearl Cove. She orders equipment locally and electronically. If she shops locally for clothes or cosmetics, she pays cash. The farm has open accounts at several places in Broome."

"What kind of payment record?"

"Pretty good. Not great. Just okay. The last year must have been hard. Some of the accounts started dunning."

"How serious is it?"

"Pearl Cove is on a cash-only basis with an outfit called Smithe and Sons Equipment. The Broome Green Grocer is a little more flexible, up to one hundred dollars Australian. She orders men's and women's clothes by credit card at a virtual store that specializes in casual tropical gear. She orders books at several virtual used-book stores and book exchanges. Reads everything from science fiction to philosophy, with stops in between for Chinese poetry and girl fiction."

"Girl fiction?"

"Yeah, stories about family and marriage and love, that sort of stuff."

Archer grunted and drank more coffee. The breeze through the verandah's screen door was heavy with brine. The temperature was as close to cool as it got in Broome in late November. "Anything else?"

"If she ever saw a doctor, it was the kind who kept old-fashioned handwritten files. Len's doctor was modern. Kept his files electronically and used the virtual diagnostic sites all the time. Len's spine was slowly deteriorating. His doctor had him on morphine. If the local bottle shop is any indication, Len had himself on booze. Or is it Hannah who's heavy on the sauce?"

"If she is, you can't smell it on her breath or her skin."

"That close, huh? Fast work, bro."

"Shove it."

"Ah, there's the Archer we all know and love."

"Shove that, too," he said without heat. "I'm e-mailing a list of Pearl Cove's employees for the past year. See what you can get on them." He yawned wide enough to make his jaw crack.

Kyle snickered. It wasn't often he had his oldest brother at a disadvantage. "Bet you're not going to be a chirpy little camper at dawn tomorrow the way you usually are."

"No bet." Archer rubbed eyes that felt like they had gone skinny-dipping in sand. "Anything else?"

"Nope. Her name never appeared on any of the singles sites or the sexual chat rooms, so virtual sex isn't her thing."

"She could have used an alias," Archer pointed out.

"Hello, this is Kyle, the brother who can spin rings around you on a computer. Remember me? I can track an alias faster than you can think."

"Good thing I can't reach you, runt."

"Runt? I'll runt you the next time I get you on a gym mat."

"Yeahyeahyeah. Lianne can dump you on your ass without breaking a sweat."

"Lianne can put me on my ass any time, anywhere, and any way she wants. Naked is her favorite."

The smug, utterly male note in Kyle's voice made Archer feel a lot more than thirty-seven, going on thirty-eight. He felt ancient, desolate, a ruin on top of a stony hill with nothing but the empty sky for company.

"I left a list of Len's phone calls for the last six months in your coded e-mail," Kyle continued.

"Cellular or land phone?"

"Both."

"Right. Thanks."

"Right, huh? Less than a day and you're sounding like an Aussie."

"It's called camouflage," Archer said dryly.

"You'll need it. Be careful, bro. Very, very careful. My gut wants you the hell out of Australia."

"I'm always careful. 'Bye, Kyle. And thanks."

Archer turned off the cell phone, opened his own computer, accessed the e-mail, and studied the lists of phone calls Len had made. Often the names were familiar. Pearl players, for the most part. Many were honest. More were honest only when they had to be. The rest were strangers. All in all, Len had known—and dealt with—some unsavory-to-dangerous men. Smugglers, government fixers, triad "interfaces," people who lived well outside the law and liked it that way.

Nothing in the lists reassured Archer that the job of finding Len's killer would be easy. Nor did he dismiss Kyle's gut feeling that there was danger. His brother's hunches were better than most men's solid facts.

Another day here, at most. After that, the word would be out that Archer Donovan was at Pearl Cove. Isolated. Working alone. The predators would descend and it would simply be too dangerous for him to stay on.

Unless Len had been working for Uncle. That would give Archer more time, more leverage to use against whoever had wanted Len dead.

Uncle.

Archer stared at his cell phone as if it was a grenade with the pin out and the spoon held down by a frayed thread. Then he picked the phone up and punched in the number he hated to use.

Because as long as he used that number, Uncle Sam would have his number, too.

"What did you say?" Archer asked, turning suddenly toward Hannah. She had come into the kitchen a few minutes ago and silently fixed a pot of coffee. Her nap had left creases on the right side of her face, as though she had fallen into bed and not moved once. Her shorts and tank top were a silvery gray that reminded him of pearls.

"I asked how you liked our computer," she repeated.

" 'Our' as in Len's and yours?"

She swallowed a yawn and rubbed the right side of her face where sweaty skin itched. "Right."

Archer stared at the computer like it was a loaded gun. Knowing Len, it could easily be just that. Yet it had seemed very innocent sitting on a rattan table in an alcove off the kitchen. And it had worked well enough for him on Pearl Cove's accounts. Hannah's simple password "Today" had opened up everything on the hard drive.

It had taken less than an hour to verify that, as a business, Pearl Cove was ninety-eight percent in the toilet. Len had borrowed against everything at least twice, and that included pearl futures.

Of course, there could be another set of books somewhere. In fact, Archer would have bet a lot on it. The question was where.

He glanced at Hannah. Her nap had helped to focus her, but she was still nearly dead on her feet. "So you both used this computer?" he asked, hardly able to believe it.

"Yes." She poured more coffee in her own cup and held the pot out to him, silently asking if he wanted more. Her eyes looked huge and dark against her pale skin. Despite her fragile appearance, she handled the coffee pot and cup without clumsiness.

"No, thanks," Archer said, shaking his head. He looked back at the computer screen. Caffeine could only go so far in curing jet lag. He was well past that point. "I'm surprised you didn't have separate computers. Len didn't like sharing."

Hannah shrugged. "Money. Every penny we had went into his pearl experiments."

"I went through all the files on the hard drive while you

were asleep. I didn't see any that were Len's. Frankly, I would have expected him to booby-trap his computer."

"He kept his work on a separate storage disk." She went to what looked like a cookie jar, took off the scarlet lid, fished around for a few moments, and pulled out a disk that fit easily in her palm. The disk had been wrapped to protect it from cookie crumbs. Absently she wiped the package on her thigh.

"Chocolate chip?" Archer guessed, looking at the dark smear on her skin. The thought of licking it off sent a shaft of heat through him. He wondered when he would get too tired to respond to her or if exhaustion, like time, wouldn't be enough to kill his response to his half brother's wife.

"Yes, it's chocolate chip," Hannah said. "How did you know?"

"Len's favorite. Mine too."

Smiling rather sadly, she smoothed a spike of chestnut hair behind one ear and rubbed a sleep crease on her neck. "They're a little stale. I haven't made cookies since Len . . ." Her breath went ragged. "Anyway, if you want some, feel free."

"I'll take homemade chocolate chip cookies any way I can get them."

Without a word she set the jar on the floor next to Archer. He reached in and came up with a fistful of cookies.

"Did Len have any particular ritual for loading the disk?" he asked around a big bite of cookie.

As she had said, the cookie was stale. It tasted wonderful, like childhood, when he and his brothers had hidden cookies everywhere in the house to make sure they got more than their fair share. Sometimes they didn't find all of the cookies for days.

"Len turned on the computer," Hannah said, "put his disk in the drive, typed in something, and went to work."

"Code word. Or words." Archer wiped his fingers on his shorts and then rubbed his palms over his eyes. They couldn't possibly be as dry as they felt.

After hours of staring at computer screens, the last thing he wanted to do right now was have a go at Len's records, but there wasn't much choice. Uncle hadn't returned his call. Until he knew whether his half brother had been working for the

U.S. government when he died, Archer couldn't realistically assess how dangerous staying in Pearl Cove was. If the motive for killing Len had been politics rather than business, Hannah might not be in danger.

"Don't suppose you know what his code is?" Archer asked, biting back a yawn. Maybe he should take her up on that coffee. Or maybe sugar and grease would get the job done. He finished off the second cookie and started in on a third.

"Like you said, Len wasn't big on sharing. Once I got the disk for him, I left. His code was his secret."

Archer would have been surprised by any other answer. That didn't mean he liked it. Kyle was across the biggest ocean on earth and sound asleep again. Archer's hacking skills were distinctly average. Knowing Len, average wouldn't get the job done.

But he would try anyway, because he didn't want to examine the pearling shed where Len had died until tonight, when it was full darkness and there was no excuse for any of Pearl Cove's employees to be poking around the wreckage. He didn't want them watching him, noting what interested him, suspecting what he was really after.

"Any guesses on the code?" he asked.

Hannah shook her head, sipped coffee that was almost as steamy as the air outside, and waited. It was early evening, she had had a nap, and she felt like she had been up forever. Archer must have felt the same, but it didn't show except in the darkness beneath his eyes. His thick, short hair was rumpled by casual, raking swipes from his long fingers. His beard was too short to show any lack of combing. Sweat gleamed, caught like dew in the black thatch of hair across his bare chest.

As she watched, several drops gathered at his breastbone and trickled down the narrow line of hair that vanished beneath the waistband of his shorts. Loose, dark blue, and thin enough to dry in minutes, the cloth clung to him almost as closely as sweat.

She couldn't stop looking. He was beautifully made, neither too heavy nor too lean . . . supple and powerful, entirely and elementally male. She wondered if he was like Len when it came to sex: hard and fast and furious, as though he couldn't finish soon enough. Then the accident had come and the end of anything sexual.

Hastily Hannah looked at her coffee, unsettled by her own thoughts and the fugitive heat pulsing out from the pit of her stomach. Now was the wrong time for her body to wake up from its long hibernation. Even if it had been the right time, Archer was the wrong man to be looking at. He was too hard. Too cold. Too ruthless.

She couldn't survive another Len.

When Hannah looked away, Archer let out a breath he hadn't been aware of holding. The fundamental female approval in her eyes had him halfway to an erection before he knew what hit him. The faint flush high on her cheekbones didn't help him to cool off. He wished he could pull her shorts down, open her legs, and push into the sultry velvet deep inside her.

With an impatient curse at his own unruly lust, Archer forced his thoughts back to Len's computer. It wasn't a cold shower, but it was close enough. After a few minutes of thinking about various possibilities for entry codes, his body slowly relaxed again.

He shoved in the disk. As he settled deeper into the chair, broken wicker strips poked into his legs, homing in on the same tender places like heat-seeking missiles. He wondered how Len had tolerated the ridiculous chair. Then he remembered—the nerves leading to his brother's legs had been severed years ago. The only thing he sat in was a wheelchair.

The screen lit up. The cursor flashed in a little box, urging him to enter the user code. He started with the simple stuff first. When the first two tries failed, he turned off the computer, waited, and rebooted.

Hannah waited until the fourth time he restarted the machine before she asked, "What are you doing?"

"Using Len's name with variations based on elementary codes."

She blinked. "Oh." After five more tries, she said hesitantly, "Len didn't think much of codes. Said they were for little boys in tree houses."

Archer grunted, shut down the computer, and rebooted.

"Why do you keep shutting down the computer?" she asked.

"Even the most paranoid password programs will give you two tries before they fry circuits. Kyle has a way around that, but he isn't here. I'll just have to do it the hard way for a while."

"I see." She sipped coffee that was now the same temperature as her tongue. "This could take a long time."

He slanted her a sideways glance that reflected the tropical blues and greens of the tiles in her kitchen floor. "Yeah. You have something better to do?"

"Watch flies land?" she suggested.

Smiling, he tried two more variations. Nothing.

Fifteen minutes later, he shut down the computer and turned to Hannah. "Okay, his code probably isn't a variant of his name or birthday, the date of his marriage or the date he was paralyzed. It's not a variant of your name or birth date, either. You don't have any pets, so—"

"My name?" she cut in. Her eyes widened into startled, navy blue pools. "Why mine?"

"People have lousy memories. When it comes to passwords, they use names and dates that are important to them."

She laughed out loud. "Forget my name. I wasn't important to Len. Not that way."

"You were his wife."

"We shared a computer."

"And a house."

"Not in the last few years. He pretty much lived out in the main pearl-sorting shed. There's a small loo, a sink, a hand shower, a bed." She smiled thinly. "All the comforts of home and none of the drawbacks."

"Why didn't he keep the computer in the shed?"

"He didn't want anyone to know that he could use it."

Snake tongues of adrenaline flicked through Archer. He looked at the computer and wondered how many of the answers he needed lay inside. "You're sure of that?"

"That he wanted his computer use kept a secret?"

"Yes."

"Positive."

"Why?"

She shrugged.

"Guess," he said curtly.

"Guessing implies that Len and I have—*had*—enough thought processes in common for a guess to be effective. I gave up guessing at Len's reasons for doing anything years ago. He and I didn't think alike." Hannah's eyes focused on Archer in dark speculation. "You would have a better chance at it."

"Are you saying I'm like Len?"

The bitterness in Archer's voice caught her by surprise. "I didn't mean it as an insult."

He let out a soft, hissing curse and reached for another cookie. "I'm not Len. I repeat. Not. Len. If I saw things the way he did, I'd have stayed in the field or gone private with him when he asked me to."

Hesitantly, Hannah touched Archer's hand, where he still held his fourth cookie. Or maybe it was his sixth. A melting chocolate chip touched her fingertip like a tiny, soft tongue. "Right. You're not Len. But you're cool, efficient, and merciless. That requires thinking a certain way, doesn't it?"

Cool. Efficient. Merciless.

Archer smiled grimly and looked at his watch. He didn't know how much time he had left at Pearl Cove. He knew it wouldn't be enough to get into Len's computer, unless he got pig-lucky. "I can be all of those things. It hasn't helped me get into that damned disk. The things that should have been important to him . . . weren't."

"What do you mean?"

"His wife," Archer said succinctly. "You should have been important to him." *And so should his unborn child.*

But Archer didn't say that aloud. For her it had happened seven years ago; she had healed. For him, it was a fresh wound.

Hannah shrugged off the suggestion that she should have mattered to Len, but her eyes were haunted. "Some things just don't work out. Only one thing was important to Len. Pearls."

Archer's eyes narrowed. He turned back to the computer. He fed in variations on the theme of pearls, Pearl Cove, black pearls, experimental pearls . . .

"Wait!" Hannah said, grabbing his shoulder and leaning toward the screen in sudden excitement. "Try the words *Black*

Trinity. Nothing mattered more to him than making that necklace perfect."

The keys clicked quickly as Archer fed in the words. Quickly the screen changed, listing various files and applications.

"Bingo."

Hannah sensed the triumph vibrating just beneath his control. She turned toward him. He was focused on the screen as he opened the file that had been used most recently. The screen blinked and filled with . . .

Gibberish.

"Shit." Archer raked his hand through his hair. "More code."

He looked outside. In a few hours evening would descend like a purple and orange freight train. Then it would be dark enough to check out Len's home away from home, his steel shell against the world.

For a moment Archer wondered if oysters felt secure inside their shells, or simply trapped.

"Now what?" Hannah asked.

"Now I tie up my cell phone for a few hours."

Mystified, she watched while he plugged his cell phone into the computer, punched in a number, hit some keys, and stood up.

"That's it?" she asked.

"Yeah."

"Now what?"

"We wait."

Seven

*H*ours later, Archer unplugged his computer from his cell phone, tossed it on the counter next to Hannah's phone, and went to the stove for more coffee. Flynn had called in an hour earlier, claiming he was crook—sick. Archer didn't believe it. Nor did he care enough to do anything about it. He and Hannah weren't going to be in Australia long enough for Flynn's report to matter.

Just as Archer started pouring the thick brown coffee into a mug, his phone rang.

"I'll get it," Hannah said, slipping past him. When she saw that it was his cellular, not hers, that was ringing, she hesitated. With a shrug, she answered it. "G'day."

"Archer Donovan." The woman's voice was clipped. She wasn't asking, she was telling.

"Who's calling?"

"It's his uncle returning his call."

"Sounds more like his aunt."

"Is Donovan there or not?"

"Yes." Hannah turned to Archer. "It's your uncle," she said clearly, handing him the phone.

The change in his eyes made her realize just how warm they had been. She looked at the phone in his big hand and stepped back away from it. From him. Neither the phone nor the man was her business, no matter how curious she was about both.

She headed for the bathroom, saying over her shoulder, "I need a shower."

Archer glanced in the readout window on the cell phone. There was no number for the incoming call. It was in the clear, unscrambled, available to anyone who wanted to overhear.

"This is Donovan," he said. His voice said a lot more. Impersonal, leashed, merciless. "How the hell are you, Uncle?"

Though Archer didn't watch Hannah, he was aware that she had withdrawn. Just to make sure the distance was far enough, he walked out onto the verandah. Against the blazing sunset, the new screens gave the land and sea a metallic, surreal glow.

"You waited a long time to call," the woman told him.

Silently he absorbed the fact that the U.S. government already knew something about Pearl Cove and cared enough that they had been hoping he would have to ask for help.

Not good.

"If I'd known you were waiting, I would have called sooner."

"Save it for someone who believes you, slick."

"Slick, huh?" He smiled thinly. The agent who had reluctantly helped Kyle chase ancient Chinese jade had called both Donovan men "slick." April Joy had been in and out of Donovan lives several times since then. She was a very beautiful, very intelligent, and very ruthless agent. At one time he would have been attracted to her. He was a lot older now. "I thought your specialty was jade."

"That's why I'm not happy. As far as I'm concerned, pearls are the end product of constipated oysters."

Archer smiled thinly. "My requests are simple. Do you want them in the clear?"

"Knowing you, I doubt it."

Static poured into his ear before a status light blinked on his phone and words came out instead of electronic garbage. Obviously the two computers had found a code they both could translate.

". . . understand?" she asked.

"Loud and clear. Ready?"

"I was born ready."

He didn't doubt it. "Two passports. Married couple. Mine should have blue eyes instead of gray. Hers should be brown. Black wig, long enough to put in more than one hairstyle. The woman is five feet ten inches, one hundred and twenty-five pounds, brown hair and brown eyes, thirty-four, dressed like designer sin. Expensive." With a faint curving of his lips, he wondered if Hannah would object to having five years, one inch, and some odd pounds piled on her life, plus a courtesan's clothes. "One pair of brown contacts. One pair of dark blue. Tickets from Broome to Darwin under one alias. Tickets from Darwin to Hong Kong under the second alias."

"Got it. You'll be Mr. and Mrs. Murray on the flight from Broome to Darwin. Darwin to Hong Kong you'll be Mr. and Mrs. South. Where to after Hong Kong?"

"I'll take care of it from there."

There was a humming silence on the other end of the call that told Archer he wasn't making April happy.

"How soon?" she asked, her voice clipped.

"Yesterday."

She snorted. "Next week."

"Tonight."

"Tomorrow, Mr. South, and you should be thanking me on your knees with your face buried in my deepest cleavage."

Archer smiled despite the urgency gnawing on him. "South. Right. I have a rental car. White Toyota, left rear taillight will be broken."

"Careless of you."

"I'm a careless kind of guy."

April laughed at that, a sound of genuine amusement.

"The car will be parked in the airport lot at Broome," Archer continued, "as close to the entrance of the lot as possible."

"Do better. I'm not sending some joker cruising the airport parking lot for hours, looking for a broken taillight."

"You ever been to Broome?"

"No."

"You can cruise the whole town in five minutes, max."

"East Bumblefart," she muttered. "Anything else?"

Archer gave her a few more items, waited, and asked, "What do you want from me?"

"The betting is that you know all about Len McGarry's background."

"Until seven years ago, yes."

"Okay, slick. Listen up. Uncle never heard of Len McGarry."

Archer grunted. That wasn't good news. "Especially in the past seven years?"

"You catch on. Make damn certain no one else does."

"Yeah, folks get really testy when friends spy on friends."

She muttered something in Chinese, which made Archer wish that his sister-in-law Lianne was along to translate.

"Slick," April said, "you sit down at a table where China, Japan, and Australia are playing pearl poker, and you can count your friends on your cock. McGarry was a loser, but he was a useful loser. Sometimes. Most of the time he was just a hemorrhoid. He took money from everyone at the table and some who weren't. He was a player without a handler."

Nothing new there, Archer thought. Len had never liked taking anyone's orders, no matter how compelling the reason.

"What does Uncle say?" Archer asked.

"We know French Tahiti's pearl farms are getting raped by international pirates—mostly Chinese businessmen in league with the triads. We're not crying. The French told the world to go to hell when they nuked that atoll. Now we're returning the favor."

"Just so I don't accidentally eat Uncle's lunch," he said, "all you're interested in is keeping Len's past quiet?"

April hesitated.

Shit. But what Archer said aloud was, "Right?"

"I'll get back to you on that."

"Don't wait until a postmortem."

"You planning on killing someone?"

"I'm planning on staying alive. Pass the good word."

"I will." She hesitated, sighed, and stuck her neck out. "Don't turn your back on anyone. *Anyone.* Pearls in general, and unique black pearls in particular, have become a very valuable bargaining chip at certain international tables. That could change in a week, a month, or a year. Until it does, there are some fairly lethal folks out there playing pearl poker."

"Does Uncle favor any of the players?"

"So far, we're just kibitzing."

"Let me know if that changes."

"I hope it doesn't, slick. Odds are we wouldn't be on the same side."

Archer wondered if the U.S. favored China, Japan, or Australia in the black pearl free-for-all. But there was no point in asking. April had already said more than he had expected her to. More than she should have.

"Thanks," he said simply. "When this is over, I'll arrange a tour of the Tang jade collection, if you're interested."

"Am I breathing?"

He laughed.

"Stay alive, slick. I dream of seeing Wen Tang's jade."

"There it is," Hannah said, pointing.

Crouching on his heels, Archer ran his fingertips very lightly over the bent metal that once had been the door to the biggest pearl-sorting shed. Though the sun had long since fallen off the hazy western edge of the horizon, the metal was still hot.

He set down his backpack, opened it, and took out the small flashlight again. An intense beam of light leaped out, sweeping over the metal like a second noon. Holding the light almost parallel to the warped door, he examined the salt-stained steel.

"What are you looking for?" Hannah asked.

"Tool marks."

Anxiously she glanced over her shoulder. No one was nearby. No one was walking toward them. The ocean lay in shades of black with molten silver highlights. A fugitive moon winked between pillars of clouds. Fitful fingers of breeze combed water and land alike. The cooling air was silky, heady, laced with salt and the earthy scent of tidal flats bared by the retreating tide.

Intent on the remains of the shed, Archer was aware of the heat and rushing night and silence, but he didn't really notice it. He wouldn't, unless something changed in a threatening way. With small, smooth motions, he shifted the light from the lock and door handle to what was left of the hinges.

Between one heartbeat and the next, the chemical heat of adrenaline slid silently into his blood, bringing his whole body to a heightened awareness. It was just a small flick of the adrenaline whip, nothing like he had known in the past, but it was very real. The echoes and memories it brought reminded him of everything he had tried to leave behind.

"What is it?" Hannah asked, caught by Archer's absolute stillness.

"Looks like somebody went after the hinges with a hammer and chisel."

Swiftly she crouched beside him. The surface of the ruined door was like a road map of chaos—dents, scrapes, lines, gouges, pits, everything that a violent, debris-packed storm could do to metal.

"How can you tell?" she asked. "The whole door is scratched and banged up."

"Storm damage is random, not symmetrical."

As Archer spoke, his long index finger traced the faint, repeated parallel gouges that radiated out from—or into—the top hinge. The marks of purposeful damage were repeated on the middle hinge, as well.

Hannah shivered convulsively and stood up.

Without standing, Archer looked at her pale, drawn face. "You're certain that Len was inside the shed when the storm struck?"

She nodded jerkily.

"Alone?" he asked.

Again the jerky nod.

He watched her for a minute, wondering why the discovery of the marks had upset her. Earlier, when he had told her that someone had knifed Len and then rammed a fragment of oyster shell between his ribs to disguise the wound, she hadn't shown much response. Maybe she had just been too tired.

A soft breeze tugged at her hair and flattened the thin white tank top over her breasts and belly. She had changed from shorts to cutoff jeans. Her legs were racehorse-long, beautifully shaped, and bare. He wondered what she would do if he ran his palms up the back of her legs, over buttocks hugged by worn jeans, beneath the tank top to her shoulder blades, then slowly around to the high breasts that were as naked as his tongue beneath the tank top.

With a silent curse Archer yanked his mind back to the business at hand. The steel door had buckled along the side, between the hinges. The damage could have come from a crowbar or from the storm itself, after some hinges had given way. He was betting on the crowbar. Once the door was pried partly open from the hinge side, the violent cyclone would do the rest.

Absently Archer fingered the frayed wires of what had once been the door's electronic lock.

"Most electronic systems freeze in the locked position if the power goes out," he said. "Is that the way the shed was set up?"

"Yes."

"Is there a manual release on the inside?"

"Yes."

"Did Len spend a lot of time alone in the sorting shed?"

"Yes."

"Did everyone know it?"

"Yes."

"Not much help there."

She didn't respond.

"Hannah."

Though Archer's voice was soft, she flinched. Then she looked at his eyes and flinched again.

"What's the problem?" he asked. "You called me, I came, yet more often than not I feel like I'm opening oysters with my bare hands when I ask you questions."

Visibly she took a grip on herself. "I was all right before you came. I knew I had only myself, that I couldn't let down. So I didn't. But now . . ."

Archer knew that she hadn't been all right. She had been running on nerve and adrenaline, headed for a big crash. Yet all he said was, "Want me to leave?"

"No." The reply was instant, certain.

"Good. I wasn't going to go even if you asked."

Startled, she stared at him. What she saw in the reflected glow of the flashlight both frightened and reassured her.

"Len was murdered," Archer said evenly. "I'm in this for the whole distance, with or without your help."

"I know," she whispered. "I knew when you came back from Broome. You looked the way Len used to look. The way you look now. Deadly. But you're sane and he wasn't, not always. Not even most of the time." She rubbed her hands over her arms. "God, I hope I did the right thing by calling you. I don't want more death. I just want the Black Trinity."

"I'm not planning on Old Testament justice. The modern kind will do just fine."

Hannah's long eyelashes swept down as she let out a breath in a relief she couldn't hide.

"But one way or the other, there will be justice," Archer added softly. He stood and snapped off the flashlight. "Show me what's left of the main shed."

Without a word she turned and walked back to the path leading down to the water. Crushed oyster shell crunched softly underfoot. He walked just behind her, trying not to notice the rhythmic, elementally sexy arc of her hips. He knew that she wasn't swinging her ass for his benefit.

You look the way Len used to look. Deadly.

Archer didn't need to ask how that made Hannah feel about him. She needed him, but she didn't like it—or him—one bit. He didn't really blame her. He was associated with the worst hours of her life, when Len had begun the transformation from a vital, virile husband to a bitter, crazy shell of a man.

Hannah wouldn't be the first one to shoot the bad-news messenger. Archer understood too well how she felt, nerve and resentment all tangled up, the child beneath the adult crying, *I don't want to go there!* He had spent years trying to put his past where it belonged. Behind him. Coming here, seeing Hannah, seeing Len, brought it all back in savage clarity. He didn't want to go there again.

But there he was.

The only thing he could do was wrap this mess up as soon as possible, then get out before all the sad, dark echoes of his past deafened him to the possibilities of the present. That had nearly happened once. He had nearly gone under, lured by the siren call of adrenaline and danger, until nothing was real but a world where treachery was the norm, multiple identities were the rule, and death was the sole judge of who won and who lost.

Some people thrived on that life. He wasn't one of them.

But he had left Len mired in that brutal, covert world. He hadn't been able to pull his half brother out until it was too late. Len had gone under, and Archer felt a guilt at escaping that was as irrational as it was powerful.

"How much warning did you have before the storm?" he asked neutrally.

Hannah's steps hesitated, as though she was startled to find herself not alone. Or maybe it was the emotions she sensed battling just beneath Archer's level voice that made her pause.

"We had several days," she said, "but we were expecting just a tropical blow, nothing to get excited about. The storm was supposed to hit land about two hundred kilometers north of here. That changed in a matter of hours. Even then, the force of the wind caught everyone off guard. No one was expecting a big one."

Archer came alongside Hannah as the path widened down toward the beach. "So Len's murderer didn't have a lot of time to plan."

Though his voice was low, carrying no more than a foot or two, Hannah looked around hastily to make certain no one could overhear.

"Don't," he said.

"What?"

"Keep checking to see if anyone is nearby. You're just show-ing your partner the storm damage so I can assess what can be salvaged and what's junk, remember? Why would you care if anyone overheard us?"

"But what if—"

"No worries," he cut in ironically. "I have eyes in the back of my head. If people are watching us, they're doing it at a distance."

Hannah hesitated, then strode forward again, matching strides with Archer's longer legs. "We could see better in day-light," she pointed out.

"We do that tomorrow, if necessary." And if they were still at Pearl Cove, which Archer doubted. But he didn't want Hannah to know they were leaving until they left. April Joy's warning had been quite clear. *Don't trust anyone.* In any case, he didn't want people to know Hannah was going until she was gone. "We can see things in darkness that full light hides."

"You sound like you've done this before."

"Done what?"

"Look for murderers."

"I've looked for a lot of things."

When he said nothing more, she glanced up at his face. Moonlight and the abrupt tropical night had turned his hair to absolute black and his eyes to silver. Beneath the short, sleek beard, the line of his mouth was hard enough to cut glass. He looked like what he was, moved like what he was, like Len once had been: a man trained to kill other men.

The ruined shell of the sorting shed appeared almost welcoming by comparison. She hurried forward, only to feel Archer's hand wrap around her upper arm, pulling her to a stop.

"Wait," he said, his voice as soft as the breeze lifting off the coal-dark sea.

"Why—"

A curt shake of his head cut off her words. "Talk in a normal tone about Pearl Cove, how it works, what you do. Don't mention Len's death."

For a moment Hannah could only stare at Archer's face, her thoughts scattering like moonlight on water. His fingers squeezed gently.

"Start with winter," he suggested softly. "What do you do then?"

"I—we—" She took a breath. "Um, in June, July, and August, we harvest shell that was seeded two years ago."

"Why do you harvest in winter?"

"Because nacre is laid down thin in colder water, and thin nacre has the greatest luster." She fell silent.

"How was the harvest this year?"

"I don't know. Len always handled that end of the job while I seeded new oysters. He didn't trust anyone but me with his experimental babies. And sometimes Coco."

Adrenaline licked in Archer's blood. *Experimental.* Maybe those oysters held the secret of the extraordinary melted rainbows shimmering beneath black glass. But that wasn't a conversation he wanted to share with whoever was cat-footing through the ruined shed right now.

"Two years from seed to pearl?" he asked, as though he didn't know.

"Right. It can be done faster—some of the Japanese Akoya oysters are harvested after only six months—but to get a top-quality pearl, the nacre has to be thick enough so that ordinary use won't dull the pearl's luster. That means the ratio of nacre to the bead has to—"

"Bead?" Archer cut in, trying to slow the nervous rushing of her words.

"The round piece of American mussel shell we use to 'seed' the oyster is called a bead once it's surrounded by nacre. That is, once it's a pearl."

He made a small sound of understanding and waited. Hannah didn't take the hint and resume talking. He squeezed her arm again, silently asking her to focus on the here and now, rather than on whatever shadows haunted her voice, her mind.

"The ratio of nacre to the bead . . . ?" he invited.

"Um," she said, distracted by the gentle pressure of Archer's fingers on her arm. They felt firm, warm, almost caressing. The contrast between the tenderness of his touch and the remote mercury sheen of his eyes was disorienting. "The, um, the nacre should be ten to fourteen percent of the total diameter of the pearl. Natural pearls are one hundred percent nacre, of course, except for the original irritant. The finest, most costly cultured pearls have forty to fifty percent nacre. Those pearls are worth much, much more than a pearl of similar size and shape that lacks the fine orient that only many layers of nacre can give."

Lightly Archer stroked his fingers over Hannah's smooth skin, telling himself he was only soothing her and at the same time reminding her to keep talking.

He didn't believe it. Fooling himself was something a smart man didn't do. But his fingertips kept on moving anyway, sipping lightly at the silk and warmth of her skin.

"If an extra eighteen months in the water makes for high-end pearls," Archer said calmly, "why doesn't everyone just leave the oysters in the drink and make a lot more money?"

"The longer you wait to harvest, the greater the chance that you'll get a pearl that is blemished or off round in shape. Two years is what Len decided was the best return on our investment."

"Which still makes Pearl Cove's harvest a very high-end product," Archer said.

"The—" her voice hitched "—best."

Gooseflesh rippled up Hannah's arm and shivered down to the pit of her stomach. Archer was making tiny, tiny circles on the sensitive underside of her arm. She would have pulled away, but she couldn't move. She was having enough trouble just breathing. It had been a long time since a man had touched her so gently.

Even as the thought came, she knew it wasn't true. It hadn't been a long time. It had been forever. She hadn't even guessed a man could have such tenderness in him.

Breath held in something that was closer to anticipation than anxiety, Hannah looked up to Archer's eyes. He wasn't watching her. He was watching tropical night sweep over the land in a dark, silent rush of extinguished light. The intent stillness of his body told her that he was waiting for . . . something. If it hadn't been for the slight, continuous caress of his fingertips, she would have said that he didn't even know she was there.

"Keep talking," he said very softly.

Hannah filled her lungs as though she was going to dive below the warm surface of the sea to the shadowed depths. "After we seed and harvest, and even during, we're constantly turning all the oysters in their cages."

He made a sound that meant only that he was listening.

She didn't doubt it. She just wondered what he was listening to, because she didn't think it was her. At least, she hoped not. In the darkness and reflected light, Archer's eyes looked predatory.

Then Hannah heard a small noise from the shed she had turned her back on. Fear raced icy over her skin and slicked her spine with sweat.

Eight

"No," Archer said softly.

But even before he spoke, his hands clamped around Hannah's upper arms, preventing her from turning toward the sound.

"There's some—"

"I know," he cut in, his voice still soft. "Talk to me. Tell me about Pearl Cove. Or else I'll have to kiss you. Either way will work as a cover for standing around out here, but it's your call."

Hannah realized two things at once. The first was that Archer had known a prowler was in or around the shed from the moment he asked her to talk about Pearl Cove. The second was that the idea of kissing him sent heat chasing after the chill of fear. She told herself she was losing it, that the last thing she needed in her life was another Len.

Yet she wanted Archer's kiss. She wanted the heady combination of his gentle touch and dangerous eyes, his cool restraint and a body that radiated vital heat.

I'm crazy. Absolutely crackers.

Hannah took a deep breath and began talking. Fast. "We turn the oysters to improve our chances of getting a round pearl. We also clean the shells to get off whatever is clinging to them. Later, in October, we move the rafts so that the water temperature will stay as close to ideal as possible."

"How big are your rafts?"

"Standard size."

He gave her a look that reminded her to keep talking or start kissing.

"A raft is made up of ten parts," she said hurriedly. "Um, each part is about twenty by twenty feet, and has a hundred separate baskets which hold a thousand oysters total. Ten per basket." She swallowed and thought quickly. "The rafts are held in place by anchors and kept afloat by big metal drums."

"A regular farm," he said, telling himself that he wasn't disappointed by her choice of talking over kissing. It was better this way, much better. He forced himself to look past her to the shed. "Do you feed your oysters, too?"

"The ocean takes care of it for us. The huge tidal shifts send a lot of water over the oysters. That's why the west-coast oysters are so big. Lots of nutrients. Oysters are filter feeders. All they have to do to eat is suck the tasty bits out of the big saltwater smorgasbord that rushes by them as the tide moves in and out."

Archer smiled slightly, a white gleam in the night. Hannah thought of the kiss she had turned down and told herself she didn't regret it.

"After the operated shell—um, the oysters we just seeded—rest for about a month," she continued huskily, "we move the survivors to the growing-out area."

"Survivors? Do you lose a lot?"

"The norm is somewhere between twenty and thirty percent, but Pearl Cove loses only eleven percent. Coco and Tom are very, very skillful. It's rare for them to injure the tiny pea crab that lives inside each healthy oyster."

"So you've seeded and the crabs are happy. Now what?"

"Prayer," she retorted. "Oysters would much rather reject foreign bodies than make pearls. That's why we slip in a tiny bit of living mantle tissue from a donor oyster of the preferred color. It grafts onto the mantle near the seed and—"

"You lost me. Color?"

Hannah doubted she had lost Archer, but she wasn't going to argue the point. Not when his eyes were narrowed, intent on something over her shoulder. She cleared her throat against the fear that kept crowding in.

"The pearl's color reflects the inner shell color of the oyster." Her voice frayed, then steadied. "Some oysters make silver-white gems. Some pink. Some gold. Some black, and so on. The mantle—the outer surface of the living animal—is the nacre factory. Mantle from an oyster with pink nacre on its inner shell will produce a pink pearl, even if it's put into an oyster with a black shell. Len also did some biogenetic sleight-of-hand with the mantle so that—"

"Right," Archer cut in, heading her off from dangerous territory. "So we have a seed and a bit of mantle that is actually a biological work order for a certain color of pearl."

"Close enough," she muttered. "Most people lose about twenty percent of the grafts. We lose just over seven percent."

"Good hands?"

"The best."

Silently Archer doubted if even a fantastically skilled technician could lower the odds that much. Waving the flag of skill and biogenetics was a way of explaining how a medium-sized operation such as Pearl Cove ended up with more than its share of pearls. But he didn't get the feeling that Hannah was lying. Wherever the truth lay, she believed what she was saying.

Len had always been a very smooth liar. Where he came from, it was a survival skill.

"We also do well on the quality of the pearls," Hannah said. "More than sixty percent of our pearls are good. The average for other farms is thirty-five percent. Another ten percent produces junk. Our percentage of junk is just under six."

Archer grunted. Len must have loved throwing his pearls on the table and daring any of the other farmers to prove that they were the result of anything other than exceptional skill.

"Len was always working on our percentages," Hannah continued. "He said they were good, but not good enough. Even for us, pearl farming wasn't a sure thing."

Absently Archer nodded, but his eyes were looking past her. She took another breath and tried to think where she had left off in describing the yearly cycle of pearl farming.

"Growing-out area," he said so softly that she barely heard.

"Oh. Um. Growing out. That's where we have long lines snaking through rows of buoys. Panels of oysters hang down off the lines. They dangle there and grow while we begin the year fishing for wild shell—oysters—in January and February."

"Wild oysters." He smiled slightly. "You make it sound like something you have to chase down and lasso."

Hannah's laugh was as soft as the air. And like the air, it rippled over Archer, bringing all of his senses alive.

"Almost," she said. "Behind a ship the men dangle off long ropes, towed only a few feet off the bottom. The trick is to stay close enough to the bottom to see the wild shell—and oysters could teach a chameleon how to hide—but not so close as to stir up the silt because then you can't see anything at all."

"So you just go out there and grab what you can?"

This time her laugh wasn't soft or amused. "Not a chance. The government licenses growers to take a certain amount of wild shell and to raise a certain amount of domestic shell. Some growers get a higher quota than others, according to a formula only the government can understand."

"Politics."

"It's a government, isn't it?"

"Which, translated, means that the licenses can be used to reward or punish."

"The bureaucrats will deny it to the last breath."

"Did Pearl Cove have trouble getting wild shell licenses?" he asked.

"We didn't get quite enough to survive, much less to grow. That's why Len had to find other ways to bring up our production in relation to other pearl farms."

"Why was the government giving you a hard time?"

"They thought Len was holding back the best of his pearl production and selling it outside the Australian-Japanese cartel."

Silently Archer wished he had never raised the question. But having done so, it would seem odd to an eavesdropper if he just let the matter drop.

"Was he?" Archer asked, but the sudden pressure of his fingers on Hannah's arm said, *Be careful.*

"No."

He relaxed his grip and returned to the tiny, hidden movements on her skin that pleased his fingertips. "Governments are always suspicious."

"They had reason to be. Less than half of our oysters were for normal sales. The rest were experimentals. Experiments fail a lot more often than they succeed."

"After you collect wild shell, what do you do?" Archer asked, wanting to move on to safer topics.

"We let it 'rest' for a month or two, to recover from the trauma of being handled and moved to a new place. The shells have to be watched and cleaned. And the shells we seeded the previous year have to be X-rayed to see if the bead has been rejected. If so, we seed again."

"One shell, one bead, one pearl?"

"Some of the farmers use several beads, but the result is almost always inferior to just one."

"What's wrong with them?"

"The pearls or the farmers?" Hannah asked dryly.

"The pearls. I've given up trying to understand people."

She smiled and laughed softly. Archer's fingers stilled for a moment, then began moving again, enjoying. Caressing.

"The Japanese started multiple seeding with their little palm-sized Akoya oysters." Hannah's voice hitched at the feel of his hands moving lightly on her skin. "They can get lots of pearls from one shell, but the pearls just aren't good. Even big oysters like the ones we have in the South Seas don't seem to be able to produce more than one quality pearl at a time. The nacre gets too thin or the shape is off or the beads are rejected by the oyster. Len was working on the problem. So is the government. As far as I know, no one has found a solution."

"So you've lassoed wild shell, pampered it, seeded it, pampered it some more, repeat as necessary. Now what?"

"Now it's around April, the water temperature is dropping

with the onset of winter, and we're letting the shells rest. That's when engines are overhauled, hulls are cleaned, rafting equipment is checked out, and whatever has to be built or repaired is taken care of. In May it's back to the grindstone, cleaning shells, turning them, checking the long lines and the cages for damage, gearing up for the harvest and seeding time, and so on. Before you know it, it's June again, harvest time. Full circle."

"Sounds intense."

"It is."

"You like it?"

Hannah hesitated. She had never thought about liking or not liking; it was just the way life was. "Pearl farming is relentless, but it kept me sane. Yes, I guess I like it. I know I needed it."

Archer heard the emotions tightening her voice, felt them in the tension of her arms beneath his hands. He wanted to pull her closer, soothe her, and then kiss her blind.

Slowly he lifted his hands from her tempting flesh and looked past her to whoever was prowling through the ruined shed. Or had been. The sounds had slowly receded, as though someone had used their voices to cover any small noises he made retreating from the shed.

Archer had heard that kind of furtive shuffling too many times before, in too many places where violence prowled in the shadows of civilization. He had vowed never to go there again.

And here he was.

Full circle.

"Show me the shed where all this hard work paid off," Archer said.

Hannah stared at him for an instant, then turned away quickly. If she had felt cool when he took his warm hands from her arms, she was thoroughly chilled by the quality of his voice. It was Len's voice, the voice of her nightmares, utterly neutral, inhuman in its absence of emotion.

She stumbled over a piece of debris, caught herself, and hurried on. She didn't have to look over her shoulder to know that Archer was following her. He was like Len. Nothing would turn him away him from what he wanted.

And what Archer really wanted was Len's killer, not Len's

widow. She would have to remember that the next time she found herself close enough to feel Archer's heat, close enough to taste his breath, close enough to see his pupils dilate when her breasts brushed against his chest. Way too close.

Not nearly close enough.

Rather bitterly Hannah wondered if she shouldn't have used Coco's approach to sex—screw Archer on the ground, then jump up and dust herself off, ready to go back to whatever she had been doing before she was distracted by a clitoral itch. But it was too late to acquire the years of experience and nonchalance that Coco had. Hannah was stuck with being what she was, a woman who had had sex with only one man, and only for a few years.

Her choice, she reminded herself. She paid her way out of the rain forest with her virginity. And while sex was exciting at first, it wasn't worth the rest of it.

Nothing was worth the rest of it.

She stumbled over a broken board, recovered, and wished that she had thought to bring a flashlight.

"What's the rush?" Archer asked behind her.

Only then did Hannah realize that she was all but running through the darkness toward the ruined shed, fleeing as though every mistake she had ever made was chasing her. She forced herself to slow down.

"The door was here," she said, pointing toward a gap in a wall.

Silently he measured the distance from the shed to the place where the steel door lay crumpled next to the path. "That was one hell of a blow you had here."

"It was as big as I ever want to see. Actually, *seeing* is the wrong word. Once the rain hit, I couldn't see beyond the porch. But I could feel it. The house shivered and jerked like a Tahitian dancer."

Hannah stepped through the gap that had once been a door leading into the shed. Even though almost half of the roof was gone and one of the corner pilings had sheared off, taking down most of the two walls nearest the door, she felt like she was stepping into a coffin. The claustrophobia that had begun with

Len's death rose up and filled her throat with raw fear. She froze, unable to take another step into darkness.

To Archer, her sudden stillness was like a warning scream. Swiftly he pulled her behind him. It wasn't much protection, but it was all he could do until he knew the source of the danger. Legs slightly braced, body relaxed, weight poised on the balls of his feet, he waited for whatever might come.

Nothing came but the silent, intangible blending of tide and time and night. No movement, no furtive scuff, no rush of breath held too long.

"It's all right," Hannah said, belatedly realizing why he had shoved her behind him.

"The hell it is. You froze like you had been shot."

"Just nerves. Since Len died . . . claustrophobia, that's all."

Archer heard what she didn't say, all the things that had come crashing down around her in a few short hours. The devastation of the cyclone tearing Pearl Cove out by its roots. The horror of finding Len's ruined body. The certainty that his murderer would kill her as soon as he discovered that she didn't know the secret of the experimental pearls.

"Can you take a few more minutes in here?" Archer asked softly.

"Of course."

Her voice more than her words told him that was how Hannah faced life: whatever was required of her for as long as she could give it. He turned, touched her cheek for an instant, then stepped back before she could do more than take a startled breath. His penlight switched on, slicing through the tropical night. Everything the light touched was broken, bent, battered, and water stained.

"Describe the shed for me, the way it was," Archer said.

Hannah let out the breath she had taken when he touched her face so unexpectedly, so gently. "There was only one door. Tables with trays of pearls went down the center aisle. The pearls are sorted for shape, color, size, and surface. We do the color sorting with natural light. Fluorescent light for orient and spotting blemishes on the surface. Indirect light, of course. With pearls, direct light hides more than it reveals."

While she spoke, the blade of light Archer held moved slowly across the interior of the shed.

"Where did you work?" he asked.

"Over there." Hannah's narrow, elegant hand flashed through the beam as she pointed toward a missing wall. "There were windows. Screens, actually. I worked with the best of the pearls, matching colors for necklaces or brooches or bracelets."

"Were the pearls left out or locked up at night?"

"Locked up."

"Where?"

"There."

With her hand over his, she moved the flashlight toward the place where the roof had collapsed. When Archer realized what he was looking at through the jackstraws that had been lumber, he whistled. Poured-concrete base, steel walls, tumbler locks and industrial-strength handles on all the locker doors. Ten feet high if it was an inch. Even with the outer door ripped off and the drawers yanked out and strewn around, the safe still looked as intimidating as the inside of a bank vault.

"That's a hell of a lockbox," he said.

"Len wasn't a trusting kind of man."

Archer gave an odd crack of laughter. "I take it the pearls were in the drawers when the storm hit?"

"Not all of them. Not even most of them. When the storm hit, pearls must have scattered all over the place."

"You weren't here?"

"No. Len kicked everyone out, locked down the storm shutters, and then did whatever he did when he was alone."

"What does that mean?"

Hannah sighed and wondered how she could explain in a few words the husband she had never understood in ten years. "Len was forever pulling security checks, sending everyone outside and searching them for pearls. Sometimes, for no reason anyone could discover, he would just throw them out and spend an hour or two in here alone. He ate here, slept here, lived here."

"Sounds like he was worried about something being stolen."

"Pearls. And he was right. They're gone."

"Stolen?"

"The insurance people said the storm hit before Len could close up the safe. Everything was washed out to sea. An act of God. Uninsured, of course. So sorry, luv, and your next premium will be due on the twelfth."

Archer's mouth curled. "Sounds like every insurance agent I've ever known." Then, in a low voice, he asked, "What about the chisel marks on the door?"

"It's hard to find what you're not looking for."

"Yeah, that's what I thought." He swept the light from side to side, looking for a fugitive glimmer of pearl. Nothing came back but shades of black. "How did they explain all the open lockers and drawers?"

"Simple. Obviously Len was checking the inventory when the cyclone ripped the place apart. A lot bigger things than pearls went missing in the wind."

Part of Archer's mind enjoyed the symmetry and utility of the explanation: whatever happened, the cyclone did it. If he hadn't seen the chisel marks on the door and felt the ease of his knife's passage between a dead man's ribs, he would have been tempted to accept the explanation himself.

"A variation of the SODDI defense," he said softly.

"What?"

"A defense lawyer's favorite explanation. Some other dude did it. In this case it's a storm, not a man. No worries, mate. Certainly no murder. No insurance money. Just an exhausted widow, a destroyed farm, and shrugs all around, because what else can you do? Life's a bitch and then you die."

Hannah wanted to laugh but was afraid she might not be able to stop. He had caught the man's tone so exactly. "Sure you aren't an insurance adjuster?"

"Dead sure." Archer waited for her to ask what he did. When the silence stretched, he smiled thinly. She assumed he was like Len had been before he was paralyzed—employed by people who didn't want to know his real name and sure as hell didn't want him to know *theirs*. "Occasionally I work in my father's business, Donovan International. It's an import-export business with emphasis on raw materials. My brothers and I have our own business, Donovan Gems and Minerals."

"You're not . . . what Len used to be?"

"A mercenary? No, I never was."

"Len said you were."

"Len hired out to the highest bidder. As long as that was Uncle Sam, we sometimes worked in the same vineyards. When Len went freelance, I stayed behind. After a few more years I got out entirely."

"Why?" she asked.

"Why did Len leave?"

"No. Why did you?"

"I wasn't strong enough."

This time Hannah couldn't help laughing out loud.

Archer didn't laugh. He had told her the exact truth. He hadn't been strong enough to survive the covert game.

Silently he played the flashlight over the jumble of lumber that covered the vault, and wondered if the flanking walls would stand up if he started moving debris around. He wanted to take a closer look at the drawers. Somehow they didn't look quite right.

"You're serious," Hannah said, no longer laughing, watching Archer's face. In the bleak flare of the flashlight, his eyes were clear, polished crystal.

"Some men can work in a sewer and come out smelling like roses," he said evenly, running the blade of light over the ceiling. There were gaps, rips, open seams. It wouldn't take much to bring another section down. "I'm not one of them. Every day, every lie, every double cross, every seductive, addictive rush of adrenaline . . ." He shrugged. "It was eating away at me. I knew one day I would wake up, look in the mirror, and see something that turned my stomach." Something like his half brother had become, but Archer wasn't going to say that to Len's widow. He turned and looked at her. "I got out. End of story."

Hannah didn't know she was going to touch Archer until she felt the smooth pelt of his beard beneath her fingertips, then the surprising heat of his lips. She snatched her hand back. "That wasn't weakness. That was strength."

"Len didn't see it that way."

"Why would you care what Len thought?"

"Didn't he tell you?"

"What?"

"He's my brother."

For a moment she was too shocked to say anything. She had wondered about the bond between the two men, but she hadn't suspected a blood tie. Other than their size and way of moving, they hadn't had much in common physically. Never once, not once, had Len so much as hinted at a blood relationship with Archer Donovan.

Archer used the silence to listen to the sounds of night. He thought he had heard a scuffle, as though a foot had nudged into a stray piece of wood. But it could just as easily have been the wind shifting the precariously piled debris.

Letting breath slide from his lungs, he listened intently, using every sense. He heard only the random movements of wind.

"Your *brother*?" Hannah managed finally. "I didn't even know Len had any family. The first time I asked about his parents was just after the wedding. He sliced me up with a few words and walked out, leaving me in Shanghai with no food and no money in a room I couldn't pay for. I couldn't speak the language. I couldn't even read the signs. He didn't come back for six days. I never asked about his family again."

Archer hoped the impotent rage he felt didn't show in any way. That kind of rage was as corrosive as it was useless. Yet he couldn't dodge a truth that was even more corrosive: by leaving Hannah with Len, he had doomed her as certainly as if he had stripped her naked and sold her on a street corner in Rio.

He hadn't been good enough to keep his own attraction to Hannah hidden from Len. That had made her a perfect target, a sideways kind of vengeance for the bastard half brother to take on the legitimate son. And if an innocent girl got chewed up in the process, well, too bad, how sad, and nobody asked to be born anyway. Len sure as hell hadn't.

Yet Len hadn't always been vicious. That was what had hurt Archer then and still hurt him now. All those bittersweet memories of the first few years he had known Len, the quiet conversations about how to size up a man or a situation, his patient demonstration of survival skills, his deep laughter and easy silences, the smile that could melt glaciers, like his brother Lawe's smile, and Len a blond Viking just like Archer's other brother Justin . . . Even Len's way of raking his fingers through his hair was like his father's, just like Archer's, a genetic echo rolling down the years between generations.

"My father didn't marry Len's mother," Archer said neutrally. "Dad was sixteen and in full rebellion against his father, who was a wild man by the name of Robert Donald Donovan. Layla was eight years older than Dad and going for the Donovan bank accounts."

"Sixteen." Hannah's smile was as bittersweet as Archer's memories. "Must be something dangerous about that age. I was wild to get away from my parents. I would have done anything, even marry a stranger. Three years later I did."

Archer's mouth turned down at one corner. He knew all about being a teenager and determined to get out from under the old man. The good news was that most kids survived it, and the dumb choices they made. The bad news was that some of them didn't live and learn.

He walked back toward the safe, drawn by its massive bulk in the midst of ruin. How like Len to pour concrete and raise steel walls and defy the gods of sea and storm. Had he lived to see his metal roof rolled up like the top of an anchovy tin?

"Dad wasn't desperate enough to marry a stranger," Archer said, probing pools of black with his flashlight. "Life in the Robert Donovan household was loud and overbearing, but it was also warm and full of love. Probably a lot like what I grew up in."

"So Layla made her play for the gold ring and got turned down, is that it?"

"Even if Dad wanted to marry her—and I doubt that he did—he was too young to do it without his father's permission. Grandfather certainly wasn't stupid enough to give that permission. Layla thought Dad was nineteen, not sixteen. She was furious. Then she was pregnant and demanding money. When the blood tests came back with Donovan written all over them, my grandfather offered Layla thirty thousand a year until the kid was eighteen, or a cash settlement of a quarter of a million. She took the cash and ran."

"And that was that?" Hannah asked from just behind Archer.

"Until I was born, yes." He stood on tiptoe and shined the light through a break in the tangle of smashed tables, broken chairs, and other less identifiable debris. "Dad was about twenty-five then. Seeing me grow made him think about the son he had never known. He hired people to track Layla down. It took seven years to find her. She was dying of alcoholism. She didn't have Len. He had run away."

"How old was he?"

"Fourteen," Archer said absently. There were scratch marks on the drawers. No surprise there. The vault had taken a hell of a hammering from flying metal chairs, among other things. "Dad started looking for Len. He was still looking when I graduated from college with a lot of language skills and a restlessness that could only be satisfied by roaming."

"You found Len."

"Did he tell you?"

"No. I just can't imagine you not getting what you want."

"Imagine it. It happens five times a day." And it had been happening a hell of a lot more frequently since he had landed in Broome and seen Hannah McGarry's haunted eyes and long, bare legs. "Who opened the top drawers for Len?" Archer asked.

"I did. He hated that, having to ask me. Just like he hated having to depend on my eyes for color matching."

"Len always was hell-bent on standing alone. Sometimes that's the best way to get a job done, especially some of the jobs he did. But it's a lousy way to live. Have you checked the top drawers since he died?"

"Yes. There were some pearls in them, but not the best. Len kept those within his reach."

"What happened to the best pearls?"

"Nothing left but the drawers. Empty."

"That was one busy cyclone."

"Greedy, too."

The corner of Archer's mouth turned up. "Where's the ladder you used to reach the high drawers?"

Her hand closed over his wrist, pushing the flashlight in

another direction. "There, along what's left of the wall, behind that stack of shutters I thought might be saved."

Though the feel of her fingers sent heat licking through Archer, all he said was, "I assume Len had a room somewhere in the shed."

"Yes. It's over there. Or was."

Archer looked at the emptiness of a destroyed wall. He could just make out twisted bits of plumbing sticking out of the floor. Turning away, he concentrated on what the storm had left behind rather than what it had taken.

He crossed the shed, examined the shutters leaning against the ladder, and began shifting them to the side. There was no way to do it quietly. That made him uneasy, like the rising kick of the wind. Soft, furtive sounds would be buried in the background noise.

The wind gusted in a long exhalation that made the shed creak and debris settle in a slightly different way. Archer froze, listening. He would have sworn he heard footsteps rushing with the wind.

"Get out," he said to Hannah.

"But—"

"Now." Archer grabbed her and began running for the door.

It was too late. A wall buckled and the metal roof came hammering down.

Nine

*B*efore Hannah understood what was happening, she was facedown on the floor with something heavy covering her from head to heels. Even as she realized the weight was Archer, metal thudded and clanged around them.

She tried to look up. She couldn't. She was completely wedged beneath him. There was barely enough room left over to breathe. Claustrophobia swept through her in a wave that stiffened her whole body.

"Easy, Hannah. Don't fight me. I won't hurt you, but what's left of the roof sure as hell might."

The calm voice reassured her at a level too deep for words. She made a questioning sound that wasn't quite fear.

"It's raining big chunks of metal," Archer said against her ear. "I'll let you up as soon as it stops. Okay?"

She nodded.

"Sure?" he asked.

"Yes. Sorry. I—"

"You have nothing to apologize for."

It was the brush of his mouth against her ear more than

the words that silenced her. Like his fingertips had been, his lips were warm, gentle, demanding nothing of her. She let out a broken breath, and with it, most of her fear.

She waited, listening. The gritty tile beneath her body was cold and hard. The man covering her was hot and supple. The contrast was as disorienting as being thrown to the floor while the roof came down around her ears.

Archer shifted slightly on his elbows. Debris clattered and slid off his back. A piece of metal the size of a dinner table groaned. He arched his back, testing the weight of junk covering him. Metal grated against tile.

Footsteps retreated at a dead run.

It sounded like only one person, but Archer couldn't be sure. For an instant he considered jumping up and running down whoever was fleeing. He shoved the impulse aside because it was the result of adrenaline, not thought. If he chased the intruder, Hannah would be left alone. Vulnerable. A woman who smelled like cinnamon and sunshine shouldn't be left to face the darkness alone.

"Archer?" she whispered.

"Not yet."

Silently she waited while he listened and listened and listened. She felt suspended, almost dazed. Then—ridiculously—sleepy. Sliding down a long slow tunnel, darkness going by at a greater and greater speed. Distantly she supposed she should be afraid, but she couldn't work up the strength. Except for her nap earlier today, fear had kept her from sleeping more than ten or fifteen minutes at a time since Len had died. She simply didn't have the energy to be afraid anymore.

Or the need. Archer wouldn't kill her while she slept. And a little catnap would be a wonderful thing.

"Hannah? *Hannah.* Come back to me, sweetheart. Tell me where it hurts."

When her eyes shot open, a white light sliced into them. Quickly she tried to turn her head and shield her eyes from the flashlight, but she was still pinned in place by Archer's weight and strength. All she could do was close her eyes again. "I'm not hurt."

"You fainted."

Her mouth curved in an off-center smile. "Not quite. It was so quiet and dark and . . . safe. I just let go. Next thing I knew, I sort of fell asleep."

Archer absorbed that while he checked her out. Her skin was flushed rather than bloodless. Her pupils both had contracted to black pinpoints beneath the relentless light. Smiling with a combination of understanding and amusement, he twisted the top of the flashlight, dimming the power. "Asleep, huh? On a cold tile floor with a falling roof for a blanket? You have to be one tired puppy."

"I am. And it wasn't the roof covering me. It was you. That's how I knew I was safe. You were protecting me, not trying to hurt me."

"Some protector. I nearly got you killed."

"How do you figure that?"

"I took you for a walk in the dark. I won't make that mistake again."

Archer rolled off Hannah in a clatter, grind, and clash of metal debris. Braced on his side, he waited to see if the motion would send anything else raining down. Nothing of any size moved. The metal storm was over.

He shoved everything he could reach aside and came to his feet in a single motion. As soon as the adrenaline wore off, he would notice the cuts, bruises, and dents his body had taken when the roof fell, but for now all he cared about was that neither one of them was badly injured. They had been lucky.

"Can you stand up or do you need help?" he asked.

Instead of answering, Hannah scrambled to her feet. She winced once or twice, but didn't stop or catch her breath in sudden pain.

"See? No damage," she said.

"Stay here. I'm going to check outside."

"I'll come with you."

"You'll stay here. I'm quieter in the dark than you are. Don't move around. I'd hate to take you down by mistake."

Hannah didn't want to stay inside the shed alone, but she didn't object. Being knocked to the ground and covered by his weight for her own safety was one thing. Being his target in the dark was quite another.

Her fingers curled around a piece of metal-tipped wood that was as long and thick as her arm. She hefted its weight and felt better.

"Hannah?"

"Yes," she whispered. "I'll stay here."

"I'll be as quick as I can. I know you don't like feeling closed in."

She almost laughed. "There's not enough roof left anymore for me to feel claustrophobic."

His smile gleamed faintly as he noticed the makeshift weapon in her hands. "I'll warn you before I come back," he said before he turned away. "I like my head right where it is."

"Archer?" she called softly.

He spun toward her.

"Be careful," she said.

Warm, callused fingertips brushed from her cheekbone to her mouth. Then he was gone.

Archer waited in the dense shadow behind a leaning wall, listening, listening. He heard nothing but the murmur of ocean and the soft exhalation of cooler air displacing warm. He toed out of his sandals and went barefoot. Without hard soles to grate over sand and crushed shell, he made virtually no sound.

After two complete circuits of the shed, he was convinced that no one else was nearby. He put on his sandals and went back inside the shed. All he could see was black debris standing raggedly against the slightly more pale sky.

"Hannah?"

A tiny, startled sound was his only answer, then a long sigh. "Here."

"Can you see me?"

"Barely."

He held out his hand, a lighter shade of darkness. "Come on. There's nothing out there but the wind."

She started to ask if he was sure, then almost laughed aloud. Of course he was sure. A man who could move that quietly, that quickly, must have eyes like a cat.

"Now what?" she asked.

"Now you get some real sleep. If I'm still curious, I'll look over the shed again in daylight."

"Do you think . . ." Hannah's voice died. Fatigue swam behind her eyes like another kind of night.

"What?"

"Was it intentional? Or did the wind just bring down more of the shed while someone was sneaking around trying to hear what we were saying and he panicked and ran?"

"If it wasn't the wind, assuming that it was could get us killed."

She tried to frame another question, but the cool gusts of air distracted her. Suddenly it was just too much effort to think, to walk, even to stand. It was all she could do to breathe the dark, wet air.

And then she was breathing that other kind of night, speeding down a long tunnel, free-falling into the deep sleep her body demanded.

Archer caught Hannah when her knees buckled. She didn't wake up when he carried her into the house, put her on her small bed, and covered her with a sheet. She didn't even stir while he took her pulse, counted the steady beat of her life, noted the warmth of her skin, and released her wrist with a slow caress.

"If you have dreams," he said softly, "don't remember them."

Quietly he walked out of her room, checked all the locks in the house, and set up some simple mechanical alarms at the doors and windows. Then he sat in the darkness.

Listening. Thinking. Planning.

Two hours passed in silence before Archer went to the cell phone that still lay next to Len's computer. The data had long since been transmitted to Kyle. Archer doubted that his brother would have found out much more this quickly, but any information was better than none.

Archer punched in a string of numbers. The encoding function blinked.

Two seconds later Kyle answered. "Our recently deceased half brother was a paranoid son of a bitch."

Archer grunted. "Problems?"

"Not with the wife. Hannah didn't have any trapdoors or shunts or guards or cookies or anything at all on her computer, not even for banking," Kyle said. "Her password is 'Today.' After that, it was in the clear all the way."

Archer didn't ask how his brother had teased private information out of the virtual world. The last time Kyle had tried to explain, Archer had listened, and listened, and *listened*, and come away as much in the dark as before. The talent Kyle took for granted was a mountain Archer could admire, but never climb.

"Our half brother is a different matter," Kyle continued. "There are some boring files on Pearl Cove, a few scrambled files on pearls as the new miracle cure for everything from cancer to a limp dick, and then nothing but blank walls. He had lots of trips, traps, and bombs laid on for anyone trying to tiptoe through his virtual tulips. Completely toasted two hard drives before I gave up. Anyone who accesses his stuff will have to be a lot better than I am or have more than his entry code to work with. Can Hannah help?"

"She didn't even know his entry code. Len wasn't a sharing kind of partner."

"No shit." Kyle's voice was ripe with disgust. "You sure he wasn't working for Uncle Sam?"

"Recently?"

"Yeah."

"Why do you ask?"

"There are some very fancy ciphers out there, and Uncle has a lock on most of them. One of Len's looked kinda familiar."

"Have you been playing with Uncle's ciphers?" Archer asked dryly.

"Somebody has to."

"Don't get caught."

"So far so good. Any chance of Uncle helping us on this one?"

Archer thought of what April had said. *Odds are we wouldn't be on the same side.* "No. Uncle would just as soon we dropped off the pearl scope."

Kyle sighed heavily. "Gotcha. I'll do what I can with the files you sent me. Nothing useful on any Pearl Cove employees yet."

"Thanks. How's Lianne?"

"Beautiful. She worries about you."

"Me? Why?"

"She thinks you've shot more than your share of troubles."

Weariness folded around Archer, darker than the night. "Give her a hug for me. A big one."

He disconnected and sat in the darkness, thinking about Len's cutting-edge ciphers and Uncle Sam.

Odds are we wouldn't be on the same side.

Blue on blue on blue, shades and tints, hints and tones, blends and startling curls of a pure primary color; the ocean surrounded Archer and Hannah in a huge embrace. Above them the surface of the water was a shifting, incandescent silver. Below them it was a deeply radiant turquoise. As they drifted with the tide, the bottom took a very gradual slide off into indigo mystery.

Archer floated about thirty feet beneath the silver ceiling. One of his hands was wrapped around a long line that trailed down from the small lugger Nakamori was piloting through the calm sea. Hannah trailed off the other side of the lugger. Using long flippers, she positioned herself in the sea with the economical, almost lazy movements of a seasoned diver. Silver and crystal bubbles swirled up from her in easy, rhythmic puffs. The yellow and black of her wet suit made her look like an exotic fish hanging in a huge turquoise aquarium.

Bathwater-warm at the surface, the ocean was cooler the deeper a diver went. Even if it hadn't been, divers still would have worn lightweight wet suits and protective gear for whatever flesh the wet suit didn't cover. Australia's warm, immense pearling grounds were home to Irukandji, a stinging jellyfish that injected nerve toxin into anything careless enough to get within range. Even though every dive ship carried an antidote, it wasn't unusual for divers to end up in the hospital with a case of Irukandji poisoning.

The only reason Archer was diving with just half of a wet suit was that no jellyfish had been sighted. If that changed, he would be in the lugger just as fast as he could cover the thirty feet to the surface. The narrow strings and hand-sized pouch that was Western Australia's standard swimwear for men didn't offer much protection. The stretchy black cloth covered less than a jockstrap.

Nakamori had chosen the relatively calm part of the daily tidal race for the dive, which meant that the bottom wasn't churned up and visibility was good. Yet after several drifts over the search area, they hadn't found any man-sized rectangular baskets of oysters sitting on the bottom.

Archer shifted his grip and looked away for a moment, letting his eyes rest. When he looked back, he didn't try to focus sharply. It was better to let the sea floor slide by with its shapeless lumps and liquid blue-green bouquets of life. Nature was fluid, quintessentially feminine; it was only man that created right angles and rectangles. An unfocused eye picked out the difference between nature and man more quickly than an intent, narrowed eye.

Perhaps thirty feet away from Archer, Hannah was also looking without focusing, floating, letting the sea flow around her. She loved the drifting, boneless feeling. It made her feel as supple as water, as weightless as sunlight, free all the way to her soul. Though her attention didn't wander, a dreamy kind of peace filled her.

When she spotted the sinuous ribbons of three sea snakes swimming along at the edge of her vision, her heartbeat didn't even pick up. The snakes were among the most deadly creatures on earth, but usually they were placid as milk cows. Some divers—Flynn among them—even amused themselves by handling the reptiles. The divers called the snakes Jo Blakes, using the rhyming Cockney slang that was impenetrable to outsiders. Jo Blake Roulette was a popular game among a certain stripe of diver. The fact that divers occasionally came across a cranky snake only made the game more interesting.

Hannah glanced over at Archer, wondering if he had seen the snakes or even knew they were poisonous. In the first instant of focusing on him, her stomach clenched: Len's wet suit was unique. Like a predatory fish, Len's dive suit was dark blue on the back and creamy silver along the belly. To a diver swimming above or below, the wet suit blended in with the lighter ceiling or the darker sea floor. She had seen Len swimming many times. In the water his strong arms made up for his useless legs. Diving gave him the freedom that he craved more than the morphine and booze that dulled the corrosive pain of his body. And his mind.

It's not Len, Hannah told herself fiercely.

Len was dead, beyond the reach of her fear or pity or sad dreams of what could have been if only she had been able to reach into the man she had married and lance the abscesses on his soul. But she hadn't been what he needed. Whatever chance there might have been for Len to heal the darkness within himself had vanished when he took pity on an innocent girl he had seduced and married her.

Forcing away the clammy veil of memory, Hannah looked again at the man who drifted nearby. Yes, there was a resemblance. Both men were broad shouldered, with unusual strength in their backs and shoulders and arms. Once, Len's legs had been powerful, too. Once, he had eaten the ground with his long strides, pulling her along at a trot until breath was a knife in her ribs. Once, he—

Again Hannah wrenched her thoughts back to the here and now, to Archer and the vast turquoise sea. And murder. She never forgot that.

Yet in the blue-on-blue dream of the ocean, she had a hard time focusing on death as an absolute evil. There were worse things than sliding into the radiant blue, feeling each shift of tone as a separate caress, shades of turquoise dissolving her slowly, slowly, until her eyes finally closed . . .

And opened as pearls, sightless and serene. No grave on earth could be more beautiful, no memorial more perfect.

And no man could be more compelling in her eyes than Archer, a man she shouldn't want at all. Swimming in the serene womb of the ocean, she could admit to herself what had always been true: she wanted Archer Donovan. She wanted the strength and the gentleness that surprised her each time he revealed it. A gentleness that disarmed her, made her yearn . . . and then his ruthlessness would surface, sending a chill that went all the way to her soul.

She couldn't risk her unborn children on a man who could shut off his emotions between one heartbeat and the next. Like Len, so much like Len.

And yet . . . and yet . . .

Different.

Len had made a naive girl dream. Archer made a woman hunger, even though experience had taught her how quickly such hunger vanished in the face of life's demands. Like a comet across night, sexual desire was wild, beautiful, and utterly doomed. No one risked their future on a comet, but surely she could risk a few days, a handful of weeks, however long it took to drink the wine of passion to its last bittersweet drop.

Surely she could risk that much. All she would lose riding the comet with him was time, time that would pass in any case, with or without the blazing arc of passion.

The risk was hers. The choice was hers. She was no longer a girl whose possibilities were limited by her parents. She was no longer a wife whose possibilities were limited by her husband. She was a woman who answered only to herself.

She didn't have to marry in order to enjoy passion. She was free.

An angular line at the edge of Hannah's vision sliced through her reverie. She turned toward it, focusing eyes and mind. At first she saw only the graceful undulations of sea snakes. Then she saw what could have been a right angle.

Even before her eyes were certain, she yanked her tow line twice and released it. Above and ahead of her the ceiling churned as the lugger's propellers kicked over, turning against the water rather than passively drifting. The signal to stop had been passed to Nakamori, who would attempt to hold the lugger stationary on the shifting surface of the sea.

The instant Hannah let go of her line, Archer swung toward her. He released his own line and finned after her. When he saw where she was heading, he doubled his speed. It wasn't the rectangle of the oyster cage that galvanized him. It was the graceful, deadly streamers of snakes playing above the cage.

Hannah reached the cage first. Finning rhythmically, easily, she approached the snakes even as she ignored them. One of them swam gracefully through the cage as though taunting the stolid oysters within. The other two snakes simply fluttered like ribbons in a dreamy wind, ignoring everything. Since nothing preyed on the snakes, they had no fear of anything, even man.

While Hannah snapped an inflatable float onto the cage, the natural drift of the tide over the sea floor slid the two snakes away from the cage like decoys painted on a carnival conveyer belt. The third snake, caught by whatever passed for curiosity or play in its reptilian mind, twined around the cage for a while before swimming free and drifting off with the restless tide.

Archer took a breath, discovered that it had been too long, and took another. Bubbles whirled around him with the grace of laughter, but he wasn't feeling humorous. Hannah must have known how deadly the snakes were, yet she had gone swimming with them as though they were pets. The feeling of helplessness he had had while he watched was as bad as anything he had ever known.

She triggered a carbon dioxide cartridge and watched the rapidly growing yellow float shoot to the surface. A thin line trailed down from the float, anchoring it to the cage. Soon a heavier line would sink down from the lugger. She would attach it and then let herself be towed up with the cage.

Wishing he could haul her off "upstairs" and yell at her for being a reckless idiot, Archer swam past Hannah. Without a glance in her direction, he started examining the heavy wire strands of the cable that had once connected the cage to a grid of huge floats. He didn't bother to check the health of the oysters jumbled inside the framework. The water wasn't deep enough or cold enough to kill them. Even if it had been, the oysters and their potential treasure weren't what fueled the urgency driving him.

He needed to find out as much as he could as quickly as he could. He couldn't shake the certainty that Pearl Cove wasn't a healthy place to be for Hannah. Or himself. The "accident" in the shed had been a warning as plain as a shout.

After a few moments Archer found the end of the cable snarled beneath the heavy cage. He shoved and pushed, trying to free enough of the cable to see the severed end. If it had been pulled apart by the force of the cyclone, the cable would be ragged and frayed, with fine wires going every which way, because each strand would have snapped separately.

It took only a glance to see that the end of the cable was as smooth as glass.

Ten

"Cut," Archer said curtly.

He yanked the screen door shut behind him and stalked through Hannah's living room with his borrowed fins jammed under his arm.

"What?" she asked, following him.

"The cables."

"What are you talking about?"

"The cables were cut. That's why the raft came apart in the cyclone. The cables that weren't cut somehow pulled free of the grid. If I thought it was worth the exercise, I'd check the ruined grid cables. But my gut already knows what I'd find."

Hannah hesitated, then gestured for him to follow her into the bathroom. "You think they were cut, too?"

"I sure as hell do."

She dumped her fins in the bathtub and ran her hands up and down her wet suit as though trying to rub up a little warmth. She was always cool after a long dive, but not like this. Not queasy chills. "Why would anyone slash the rafts apart? That's killing the goose that lays the golden eggs."

"Len's gold. Not theirs." Archer's fins made a smacking sound as they landed on top of Hannah's.

She stepped into the tub, grabbed the shower wand, and began rinsing off the wet suit she still wore. "Is it that simple?"

"Greed usually is. The question is, who? Did Len talk with you about his plans to sell the special pearls?"

"He didn't plan to sell," she said as she bent over to rinse out her hair.

"Ever?" Archer asked.

"I don't think so." Her voice was muffled by water. "The rainbow blacks were . . . a religion to him, I guess. As close as he came to God."

"What did he want from his religion?"

"Want? What do you mean?"

"Len wasn't raised in any church. Converts almost always have an agenda. Wealth, acceptance, power, happiness, peace, health . . ."

Health.

For a minute there was only the sound of water dripping and splashing on porcelain.

"I didn't mean religion in the literal sense," Hannah said. "A church, a set of ceremonies, that sort of thing."

"Yet you called pearls his religion."

She shut off the water and combed wet fingers through her dripping hair. "It's the only way I could think of to describe his intensity about them. He collected and perfected the Black Trinity as though his next breath depended on it."

"How insane was he in the last few years?" Archer asked quietly.

Hannah bit her lip. "On a scale of one to ten?"

"Yes."

"An eight," she said bleakly. "Some days, worse. A nine, maybe. But he wasn't consistently insane. Except on his very worst days—when he locked himself in the shed—he could talk very intelligently about the problems of periculture and the nuances of the pearl-marketing monopoly."

"What were his crazy areas?"

"Black pearls. The rainbow kind. He could never have enough, or have them perfect enough. It was an obsession."

She slicked water from her wet suit. "No, it was beyond obsession. It was a sickness. Except for the pearls that escaped his security measures, he destroyed any rainbow pearl that was less than perfect. Considering the rarity of the rainbows, he must have ground several million dollars into dust. And this was at a time when we could barely meet our bills."

Archer whistled softly and thought of what Kyle had discovered in Len's files: the articles on pearls as a medicine for every ill. "Did he ever talk about pearls as a cure for certain diseases?"

"He talked about pearls as his 'little miracles,' but he didn't take them like vitamins or anything. At least, I don't think he did. He could have. Some of the Chinese divers grind up the inferior, usual kind of pearls and drink them in a potion."

"What about the Black Trinity? It must have represented something very special to him."

Hannah frowned. "Last week, when I was color-matching the strands of the Black Trinity yet again—something he made me do at least twice a week—I said it couldn't be any better. The last harvest hadn't added even one pearl to the strands."

"Odd. Most matches can be better."

"That's the beauty of the rainbow pearls. The orient—the mix of color overtones—on all the rainbows was usually quite close. All that really had to be matched was size, surface perfection, and shape."

That kind of identity was rare, except with clones. Archer made a mental note to look into experiments to clone oysters. "Go on," he said.

Frowning, Hannah slicked back her hair with her fingers. Still salty. She turned on the water and bent over to rinse more thoroughly. Her words mixed with the silvery splash and drip of water. "Len refused to believe that the new harvest of experimental pearls couldn't improve the size or perfection of the Black Trinity. He started screaming at me to look again, it wasn't perfect, it couldn't be perfect, *because if the Black Trinity was whole, he would be, too.*"

A chill went over Archer's skin that had nothing to do with his recent dive. "That explains what he wanted from his religion. A miracle."

"That's . . ."

"Insane?" Archer asked softly. "We've already agreed that Len wasn't a poster boy for mental health."

Hannah straightened, dripping and flushed, and handed Archer the shower wand. "Your turn," she said, stepping out of the tub.

Archer stepped in, picked up the wand, and began rinsing off his diving gear. "Tell me about Len's enemies."

"Everyone he met became an enemy, sooner or later."

Frustrated, Archer raked his hand through his rapidly drying hair. Salt made his scalp itch, but he noticed it only at a distance. He had more pressing problems than dried brine irritating his skin. No matter how he arranged the information in his mind, it came up with red flags sticking out all over.

He held his wrist under the water, rinsing off the watch that had gone diving with him. Seconds were fleeing while he looked, seconds turning into minutes, minutes turning into hours, hours turning into too much time lost and not enough information found. He was no closer to an answer than he had been when he arrived yesterday.

The watch told him that he had wasted several hours diving.

Maybe it hadn't been a complete waste. Before diving he had guessed sabotage. Now he knew it. What he didn't know was who and why.

"My guess is that it took more than one man to cut those cables before the full force of the cyclone hit." Archer flipped the fins over, cleaning them thoroughly before tossing them out on the floor. He didn't worry about making a mess. The tile floor slanted down to a small grate, which funneled water into the darkness beneath the house. Standard plumbing in the rural tropics for everything but toilets. "Are any of Len's enemies good friends with each other?"

"Are we talking about personal enemies or business competitors?" Hannah asked, using her fingers to comb her wet, seal-dark hair away from her face.

Archer thought about the fluid alliances among pearl producers. The Chinese, the Japanese, the French, the Indonesians, and the Australians all had periculture ventures. Even the Americans had set up a pearl-farming business in Hawaii.

Len's coalition of small farmers wasn't much by itself, but given the right opening, the independent pearlers could shift the balance of marketing power in one way or another by joining with one of the larger alliances.

No doubt that was what Len had been trying to do in his sane periods, which meant that any of the big pearling operations might have decided they could live well without him. The quickest way to find out was to catch the murderer and convince him to talk.

"Personal," Archer said. He knew more about the rest than Hannah did.

She opened her mouth, hesitated, and sighed. "Except for me, Len didn't know anyone personally, only through the pearling business."

"Too bad. Murder up close is a real personal kind of crime."

Bending to get his head and shoulders within reach of the wand, he let the tepid water sluice over him. While he rubbed his face, he thought about shaving his beard. Teddy Yamagata was right. A beard itched in the tropics. But then, so did razor burn, which was what had made Archer give up shaving in the first place; he had inherited his father's touchy skin.

When Archer cleared the water from his eyes enough to see again, he nearly dropped the wand. While he had been sluicing off, Hannah had been peeling out of her dive gear. She was down to tropical Australia's second uniform—a handful of string and three patches of indigo fabric that were smaller than his palm.

He had seen women wearing less, but he had never wanted one of them more.

Then Hannah turned away and he saw bruises along her left shoulder and hip. He remembered last night, when he had knocked her off her feet and slammed her to the floor while pieces of roof rained down. He had shielded her head from the hard tile, but not the rest of her. There simply hadn't been time.

"I'm sorry," Archer said.

The emotion in his voice surprised her as much as his words. "For Len's enemies?" she asked, looking over her shoulder.

"No. For this."

Hannah didn't understand until she felt his fingertips tracing her bruises with a gentleness that loosened her knees. She started to speak, couldn't, and tried again. "Not your fault," she managed.

"The hell it wasn't. I knocked you down."

"Only to protect me."

"Damn poor job I did."

She turned fully around. "Don't be ridiculous. Just because I was too rattled to thank you doesn't mean that I don't know what happened. I'm still rattled. No one ever did anything like that for me."

"Knock you down?" he asked ironically.

"Protect me at their own expense," she shot back. "My parents were too busy saving the Yanomami, and Len—well, Len figured he had done enough by marrying me. If I got into trouble after that, I could get out of it the same way I got in. Alone."

Archer wondered if her pregnancy, illness, and miscarriage had been the kind of trouble she was supposed to take care of alone. He couldn't ask without raising more questions than he was willing to answer. How he knew about her past history was foremost among those questions.

Shutting off the water, he stepped out of the tub. He expected her to back away from him, because the bathroom was small. Instead she went back to collecting wet diving gear.

"Is your shoulder stiff?" he asked, looking at the bruise while she bent down to snag the last fin.

"No."

"Your hip?"

"I'm not a china doll." Hannah straightened and gave him a hard look. She was amused, irritated, and touched by his concern. And being within inches of him was making her heart beat as though she was swimming too fast. "I'm an active, physical kind of woman, Archer. I get bumps, bruises, cuts, and scrapes all the time."

"Not from me."

She made an exasperated sound. "Take off the ruddy dive gear so I can hang it on the verandah to dry."

With a hidden smile, Archer unzipped the borrowed wet suit and began peeling it off.

Hannah had spent her life surrounded by men of many races, athletic men, hunters in the Amazon and divers in Australia, men whose bodies were honed by the demanding physical necessities of their lives, men who often wore little more than a pouch to cover their sex. She was quite accustomed to the naked muscularity of a fit male.

And she was staring at Archer like a convent girl turned loose on a beach in Rio de Janeiro.

When she realized it, she forced herself to look away, or at least to look at him from the corners of her eyes under cover of her eyelashes. Then she saw the bruises striping his back and forgot everything else.

"Why didn't you tell me you were hurt! You had no business diving with—"

"I'm fine," Archer interrupted without looking up from his dive gear.

"Bloody hell you're fine. Your back looks like someone worked you over with a club."

"So does your shoulder and hip."

"That's different."

"Yeah?" He turned and looked at her. "How?"

"I know my limits."

"That's a relief," he muttered, not believing a word of it. "I *do* know mine. My shoulder is a little stiff, that's all. The rest is just colorful."

"A little stiff. What a load of bull dust."

"Bull dust? Is that what they call it here?"

"They call it stupid here when you dive injured. Just strapping on the dive tanks must have hurt you."

Archer heard what Hannah hadn't put in words: the thought of him hurting made her angry. If she could have taken his pain, she would have. The fact that he had six inches and eighty pounds on her—and easily twice her pure physical strength—didn't seem to matter to her at all.

Amusement and something much more intense rippled in his voice when he spoke. He liked the concern in her eyes. He would like even better to turn it into sexual need. "You saw me dive. Was anything wrong?"

She took a deep breath, ready to chew him up one side and down the other for being a macho idiot.

"Was it, Hannah?" he asked calmly.

Her breath came out in a rush. "No. You dive like you were born to it. It's just . . ."

He waited.

"No one ever . . ." She moved one hand jerkily. "I'm not used to being . . ." Her voice died.

"Helped?"

"Protected. I don't need it."

"Everyone needs it."

"Even you?" she retorted.

"I must."

"What do you mean?" she asked warily. There was something beneath his calm that made her breath catch.

"You raced to beat me to that cage full of snakes."

"I didn't know if you knew that they were . . . um . . ." Her voice faded again. She almost smiled despite the turmoil that had come when she saw his bruises and remembered how he got them. Protecting her.

And now he had boxed her in quite neatly, using her own reasons, her own rules.

"You wondered if I knew the snakes were lethal?" Archer asked with superficial calm. "As in the deadliest damn venom on the planet?"

"Um, yes."

He took a half step forward. It was all the small room allowed. The palms of his hands slid across her cheeks as his fingers probed through her short, wet hair. He tilted her face up so he could see into her dark, dark eyes.

"Let's make sure I understand what you're saying," he said. "You can play with sea snakes so that I won't have to, but I can't take a few lumps for you when the roof caves in."

"That's right," she said defiantly.

"Wrong answer. Try again."

"Archer—" Her voice broke. She had thought his eyes were like gray-green stone, hard and cold. Now she was close enough to see flashes of blue, gemlike shards buried in the smoky crystal iris. "You have blue in your eyes."

"That's because the bathroom is blue. Stand me up in a greenhouse and my eyes are green. Make me mad enough, and I'm told they go steel gray. About that answer, Hannah."

"I hate knowing you were hurt because of me," she said in as calm a voice as she could manage.

"What do you think it does to me knowing that you could have been killed by that roof? What do you think it does to me knowing that I should have yanked you out of here the instant you called me in Seattle? What do you think it does to me when I see bruises on you and know I—"

Her fingertips on his mouth were light, but they cut off his words like a fist.

"I want Len's killer, too," she said. "Whatever happens to me along the way is my responsibility, not yours."

Archer closed his eyes for an instant, not trusting himself to look at her without kissing her. If he kissed her, he wouldn't stop until she was naked and wet and he was buried so deep in her heat that he would forget what it was like to be separate, cold.

"Hannah."

The huskiness of his voice sent tongues of fire licking through her. It had been a long time since she had lain under a man, but she hadn't forgot the glittery excitement, the hot rush, the rhythmic urgency of body against body.

"If you keep looking at me like that—" Archer began.

"Like what?" she cut in.

"Like you're wondering what it would feel like to have me inside you."

"Are you wondering?"

"I've been wondering for ten years."

Her eyes widened. Ten years.

Len.

Memories broke over Hannah in a cold, endless wave, drowning her heat. She had been so sure of herself ten years ago, so certain that Len was right for her. And now she was standing a breath away from a man who was just as hard, just as ruthless as Len.

Len, who had been so wrong for her.

Len, who hadn't cared when their child died at birth. He literally *had not cared.* Though she was so ill her baby died and she nearly did, he had dumped her in a hospital where no one spoke English and took off. As always, he was pursuing another hot rumor about a black pearl whose orient was all of God's rainbows wrapped together.

God's or the devil's. She still wasn't sure which. She no longer even cared. She had learned not to care. Just as she had learned not to risk any more unborn children to the whims of their careless father. She would never forgive herself for that. No punishment could be too great for such misjudgment, even the hell of living with Len McGarry.

In the instant before Hannah stepped back, Archer felt the change in her—resistance where there had been fluid ease, restraint where there had been hunger, distance where there had been heat. He let her slip between his hands like fire, because like fire, he couldn't hold on to her without being burned.

"What did Len do to you?" he asked softly.

Eleven

*F*or several heartbeats Archer thought Hannah wouldn't answer.

And so did she.

Then she remembered the freedom she had discovered floating deep in the turquoise sea, and she wondered if she would ever find the courage of that freedom on land, face-to-face with the man she both feared and desired.

"Len taught me to be careful," she said finally. "Very, very careful." Her voice was ruthlessly neutral, concealing the stark female hunger and the much more complicated yearning that coiled just beneath. "Not a bad thing to learn."

"There's such a thing as being too careful."

"Sure, I'll bet you know all about it." Her tone was sardonic. "Turn around so I can check the bruises on your spine, the ones you got by being so bloody *careful*."

Despite Hannah's brisk words, her hands were gentle as she turned Archer around. The simple heat of his body and the complex slide of his muscles beneath her palms made her wish that Len hadn't taught her how necessary it was to protect her soft center beneath a harsh shell of experience. Touching Archer made her yearn for things she couldn't name, only feel.

"I was careful ten years ago," Archer said. "I've regretted it as I've regretted nothing else in my life."

Hannah's hands paused in their slow probing of his back. "What do you mean?"

He moved so that they were facing each other again. The feel of her fingers sliding on his bare skin did nothing to cool his blood. When she lifted them, he had to bite back a protest. The depth of his hunger for her would have shocked him, but right now he could feel nothing except his own heat, see nothing except her eyes shadowed by a past he couldn't change.

Too late. Too damned late for everything except pain.

"Len and I had a complicated relationship," Archer said evenly. "I didn't know how complicated until it was too late."

She frowned, not understanding.

He lifted his hand, wanting to smooth the lines between her shiny brown eyebrows. Yet he didn't trust himself to touch her in even so casual a way.

And he touched her anyway, tracing the frown lines with a fingertip that was callused and gentle. Her eyes widened in surprise, but she didn't pull back.

"I was raised," he said quietly, "in a big family with love and shouting matches and laughing and hugs, grandparents and aunts and uncles and cousins, parents and brothers and sisters, dogs and cats and car pools. Len was raised by an unloving woman who began life as a calculating piece of ass and ended up as a bitter, alcoholic whore."

Hannah listened with complete attention. She had often wondered about Len's childhood. She had learned not to ask. She had learned so many things.

And Archer was teaching her other things now, with the gentleness of his touch despite the blunt woman-hunger that had tightened his whole body.

"When I found Len and told him who I was, he just stared at me," Archer said. He brought up both hands, barely touching Hannah's cheeks, tracing her sleek eyebrows with his thumbs. Her sudden breath brushed her breasts against his chest. He went still for an instant, then resumed the soft not-quite-caress of her eyebrows. "I told him that he was welcome in the Donovan household, that Dad had spent years looking for him."

"What did Len say?"

"'Too late, kid. Time only goes one way.'"

She winced. "That sounds like Len."

"I tried to convince him to come home," Archer said, looking at Hannah's eyebrows, her dark chocolate eyelashes, the pink curve of her mouth. "He said he was already there."

"Where was he?"

"In a hellhole in Kowloon."

Her mouth thinned. The fever that had killed her pregnancy had begun in Kowloon. It had ended in another country.

And now it all seemed very far away, the world shrinking to one room, one man, the gritty depth of his voice and his eyes watching her as though he had just discovered life.

"I didn't give up," he said. "I'd been looking for Len too long. I couldn't just let him go. He was a blond Viking like Kyle and Justin, with the Donovan smile, his way of looking over his shoulder, even his laugh. I couldn't believe that Len wasn't like the rest of my family."

"Believe it," Hannah said huskily. "He wasn't. At least, for your sake, I hope he wasn't."

"Though he looked like us, Len was different. I know that now. Too late to help you." Archer's fingers trembled on Hannah's face. "Way too late to change the pain. There was something bent or broken or missing or stunted in Len. Part of it was the way he was raised. Part of it was the sum total of all the choices he made when he was old enough to know better. The whys don't matter anymore. What I learned too late does matter."

Hannah watched Archer's eyes change, felt him retreat from her even though he didn't move an inch physically. The emotion beneath his neutral voice made her heart twist. She knew what it was like to bleed silently beneath the careful mask she showed the world.

"Too late," he said, "I learned that Len resented me as much as he liked me. Instead of seeing us as a team, he saw us as locked in some kind of destructive competition. He was always playing all the angles to come out on top."

"He wanted to prove that he was the best man around," she said.

For an instant Archer's eyes shut, veiling the shaft of guilt and pain. "Is that what he said?"

"Not in so many words. But he used to taunt me for choosing the wrong man in Rio. If there was a wrong man in Rio, there must have been a right one. You."

Wearily Archer swore beneath his breath and started to step back. The bathroom was too small for him to move. Hannah was too close, her hands over his, holding his palms against her cheeks. Holding him close. He felt as though he was absorbing her through his palms pressed against her skin. Her warmth and softness and strength went through him like a double shot of whiskey, making his blood ignite and his heart speed.

"That was another thing I learned too late," Archer admitted huskily. "Len knew how much I wanted you before I admitted it to myself. You were so young, so vivid, so—"

"Stupid," she cut in.

His smile flickered and vanished. He lifted her right hand and kissed the cool center of her palm. "You were innocent. That's why I couldn't admit I wanted you. So I had a hell of a shouting match with Len. I was going to send you to the Donovans. They would have taken care of you."

The feel of Archer's lips against her palm made Hannah light-headed. "I was nineteen. An adult."

"You were raised with a Stone Age tribe. You weren't ready for the tenth century, much less the twenty-first."

"It wasn't that bad."

"It was worse." Tenderly he bit the pad of flesh at the base of her thumb. The swift breaking of her breath went through him in a shock wave of desire. He hadn't expected her to respond so quickly, so openly. Not after living with Len. "You'd never seen a flush toilet, never seen a sink, never seen a computer, never watched television, never flown in an airplane, never driven a car, never—"

"I remember better than you," Hannah interrupted, hearing the huskiness of her own voice, knowing its sultry source, not caring. If she didn't use her newly discovered freedom, it would become just another kind of cage, one filled with regrets and might-have-beens. "Anyway, my parents had a radio phone."

He laughed softly and bit her again with great care. "For emergencies, right?"

She watched his teeth close on her flesh for a third time. Warmth flashed through her with an intensity that made her bones loosen. "Yes," she whispered, though she had forgotten the question. Somehow she was so close to Archer now that she could feel his body heat, breathe in the salt and mystery of his scent, feel the stark reality and lure of his erection brushing against her with each deep breath.

"Ever use the radio phone?" he asked.

She shook her head, watching his eyes the whole time. If fog could burn, it would look like that, a hot silver glitter. "Technologically," she said, "I was innocent. But in other ways, I wasn't innocent at all. I knew more about life, death, and sheer human endurance than most technological types ever have to learn. I also knew about the other world, the civilized one out there beyond the rain forest, because Mother and Father kept telling me how evil it was, how decadent, how godless, how riven by greed and malice."

Archer turned Hannah's hand and began to taste each one of her fingers in turn. "Didn't it scare you?"

"The outside world?" she managed, despite the vise of desire squeezing her throat. The velvet rasp and gentle suction of his tongue were a sensual revelation. The contrast between his neutral conversation and elemental sexuality made her dizzy. His control was utterly unexpected. Len would have had her on her back by now, driving toward his own satisfaction.

"Scare me?" Hannah repeated, her voice as raspy-sweet as Archer's tongue. "No. The world beyond the rain forest fascinated me. A place where you could go thousands of miles in a few hours instead of a few miles in days. A place where every book ever written could be conjured up on a screen and read. A place where people looked like me, yearned like me, *needed* like me."

He tasted her little finger, decided that he liked it best, and tasted it again, deeply, before slowly letting it slide free of his mouth. "What did you need?" he asked finally, looking at her, focusing only on her.

"I . . ." Her breathing frayed as a shiver trembled through her body. She had never been looked at like that, as if she was the very center of life. "I don't know. But I knew I wouldn't find it in the rain forest."

"Did you find it beyond the rain forest?"

She closed her eyes. "I grew up."

"That's not the same thing."

"It has the same result."

"Which is?"

"You stop looking."

When Archer would have asked another question, Hannah put her fingers against his mouth. He kissed them and waited.

"Turn around," she said in a low voice. "One of those bruises looked deep enough to need attention."

Slowly he turned his back to her. Again he felt her cool, light fingers smoothing over his skin, probing gently, testing the bruises. He tried not to think how good it would feel to have her hands all over him. Not soothing him. Measuring him. Teasing and arousing, enjoying and demanding.

A decade of remembering her voice, her laughter, and her grace had been bad enough, but this was the most exquisite kind of torture he could imagine. Standing nearly naked, breathing in her cinnamon-and-sun scent, feeling her delicate touch on his skin, thinking what it would be like to pull her arms around him and kiss her until neither one of them could stand up . . .

He could barely breathe, barely think, only drown in a combination of lust and tenderness that was like nothing he had ever felt for a woman. Eyelids half lowered, aching and oddly at peace, he steeped himself in the moment. When her breath washed warmly down his spine, he couldn't prevent a shiver of pure sensual pleasure. She was a dream he had never allowed himself to have, a warmth he had always needed and never known, the essence of everything he yearned for that had no name.

"Does that hurt?" she asked when he shivered again.

"Yes."

Elizabeth Lowell

Without stopping to think, she bent and brushed her lips over the bruised skin. "I'm sorry. When I asked you to come here and help me, I didn't think you would be hurt. I thought you were too hard to ever be hurt."

Slowly Archer turned around. "Don't be sorry." He eased his fingers into her wet, dark hair and tilted her face up. "It's the best hurt I've ever felt."

Hannah started to ask a question, but the words never formed. His mouth was brushing hers, his tongue was tracing her lips, and all she could think of was getting closer to him. Whispering his name, she stood on tiptoe, wrapped her arms around his neck, and buried her mouth in his.

With a thick sound of pleasure, Archer pulled Hannah hard against him and returned the kiss as deeply as she gave it. His teeth nipped at her tongue before his own tangled with it, teasing and tasting her until she had no thought but to get more of him, get it deeper, get it *now*. What she needed, a kiss couldn't provide, no matter how hot and greedy the mating of mouths. Whimpering, demanding, she moved against him in a haze of hunger.

The bathing suits that had seemed so minimal were suddenly intolerable. He stripped her bikini top off, caressed her breasts, and tugged at the nipples. Helplessly she arched, pinning her hips against him, moving hungrily until the scent of her arousal infused the air. He breathed it in even as he pushed his hand beneath the bikini cloth that barely covered her soft, moist center. When his finger penetrated her, she cried out and silky heat spilled into his hand.

Hannah's reckless response made Archer fight for breath and the self-control that he usually took for granted, the same control that was sliding away even as he reached for it, like her bikini bottom falling to the floor. She was so close, nearly his, caressing him with every glide and clench of her response to him. Unable to stop himself, he probed more deeply, pushing into the tight, slick satin of her body. Hidden muscles gripped, begged, demanded.

She was more than ready for him. He could take her now, right now, filling her, ending the agony of always wanting what he couldn't have. Yet he knew that she was off balance, frightened despite her courage, emotionally exhausted beneath her sexual hunger. Vulnerable.

And he had come to Australia to protect her.

With the last of his control, Archer pulled his mouth away from Hannah's until there was just enough space to speak. "If you don't want to finish this, tell me now."

It took a moment for the words to get past her sensual daze. *"I want you."*

"You've got me. But I don't run around with a pocket full of condoms, because I'm too old to look at sex as a game. Unless you're protected, we're real close to making a baby right now."

The thought of his own child teething and drooling on his knuckles aroused Archer as much as Hannah's sultry feminine core rubbing against him. His hands contracted on her hips, lifting her against the erection that had outgrown his swimsuit. He fought against the climax pulsing at the base of his spine. He wanted to be inside her when he came. Naked. All the way naked. Naked as his tongue. He had never been like that with a woman in his entire life. He could only guess at how good it would feel.

"I'd like a baby, Hannah, but only if it's what you want, too."

Her eyes widened. The thought of having a baby had knocked her breath away, leaving her gasping. "I—I'm not—I haven't—seven years—"

Archer wasn't surprised that she had no handy means of birth control. Everything Kyle had discovered suggested that she hadn't taken lovers. That was why she felt so tight when he pushed his finger into her sweet, hot center. So soft and yet so strong, so supple. She could take all of him and they both would know only a blinding pleasure.

"Your call," he said huskily.

But he couldn't help probing between her legs once more, tempting her with what she didn't yet have. The hot, helpless rush of her response spilled over his hand. He gritted his teeth against a groan of need. Her hidden flesh clenched rhythmically around his finger. The sultry rain of her pleasure licked over him again, this time kissing the broad, bare head of his erection.

He stopped breathing.

"Hannah?" he said thickly.

"Don't worry—" pleasure arced through her, making her rigid, shattering her voice "—about a baby. I don't expect— Oh, God, *take me.*"

His thumb moved, two fingers probed deeply, and the tension coiled inside her burst. Shaking, making broken sounds that could have been his name, she clung to him while waves of violent pleasure convulsed her.

Watching her through narrowed eyes, Archer smiled despite the sexual heat that sent sweat sliding down his spine. He wasn't inside her, but he was so close that her climax kissed his penis with hot, teasing pulses. All that kept him from pushing her against the wall and taking her was a need he had just discovered. He wanted to see her eyes while he buried himself inside her, to watch them widen and then go hazy with pleasure when she discovered just how good it felt when they were completely locked together.

"Put your legs around my waist."

Hannah hardly recognized the rough voice as Archer's, but she tightened her arms around his neck and drew herself up his body. She couldn't have done it without the strength of his arms supporting her, his big hands lifting and spreading her legs until she could cross her ankles behind his waist. The hard, smooth head of his erection nuzzled against her undefended core. She was entirely open to him, entirely vulnerable. . . .

And she smiled. She had been helpless in his arms before, and he had given her pleasure. Pure, blazing fire.

She wanted more.

Archer was heading for the bedroom until Hannah shifted herself against him, shivered, and hitched herself over him, all the while watching him like a cat that had just discovered cream. The sensation of her slick heat on his aroused flesh made his heart stop.

"That's it," he said hoarsely.

"What?"

Her voice was as husky as his. He sank to the floor, never releasing her, never letting the blunt head of his erection move from its lush nest. "I was going to give you a bed."

Cool tile met her sweaty back. "I don't want it."

"Your back—"

"Your front," she cut in.

He blinked. "What about it?"

"Mine," she said. Her hands went to his hips and her fingers pushed beneath his swimsuit, fully freeing him. He jerked against her, groaning. In fiery silence she measured him, wondering if it had been so long since Len was capable that she had forgotten what an aroused man was like, or if Archer was simply big. She could hardly wait to feel herself stretching around him, discovering all the other things she had forgotten about sex . . . and discovering other things she had never known. Like this slow, teasing sensuality. It was completely new to her, completely delicious. "Definitely. Mine."

He gave a crack of laughter even as he shuddered with the pleasure of her hands stroking him, savoring him with frank female approval. "Yours, huh? I don't know how to break this to you, sweetheart, but I come with it."

She fought against a delicious bubble of laughter. "You sure?"

"Damn sure."

One fingertip circled him like a lazy tongue, spreading the few drops he couldn't hold back. "Then I guess we'll just have to share."

Sweat gathered and ran over Archer's clenched body. He was so close to the edge, closer than he had ever been without giving in. With each heartbeat, the head of his penis nudged against her sultry core. Each heartbeat told him what he already knew. She was hot, wet, ready.

And the climax was pulsing up the base of his spine.

"Hannah, *look at me.*"

Her half-closed eyes opened wide as he thrust into her, hot and deep and hard. She felt even better than he had expected, so tight he knew he should be afraid of hurting her. But it was much too late for fear. He could no more pull back from her than he could strip off his own skin.

He hooked his arms beneath her legs, lifting them, opening her even more, stretching her around him. Her eyes went dark, then blind with pleasure. Hot ripples licked up from her core, sensual contractions that drew him deeper. The feel of her trembling and tugging at him made him wild. His eyes and mind went blank and he felt nothing but the slow mating of their bodies.

Then he was buried deep within her, fully sheathed. The first pulse of release ripped through him. He tried to hold back, wanting to stop time so that he would always be as he was right now, feeling her climax radiate in delicate convulsions, feeling his own power pulsing, pulsing, pulsing, pleasure consuming him, overpowering him, devouring him.

And then it freed him in a world gone red and black and blind.

Smiling even as she fought for breath, for sanity, Hannah kissed Archer's eyelids, his nose, his lips, his neck beneath the sleek black beard. Her fingers combed over his hair and down his back, then up again, and with every stroke she nuzzled against his beard, licking and nibbling. When he began to get up, she made an unhappy sound and tried to hold him right where he was.

"Even with my weight on my elbows, I'm flattening you," Archer said.

Hannah shook her head. She didn't want him to get up, didn't want the closeness to end and the cold to begin. She had learned with Len that it might be weeks before he came to her again. "You feel wonderful."

"You feel better." Archer shifted his hips just a bit and smiled to hear her breath break. He was still hard. She was still soft. The combination was dizzying.

For both of them.

"Impossible," Hannah said, her voice husky. "There's no word for better than wonderful."

"Yes, there is."

"What is it?" she challenged.

"Hannah."

She laughed softly and went back to exploring his face with her mouth. Len had rarely allowed this kind of sensual freedom, and never after sex, but Archer wasn't pushing away from her. In fact, he seemed to be enjoying it. She liked that as much as she liked having him stay deep inside her.

Eyes closed, smiling, Archer enjoyed Hannah's caressing hands and nuzzling kisses, her tongue tasting first his beard, then his neck, then the tender skin behind his ear. When she nibbled around his ear and explored the center with her tongue, heat flickered over his skin like lightning.

"You keep that up and you're going to wish you weren't on the bottom," he said.

Her answer was a low, questioning sound, because she was too fascinated by the contours of his ear to bother shaping words. Then she felt his hips clench. Suddenly he was locked hard against her, moving in short, powerful jerks that made her limp with a shocking pleasure. But nothing was as shocking as feeling him stretching her again, as though it had been weeks since his last climax.

"Archer?"

"Hang on." He rolled over onto his back, taking her with him, shifting her until she lay on top of him, thigh to thigh, chest to breasts. When the tile hit his back, he grunted, but it wasn't his bruises that bothered him most. "You should have told me."

"What?"

"How cold the tile was."

"I didn't notice."

"The least you can do is return the favor."

Reluctantly Hannah started to get up. Big hands held her where she was, pinned against him, still deliciously impaled on him. She gave him a questioning look.

"Make me forget about the tile, Hannah."

She didn't understand until she looked at his eyes. And then she could hardly believe it. The intensity of his hunger made her whole body tighten with pleasure, stroking him where he lay buried within her.

"That's a good start," he said, his voice raspy.

He shifted his feet until they were between her ankles. Slowly he opened his legs inside hers, stretching her wide. Her eyes came fully open in startled pleasure. He was hard against the violently sensitive knot of her clitoris. The more he pushed apart her legs, the more pleasure licked through her, and the more need gnawed at her. She moved as much as she could against him, inching her hips back and forth until she shivered against him, around him.

It wasn't enough. She could tease both of them to the edge of release, but no more. Trapped on a sensual rack, she writhed slowly, seeking release and at the same time luxuriating in a ravishing kind of pleasure. She knew nothing about making love like this, about need that grew and grew and grew, climax leading to climax and yet nothing was enough, never *enough*, until she was shaking, whimpering, struggling against and with him, crying and wild.

And then she was free, grinding against him as wave after wave of pleasure slammed into her. She would have screamed if she could have, but all she could do was arch her back and give herself to the endless, wrenching ecstasy.

Archer watched through burning gray-green eyes, moving just enough to drive her higher, rubbing against the sleek, hot pearl of her pleasure until she was abandoned, crying, utterly surrendered to him and wholly victorious at the same time, driving him as surely as he drove her, taking him to the same shattering completion she knew, holding him there, burning, pulsing, drowning him in ecstasy.

It was a long, long time before either of them noticed the tile floor again.

Twelve

he bathroom was still steamy from their shared shower. So was Hannah. The fact that Archer had been obviously ready for sex again by the time he left the shower hadn't helped to cool her off. Wistfully she toweled herself dry and watched the closed bathroom door. She hadn't expected him to want her again. Not so soon. That he did both surprised and aroused her.

He might be as ruthless as Len, but Archer was certainly different when it came to sex. She liked that difference. A lot. Knowing that he wanted her even before the sweat dried from the last time made her light-headed with too many emotions to name, even if she had wanted to.

She didn't. The shimmering sexuality she had discovered within Archer—and herself—was more than enough for her to cope with at the moment.

"No wonder Coco can't wait to get past a man's fly," Hannah muttered, wrapping the towel around herself.

"What?" Archer asked from beyond the door.

Even as she flushed, she smiled a cream-licking kind of smile. It was still on her face when she opened the bathroom door. "I said, 'No wonder Coco can't wait to get past a man's fly.' "

He smiled despite the familiar stab of heat in his crotch when he saw the rise of her breasts against the white towel, a towel that was too small to entirely cover the dark nest of curls between her legs. All that kept him from kneeling and burying his face in those curls was the clock ticking in his head, the damned clock that told him he was running late. They should be on their way to Broome by now. Yet there were so many things he wanted to do to her, for her, with her; a whole world of sensuality waiting for them.

It had waited for ten years, Archer told himself. It will wait a little longer. The fact that he wanted to suck on her tender flesh now—right now—was too damn bad. He was old enough to control himself.

Or he had been, up until an hour ago, when he had laid her down on the tile floor and found out just how much he had been missing in life.

"What do you usually wear when you go to Broome on errands?" he asked.

Hannah didn't miss the thickening of his voice, or the silver flicker of heat in his eyes as he looked at the bottom of the towel that almost covered her. "Shorts. A tank top. Sandals."

"The usual, huh?"

She nodded.

"Underwear?" he asked.

"Bikini bottoms. Bras are too hot in the rain months. Why? Do you have some kind of thing for underwear?"

He laughed even as his body tightened. "If it's yours, I have a thing for it."

"And I know just where you keep it." Smiling, she looked at the Aussie walking shorts he was wearing. It was her new smile, the one that told Archer just how much she had enjoyed being his lover. And that she was looking forward to being his lover again.

Soon.

"Get dressed, Hannah. My good intentions are getting even smaller than that damned towel you're almost wearing."

"Who needs good intentions?"

"I do. It had been a long time for you. You're going to be sore enough without an instant replay."

"How about a slow replay?"

"Even worse."

"You sure?"

"Positive."

"Damn." She sighed. "I'll get dressed."

She turned away, only to go still when Archer's palm slid up the inside of her thigh and tenderly cupped the soft curls.

"I'm sorry I was rough," he said quietly.

She stared over her shoulder at him. "You're kidding, right?"

"No."

"Archer, have you looked in the mirror? I left marks on you!"

He grinned. "Did I forget to thank you?"

"Yes. No! Bloody hell, the point is you didn't bite me or scratch me. I was a lot harder on you than you were on me."

"I'll make it up to you when you're not sore." Gently he skimmed her hidden sex, parting soft folds. The flesh heated, moistened, until his fingertips were damp, too. "God, I wish this was my tongue."

Her eyelids flickered down and her legs trembled as she focused on the sweet caresses he was giving her, barely penetrating her with a fingertip, for all the world as though he was tasting her. "How do you know just how to touch me?"

"I've had ten years to think about it."

He entered her tenderly once, twice, then withdrew so slowly that her head tilted back as though it was suddenly too heavy to hold upright.

"Get dressed, sweetheart. Think of me thinking about you. Think of all those things I want to do to you. Think of things you want to do to me. I'll wait for you outside."

Archer turned and left the room quickly, while he still could. The sweet heat and ease of her response made his blood burn and his mind go blank.

The front door closed hard. Hannah sighed and opened her eyes. She was alone in the bedroom.

And she was thinking about Archer thinking about her.

She dressed by habit, picked up her purse, put on her sunglasses, and headed for the front door. When she stepped out into the white violence of the sun, she stopped dead. Archer was there as he had said he would be, backpack slung over one shoulder, waiting for her.

And Coco was standing close enough to him that her hard-tipped breasts rubbed his bare chest every time she took a breath.

"Something wrong, Coco?" Hannah asked.

Coco's black eyes gleamed as they roamed again over the man who had introduced himself only as Archer, the man who had neither backed up nor moved toward her. He was tall and rangy, with the kind of strength that made her wonder how long it would take to wear him out with sex. Men were strange that way. Some of the big ones were used up quick. Some of the wiry ones had amazing stamina, like Tom Nakamori, whenever she got around to allowing him in her bed. Whichever kind Archer was, he was obviously and impressively aroused.

"Coco?" Hannah repeated, her voice sharp. Normally Coco's effect on men was amusing, but seeing Archer standing so close made her angry.

"The dive," Coco said, reluctantly shifting her attention to her employer. "Was it good?"

"It went fine," Archer said before Hannah could answer. "We found some shell."

"Much?"

"Not enough to make a difference," Hannah said briskly. "Where's Christian?"

"He still bad."

Hannah made an impatient sound. When Christian had called and begged off giving her a report because he was feeling ill, Archer hadn't believed him. Neither had she, but there wasn't a great deal they could do right now.

"We won't be able to decide how to put Pearl Cove back together until he finishes his report," she said curtly. "Has he seen a doctor?"

Coco shrugged. "That one? I no think so."

"Bloody hell," Hannah muttered. "I'm going to Broome to run errands. Anything you need?"

With a lazy kind of thoroughness, Coco looked Archer over again. *"Oui,* but is not in Broome."

Hannah knew she should laugh and leave Coco to it, as she had so many other times with other men. Yet even as Hannah lectured herself, she couldn't look at Archer. If he responded to Coco's open invitation, Hannah didn't know what she would do.

Expression neutral, Archer watched Coco. Despite his body's stubborn arousal and her lush breasts brushing against him, he didn't want her. It was Hannah who made his blood heat, not the undoubtedly accomplished Ms. Dupres.

"Ready, sweetheart?" Archer said, turning away from Coco.

Coco saw the change in him when he looked at Hannah. The heightened tension, the narrowed eyes, the sheer sexuality radiating like heat boiling up from a fire. With a shrug, Coco conceded the field to Hannah. For now, anyway. Archer wasn't the first man to sniff after Sister McGarry. When he realized that she wasn't interested in sex, he would remember Coco.

And she would remember that he had once turned his back on her. She would make him pay before she climbed on and rode him until he was raw. The thought made her smile and stretch like a lazy cat.

"When will you be back?" Coco asked Hannah.

"Tomorrow," Archer said.

Hannah gave him a surprised look. "I shouldn't be gone that long."

"You need a break."

She looked at his eyes, more steel than heat now, silently commanding her to agree. "I hear the hotels along Cable Beach have Jacuzzis in the rooms," she said after a moment.

His smile gleamed whitely against his sleek beard. "Big enough for two?"

Dubiously Hannah measured Archer's length. "I don't know."

"I'll take the bottom. You take the top. Plenty of room that way."

The thought of having Archer in a Jacuzzi with water fizzing all around appealed to Hannah. She smiled slowly, thinking of the possibilities. It was her new smile, the one that made Archer want to strip off her shorts and take her right there.

Coco stared at the transformation in her employer. She had the look of a woman who had just acquired a very good, very personal sex toy, and his name was Archer. Ian wasn't going to like hearing about this.

But she sure was going to enjoy telling him.

Chang and Flynn sat in a private room off the Blessing Crane's small public dining room. None of Chang's anger at finding out that Hannah McGarry had finally taken a lover showed on his face. The least important part of his anger was personal and male. The majority of his ire was professional. The Chang family was counting on him to discover the secret of producing rainbow pearls. With that, they could increase their importance to mainland China. With more importance would come more contracts, better contracts, and a strengthening of *guanxi*, the all-important connections that were the basis of power in China.

Despite his darting thoughts, Chang's face was impassive as he ate, wielding chopsticks or knife and fork with speedy precision, depending on the dish in front of him. Flynn did the same. Cigarettes smoldered in the ashtray between the men, adding to the stale smell of the room. The fact that the food was second rate didn't matter to either man. If they wanted really good food, they abandoned Broome for Darwin or Kowloon or even Perth.

Both men were silent. They had nothing useful to say to one another. McGarry's death was old news. The missing rainbow pearls were old news. The fact that each man's government was pressuring him to come up with the pearl prize was taken for granted, as was the fact that Flynn and Chang were in competition.

They hadn't come to the restaurant to socialize. They were here because a third player in the pearl game had "requested" it. Until the third representative arrived, there was nothing to do but smoke and eat and drink lukewarm beer.

The door to the private room opened. Without a word of greeting, a third man walked in, sat down, and picked up a plate to help himself from the varied dishes at the center of the dark table. Whatever Maxmillian Barton thought of the food, he kept it to himself. He had been raised on Tex-Mex cuisine and had graduated to coconut milk and nuclear Thai curries while doing several duty tours for the U.S. State Department. No matter how hot the spice or how cold the company, Barton ate and listened, both eyes wide-open for the main chance.

"Is Archer Donovan working for the U.S. on this?" Chang asked Barton without preamble.

"Not so far as I can tell."

"How far is that?" Flynn asked.

"Far enough to know that he has no official ties with the U.S. government."

Chang picked up a tree ear with his chopsticks, chewed the nutty fungus, and swallowed. "What about unofficial ties?"

"He's not ours off the books, if that's what you mean."

Chang grunted. McGarry had been an off-the-books agent for the United States. Sometimes. Most of the time he had worked for himself. Chang wondered if anyone else at the table knew.

"Archer Donovan's a Yank through and through," Flynn said. "He'll help out his government."

Barton shrugged. "Maybe. He's turned 'em down flat in the past."

Flynn's blond eyebrows rose. "You let him get away with yanking your chain like that?"

"It's a free country," Barton said blandly.

"Balls."

"Len was a Yank, too," Chang pointed out to Flynn. "He didn't help anybody but himself, no matter who happened to be employing him."

Flynn made a disgusted sound. If there was anything that made a government crazy, it was foreign or domestic agents who wouldn't stay bought. But it was a hazard of the business. "I still say Donovan somehow got McGarry killed."

"If he did," Barton said, avoiding an opaque clot of tofu in favor of anonymous animal protein, "you better pray he never wants your pecker in his collection. We looked, and we looked hard, and we couldn't find one single goddamn piece of evidence that Donovan had a hand in McGarry's death."

Flynn started to object.

Barton looked up, still chewing. His black eyes reminded the other men that he once had been a contract assassin. "We would love—just flat fucking *love*—to have a twist on Archer Donovan. He was about the shrewdest damn analyst we ever had, as well as one effective son of a bitch in the field. Having that kind of talent running around without a handler makes us nervous. So if you're thinking we didn't look hard enough, think again."

The palm of Flynn's big hand came down on the table with enough force to make silverware jump. "Then who in Jesus and Mary's name killed Len McGarry?"

Barton smiled thinly. Beneath his thinning gray hair his scalp gleamed. So did his teeth. "We have two pools going. The first is betting on the Chinese triads, compliments of one of the Overseas Chinese's foremost trading families."

Chang speared tofu, chewed once, and swallowed as though he didn't understand that Barton was accusing *his* family.

"The second pool," Barton said, watching Flynn idly, "is on the Aussies doing the dirty. Specifically the marginally bright, no-longer-young Turk who needs a gold star in his file to go up in rank."

"Bugger yourself," Flynn said without heat. "If I killed the wanker, you'll never prove it."

Chuckling, using the chopsticks as deftly as Chang, Barton flicked a lump of noodles from his plate to his mouth. "What are you going to do about Donovan?"

Flynn didn't say a word.

Neither did Chang.

Barton sighed. "Listen up, boys. For the moment, the U.S. wants Archer Donovan alive and kicking ass."

Chang glanced up and mentally began revising his phone summary for Sam Chang. "Why?"

"Yours not to reason why," Barton retorted. "Just make bloody sure that if Donovan goes tits up, you don't have any part in it. If your Daddy doesn't like the good word, tell him to call my boss. She'll tell him just what I'm telling you. Lay off Donovan until you hear otherwise." Black eyes glanced at Flynn. "Same goes."

Flynn shrugged. "I don't take my orders from a Yank."

"Your country takes loans, lots of them, in U.S. dollars. Would you like to be the one to explain to your finance minister that you personally fucked up some multibillion-dollar development loans because McGarry's widow liked Donovan's cock better than yours?"

Flynn's head snapped up. "So Donovan *is* working for you."

Barton's laugh was as cold as his eyes. "Not yet, but we're giving him rope and lighting candles in hell. The instant he screws up, we'll be there. And he'll be ours."

"What about Hannah McGarry?" Chang asked.

"What about her?" Barton retorted.

"Is she off limits, too?"

"Nothing was said about her."

Chang flicked a prawn into his mouth, eating it in the Chinese manner—head, shell, and all. He chewed thoughtfully, savoring the intense flavor of the shell and the succulence of the flesh. "Ms. McGarry is the owner of record of a very special, very valuable piece of the pearl trade."

"Too bad Donovan showed up," Barton said cheerfully. "She isn't likely to make an alliance with either of you now."

Neither Chang nor Flynn looked at each other, but each was thinking the same thing: Barton didn't know that Donovan was half owner of Pearl Cove.

And Hannah McGarry had just been thrown to the wolves.

Barton stood up, tossed some Australian money on the table, and walked out. Every step of the way he cursed April Joy for her latest intricate game. It wasn't the first time he had cursed her. It wouldn't be the last.

The hell of it was, she was right. Getting a handle on talent like Archer Donovan was worth bending a few rules.

Red dirt flew by on either side of the road, which was also red dirt. Low, ramshackle buildings circled Broome and crouched rather drunkenly along the waterfront. Many of the buildings were remodeled pearling sheds. New buildings stuck out like castles in a shantytown. These were the small hotels and restaurants, stores and bars that had been built recently with the tropical tourist in mind—potted palms, French doors, bamboo or rattan furniture, breezy rooms, lots of shade, and a cross between rustic frontier and clean-lined Asian decor.

The airport wasn't one of the castles.

Like the World War II Quonset hut that served as a terminal, the airport parking lot was unadorned and unshaded. It sucked in heat and held it, returning it redoubled to anyone unlucky enough to stand on the sun-softened surface. Even through the mercury-colored heat haze, sunlight was a staggering burden over land and man alike.

While Archer locked the car, Hannah looked around the parking lot. Though Archer said nothing, he was feeling every bit of the temperature difference between Seattle and Broome. Sweat gleamed on his face, his arms, his legs. His tank top and shorts were a wet second skin. He couldn't have dripped more if he had just walked out of the shower.

"Is this where you tell me why we're in Broome?" Hannah asked.

"No."

She lifted her eyebrows, shifted the airy straw hat that shaded her head, and waited.

He held out his hand, silently apologizing for his curt answer. "A flight just came in."

"So?"

"So what passes for a taxi service should be waiting out front for passengers."

Hannah looked at the car they had just gotten out of. She looked at Archer. He didn't say a word. She took his hand and headed for the ragged jitney that would ferry them to town.

When the van left the airport, there were only six people sitting on the cracked, sticky seats. The other four passengers were two couples who had nothing in common but the slammed feeling of having been on a jet for too many hours, through too many time zones, and then walking out of stale air-conditioning into the tropical sauna of Broome air in late November. Overdressed for the time and place, they watched the world outside the jitney windows with the glazed eyes of people who would remember nothing of their surroundings until they slept for eight hours.

When Hannah would have spoken, Archer swiftly bent and

kissed her. Then he murmured against her ear, "Look exhausted, sweetheart."

She gave him a sideways look and settled her head against his sweaty shoulder to punish him. Exhausted women slept, didn't they? A little thing like 99 percent humidity and a temperature to match wouldn't stop a really tired woman from curling up against her man.

Archer stroked Hannah's hair and caressed her cheek with his fingertips. He watched the passengers and the view outside without seeming to do either. The other couples talked in fragments, too tired to finish sentences. Neither he nor Hannah spoke until the jitney left them off in the heart of Broome.

"Now what?" she asked, turning away from the jitney's ripe black exhaust.

"We kill some time."

"Why?"

"I'm waiting for someone."

"Who?"

"I don't know," Archer said.

"That will make it hard to meet him," Hannah said dryly. "Or her."

"I don't know that, either." He glanced at his watch. If April Joy was on the job, someone was cruising the airport lot right now, looking for a white rental car with a broken left taillight. "We won't be meeting this person in the flesh, but our car will."

Hannah blinked, tilted her head, and stared up into his gray-green eyes. "Want to run that by again?"

"It won't make any more sense the second time."

She sighed.

He smiled. The speckled sunlight and shade from her straw hat made her look like she had white-hot freckles sprinkled across her face.

Before she could ask another question, a trio of men dressed in the Outback uniform staggered toward them. Two of the men were drinking beer. The third was knee-walking drunk. They were staring at Hannah like she had a For Rent sign tied to her butt.

"Time to go sightseeing," Archer muttered. The last thing

he wanted was to call attention to himself by brawling with three randy drunks.

Broome's Chinatown was a cluster of whitewashed corrugated roofs, red grates and trellises, and palm trees that had weathered many cyclones. The Asian cemetery, where so many pearl divers were buried, had the weary dignity and ageless power of a place where too many hopes had died.

Hand in hand, silent, Archer and Hannah walked slowly through the cemetery. The hot, wet breeze felt heavy with the secrets of men long dead. Under other circumstances, he would have walked quietly through the cemetery, reading the markers he could and appreciating the mystery of the ones he couldn't. How people chose to meet the darkness that came at the end of the lightning stroke of life had always fascinated Archer, but even if he had been able to read Chinese, the messages engraved on headstones would have remained a mystery. The complex ideographs had been worn to shadows across the faces of the slowly, slowly dissolving stones. Canted every which way, poignant, elegant, the headstones gleamed redly above their rough, untended graves.

"Will Len be buried in Broome?" Archer asked quietly.

"No. He wanted his ashes scattered at sea." Hannah closed her eyes and let the sultry air flow over her face. "He didn't want any kind of ritual or ceremony. Said he wouldn't need it."

"But the living do need it."

Something burned behind her eyes, something she refused to recognize as tears. She was finished with crying. It accomplished nothing. The past was beyond redemption and the dead were beyond tears.

"Tell me about him," Archer said quietly. "Tell me about the good times."

"It was . . . a long, long time ago."

"Have you forgotten?"

Hannah's silence grew and grew until Archer accepted that she wasn't going to say anything about Len. Then she sighed, laced her fingers more tightly with his, and began talking about the man they had both loved before they understood that he could neither accept nor give love.

"Len was mad for lemonade." She laughed oddly. "I don't

know why that pleased me, but it did. He would hover around like a big kid while I squeezed lemons, then he would drink so hard and deep he would have a sticky mustache and drops of lemonade on his chin. I'd watch his pleasure and dream of having a little girl or boy who would hug my knees and dance with impatience while I fixed lemonade."

Archer thought of the pregnancy that had ended in sorrow and agony for Hannah. His throat ached with all that he couldn't say, couldn't do, couldn't change.

"Len taught me to dance," she continued after a few moments. "He had a penny whistle and an ancient Asian flute. When he was pleased with a project, he would play jigs on the whistle and we would dance until we were breathless, laughing. . . . He had a wonderful laugh, big and free." Her breath squeezed. It had been years since she had heard Len laugh, really laugh. "When he played the Asian flute, I knew that he was almost sad."

"Almost?"

"Melancholy, but not really depressed. More like . . . gently haunted. As though he was thinking about things that he had never seen or done and never would, but it was all right. He accepted it. And he played so beautifully, conjuring dreams with just breath, wood, and fingertips."

"Yes," Archer said, smiling and sad. "The first time I heard Len play, I thought of Lawe and Kyle. Lawe especially. Put a harmonica or a flute in his hands and he'll make you laugh and weep and yearn for everything that doesn't have a name."

"That was Len." Hannah made a soft, aching sound and looked around the cemetery that was both empty and full. After Len was paralyzed, he had never played again. He had never laughed again, not his real laugh. He had never touched her again.

But Archer had asked her to remember the good times, and that was right. Thinking about the bad times didn't solve anything. Remember the good, accept the bad, and walk on, because there wasn't another damn thing she could do except hate herself for not being what Len had needed.

"He could dance me into the ground," she said huskily, "wipe the sweat off his forehead, and start all over again, laughing out loud, loving just being alive. That's when I loved him the most, when I could all but touch the life pouring through him. He was . . . incandescent."

"I saw Len like that, but it wasn't dancing. It was hell's own bar brawl in Kowloon. Len and I fought back to back against a roomful of strangers. I fought because it was the only way to get out of the place in one piece. Len fought because he simply, fiercely, enjoyed the physical contest of man against man."

Hannah nodded. "That was Len. He really loved a good fight. He'd come home grinning with a shiner the size of a pie plate and his arm around the bruiser who had given it to him." She smiled slightly. "Are you sure Len didn't start that bar riot?"

Archer smiled even as he realized that Len undoubtedly had done just that. "I'll bet he did it as a way to test his newly discovered half brother."

She looked at Archer curiously. Her eyes were a blue so dark it made him think of twilight sliding into night.

"I didn't let him goad me into a fight with him, one on one," he explained calmly. "He called me a coward. I just laughed at him and said I didn't fight with family that way, no holds barred. I think the bar brawl was his way of finding out what I was made of."

"Did he try to get you to fight him after that?"

"No." Though Archer didn't say any more, he was remembering the few times Len, without trying, had come real close to getting a brawl. All of those times had involved Hannah.

"Guess he figured out real quick that you weren't a coward," she said. Despite the sadness that clung to her memories like cold to ice, she smiled.

"Guess so."

"You don't hold it against him?"

Archer shook his head. "It would be like holding thunder against lightning. Len was what he was. Strong. Tough. Reckless."

"You sound like you admired him."

"Some of Len was worth admiring, worth remembering." The rest wasn't, but Hannah knew that even better than Archer did.

She hesitated, then sighed and laced her fingers more deeply with Archer's. "Yes, some of Len was worth remembering." She lifted his hand and brushed her lips over his knuckles. "Thank you."

"For what?"

"Giving the best of Len back to me."

Archer lifted Hannah's chin, kissed her very gently, and hoped that both of them lived long enough to enjoy the gift.

Thirteen

*A*rcher opened the small duffel bag that some nameless agent had left in the rental car while he and Hannah walked through Chinatown's windswept graveyard. If April had followed directions, there should be at least two changes of clothes for them.

"This should do it for the first round," he said.

He pulled out uncrushable white slacks and a colorful floral shirt of the kind favored by tropical tourists. The wig that went with the clothes was black and breast length. A stiffened straw pith helmet—again, a tourist favorite—and black-rimmed sunglasses completed Hannah's outfit. He added a handful of makeup for the finishing touches. Ruthlessly he stuffed everything into the pith helmet.

"Have you ever worn a wig?" he asked, holding helmet and all out to her.

She stared at the black hair trying to crawl out of the pith helmet. "No. It looks hot."

"It is."

She glanced around. The coffee shop they were in held a

few hardy tourists whose vacations hadn't coincided with Broome's cool, dry season. The rest of the people were locals who apparently had nothing better to do than smoke cigarettes and drink coffee or beer until the sun gave up its grip on the land. Seashell ashtrays overflowed, testament to the patrons' grim dedication to killing time.

"Bathrooms are back and to the left," he said. "I'll meet you out on the sidewalk."

Silently Hannah got up, leaving her coffee and a half-eaten roast beef sandwich behind. Archer stretched lazily, though his gray-green eyes searching the room were anything but indolent. No one so much as glanced in Hannah's direction. He stood up, paid the bill, and went outside to wait.

A flock of sulfur-crested cockatoos burst from a nearby tree and swooped upward, spinning and swirling like noisy white leaves on a storm wind. After a few minutes the birds vanished into the part of the sky where the sun's burning disk transformed humidity into a blinding curtain of light.

"The hat is too big," Hannah said from behind him.

"When my turn comes it will be too small."

She was still thinking that over when Archer led her to the front window of a tourist store, straightened her wig with a tug, and smiled at her haphazardly applied makeup. "You don't wear makeup much, do you?"

"In the rain forest, men wore the paint, not women."

He smiled. "And after the rain forest?"

"Why bother? Makeup lasts about two minutes in the tropics."

"Not this stuff," he said, holding up the duffel. "It's waterproof."

"Miraculous," she said with a total lack of interest. "How do you get it off?"

"Oil. When we go in, pretend to be interested in the junk. But keep your sunglasses on. Your eye color is too unusual. Someone might remember it." He thought of giving her the contacts now, and rejected it. There would be time enough later to introduce her to the tearful joys of contact lenses.

Not to mention the basics of using makeup as both art form and disguise.

Before Hannah could ask Archer why she was wearing bad makeup, a wig, and pith helmet, he walked two doors down—another bar—and vanished inside. He took the duffel with him.

Dutifully she walked into the tourist trap and looked through the goods. There were the usual kangaroo and koala designs on everything from T-shirts to teaspoons. There was a heap of tropical shells gleaming in shades of white, cream, peach, vague gold, and every tone in between. Though many of the shells were quite beautiful, she wasn't tempted to buy any. The shells were perfect, which meant they had been taken from living animals. She would rather find her shells on the beach, imperfect.

The only thing that interested her even slightly was a display of pearls from *Pinctada maxima*, the most common Australian pearl oyster. The shell was as big as a turkey platter and colored inside like a gentle tropical dawn. The choker necklace resting on the shell was made of pearls as big as a thumbnail. And like a thumbnail, these pearls lacked the satin iridescence of a quality gem.

On first look the necklace was flashy and a tremendous buy. On second look it rather resembled a tiny version of china eggs, the kind women once used for darning socks or fooling hens. On third look, the necklace was way overpriced. The pearls were big and fairly round, but their luster was dismal. Like chalk.

"Need any help, luv?" asked the shopkeeper.

Hannah turned around and saw a woman wearing hair an unlikely shade of red, a T-shirt proclaiming the joys of camel riding in the moonlight, and the kind of skin that came from fifty years of sunbathing. "Uh, well . . ."

"Oh, no," Archer said from behind her. "You aren't going to start whining about me buying you pearls again, are you?"

The voice wasn't like his usual one. It was higher, long-suffering, and grudgingly indulgent.

It didn't take Hannah two seconds to catch on. She spun around and put her hands on her hips. Her mouth was set in a hard-edged pout, which was a good thing. Otherwise it would have dropped open at the sight of him. Loud sport shirt, safari pants, and no facial fur except for a thick mustache.

"I told you, baby," he continued. "Pearls cost more in Broome, not less."

When Hannah spoke, it was with a pronounced whine. "I could be in Tahiti sipping gin and watching men in G-strings juggle torches, but no, *you* had to come to Australia. *Adventure*, you said. Exotic *animals*. Thousands of miles of *pristine* sugar-sand beaches. So I came, and what did I get? Mudflats, sweat, and nasty flies. But have I complained? Hell no. The least you could do is buy me some pearls!"

He looked at the choker, grimaced, and looked away. He would rather have owned the shell the pearls came from. "Too much. It would max out our plastic."

"We're having a special on pearls, luv," the shopkeeper said quickly. She sized up the couple's clothes, the irritation reddening the lady's cheeks, and the guilt on the man's face. "Thirty percent off. But since your sheila's been such a good sport, I'll make it forty."

He looked at the pearls, hesitated, and shook his head.

"Half, then," the shopkeeper said instantly. "You're a shrewd man in a bargain, mate."

Archer shook his head, but his eyes gleamed with amusement only Hannah could see, egging her on.

"Hon-ey," she said, drawing out the endearment. Her tone was both sexy and threatening. What she threatened was an embarrassing scene if he didn't buy the pearls. "You *promised*."

With a few curses under his breath, he reached into one of the eighteen pockets decorating his wrinkled safari pants, hauled out the wallet he had seen for the first time a few minutes ago, and handed over a debit card to the shopkeeper. Hannah gave him a sultry smile, put one arm around his waist, and began whispering against his chest.

"Is that your card?" she asked.

"Never seen it before in my life."

Her eyes widened and she asked anxiously, "Do you know the PIN number?"

"A little late to be thinking of that, isn't it?"

She looked stricken.

"Don't worry, sweetheart." He kissed her lips, then slid his tongue along them. "It's all taken care of. Uncle is thorough."

A few moments later Hannah left the shop with a cheap—but not inexpensive—pearl choker around her throat. Despite the inferior quality of the pearls, she liked the heavy, cool feel of them against her skin.

"What are you smiling about?" Archer asked. "You throw away better pearls than that every day."

"Yes. But this is the first time I've owned any."

"Out of all the pearls you've seeded, sorted, color-matched, doctored, you never owned one?"

"Everything that was worth selling got sold. Except for—"

"Yes," he cut in quickly, thinking of the black rainbows. He touched the choker with gentle fingertips. "If I had known, I would have bought you a good necklace." Then he laughed. "No, I wouldn't have. Anyone who follows us will be looking for people who know about pearls. No one who knew anything about pearls would buy that necklace."

She didn't argue, but she kept smoothing her fingers over the pearls just the same, enjoying them.

Smiling, Archer looked at his watch. "Time to go."

"Where?"

"The airport." He handed over a small cloth purse. "Your California driver's license and credit cards are inside if anyone wants ID at the gate."

She blinked. "Gate. As in airplane?"

"Yeah. We're going to Darwin."

"Why?"

"Because when they don't find our names on a flight out of Broome, they'll assume we drove to Derby, so they'll look for us there."

"Who will be looking for us?"

"Should be interesting to find out."

"Is that why we're going? Just to find out if anyone follows?"

"No."

Hannah dug in her heels and stopped. "I can't just walk away from Pearl Cove and have a little holiday."

"That's what everyone thinks."

"Except you," she retorted. "I don't know what you think at all."

"I think we'll be dead in two days—one week max—if we stay in Pearl Cove."

A chill went over her that the sun couldn't touch. She looked at his face, hoping he was making a bleak joke. Nothing she saw reassured her. Without the beard, the harsh beauty of his face was fully revealed: angular, balanced, strong, unflinching, framed in darkness. His eyes were clear and remote, reflecting the torrid sky. And like the sun, his eyes were relentless. The man who had laughed with her, teased her, loved her, was gone as though he had never existed.

"Very soon Flynn, Chang, and whoever else has bought in to the game will have had enough time to ransack what's left of Pearl Cove," Archer said calmly. "When they come up empty, they'll have to admit that the secret to the black rainbows isn't in the ruins. That's when they'll come after you."

"But I don't know!"

"I'm sure they'll believe you, eventually. Unfortunately, by then you'll know too much about who killed Len, who has been creaming Len's pearls, and who has been laundering pearls through him. You'll be a liability who is known to enjoy diving. Alone. If they're feeling kind, they'll let you die that way. If not, they'll simply feed you to the sharks."

Hannah opened her mouth to speak. Nothing came out but a hoarse sound.

His expression gentled. He brushed the backs of his fingers down her cheek. "Don't worry, sweetheart. I'm taking you to a safe place."

She heard what he didn't say. "What about you?"

"I'm a big boy." He glanced at his watch. They were cutting it fine. "When we get on the plane, don't talk about anything that has to do with pearls."

"I thought you said we would be safe."

"I'm working on it."

Darwin had paved streets, more people, bigger buildings, and the same climate as Broome. The gunmetal sky promised rain; the inhabitants prayed for it as a temporary relief from the merciless seasonal buildup of heat and humidity. The clothes in the store windows and on the pedestrians were a decade or two more fashionable than Broome's. Despite the punishing climate, people darted from building to building with a purpose greater than merely getting in out of the heat. Darwin didn't have the pace of Seattle, much less of Manhattan or Tokyo, but the beat of life was faster here than Broome's no-worries-mate indolence.

Archer looked in the window of a jewelry store, but it wasn't the Australian pink and green diamonds that held his eye, or even the silky, lustrous Australian pearls in every shade from moon white to midnight black. What interested him was the store's thick plate glass. It made a decent mirror, which meant that he didn't have to crane his neck to check for followers.

The street behind them was busy enough so that he and Hannah didn't stand out, yet not crowded enough to make a tail's life easy. Archer was eighty percent certain that someone had followed them from the airport. April Joy's man, probably. As the person who supplied the tickets, passports, and clothes, she was the only one who would have a clear idea who to look for and where to look for them.

"See anything, er, darling?" Hannah asked. She didn't know what else to call Archer, because his real name didn't match his present ID.

"Just some pretty jewelry."

She let out a long sigh. "Good. Could we go to our hotel or wherever we're staying?"

He smiled slightly. "Tired?"

"Hungry, too." She glanced around furtively. "And this wig itches like fire ants."

He looked at his watch, took her arm, and headed for one of the run-down bars he had noticed during a taxi ride along the waterfront. If anyone followed them, Archer couldn't pick the shadow out of the pack of normal citizens.

"Here," he said.

She glanced at the dirty neon lights flashing dim messages about beer and fun. "I'm not sure I'm this hungry,"

"We're not here to eat."

"Small comfort," she muttered.

She followed him into the dim bar. It was surprisingly full of people. Most of them had the look of serious drinkers seriously intent on maintaining an alcohol haze. The air-condition-ing wasn't up to the demands of sweat and cigarettes.

"I've smelled better oyster dumps," Hannah said under her breath.

Archer didn't argue. He just kept taking her deeper into the barroom. He caught a server's eye, held up two fingers, and pointed toward an empty booth. As soon as the server brought two beers, he paid, left a tip on the table, and kept on watching for new customers coming in the door.

Sipping her beer, Hannah looked around the bar with a com-bination of disbelief and sympathy. Disbelief that anyone would choose to spend time in such a hole, and sympathy that they had no more appealing choices.

The three women sitting together at the bar were especially hard for her to watch. Their hair was dyed, lacquered, and hadn't been combed for too long. They smoked constantly, squinting through eyes that had seen too much, none of it good. Their mouths were painted on in bright, hard colors. So were their clothes.

When a man walked up, squeezed one of them low on her hip, and held up a twenty-dollar bill, the women glanced among themselves as though deciding whose cigarette break was over and who was still off duty. Finally the woman with the biggest hair tossed her cigarette on a mound of dead and dying butts and strolled toward the door at the back of the bar. The man followed, already reaching into his fly.

Hannah looked at the tired bubbles that barely covered the top of her mud-colored beer, but it wasn't the beer she was seeing. It was the past, when a young girl had taken one look at Len McGarry and decided that he was her knight in shining armor, come to rescue her from the green dragon of the rain forest. And no matter how much the voice in the center of herself warned, *Not this man*, she simply ignored it.

Len was the first western man she had met in three years who wasn't a Catholic priest, married, or old enough to be her grandfather. It was Len's wildness that drew her. It was his laughter that convinced her. It was determination to escape the green hell that made her endure the first uncomfortable bouts of sex. It was her own sexuality that finally ignited, surprising Len even more than it surprised her.

She decided to make Len hers, and to hell with the consequences and the voice whispering inside her, *Not this man*. Surely nothing could be worse than eating monkey parts stewed over a sullen fire.

Very soon she discovered that there were worse things. One of them was confronting the streets of Rio de Janeiro alone and broke, seeing her own future in the jaded, opaque eyes of prostitutes. Then Len came back with cuts and bruises on his face and said, *Fuck it, why not get married? It's the one thing I've never done.*

She was so relieved she almost blacked out. When she could focus again, she was clinging to him, watching him as though he was fire and she was freezing. She didn't notice the other man with him until Len dragged her arms from around his neck and introduced her to Archer Donovan.

The anger in the other man's eyes struck her like a blow. Archer didn't want her to marry Len. She didn't know why, but she was sure of it. Just as she was sure that something about Archer fascinated her. He watched her with such darkness, such savage intensity, silently demanding . . . what?

She didn't know.

Couldn't know.

Wouldn't know.

So she turned her back on Archer and watched Len with eyes full of hope, certain that everything would turn out all right now. Yet when she dreamed that night, it was Archer's face that haunted her, Archer's silver-green eyes that followed her, Archer's hands that ignited the newly discovered fires in her body.

She hadn't understood her reaction then. She didn't understand it now. But it was real, as real as the quickening of her heart and her body each time Archer touched her.

"What are you thinking?" he asked softly.

Hannah jolted, then sighed. "The day Len came back for me in Rio."

He followed her glance toward the bar, where the two remaining prostitutes lit cigarettes from the smoldering ends of other cigarettes. "You wouldn't have ended up like that."

"I was one night away from it," she said simply.

"Len and I were both looking for you. He found you first."

Shocked indigo eyes focused on Archer. "He never said anything about you looking for me."

"No, he wouldn't have."

"Is that why you were so angry with me when you first met me? Because you'd spent the night looking for me?"

"You were innocent, terrified, and completely alone. Len never should have abandoned you. That's why I was angry. It was as close as I ever came to giving Len the fight he thought he wanted, no holds barred. All that kept me from beating him unconscious was that two of us had a better chance of finding you than one."

In the dim light of the bar, Archer's eyes were narrowed, feral. Dangerous. Hannah swallowed uneasily. "I've often wondered why Len came back. At first I thought it was because he loved me. But he didn't."

"You touched everything that was good in him, Hannah. That's all anyone can ask."

Pain drew her face into taut lines that the black wig made even more grim. "It wasn't enough. I wasn't what he needed. I only made him worse."

"No."

"Yes," she countered bluntly. "After he was paralyzed he needed someone older, someone who needed him less and could help him more."

"Paralysis changed Len's body, not his soul. He wasn't an easy man when he could walk. He wasn't an easy man when he went on wheels. You didn't make him what he was. You couldn't make him different. Only Len could do that, and Len didn't want to."

"If I hadn't made him marry me—"

"You didn't make him marry you," Archer cut in. "No one ever made Len do one damned thing he didn't want to." He glanced down toward the dim, narrow hallway where the prostitute and her trick had disappeared. Nothing moved in the shadows. "Come on."

Relieved that they were leaving the depressing barroom, Hannah stood quickly. She made a sound of dismay when Archer turned her away from the front door. Instead, he urged her down the reeking hallway, opened the door to the men's bathroom, and looked around.

Empty.

Without a word he dragged Hannah past a stained urinal toward the single stall. What the place lacked in size, it made up for in sheer quantity of dirt.

"What if someone comes in here?" Hannah asked, jumpy as only a woman can be in a men's public toilet. "What will he think?"

"When you change into this, he won't have to think. He'll be sure I hauled you in here for a quickie."

While Archer talked, he rummaged in the duffel. Rapidly he pulled out a short black skirt, black lace bikini panties, and a black-and-pink striped crop top so tight there wasn't room for a bra beneath. A pair of black high-heeled sandals completed the outfit. What there was of it. Without the jacket—which Archer left in the duffel—there wasn't much more concealment in the clothing than in an Australian bikini.

"What is that?" Hannah asked, staring at the hot pink and black stripes.

"Clothes. Yours, to be precise."

"I don't think so."

"Screaming pink isn't my color," he said blandly, dangling the stretchy top from his index finger. "Stripes don't do much for me, either."

"I think you'd look smashing in that. Every man needs a jockstrap that looks like an embarrassed tiger."

"It's not a jockstrap." He held it out to her. "It's a blouse."

"No."

"And this is the skirt that goes with it."

"Not until you tell me why."

"Pink turns me on."

"We didn't have it earlier and you did just fine."

He smiled a remembering kind of smile. "Yeah, we did. Imagine what we'll do now."

Hannah hesitated, then gave Archer a smile that made him

wish they were in bed. "I'm imagining." She reached for the buttons on her blouse. "Want to imagine with me?"

"Hell, yes. But I know better."

Reluctantly he turned his back and went to the pitted sink. If he watched her undress, he would do something really stupid, like take her right here, right now, as though she was bought and paid for with a twenty-dollar bill.

A turn of the tap told him this would be another cold-water shave. Grimacing, he pulled out the disposable razor—April Joy had only sent one—and shaved off his mustache with swift, painful strokes. He rinsed the sink carefully before he pulled out his own disguise and looked it over.

The change of clothes began with simple and shockingly expensive black slacks and a white silk shirt. A Krugerand on a heavy gold chain told him that he was expected to wear his shirt in the European style, unbuttoned halfway to his belt. He wondered if April knew that the chain would nip and gnaw at the hair on his chest.

The shoes answered his question. Though they took up most of the space in the duffel, they were a size too small.

April must have laughed herself into a coma at the thought of his discomfort. She knew everything about him, including his shoe size. She certainly knew him well enough to be sure that he wasn't the type to flash a chunk of gold against his hairy chest. But once he was dressed, he would be a fit partner for Hannah's outfit: money and barely bridled sex.

When he turned around, she was struggling to zip up the skirt's back zipper. He stood where he was and stared. Just stared. He had had her naked, had licked every bit of her, and still he was rocked back by the sexy sway of her breasts beneath the tight top and the hot curves of her long, long legs.

"Why do they put zippers in skirts this tight?" she muttered. "Why not just spray the ruddy thing on and be done with it?"

"Let me try it."

The husky timbre of Archer's voice brought Hannah's head up. The blunt male appreciation in his eyes made her feel sleek, sexy, and primitive as a cat in heat. "I wish you didn't have to shave your beard."

"Why?" he asked, walking around behind her.

"I liked the feel of it . . . everywhere."

He gritted his teeth and tried to think of all the reasons he couldn't do what he wanted to do. What she wanted him to do. The blood hammering through his body made it almost impossible to think. Carefully he pulled up the zipper.

She cleared her throat. "Thanks. My fingers kept slipping off the tab. What's this stuff made of?" she asked, running her fingers up and down the skirt, from waist to midthigh hem. "It feels like silk, looks like silk, but doesn't wrinkle."

Archer looked away from the narrow, long fingers that were running up and down Hannah's hips. "I don't know what it is. Have you ever worn contacts?"

"Nope."

He held out a tiny box to her, explained the procedure, and demonstrated by opening a similar box and putting his own contacts in. She looked critically at the result. His gray-green-blue eyes were transformed into a muddy shade of blue.

"I like the original better."

"I'll keep it in mind," he said dryly. "Give me the wig while you put in your contacts."

Trying not to think about the appalling condition of the sink, she leaned toward the dingy mirror and went to work. She had one contact in and was blinking furiously when someone hammered on the door.

"Hey, mate," called a voice. "I gotta piss."

Archer growled some words that made Hannah wince. She put in the other contact and looked at herself. A pair of brown eyes looked back at her.

It was unnerving.

"Put this on," he said, holding out the wig.

She looked from the neat French braid Archer had made in the wig to his blue eyes. "You keep surprising me."

"Wait until you see what I can do with cosmetics."

"You're joking."

He reached into the duffel and came up with a handful of makeup. "Tell me that in a few minutes."

A few breathless minutes later—Archer stood very close while he put makeup on her—Hannah looked at herself in the mirror again, made a startled sound, and leaned in closer over the sink. Like the clothes, her makeup sent a message of expensive sex. Very expensive. Very sexy. "You weren't joking."

Archer looked at the skirt flirting with revealing her tempting cheeks as she bent over the sink. Before he knew he was going to do it, he slid one hand up between her thighs. The skirt was like her, so tight that there was barely room for him inside.

She made a startled, husky sound as he eased aside the slim thong of her underwear and stroked soft flesh until she shivered. Her eyes met his in the mirror while liquid silk licked over his fingertips.

"I don't have much won't power where you're concerned," he said, his voice gritty.

"Won't power?" she asked huskily.

"As in I *won't* bend you over my arm and make you scream with pleasure."

She hesitated, then sighed. "Are you sure?"

"No," he admitted.

The hammering came on the door again.

With a curse, Archer forced himself to stop teasing both of them. "Put this on."

Hannah took the pink jacket that dangled from his big hand. It fit her perfectly. The hem of the jacket skimmed the hem of the skirt. Now she looked like ultra-high-class sin, the kind only kings or mafia princes could afford.

Archer whistled softly. April Joy had outdone herself. It almost made him forgive her for the black loafers that were gnawing on his toes.

"The pearls have to go," he said after a moment. "Someone who looks like you wouldn't be caught dead in anything less than the best."

Hannah made a face at him, but removed the pearls and watched them vanish into the duffel. He pulled out a tiny, sleek, black leather purse with a long braided strap and solid gold designer initials on the side.

"Your passport is inside," he said.

She froze. "Passport?"

Rather than answering, he opened the bathroom door and ushered her out. The man pacing the hallway began swearing.

Then his bleary eyes focused on Hannah. His jaw dropped and he forgot all about the beer stretching his bladder. He stared at her until she vanished out the door into the alley.

Archer smiled rather grimly to himself as he shut the back door behind them. The man would never forget Hannah, but he wouldn't be able to describe anything more of her than the swing and sway of a very nice ass.

When they were out on the street, Archer smiled. "You look very nice, Mrs. South."

"Thank you, Mr. . . . ?"

"South."

"We're married?"

"It says so on the passports." He took a ring box from his pants pocket. "Here."

Hannah flipped open the velvet lid, stared, and looked hastily at Archer. "Are these real?"

"Probably." Considering that April Joy went shopping with Archer's money, almost certainly. April would have relished spending every dime. But there was no need to tell Hannah that. She was nervous enough about the rings as it was. "Want me to get them appraised?"

Openmouthed, she stared at the rings. The stones were set in what looked and felt like platinum—cool, heavy, hard. The wedding band was a wide circlet set with flush-mounted, square, colorless diamonds. The engagement band featured a marquise-shaped silver-blue diamond that was at least three carats, set with large, triangular, colorless diamonds on either side.

"I can't wear this," she said, swallowing.

"Wrong size?" He picked up the rings and her left hand. Easily he slid the rings into place. "Nope. Perfect. Let's go, sweetheart. We don't want to miss our plane."

She braced herself and didn't budge. "Not until you tell me what's going on."

"Simple. We're going after the Black Trinity."

Fourteen

F rom the air, Hong Kong was a silent, glittering white dream sleeping between blue ocean and black land. From the ground, Hong Kong was an exhilarating nightmare. Noise. Traffic. Smells. Crowds. Urgency. The rapid rise and fall of the Chinese language ran like a seething river through the city's high-rise canyons. There was calm to be found inside walled residences, those private oases of proportion and elegance and silence. There was no calm on the streets. The streets were for reckless commerce, sharp-edged and unapologetic.

The change in government known as the Turnover hadn't diminished Hong Kong's wealth or ambition. The newspapers printed communist sentiments and exhortations daily, but the city was fueled by a breathtaking capitalism. Hong Kong was a neon-flashing city of gamblers whose sheer dedication to money made Las Vegas look like a sixty-five-watt bingo parlor run by parish priests.

The streets boiled with pedestrians locked in unequal battle with delivery trucks, taxis, buses, motorbikes, bicycles, and private cars. Beneath the haze of vehicle exhaust, white was the most common color of the buildings. Dazzling rainbow bursts of neon signs climbed entire buildings, calling attention to commerce. Black was the usual color of clothes. Smoke blue was the color of the air in the streets where sidewalk vendors grilled snacks on braziers for the endless, restless, relentless tide of humanity.

Archer tapped the taxi driver on the shoulder and pointed toward the sidewalk. Without looking at traffic, the driver pulled over. Hannah tried not to look, either. Despite her dislike of the rain forest's primitive villages, she had never been comfortable in big cities. They were exciting. They were fascinating. They were exotic. But after a while, a numbing sort of overload set in. Then all she wanted was silence and space. Cities offered neither.

"Almost there," Archer said. He tugged down the black cowboy hat he wore. He had picked it up from one of Hong Kong's remarkable street vendors. Wisely, he had declined the dazzling diamond "Rolex" the same vendor was ready to part with for *ver' tiny cash, sir-sir, ver' tiny.*

"Anyone following us?" Hannah asked.

"We lost the last one in the meat market, when those German tour buses unloaded."

"Did you recognize him?"

"Them," he corrected. "No. I just recognized the moves. But you could lose an elephant in that market. That's why I went there."

Hannah swallowed and said nothing. Hong Kong's immense open-air food market had reminded her of a jungle without trees, Genesis without pages. Every kind of creature that walked, flew, jumped, swam, or slithered waited in cages for housewives and cooks to bargain over the cost of fresh protein for dinner. The cats and dogs were difficult enough for her to bear, but the monkeys were the worst, so nearly human in their silent pleas to be freed from the cage of heat and smoke and noise. Eventually, this meal or the next, they would get their wish.

Shuddering, Hannah put the memory of the cages out of her mind.

"Over there," Archer said.

She followed his glance and saw the store without even having to stretch her neck; when they weren't being followed, being tall enough to look over the heads of most of the street crowd was an advantage. She couldn't translate the ideographs that flashed over the shop, but the owner obviously had his eye on world trade. Translations of the Chinese symbols were provided in Japanese and Korean ideographs, the Russian Cyrillic alphabet, plus the more familiar alphabet used by the French, German, Portuguese, Spanish, Italian, and English speakers.

"No Arabic," Hannah said.

"No Arabian buyers."

"Why? Do they like hard gems?"

"They like diamonds as well as the next guy, but the Arab princes and oil sheiks have treasure rooms that are jammed with ropes of natural pearls," Archer said. "They've been harvesting naturals for two thousand years in the Red Sea, Persian Gulf, and Gulf of Aden."

"Bet they hated Kokichi Mikimoto."

Archer looked around. Despite being literally shoulder to shoulder with other pedestrians, he and Hannah might as well have been alone. The people dividing around them were talking fast in Chinese, walking faster, and smoking as though there was a million-dollar prize for finishing the most cigarettes in a day.

"Are you talking about the guy who patented the technique for culturing round pearls?" Archer asked.

She nodded.

"You're right," he said. "Mikimoto's not a hero in the Gulf. He blew the bottom out of the pearl trade when he destroyed the rarity of the pearl."

"But not the beauty."

"The child of moonbeams. Tears of the gods. The soul of the sea." Archer smiled. "Pearls are all of that and more."

"But not cultured pearls, is that it?"

"Not to the Arabs. They say cultured pearls are inferior to naturals, and they'll say it as long as they have natural pearls supporting their currency along with the rest of the royal treasury."

"What do you think?"

While people jostled and chattered and poured by on either side in a human tide, Archer looked across the bobbing heads at the window where a gleaming South Seas necklace was the centerpiece of one display. The choker was made of round pearls that had an unusual, almost tangerine orient. "I think that gem-quality natural pearls are far too rare—and therefore astronomically expensive—to support any kind of extensive pearl trade. Fortunately for Chang's Sea Gems stores, the rest of the world isn't prejudiced against cultured pearls."

"I admit to a prejudice in favor of black pearls," Hannah said, looking at a matinee-length necklace that had a lovely dark luster. She would have liked to get closer to the window, but the crowd was like a moving, impenetrable barrier.

"Must be your American parents," Archer said. "Asians prefer silver-white. South Americans like South Seas gold. It's classic white for Europe, pink for the low-ticket American Akoya trade, and black for the American luxury trade."

She leaned very close to Archer. "If the Asians don't like black pearls, why are we here?"

"Japan loves black pearls. For the right gems, they'll pay twice what Americans would."

"Then we should be in Japan."

"Last year. Or maybe next year. But right now, the yen is very weak against the dollar. Whoever has the goods will sell them where the currency and demand are the strongest."

"America?"

Archer nodded.

"So why are we in Hong Kong?" she asked.

"When it comes to luxury goods, Hong Kong is the commercial crossroads of the world. If someone wants a quick transaction and is willing to settle for a cut-rate price, this would be the place."

"Isn't this kind of shop too, um . . ."

"High-end for crooks?" he finished dryly.

"Right."

"No matter where on the food chain you start, goods like we're chasing would end up in Sea Gems, where the clientele is rich enough to buy third-world countries but would rather have baubles."

Hannah chewed lightly on her lower lip. She was still getting used to the taste of indestructible lipstick. "Is Sea Gems part of the Chang family's holdings?"

"Sam Chang is the owner of record," Archer said quietly, "but you have to dig a long time to find that out. The store has the best pearls in Hong Kong, which is to say some of the best pearls in the world."

"Both the name Sam and the name Chang are common, especially in the westernized East. Are you sure it's the same Sam Chang? Ian's father?"

Archer nodded. "The old man owns and operates high-end pearl stores all over the world. Tokyo. Shanghai. Los Angeles. Manhattan. London. Paris. Rome. He was going to open up one in Moscow, too, but the ruble keeps crashing."

"What about your father's company?"

"Donovan International?"

"Yes."

He shrugged. "We have offices in every country that has significant mineral reserves, if that's what you mean."

In mock salute she touched the brim of the wide, floppy black hat she had picked up in the airport. "Impressive."

"That's The Donovan, all right," he said, forcing a path through the crowded sidewalk so that they could stand close to one of the many display windows. "Impressive. Like that pearl choker."

He stepped back just enough to let her look past him into the display window. To the right, next to a long strand of golden pearls alternating with glittering diamonds, she saw a black pearl choker. The pearls were at least eighteen millimeters, as big as the choker Archer had bought for her in Broome. After that, all similarity between the two necklaces ended. These pearls had a fine luster, an iridescent blue-black color, and a fat six-figure price tag.

Frowning, she went in closer until she was all but pressing her nose against the glass. The city heat was so intense she couldn't have steamed up the glass with her breath if she tried.

She looked at the necklace with such concentration that the rest of reality just faded into background.

"What do you think?" he asked after a few minutes.

"Quite nice, despite the fact that the color match across the strand is only good, not excellent."

He turned, looked at the necklace appraisingly, and then at her. "Only good?"

"Yes," she said, not glancing away from the window. "There was no hesitation in her voice. "I can't tell from here, but I suspect that the surface isn't quite up to the price on one or two of those pearls. If so, it would explain the less than superior color match."

A slow smile spread across Archer's face. He thought of how quickly she had become a pouting tourist for the shopkeeper in Broome. He was accustomed to working alone, but he was beginning to appreciate just how useful she could be in catching pearl traders off guard.

"Can you play the part of an ultrafussy, not-too-classy rich bitch without revealing how much you really know about pearls?" he asked.

"You mean the kind of spoiled brat who knows what she likes, never sees it, and could find fault with God?"

Archer laughed out loud. "Perfect." He ran his fingertips over Hannah's cheek in a light caress. "You're looking for a very special black pearl necklace. You don't know what kind, but you'll know it when you see it."

"How special?" she asked.

He shook his head, silently telling her not to mention the Black Trinity. "As long as you don't describe right away how special the orient is, the necklace can be as special as you like."

"A real colorful black," she said, deadpan.

A smile tugged at the corners of his mouth. "You got it. Let's go make the manager chew his very expensive carpet. If he gets irked enough, he'll let us into the vault in back just to show us how important he and his pearls are and how ignorant and ordinary we are. Then we'll see how much he knows and what he's saving for his special clients."

And, depending on what Archer saw or didn't see, he would

decide if it was time to put a rainbow cat among the sleek pearl pigeons.

"How do you know this store has the really good stuff hidden in a vault?" she asked.

"Stores like this always do. What's in the windows is just the lure. Besides, I've been in the vault before. That's where they keep their virgins," he said, using the common name for pearls that haven't been drilled. "Nice goods. Really nice."

"Will someone here recognize you?"

"I doubt it. It's been years."

He pulled out a pair of clear glasses. It looked like they were bifocal, but they weren't. There was just an extra thickness of glass at the bottom of the lens. The frames were thin, black, the latest in Italian flash. The lenses were amber tinted. The glasses, like the hat, completely changed the lines of his face.

She lifted her eyebrows in silent salute. "Spoiled, bitchy, and way too picky. Anything else?"

"I don't know anything about pearls. And my name is—"

"Sugar," Hannah cut in quickly. "I'm rotten with names."

"Sugar?" His mouth curled up at the corners. "Okay, I can live with that. It beats buttercup."

"Buttercup?" She looked him up and down, lingering on the size and set of his shoulders. "Doesn't suit."

"Thank you. But that's what my sister Honor calls her husband when she's annoyed with him. And vice versa."

"Buttercup. Is her husband, um, small?"

"Am I?"

"No."

"Jake's the same size as me."

"Buttercup." She rolled the word around on her tongue and grinned. "I like it."

Archer had a feeling he was going to wish he hadn't let Hannah in on that particular family joke. Yet seeing her face light up with amusement was something he couldn't really regret.

The inside of the store was like a museum rather than a commercial enterprise. Instead of putting out as much merchandise as possible, the decorator had used empty space to create a feeling of importance around the display pedestals. In place of the brilliant, pinpoint lighting used by jewelers to enhance diamonds and other faceted stones, the light aimed at the pearls in their satin nests was soft, carefully color balanced, and often fluorescent rather than incandescent.

No glass caged the tops of the pedestals. Potential buyers were kept just out of easy arm's reach by burgundy velvet ropes. A very old, fabulously costly silk carpet muffled the sound of expensively shod feet. French Impressionist paintings and works by ancient masters of calligraphy hung on the walls, adding to the feeling of richness and cultural worth. Intricately carved, museum-quality folding screens separated various areas. Quietly, repeatedly, the decor let customers know that they were privileged to be part of such elegance and taste.

The interior was divided into suites. Each had its own type of pearls. Freshwater baroques from every river, stream, pond, and lake in the world, in sizes from hummingbird to chicken egg. Saltwater baroques from abalone whose rainbow orient was intense, but lacked the mystery of the Black Trinity's pearls. Small Japanese Akoya pearls, with their natural pale blue tones and their unnatural pink and silver ones. Larger Tahitian pearls, whose highlights ranged from steel gray to peacock blue to jungle green. Big South Seas pearls with their silver-whites and radiant golds—angel dreams fashioned into necklaces and bracelets, set into earrings and brooches and rings. The Australian pearls were biggest of all, legacy of the Indian Ocean's sweeping tides and the pearl farmers' skill.

Most of the suites held customers conversing in Chinese. There were a few speaking English and what might have been Italian. The suite specializing in black pearls was empty but for a man sitting at a desk. The polished brass plaque announced that he was Paul Chevalier. Archer knew that Monsieur Paul was one of Sam Chang's head pearl buyers, an up-and-comer from Tahiti who had his eye on one of the Chang granddaughters. If rumor was correct, the granddaughter had both eyes on the very handsome Paul.

Paul barely nodded to Hannah and Archer before he went back to his phone call. He left the distinct impression that he knew important customers on sight, and they didn't qualify.

Archer bent over Hannah, nuzzled and nibbled on her neck,

and said softly, "We're in luck. That's their top black pearl expert. If anyone can get us into the vault room, he can. Word is that he's a vain, self-important son of a bitch. The kind who loves to put people in their place, which is the dirt under his feet."

Her slow smile was pure acid. "Only in the colonies," she said in a calm, carrying voice, "would anyone think their great-grandmother's hallway rug was classy."

"You're the one who wanted to look at pearls," Archer said. A twang had appeared in his voice, something between Oklahoma and Texas. "We were told this was the place to look, darlin'. So look. Screw the rug."

"You never understand."

"Aw, babe. How long did I look for just the right shade of fancy blue diamond for you?"

She rolled her eyes. "I was looking right alongside you."

"Years."

"But we found it, didn't we?" She held her hand out and admired the flash and play of her rings. "Even if it looks a little off in this light. Stupid jewelry stores. Why don't they just use full-spectrum lighting?"

"Admire your rocks outside. We're looking for a pearl necklace in here, remember?" But he grinned and ran his fingertip down her arm in a slow caress to take any possible sting from his words. "You know my policy. Only the best for you, darlin'."

She made a husky, murmurous sound, stood on tiptoe, and brushed her lips against his. "You're such a sweetie."

"For you, I'm pure sugar." He smoothed his hand over her hip and squeezed with the assurance of a man fondling a long-time lover. "Go see if you like something. If not, there are other stores in Hong Kong."

She toyed with the gold chain lying against his furry chest, smiled when he winced at the hair caught in the chain, and sauntered over to the nearest pedestal. After walking around it once, she leaned in and calmly snagged the necklace off its ice-blue satin pillow.

Instantly an alarm chimed, both musical and loud. Monsieur

Paul hung up and shot out of his chair, letting loose a torrent of French with a pronounced Tahitian flavor.

Ignoring him like dirt under her feet, Hannah kept looking at the necklace. The semibaroque black pearls were beautifully matched for shape, size, color, and luster. They looked like slightly flattened planets with rings around them. Their orient had an unusual silver-blue sheen. There was a scattering of surface pits and a few cloudy spots, all of which were very minor on first inspection. The asking price was major, just under $320,000. A portion of that price was due to the pale blue diamonds set in the platinum clasp.

"What's he fussing about, sugar?" she asked without looking up from the pearl necklace.

"Beats me," Archer said, swallowing his laughter.

She replaced the necklace on its pedestal, which shut up the alarm. Without a pause she headed toward the next display area. This one featured a matinee-length necklace of matched, uniform black pearls. These had a peacock-blue sheen and a pigeon-blood ruby clasp.

"Madame," the man said quickly in English, stepping between Hannah and the velvet rope. "I am Monsieur Paul. Please permit me to assist you. Pearls are like a woman, very delicate. They must be handled carefully."

His accent was island French, legacy of his birth on the Chang pearl farms in Tahiti. His demeanor was that of a slender prince trying to be patient with a thickheaded peon. He wore a suit and tie, both of cream-colored silk. His shirt was also silk, dawn pink in color. Handsome as a soap-opera star, he moved confidently, knowing women of all races would forgive him in advance.

He led Hannah back to the first pedestal and pulled a butter-soft cloth from his inner suit-coat pocket. Deftly he switched off the alarm and wiped down the pearls Hannah had touched. Only when he was satisfied with their gleam did he settle them back into their satin-lined display and reactivate the alarm.

Throughout the whole process, Hannah examined her fingernails. One by one. The hot pink color she had applied on the plane was already showing wear. When it came to nail polish, she was hopeless. Nor did she care whether her nails were perfect or perfectly awful. She was silently, thoroughly, telling the elegant Monsieur Paul that she wasn't forgiving him for anything, no matter how beautifully he pouted.

"If pearls are that delicate, they won't last long, will they?" Archer asked Paul.

"*Mais non!* With care, they will last for generation after generation."

"Care, huh?" Archer glanced at Hannah. She was still examining the polish she had put on while he slept on the plane. "Maybe you better fill me in. My wife and I are new to the pearl game. She saw some black pearls on a French model at our last party and hasn't let up on me since."

Paul's eyes brightened. Paying celebrities and models to wear Tahitian pearls was a common, very effective way of drawing attention to pearls in a culture such as America's, which was focused on faceted gems.

"Always store your fine pearls in a soft bag," Paul said in the tone of a professor, "separate from your hard gems. But no plastic, you understand. They must breathe. They were created by a living animal. To remain beautiful, they must have moisture."

"Good news, darlin'," Archer said to Hannah. "You can wear them to your aerobics class. That should give 'em a good drink."

Monsieur Paul paled. "No, no!" He cleared his throat. "The moisture in the air is best. Perspiration, even from the most, ah, delicate of women, simply will not do. Perspiration has acid in it, which will eventually change the pearls' color."

"Handle like a baby and no sweat. Anything else?" Archer asked, looking impatient.

Ignoring the men, Hannah sidled up to the next display pedestal. She wanted a closer look at the matinee-length pearls.

"Of course, Madame knows not to put on her pearls until after she has applied her perfume or hair lacquer and cosmetics," Paul said, inching away from Archer and watching Hannah with faint horror.

"Don't tell me, let me guess," Archer said, his voice edged with impatience. "Perfume, hair spray, and makeup aren't good for pearls."

"Ahhh," Paul sighed, relieved. "You understand."

"How about swimming in the damn things?"

"In the ocean, if you must. In a pool, never. Chlorine—"

"I get it," Archer cut in. "Chlorine eats the dainty little things. So how do you keep them clean? Or are they too delicate to take that, too?"

"Use soap, not detergent, then rinse thoroughly and let the pearls dry in the air," Paul said, watching Hannah narrowly. "Never use ammonia or vinegar. It will destroy the pearls. *Un moment, madame.* I will show you those pearls."

But Archer wasn't ready to let Paul off the hook quite yet. "Sounds easier just to lock pearls in a safety-deposit box and be done with it."

Hannah smiled to herself as Paul muttered something under his breath. It was one of Coco's favorite curses, obscene and blasphemous in equal parts.

"Vaults are often very dry," Paul said with immense patience. "That is not good for pearls. If you must lock them away in a steel box, put with them a damp cloth. Moisture, yes?"

"Darlin'?" Archer called out.

"Yeah?" She leaned in and reached for another necklace.

"Stick to diamonds."

She gave both men a pouty, impatient look. "I want black pearls." An alarm chimed as she lifted the long necklace off its pedestal.

Archer sighed. "Okay, babe. If you scratch them up, I'll get you some more."

She blew him a kiss.

Outrage and greed warred for control of Paul's expression. Greed won. He was, after all, in the business of selling pearls.

Even to swine.

Fifteen

"So, tell me about this one," Hannah said, running the pearls through her fingers.

Paul saw only her unusual, high-quality diamond, not the skill and care of her fingers as she handled the necklace. "Three hundred and fifty thousand dollars, American."

"Why?" she asked.

"Pardon?"

"Why?" she repeated. "With diamonds you have a fixed color scale and carat weight to determine price. What did you do to price this necklace, pick a number out of the air?"

Paul cleared his throat. "It is a very complex process."

"Uh-huh." Clearly she wasn't impressed.

"Color, shape, presence or absence of blemishes, and size all figure into the price," Paul said stiffly.

She nodded. "Like diamonds."

"Unlike diamonds, pearls are not touched by man. Their shape and polish is as natural as the shine of water. Pearls come to you as they came from the oyster."

And pigs fly, Hannah thought sardonically. There were a

hundred ways to make inferior pearls look better than they were. But she wasn't supposed to know about that. She was just supposed to know what she liked.

"Unlike diamonds, which can be cut into many shapes, the shape of a pearl is determined solely by the oyster," Paul said, falling into his sales patter. "These are living gems, very unique, very precious. Especially the spherical pearls. Most pearls are baroque. Do you understand baroque?"

"It means they're not round, doesn't it?" Hannah asked indifferently.

"Each shape has its own beauty, its own mystery, its own admirers—" Paul began.

"Round," she cut in.

"Pardon?"

"I want my pearls round. The model's were round and black, but not really black. Lots of color."

"Spherical is the most valuable class of pearls. The ones you are holding now are spherical. They also have a peacock-blue sheen, which makes them very desirable."

"Not to me," Hannah said, handing him the pearls. "I want reds and greens and golds and pinks along with the blue. Don't you have something with more color?"

"This is a very fine necklace," Paul said through gritted teeth.

She shrugged and wandered off to the next pedestal.

"Like I said," Archer muttered, "we spent *years* looking for just the right shade of silver-blue diamond for her. That woman is downright persnickety when it comes to color. You have any idea how many shades blue diamonds come in?"

Paul managed a smile. He knew just how much a flawless, vibrant, three-carat, fancy blue diamond cost. That was why he wasn't showing these exasperating peasants to the door.

"What about that little necklace in the window, darlin'?" Archer asked.

"No, thanks," she said casually. "Some of the pearls aren't a very good match."

Paul winced and began wiping down the necklace she had just replaced on its pedestal. "Madame, I assure you, whether it is a question of shape, color, size, or orient, our necklaces are matched to the highest standards."

"Yeah? Then they're not as high as mine."

"Like I told you," Archer said cheerfully, "we searched for years. My baby has an eye for color."

Paul folded his lips and said not one word.

She stopped at a third pedestal, hesitated, then went still. She would have sworn the pearls in this necklace came from Pearl Cove. Not the experimental rafts, but the ordinary black pearls that were the most profitable part of Pearl Cove's production.

"So, all your pearls come from around here?" she asked. "Or is that just publicity crap?"

Hannah's question pressed the button marked Sales. Words poured out of Paul like a swift tide. "If you speak of black pearls, you are speaking of Tahitian pearls. Tahiti has many, many pearl farms. Each of them produces a pearl that is superior to any other in the world. There is no need to search farther than my country's own beautiful lagoons for the very finest in black pearls."

"Uh-huh," she said. Her tone said *publicity crap.*

Archer watched her closely. He didn't know what she was seeing in those particular pearls, but the very stillness of her body told him that somehow, in some way, the pearls weren't what she had expected. He eased closer, ready to step in if she forgot her role and started asking too many intelligent questions.

"Sugar, are we going Down Under?" Hannah asked, turning toward Archer. "You know, that place in Western Australia where they have miles and miles of pearl farms?"

"If that's what it takes to get you the necklace you want, that's where we'll go." He smiled at the jeweler. "Good thing they don't grow pearls on the moon. Sure as hell, she'd be booking us a shuttle flight."

Paul's smile said he thought that was an excellent idea, and the sooner the better.

"Well," she said, shrugging, "just because blokes—er, folks— in this store can't tell the difference between a good color match and a great one is no reason for me to have pearls like the ones in the window."

"The black choker?" Archer asked. "The one I liked?"

"Yeah. I could do better than that with my eyes closed." She strolled past Paul, whose tongue was developing red skid marks from being restrained between his teeth.

"Darlin', you're being awful hard on the poor man," Archer said. His eyes said he was enjoying every second of it.

"At more than fifteen thousand bucks a pearl, I haven't even started being hard."

"The cost of any necklace," Paul said in a strained voice, "reflects the difficulty of matching the pearls, rather than the worth of each individual pearl."

"Yeah, matching must have been tough," she said indifferently. "Maybe you'll get it right next time."

"Perhaps Madame would show me which pearls aren't up to her exacting standards?" Paul asked. The disdain in his voice said that he didn't think she could.

Hannah flicked a sideways glance at Archer. He nodded so slightly that she would have missed it if she hadn't been watching closely.

"You sure you want me to?" she said to Paul, but her eyes were still on Archer.

"Quite," Paul said in a clipped voice.

It was Archer's tiny signal, not Paul's urging, that sent her strolling toward the front display window. Ignoring Paul darting around her like a nervous gazelle, she lifted out the expensive choker and looked around for a neutral surface to put the necklace on. The best she could do was a cream-colored satin tray she found on Paul's desk. Instead of leaving the pearls in a neat circle as they had been in the window, she made the necklace into two roughly parallel lines. Pearls that had been separated by the width of a woman's neck now lay side by side.

Saying nothing, Archer bent over Hannah's shoulder. The expression on his face was that of a proud parent watching a beloved child perform. His hand on her butt wasn't that of a parent. Absently he caressed one sleek, firm cheek.

"Like it, *buttercup*?" she muttered.

"Prime. Really prime." He squeezed gently, deeply, before he released her.

When she turned and looked over her shoulder at his eyes, there was laughter and something much hotter in them. Slowly she licked her lips and made a soft, growling-purring kind of sound. Before he could recover, she bent back over the pearls. With a casual, deliberate movement, she slid her butt firmly over his thighs. It was caress, promise, and warning in one: two could play the intimate-couple game.

Archer laughed softly and wished he had nothing more on his mind but the feel of her taut cheeks nuzzling up close to his crotch.

"See this one?" Hannah said. "It doesn't look so hot with this one."

"Note the position of the clasp, madame," Paul said quickly. "When on your neck, the pearls would not be next to each other."

Disdainfully she lifted her elegantly outlined eyebrows. "So the deal is, a matched necklace means the pearls only have to match the ones touching them? Is that what the diamond spacers are for—distraction from a so-so color match?"

Paul's teeth came together with a muted click. The bitch might have the class of a hooker, but she did have an exceptionally keen eye for color. The pearls were separated by the width of a necklace because they weren't a truly fine match. Ninety-nine people out of a hundred wouldn't have noticed that the match wasn't excellent across the whole strand. Unfortunately, this woman wasn't one of the ninety-nine.

"Pearls are as individual as people," Paul managed. "Just as no two people are exactly alike, no two pearls are exactly alike."

"Uh-huh," she said. "But I'm not asking about a matched-people necklace."

Archer snickered.

"I'm talking pearls here," she continued, ignoring him and focusing on Paul. "Is this the best color match you have?"

"The silvery blue semibaroque necklace—" he began.

"No," she cut in impatiently. "I told you, I want big, *round* black pearls with lots of color. So is this the best big, round black pearl necklace you have?"

"Black pearls are the most difficult to match. The differences in orient are very great, much more so than is the case with white pearls."

"Uh-huh. So this is the best you have." She looked at Archer and jerked her head toward the exit. "C'mon, darling. We'll just have to tell the Rothenbergs that they were wrong about this shop being the best of the best. It ain't."

"However, we just happen to have an unstrung, triple strand necklace of large, round black pearls," Paul said quickly. "They are exceptionally colorful, and exceptionally well matched."

She froze as the words echoed in her mind. Black. Unstrung. Triple strand. Large. Round. Exceptionally colorful.

The Black Trinity.

"Yeah?" Archer said, drawing Paul's attention away from Hannah. "Where are they?"

"In the vault."

She clicked back into her role. "Well, what are they doing in there? You'll never sell them that way. God, don't the French know *anything* but food and rags?"

"Excuse me," Paul said, tight lipped. "I will need assistance."

He stalked off to a back room.

Lazily Archer pulled Hannah close, nuzzled against her neck, and asked very softly, "What bothered you about that other necklace?"

The hidden, leisurely caress of his tongue against her skin sent heat scattering over her. "They looked like Pearl Cove goods."

"What do you mean? They certainly weren't rainbows."

"I can't remember every pearl I've ever sorted, but I do remember the difficult or special ones. I'd swear I've sorted pearls in just that combination of pink-orange orient and deep black background, with the faintest of parallel lines in the surface. They were a right bitch to match with the usual run of Pearl Cove product."

"Probably because they came from Tahiti, not Pearl Cove."

"Why would— Never mind. Quotas, right?"

"Bingo. Laundering pearls from Chang's Tahitian pearl

farms through Australia's Pearl Cove would be a good way to evade quotas." Archer hesitated, then gave in to temptation. With the tip of his tongue he tasted the soft, fragrant skin just behind Hannah's ear. "Or the pearls could have been stolen and then sold at bargain rates to Len. Another kind of laundering. It's possible the pearls could have been stolen from Len and sold to Chang, but it's not likely. To my eye, the orient is Tahitian rather than Australian."

"I agree." She shivered, caught between the sultry heat of Archer's tongue tracing her hairline and the cool assessment of his words. "Would Ian have known about this?"

"Likely. Why?"

"If Chang wasn't evading the quotas, if Len was fencing stolen Chang pearls . . ."

"It would be a motive for murder, is that it?"

She nodded, though the thought of Ian Chang ordering Len's murder made her cold. She had never wanted Chang as a lover, but she considered him a friend.

Abruptly Hannah turned her face in to Archer's neck, burrowing, inhaling the musky mixture of heat and soap and man. Instead of being like rough silk, he felt rough, period. The individual hairs that just barely poked out from his skin were like wire.

"Why do they call it beard burn when you only get it from a man who shaves?" she muttered.

Archer laughed softly at the non sequitur. "Are you telling me I need to shave again?"

"I'm telling you I miss your beard."

"I'll throw away my razor."

"Lovely."

"Tell me that in a week."

"Okay."

He hesitated, then gave in to a need to touch, taste, cherish. He tilted up her chin and kissed her, a kiss as soft as his voice whispering, "You're a very special woman, Hannah."

"Because I like beards?"

"Among other things."

"What other things?"

Before he could answer, the door leading into the back of

the shop opened and Paul strode out. "Madame, monsieur, if you will come this way, I will show you the finest of pearls."

"Matched?" Her voice was a nice blend of eagerness and doubt.

"Mais oui." He turned and barked out some fast orders in Chinese. Another man appeared. Like Paul, he was slender, expensively dressed, and quite beautiful except for the suggestion of a sneer on his full lips.

The man bowed briefly and took up a station near the door.

"Come with me," Paul said. "Please."

Hannah took her time following the curt invitation. Her pulse was still speeding from the hot, delicate caress of Archer's tongue and the stroke of his hand from her nape to her hips. She would have been unnerved by her headlong response to him if she hadn't felt his own swift reaction, the quickening of his pulse and the hardening of his body against her belly.

The store's vault was much larger than the ruined one in Pearl Cove. Like the store, the room leading to the vault was divided into sections. Unlike the store, the guards here were visible, for all their carefully tailored dark silk suits. Anyone hoping to grab and run wouldn't make it to the front door.

Off to the left, two Chinese men discussed the merits of three enormous silver-white South Seas pearls. Just beyond the men, a Chinese dowager measured the weight and feel of a matinee-length necklace whose pearls were all as big as a man's thumb. These, too, were silver-white pearls. A German man wearing a wool sport coat and slacks waved off one tray of undrilled pearls and demanded another. Despite the air-conditioning in the vault, the German was sweating. On the table in front of him was the beginnings of a golden South Seas necklace.

Paul gestured to a table and velvet-covered chairs that waited off to the right, just beyond the vault's door. The decor here was a modern Asian take on Louis XIV magnificence—a deep teal blue and cream Chinese rug woven in ancient cloud patterns, gilt chairs with cream silk cushions and raised blue brocade ribbing, and gilt mirrors whose faintly curved frames matched those of the chair. The walls were a rich cream silk that matched the chair cushions. Raised blue ideographs wished the occupants health, serenity, and a fat bank account.

The video cameras that covered all angles of the room were also a tasteful cream color. The thick, curved lenses looked teal blue. Seeing the cameras, Archer almost smiled. By the time the Changs checked the videotape—if they became suspicious enough to check it at all—he and Hannah would be long gone. She would be safe with his family.

And he would be the way he had been years ago: alone, moving fast to stay ahead of the other predators, every sense raised to the burning edge of clarity by adrenaline, searching for someone who was also moving fast, looking over his shoulder, every sense burning.

"Madame," Paul said with a faint sneer and a theatrical flourish, "one hundred and seventy-seven round, black, large, matched pearls."

He opened the lid on the flat, gunmetal satin jewelry box and set it in front of her. Inside, lying within three oval, satin-lined channels, were round black pearls.

Not one was a rainbow.

She fought to keep her disappointment from showing, but doubted that she succeeded.

"Hey, these look good," Archer said in a hearty voice. "A little small maybe, but not bad."

"The smallest pearl is just under fourteen millimeters," Paul said stiffly. "The biggest is over fifteen."

She didn't say anything. A single look had told her that these pearls, however beautiful, weren't part of the Black Trinity. While colorful, the pearls lacked the splendor of rainbows swirling beneath black ice. They were indeed exquisitely matched, both within and across the "strands." Someone had gathered together one hundred and seventy-seven very, very nice pearls.

But they weren't the Black Trinity.

"Madame?" Paul asked smoothly.

"How much?" Archer cut in.

"Two million six hundred thousand dollars. American, of course." Paul smiled in the manner of someone who has just trumped another player's ace.

"Ouch. Oh well, she's worth it and then some."

She gave Archer a pouty air kiss and stood up.

"Madame would like to see something less expensive?" Paul asked smoothly.

"Madame would like to see something more colorful," she said, her voice as flat as she felt.

"Madame asks the impossible. These are the best pearls the world has to offer. You will find no finer necklace anywhere."

"In your dreams, mate," she retorted, disappointed and not at all reluctant to share the pain. "It's nice enough, but it needs more pinks and golds and reds and oranges."

"I repeat. You ask the impossible. Believe me. Every year the cream of Tahiti's black pearl farms passes through our owner's hands. I personally oversee the choices for jewelry. The crème de la crème is made into matched necklaces. This necklace is the best Mr. Chang has ever assembled."

When she would have responded, Archer restrained her by giving her hand a quick squeeze. "Maybe in Tahiti it's impossible to find more colorful black pearls," he said cheerfully, "but we've heard that Australia has some really special black pearls."

Paul shrugged. "One hears many things, most of them false. One rarely sees a necklace such as this one."

"Yeah, it's a nice fistful of pearls," Archer agreed, reaching into his pocket. "But once my darlin' saw this, she never looked at another pearl in quite the same way."

As he spoke, he pulled a ring box out of his pocket. Without taking his eyes off the jeweler, Archer flipped open the lid and tipped Teddy's tear-shaped rainbow black pearl onto his palm.

Paul's expression shouted that he had never seen a pearl like this in his life. His eyes widened, his jaw loosened, and he reached automatically for the rainbow gem.

Archer closed his hand.

Hannah reeled in her own jaw and waited for a signal from him as to how to act. She knew the gem had to be one of Pearl Cove's. What she didn't understand was how it had slipped through Len's fingers.

"Where did you get that pearl?" Paul demanded.

It was exactly the question she wanted to ask.

"It must be treated," Paul said without waiting for an answer. "Has it been drilled?"

"Don't know about treatments," Archer lied cheerfully, "but it hasn't been drilled."

Paul stared longingly at the other man's closed hand.

Archer opened his fingers as coyly as a stripper playing with a G-string. Rainbows gleamed against midnight.

"May I?" Paul asked, inching closer.

"Don't go losing it," Hannah said quickly. "Nobody we've showed it to ever saw one like it."

"If it is a virgin—that is, undrilled—no dye could penetrate the nacre," Paul said. "Therefore the color would have to be natural."

Archer rolled the pearl lightly on his palm, proving that there were no drill holes.

"Virgin," Paul said reverently. "Where did you get it?"

"Card game," Archer drawled.

"Where?"

"Vegas."

"Who had it before you?"

"A guy called Stan who wasn't as good at five-card stud as he thought."

"What is his last name? Where did he—"

"Look," Archer cut in. "I don't know how y'all play poker in Hong Kong, but when I sit down for a game, we don't pass around last names and life histories. You put your cash on the table and you play until you're busted or everyone else quits."

"I've heard of such pearls, but I've never seen one before now." Paul looked hungrily at it. "May I?"

Archer acted reluctant, but finally passed the pearl over.

Paul weighed it in his narrow palm. It was an old test and still a good one; true pearls felt cool and heavier than their size would indicate. Pearls made of fish-scale paste, or plastic, or ceramic—or some unholy combination of all three—felt light and took on the temperature of whatever room they were kept in. Just to be certain that the pearl wasn't fraudulent, he lightly ran the edge of his front teeth over the surface. It had the gently gritty texture that was the hallmark of a true pearl.

"Hey, you said a pearl was delicate," Hannah objected, "and now you're chewing on it."

Wholly intent on the iridescent bit of midnight on his palm, Paul ignored her.

"That's okay, darlin'," Archer said. "The jeweler in Vegas did the same thing and didn't leave a mark."

She made a grumpy sound, even though she knew as well as either man that the tooth test was one of the most ancient ways to determine a pearl's validity.

Paul went to the nearby table, set the pearl down, and simply looked at it from all angles. After a time he opened a drawer in the table and picked up what looked like an ivory chopstick. He laid it very close to the pearl and looked for a reflection on the pearl's shiny surface. It was there, and it was deep. The nacre on this pearl was thick. Gem quality.

"*Superbe,*" he said simply.

Archer scooped the pearl up and put it back in the box. "My darlin' likes it, and that's good enough for me. So where can I find more like it?"

"Impossible. I have heard rumors, but never have I seen a pearl such as this."

"Well, shoot." Archer tucked the box in his pocket. "C'mon, babe. Looks like we'll have to go to Australia after all."

An instant after the front door closed behind them, Paul was on the phone.

"Mr. Samuel Chang, please. It is urgent."

Sixteen

Seattle lay beneath a thick lid of clouds. The moonlight that had kept the airplane company from Hawaii vanished into seamless night. It was seventy degrees colder than Hong Kong. By the time Hannah had gone the twenty feet from the airplane to the car waiting by the apron, she was shivering and wishing for the warmth of the wig she had ripped off and stuffed into the trash as soon as Archer handed her a passport in her own name.

Despite being cold, she was exhilarated. The air was fresh enough to cut into squares and eat like candy. The streets were dark and glistening with what Archer called rain, but what was merely an invigorating mist by Broome's tropical standards. It reminded her of her early childhood in Maine. She hadn't known how much she missed the climate until right now.

"Turn the heat up, Amy," Archer said to the driver. "This one is a hothouse flower."

"Not too hot," Hannah said, sliding into the sleek black car. "I like this wake-up-and-conquer-the-world temperature."

"Right," he said dryly. "That's why your teeth are chattering. Heat, Amy."

"Yessir," the chauffeur said, and cranked the heat to the max. As she turned to check on traffic, her short silver hair glinted in the airport lights. Like her haircut, her clothes were smart and casually chic—peach silk blouse, unstructured black jacket, black slacks, and low-heeled shoes. The Donovans didn't require a uniform, but Amy felt that it added a certain panache to her job. Sanity, too. Driving for a canny old entrepreneur and his unpredictable, highly artistic wife called for a level head and unflappable nerves. Amy Crow had both.

"Are The Donovan and Susa at the condo?" Archer asked.

"Yes. There's a party tomorrow night."

He thought quickly. They had missed The Donovan's birthday party, but with so many other Donovans, it was hard to keep track. "Birthday? Anniversary?"

"Well, The Donovan has hopes." Amy looked in the rearview mirror at the hothouse flower with sun-streaked chestnut hair, dark indigo eyes, and the kind of walk models would kill for. "You've never brought a woman home before. He's celebrating."

Briefly Archer closed his eyes. He had wondered how The Donovan would deal with explaining Hannah, the widow of his bastard son. Passing her off as Archer's "friend" would simplify the father's problems greatly.

And greatly increase the son's.

"Privacy, please, Amy."

A glass plate slid into place, dividing the back from the front of the car.

Silently Hannah looked at him. He picked up her chilly hands, kissed them, and slowly rubbed heat back into her fingers.

"Will you mind not mentioning the rest of it until I talk to Dad?" Archer asked.

"You mean Len?"

He nodded. "Just until I find out if Susa knows. After that . . ." He shrugged. "The Donovan is a big boy. He can deal with the past. So can his children."

"But not your mother?"

He hesitated, then nodded again. "She had surgery two months ago. There were complications. She came back from it, but she hasn't had the energy to paint yet. I don't want her knocked down again because of something that happened when Dad was sixteen."

Hannah's fingers threaded through his and squeezed gently. "I won't mention the past."

"You can talk about everything but Len's blood relationship to Dad."

"So how did you meet me?"

"You were having trouble with pearl theft in Australia, your husband was dead, and you remembered that he once told you if anything happened to him, you were to call me."

She tilted her head thoughtfully, then asked, "Why would you care?"

"I used to work with Len in some dangerous places, the kinds of places that lead to obligations and debts."

Her expression changed. She looked past him, out the mist-slicked window to the shimmering lights of the freeway. But she wasn't seeing light. She saw only darkness, felt only a queasy, sinking fear. She kept forgetting that Len and Archer were so alike. Archer concealed the ruthlessness better, but it was there just the same.

When she could trust her voice, she asked, "What if someone wants more details?"

"Send them to me."

She nodded and sat without moving, letting the night slide by on either side of her. Though she had spent most of the time on the Donovan International plane sleeping—and the rest satisfying her hunger for Archer—she was still tired. Jet lag, she supposed. Or reality lag. So much had happened in so little time. No sooner did she catch her balance from one thing than she was knocked sideways by another. The cyclone. Len's murder. The loss of the Black Trinity. The certainty that she was in danger herself. The sabotage of Pearl Cove.

And Archer.

Archer, who kept surprising her. She had never expected to find such passion and restraint in one man. Even as she told herself that it was stupid, that she had no business risking pregnancy, she could hardly wait to be in bed with him again, to pull him around her like darkness and fire, to wake with his warmth and scent and taste everywhere on her body.

Even if there hadn't been passion and release, she would have gone to him. The chance of having a child burned like hope in her soul. After years of believing that children weren't in her future, the thought of feeling a baby grow inside her was a pleasure so great it made her shiver.

Turning in his seat, Archer watched out the rear window. It took less than ten minutes to be certain that someone was following them. He punched the car intercom button. "Amy, did you tell anyone what time we were coming in?"

"Just The Donovan, sir."

"Thank you."

Impassively Archer watched the rear window. The style of the tail was federal—at least two cars shifting back and forth, passing off the lead position, dropping back, then switching again five or ten minutes later. The cars were American made, which was as good as wearing a light bar when it came to identifying cops; the West Coast of America was the home of imported cars.

Silence settled in the car like a soft, contented cat. Archer turned away from the rear window and watched Hannah rather than the freeway. In the muted golden glow of the car's interior lights, her face was an ever-changing arrangement of light and shadow. Just when he decided she couldn't be more beautiful, he found another angle, another blending of light and dark that squeezed his heart.

He was still watching her when Amy pulled up to the low-rise condominium building that served as the Donovan family headquarters in Seattle. She punched in numbers on a piece of hand-held electronics that was about the size of a hefty cellular phone.

With a half smile, Archer waited to see if they passed the electronic scrutiny of Kyle's latest invention. After a few seconds the garage door rolled up, allowing the black car to pass. He let out a long breath when the heavy steel links lowered again, shutting out the rest of the world.

Home.

The one place where the nape of his neck wouldn't prickle each time he turned his back on someone.

His past had taught him that no place was perfectly safe, but the Donovans' Seattle residence came very close. He needed that safety, that relaxation of the merciless inner alertness that had begun with Hannah's call and wouldn't end until he found Len's murderer.

As he looked back at the heavy steel grid, headlights flashed by on the street. He smiled coldly. At 3 A.M., Seattle didn't have much in the way of freeway traffic. Even the surface streets were nearly deserted. The cars that tailed them had tried to be discreet, but there wasn't enough traffic to hide in.

Amy eased the big Mercedes to a stop near a lighted entrance. Before she could stir from her seat, Archer opened his car door. A tug on Hannah's hand sent her sliding over the seat toward him. He waited, watching her without any sign of the fatigue and rising hunger that gnawed at him.

The expensive outfit she wore might have looked wilted and travel-worn around the edges, but her legs were as smooth and supple as ever. Desire turned like a knife in him as he thought of how she had wrapped those long legs around him on the plane, opening herself completely. He had pushed into her the same way. Completely.

None of his thoughts showed on his face or in his touch as he took her arm. He knew she was too tired to be tearing up the bed with him for what was left of the night. Certainly he should be too tired to be thinking about it.

He turned to his parents' chauffeur. "Thank you, Amy. Is anyone else still awake?"

"I don't think so, sir. Jake, Honor, and Summer came in just after dinner. Faith is at a designer's symposium in New York, but will be back soon." She glanced at the electronic device in her hands. "Kyle might be up tinkering with this, er, *thing* again. He has something else he wants it to do."

"Pray for us," Archer said under his breath.

Amy laughed. "I'll do that, sir. Good night."

Only family members knew the code that opened the entrance from the garage. He punched in the numbers on a lighted pad. Instantly the lock retracted and the door swung open. Hannah watched curiously as he repeated the process to get in an elevator, then again to get out of the elevator.

"Different codes each time?" she asked. "I didn't think Seattle was that dangerous."

"Kyle is that inventive," Archer said easily. "And I'm that paranoid."

"I'm going to need a native guide to get around here. For me, numbers are like names. You say them, I listen, and *fffft*, gone."

Smiling, he tucked a stray bit of hair behind her ears. The hair was soft and smelled lightly of cinnamon. "Honor threatened to take a very sensitive part of Kyle's anatomy and feed it to her cat unless he switched to voice recognition or retina patterns or something that doesn't require learning new codes at random intervals."

"She has my vote."

Laughing softly, he unlocked the door to the suite and gestured her inside. The entryway was marble; the white rug recently had been replaced with hardwood. Over the wood lay carpets from India, China, and vanished Persia. The city view from the wall-to-ceiling windows at the far end of the room was magnificent, but couldn't overcome the uncanny power of the landscape paintings that hung along one wall.

Hannah walked forward, lured by the elemental presence of art. Even if she had lived all her life among the mountains and sand dunes and plateaus in these paintings, she would have been compelled. She rubbed her eyes as though waking up from sleep. The paintings were still there, still powerful.

"Who?" she asked simply.

"My mother. This way," Archer said, keeping his voice soft. Though the rooms were well insulated to muffle noise, he had no desire to wake up the family and put Hannah through a lot of introductions when she was swaying on her feet from exhaustion.

"But—"

"The paintings will still be there tomorrow. You need sleep."

She couldn't argue, though she wanted to. She looked back over her shoulder as long as she could see the paintings. Then she sighed and wished she had half the gift his mother had.

Archer led Hannah down a hallway lined with ancient and modern black-and-white photographs of some of the wildest places on earth. The carpet was luxurious, vividly colorful, with random patterns that evoked the feeling of earth's continents seen from space. Several doors opened off the short hallway before it ended in a circle. Six doors opened off the circle.

"Everyone has separate suites." He spoke in a low voice and smiled crookedly. "The Donovans all like space. It keeps the family arguments to a minimum. Most of the time."

She saw his smile and knew that the arguments, however lively they might get, weren't bitter. "Do you all live here?" she whispered.

"Jake and Honor live up north, near Anacortes. So does Kyle. Lawe and Justin use this as their home base, but they aren't here more than a few weeks a year. Faith had a condo in San Francisco, but she moved here after Honor and Jake married. Dad and Mom have homes in several places."

"What about you?"

He shrugged. "I'm like Lawe and Justin."

"Wanderlust?" she asked curiously, looking at him with eyes that were both clear and very dark.

"At first."

"And now?"

He opened one of the doors and nudged her into the room beyond. "For me, a home has to have more than one person in it."

She smiled sadly. "Numbers don't count, Archer. There has to be love."

He yawned. "Guess I don't love myself enough, then."

She snickered. "You know what I mean."

"Yeah." He slid his arms around her and gave her a slow, easy, homecoming kind of kiss. "I know what you mean."

Still smiling, she enjoyed the kiss. He tasted of coffee and the tin of mints that someone had left aboard the Donovan company plane. She supposed she tasted of the single brandy she had taken like medicine in order to sleep.

It didn't matter. Before too long, their tastes would be the same.

"You're asleep on your feet," he said, gently ending the kiss. "Get in bed."

She looked around. The sitting area looked as though one of the couches unfolded into a bed, but it wasn't made up. The king-size bed in the room beyond was turned down for the night.

"Don't laugh," she said, ducking her head, "but what will your parents think?"

"That we're single adults with high standards who got very, very lucky." He brushed a kiss over her eyebrows. "It's all right, Hannah. Mom and Dad aren't in the business of passing judgment. If it really bothers you, though, I'll put you in Lawe's or Justin's room. I don't think they're coming back here soon."

The thought of sleeping without Archer's muscular warmth curling around her didn't appeal. She didn't know how much longer she had with him. Once they found the Black Trinity, they would go their separate ways. Then she would regret each minute she hadn't spent with him, exploring their mutual, unexpected passion.

"I want to stay with you," she said. "It's just . . . old habits."

"Good habits. Contrary to modern urban myth, there's no such thing as safe sex. For people like us, sex comes two ways—dangerous and more dangerous."

She didn't like the sound of that. "What do you mean?"

"There's no condom you can wear to protect your emotions." Very gently he kissed the frown lines between her eyes. "Go to bed, love."

"What about you?"

"You showered on the plane. I didn't."

"But . . ." Her voice faded when she looked at him. He no longer held himself as though he was ready to fight or flee on an instant's notice. He was tired. She could see it in his eyes, in the lines of his body. Despite that, he looked years younger. The wary, unwavering calculation was gone.

"But?" he asked.

She kissed him gently and put desire on hold. "Ask me in the morning."

When he understood, his body changed in the space of a few heartbeats. He pulled her closer and opened her mouth with a twist of his head, sinking into her with a heady, slow luxury. A taste of brandy, a wisp of mint, and a swirl of something much hotter, more ancient.

Dangerous.

"You're tired," she said.

"Dead on my feet. Take me to bed."

"You don't have to."

"You'd rather I sleep on my feet?"

Her smile curved against his lips. "You know what I mean."

"Nope." His tongue dipped, tasted, savored. "What do you mean?"

"It can wait until morning."

"It?"

"Sex," she muttered, embarrassed. She and Len had never talked about it. They had just done it.

"Sex can wait until hell freezes over," Archer said calmly.

She gave him a startled look. The heat and laughter and confidence in his eyes made her feel as though she was being licked all over by tongues of fire.

"Making love, now, that's different," he said. "That can't wait a minute longer."

Her smile disappeared in a kiss that was both restrained and urgent. When it ended, she was naked on the bed and his tongue was sliding over her, lingering in all the tender places, the hidden places, the secret places where scent and mystery fused into heat. His hands caressed even as his mouth tasted, hovered, tasted again, before slowly, slowly sinking into her, unraveling her in a loving that was both tender and starkly intimate.

Her breath stopped and her heart speeded as her climax uncoiled in a luxuriant whip of pleasure that arched her whole body. Seeing her lover's dark hair against her skin as he turned and bit her with exquisite care sent another slow lash of ecstasy through her, another unraveling so beautiful that she couldn't breathe. Yet somehow she said his name.

He looked up, saw the hazy indigo of her eyes, and smoothed his cheek against the sultry flesh he could still taste on his tongue. When he felt the ripple begin again, the sweet slow clenching of her body, he could wait no longer.

His name came in fragments from her lips when he entered her with a single, prolonged movement of his hips. The ravishing whip uncurled again, taking her, giving her to him. He took the gift and gave himself in turn, moving slowly, kissing her tenderly. Despite the urgency building with every leisurely stroke, he savored each moment, memorizing the scent and taste of her shimmering and crying, burning beneath him.

And then he was burning with her, pulsing in light-shot darkness, spending himself until he had no more to give, no more air to breathe, no more body to feel, nothing but her arms holding him to tell him that he was still alive.

It was a long time before he found enough strength to roll aside. Even then he didn't leave her body. He simply gathered her closer and held her against him as he turned over. She made a murmurous sound, burrowed into his neck, and took a ragged breath as the silvery aftershocks of ecstasy rippled through her again.

"You were supposed to be tired," she said huskily.

"I was. Next time you get to do all the work."

She smiled against his neck. "You'll have to tell me how. In great detail."

The thought of it made his heartbeat quicken. He laughed softly. He had never been like this with any woman. The sensual revelation was as surprising to him as anything that had ever happened in his life. He nuzzled her ear, bit delicately, and said, "If this keeps up, you're going to be pregnant for sure."

More than half asleep, she snuggled against him and said the first thing that came to her mind. "I hope so."

Relief and something very close to joy swept through him. He held her even closer, wondering if many people were ever lucky enough to know they held the world in their arms. "Good. I'll make the arrangements tomorrow. We'll be married as soon as—"

"Married." Hannah struggled upright and stared down at Archer as though he had grown two heads. "Who said anything about marriage?"

"We did. When we agreed to make a baby."

"No." She pushed away from him and sat on the edge of the bed. "I didn't say anything like that."

"If you're pregnant—"

"I'll sell my half of Pearl Cove," she cut in, "buy a house, and make my living color-matching pearls for the other farmers. It would be a good, stable job, and it would give me plenty of time to raise my child."

"*Your* child?" Archer's question was as cold as the chill he felt inside and out, everywhere that he had been warm from her. "What about me?"

Angry, frightened, feeling cornered by life and wanting to lash out in all directions, she combed trembling fingers through her hair. She didn't want to talk about this, any of it. She just wanted to go on as they had, suffused in passion, not asking about tomorrow because they both knew there wasn't any tomorrow.

Not for them.

"Damn it, Archer. What are you complaining about? Sex with no strings attached? Most men would be dancing a jig."

Sex with no strings attached.

He closed his eyes and tried to accept the fact that the woman he could have loved all the way to his soul felt nothing more than lust for him. "I'm not most men."

"I know. That's why I can't marry you."

Rage chased in the wake of pain, caught it, raced neck and neck in a headlong run toward destruction. Archer let the pain sear through him, but he fought the anger savagely. At a level too deep for words, he knew if he slipped the leash on rage, he would regret it even more than he regretted leaving Hannah to Len's mercy ten years ago.

"Why can't you marry me?" he asked evenly. "Explain it to me, Hannah."

She looked at him. Her breath caught at the drawn lines of his face, as though he had his hand in fire and was fighting not to show pain. Yet it was there. Agony. Stark and real.

Something terrifyingly like his agony sliced through her to her soul.

Then he opened his eyes. They were the color of steel. They belonged to a man who knew no mercy.

"Look in the mirror," she whispered. "You'll see why."

"Tell me."

"You're like Len!" Her breath broke on a sob. "Damn you, you're like Len! Great smile, great body, and underneath it all, as cold a bastard as ever walked the earth. That kind of ruthlessness makes love impossible. It makes everything impossible, even the most simple affection." She took a tearing breath. Tears blocked her view of Archer, but it didn't matter because all she could see was the past. "I was pregnant once. When I miscarried, I wanted to die. I almost got my wish. Later, much later, I went down on my knees and thanked God that I didn't have a child to raise in Len's cold shadow. I'll never expose my child to that kind of ruthlessness. *Never.*"

Once, years ago, Archer had been beaten to the point that it was agony to breathe, to move, even to blink his eyes. He felt that way now. "I would never hurt any child, much less my own."

She just shook her head. "You don't understand. You can't. Like Len. He didn't get up each morning and decide to be the way he was. He just . . . was."

Silence stretched, stretched, thinned. Snapped.

"Let's see if I understand," Archer said, his voice low and flat. "Marriage is out because you don't trust me and you don't like me, but you don't mind having sex with me."

She gave a broken laugh and wiped her eyes. "I trust you. That's why I called you. I know you won't kill me."

"You trust me with your body, but not your emotions, your future, and your children, is that it?"

The blunt words made her flinch, yet she didn't argue. "I like you. I didn't want to, but I do. And the—the sex is good." She shivered. "Very, very good. Can't that be enough?"

It had been enough for Archer in the past, with other women. It wasn't nearly enough now.

"Sex and protection, that's all you want from me?" he asked, driven to be certain.

Again his blunt words scraped over her emotions, touching raw spots she didn't even know she had. "Yes." Her voice was bleak. "That's all."

Archer looked at Hannah's bruised eyes and trembling lips,

at her chin tilted up and her shoulders squared. He remembered the girl who had stood on a street corner in Rio de Janeiro with empty pockets and a raw determination to survive.
With a distant sense of surprise he realized that he had fallen
in love with Hannah then: her courage and her fear, her de-
spair and her hope, the life that burned so incandescently
within her, giving her a beauty no other woman had ever
equaled in his eyes.

Nothing had changed in ten years.

Nothing would change.

He would never have the woman he loved.

The mattress hitched suddenly as Archer got up and began
dressing. "If you're pregnant, I will support you and my child."

"No, I—"

"The child will know his or her cousins, aunts, uncles, and
grandparents," he continued relentlessly, zipping up his pants
with a quick jerk. "Most of all, the child will know me." He
buttoned his shirt with quick flicks of his fingers. "If that upsets
you, I regret it, but it's not negotiable. If you wanted a child
without complications, you should have gone to a sperm
bank."

"But I—"

"See that intercom?" he cut in, pointing to a lighted panel
on the wall by the bed.

She nodded.

"If you want protection or sex, punch number six."

Seventeen

*I*an Chang shut off his car engine and got out while the red dust was still boiling up toward the gunmetal sky. As he strode over the walkway to the verandah, he ran through all the points his father wanted him to cover with Hannah McGarry—who was buying what, who was selling what, and the gradations of threat to apply at each point in the negotiation.

Sam Chang wanted Pearl Cove, even if it meant partnership with Donald Donovan's Number One Son.

Unfortunately Hannah had refused to answer her phone or return messages left on her answering machine, which meant that Ian Chang had been forced to make the boring drive from Broome just to talk to her. Irritated, he knocked hard enough to rattle the verandah door on its hinges. The thunderous sound startled a flock of cockatoos. They took off in a swirling, darting, shrieking cloud of white.

It was the only response Chang's knock got.

"Hannah, it's Ian," he said loudly. "Let me in."

No one answered. It was the same for the back door. Nothing but silence and the muted echo of his fist thumping on the door. Cursing in a sizzling mix of Cantonese and English, Chang lit a cigarette and headed for the scattering of cottages where the workers lived.

Coco waited on the front porch of the third cottage, leaning languidly against the wall. She had been leaning there since she saw Chang's car roar up to the McGarry house. She could have saved him the trip down to the cottages, just as she could have saved him the trip to Pearl Cove by returning the messages she had listened to in the middle of the night, when no one would notice her inside the McGarry house.

But Coco wasn't in a mood to save anyone trouble. She was in a mood to cause it. Especially with Ian Chang, who had forgotten their date a few nights ago. She wasn't used to a man forgetting her. Just as she wasn't used to a man looking past her to Len McGarry's pale, sexless wife. The memory still stung.

"Is Hannah diving again?" Chang demanded in English without so much as a greeting.

"No."

"Is she in what's left of the sheds?"

"No."

"Then where the hell is she?" He drew in smoke and sent it out again in a rush of silver.

Coco shrugged, but her black eyes gleamed with cold amusement. She liked seeing Chang upset. "She gone."

"What do you mean, she's gone?"

The angry demand in his voice was like wine to Coco. She had his full attention now. "Just that. Gone. *Ffft.*"

"Where?" he snarled. "Did Christian get her?"

Laughter that was both soft and hard curled out of Coco. "No, it is Donovan."

Uneasiness cooled Chang's anger. He took another pull on the cigarette, swallowed smoke, and let his temper damp down. "She's with Donovan?"

"*Oui.* They go to Broome and never come back. Cable Beach, mmmm, the rooms grand and the sheets ver' cool and smooth." She took the cigarette from him, sucked deeply, and returned it. Then she licked her lips with the deliberation of a cat grooming itself. "Maybe they in bed still, yes? He is a ver' potent man. Long time since she was a woman."

Chang didn't like to think about it—Hannah and Archer, the tangle of legs and musky sweat and pumping hips. "You should have called me."

"But why?" She smiled with pure malice at what she saw in Chang's expression. She asked in French, "Did you lust to see how well he fills the hole between Sister McGarry's white legs?"

Chang flipped the burning cigarette onto the ground between Coco's bare feet. His left hand shot out and wrapped around her throat. "Don't play the bitch with me. I haven't time for it. *Where is Hannah?*"

"Where is Donovan?" Coco countered, amused.

His fingers tightened enough to leave marks on her tan skin. "If I find out that you knew more than you told me, you'll be stuck with your half sister back on an atoll in Tahiti that's smaller than your ass. Do you understand me?"

Smiling, she inched closer to Chang, brushing her breasts against him, then her thighs. "Coco understands many things."

For a moment he was tempted to take what she was so plainly offering.

Seeing it, Coco smiled. Like the cigarette smoke curling up between her feet, her smile was cool.

Chang let go of her and stepped back a bare inch. Just enough not to feel her hard nipples against his chest. "I don't have time now. Later."

Black eyebrows rose like sleek whips. "What if I do not have time later?"

"Find it."

Coco thought of the cache of pearls she had built over the years, of the payments she had received from the Chang family, and of other payments from the pearls her half sister sold whenever Coco gathered enough to make it worthwhile. She would take Chang's money and his screwing, because he was the most interesting game in town at the moment; he wanted her, but not enough to beg.

Nakamori had been hers for years, enslaved, pleading for the sweet poison he was addicted to. Flynn was too much like her; neither of them felt jealousy as other people seemed to, something to kill or die for. With Flynn there was simple sexuality, a bull covering as many cows as presented themselves. All women were the same to him. Cows. Just as all men were the same to Coco. Bulls.

She would always regret that Len had died before she could find the key to seduce him. From him she would have had the secret of the black pearls that looked like Australia's famous black opals. And from him she also would have had the only emotion she felt deeply.

Fear.

Sighing, Coco stretched and rubbed herself against Chang. "*C'est vrai, mon cher.* Coco find time. Later."

Chang didn't bother to say good-bye. He simply turned and strode off to his car, leaving Coco with a thin wisp of cigarette smoke coiling up between her bare legs.

Before Pearl Cove vanished from his rearview mirror, Ian was calling Cable Beach hotels. Most people who demanded to know if someone was registered at a hotel would be politely told that such information wasn't given to the public. The Chang family, however, owned one hotel outright and had employees at all the others. When a Chang wanted answers, he got them.

By the time Ian sped into Broome, he knew he was in trouble. He went to his office, looked at the deceptively placid ocean until he was certain of his own self-control, and then called his father's private line.

"There is a problem," Ian said in curt Cantonese when his father came on the line.

"Increase the offer by ten percent."

"That is not the problem."

"I listen."

Ian didn't doubt it. Being listened to by Sam Chang was an experience most people didn't wish to repeat. It reminded everyone of the days when emperors were gods who anointed or executed at will.

"Hannah McGarry has vanished," Ian said baldly. "So has Archer Donovan."

The silence that came back told him that Sam was still listening.

"She is not at any hotel, motel, or rented room in Broome," Ian said.

"Not under her own name, perhaps?"

"Of course," Ian snapped. Then he reined in his impatience. He had had a lifetime to get used to one simple fact: his father thought that his Number One Son was incapable of doing anything more taxing than producing sons. It had taken five tries, but Ian had managed to get a son and heir. Unfortunately, as far as Ian was concerned, said son and heir was useless, a gambler and a wastrel whose greatest ambition was to clean out his father's and grandfather's bank accounts.

"Speak," Sam said harshly.

"Hannah McGarry is not staying in Broome under any name. No tall Caucasian woman with short sun-streaked hair and big indigo eyes has checked into any accommodation, with or without a man. No tall, muscular Caucasian man with pale eyes and short black hair and beard has checked into any accommodation, with or without a woman. Donovan's car has not been turned in to the rental agency, which means that they are probably in Derby by now. Or even Darwin."

The silence was different now. Ian couldn't say how it was different; he just knew it was. He had had many years to learn how to read his father. Right now the senior Chang was thinking hard, fast, and cruel. Ian hoped he wouldn't be on the receiving end of the cruelty, but braced for it anyway.

"Incompetence," Sam said angrily. "When will I grow accustomed to Number One Son's incompetence?"

Ian muttered the required apologies for living, breathing, and disappointing his father.

"I will find them for you," Sam said, his voice harsh. "Then you will bring me the secret of Pearl Cove."

"If I have Hannah alone, you will have your secret," Ian promised. "If Archer Donovan is with her, we will have a great problem. The Americans want him unharmed."

Sam made a curt, throaty sound possible only to a Chinese autocrat. "I will test their resolve on this Donovan."

"Please do," Ian said smoothly. "While you negotiate with the Americans, I will search Derby and Darwin for our missing pawns."

Sam grunted. "With luck, we will not need them."

Though Ian didn't move, he came to full, quivering attention. "May I ask why?"

"The manager of my Hong Kong store called. He has seen a black pearl unlike any other. It has all the colors of life and the dark transparency of time."

"Did it come from Pearl Cove?" Ian demanded.

"No. From the American gambling city of Las Vegas."

"Where is the pearl now?"

"The swine would not sell it at any price. His wife wanted an entire necklace of such pearls."

Sam muttered in disgusted Cantonese about stupid dogs and bitches in heat. "First Son, you went to Stanford in California. Tell me. Why do American men let their women run free? It is against all common sense."

"If I knew the answer to that, I would understand the West. I do not."

Sam lit a cigarette, drew hard, and blew over the mouthpiece of the phone, setting up an odd rushing-whistling sound. "You know the answer to nothing. Why have I been cursed with seven daughters and a worthless son?"

Ian didn't know the answer to that question either.

Archer was up and working long before dawn. Lawe and Justin's suite was laid out like Archer's, with a sitting room just off the hall. Because the "boys" shared the living quarters, there were two smaller, adjoining bedrooms with big beds. Thanks to the modern, angular style of the condo building, every room had privacy and some kind of a view.

But even when dawn started sending pale streamers of light over the city, Archer didn't look up from the computer screen in front of him to admire the sight of the sleeping city coming awake. It wasn't the computer that kept his attention from the cloud-shot sunrise. There wasn't anything exciting on the screen. He had been over and over the information, seeking patterns, finding them, discarding them.

Nothing new.

At the moment, the list of telephone numbers that Len McGarry had frequently called glowed on the screen. There was a name and an address beside each one. Most of the numbers traced back to pearl farms in Western Australia. Another number led to one of the Tahitian pearl farms owned by the Chang family. Archer ignored those listings. None of Len's competitors or professional "friends" had the secret of the black pearls.

A handful of numbers belonged to high-end jewelry stores such as Sea Gems. Five numbers belonged to pearl dealers whose reputations were no better than they had to be to stay out of jail. Two numbers led back to midlevel bosses of the Red Phoenix Triad.

"What were you up to, Len?" Archer muttered. "Or were you just stirring the pot to see what floated to the top?"

Len had been good at that. The man was a trouble magnet, and he took the devil's own delight in it. If trouble didn't exist, he poked and kicked until it boiled up around him. And then he laughed, because life never rushed through him so hotly as it did when he was rocketing down the greased skids to hell.

The computer cursor blinked patiently, waiting for its human master to do something.

Archer clicked the mouse and a new screen appeared. On it was a long list of names and dates, quantities, and enigmatic entries along the margin. The names and quantities related to pearl-production allowances, shell quotas, and pearl sales. He had studied enough raw data in his past service with Uncle Sam to see very quickly that the allowances and quotas had no obvious relation to the size or productivity of the pearl farms.

Some growers get a higher quota than others, according to a formula only the government can understand.

Hannah's sardonic words echoed in his mind, distracting him. He didn't want to think about her. Thinking would make the pain worse, not better. All he could do was find Len's killer and get Hannah out of his life. Maybe the ache and emptiness would go with her.

Maybe.

But he wasn't betting on it.

He dragged his mind back to the task at hand. There was nothing he could do to change what he had done in the past or her fear of him in the present.

You're like Len! Damn you, you're like Len!
Ruthless. Cold. Unworthy.

For a moment Archer's eyes closed, as though being blind would somehow make the agony less. It didn't. He accepted that, too. He had lost Hannah to Len. Twice. This time he had lost her before he ever had a real chance to win, but not before he had learned the razor stroke of love against his undefended soul.

Accept it.

Get over it.

Get on with it.

Archer's eyes opened. He stared at the information on the screen. Nothing new emerged. Pearl Cove, along with other rebellious pearl farms in every pearling zone of Western Australia, had been systematically given the short straw when it came to allotments of wild shell. The allotment of "domestic" shell, the amount of oysters a farmer could breed and raise on his own farm, had also been curtailed.

The only loophole was "experimental" shell, those oysters devoted to improving the breed. Not surprisingly, Len had designated forty percent of his farm as experimental. The truth was closer to seventy percent, a fact that even Hannah hadn't known. The shortfall in pearls was made up in Tahitian gems from Sam Chang's farms.

Nothing new there, either. No matter how much Archer might wish it, he no longer believed that the answer to who killed Len McGarry lay within Len's computer. Len had made enemies the way the ocean makes waves—effortlessly, inevitably. But only one of those enemies had killed him. Only one of them had the Black Trinity.

Find the Black Trinity and he would find Len's killer.

Archer rubbed his face as though to wake up some brain cells. His growing beard grated over his palms, bringing a surge of memories like molten glass.

Why do they call it beard burn when you only get it from a man who shaves?

I'll throw away my razor.

Lovely.

Tell me that in a week.

Okay.

Abruptly he shoved back from the computer and stood. He stretched hard, hoping to release the tension that kept tightening his body until he felt like he was being squeezed by a boa constrictor. He looked at his watch and wondered if Jake was up yet. He hesitated, then punched a number on the intercom.

"Yeah?" The voice was rough, relaxed, and alert.

"It's Archer. How'd you like to go one on one?"

"Only if we keep Lianne out of it. She dumped me on my butt last time. Lord, that female is *quick*."

Archer smiled and felt the coils of tension loosen. "Ten minutes?"

"Five. I've been awake for an hour."

Archer heard Honor's sleepy voice in the background, followed by Jake's soothing murmur. "No, don't get up, honey. I'm just going to hammer your brother into the exercise mat."

"Kyle?" Honor asked, surprised into wakefulness. "At this hour? Kyle never gets up before eight unless the place is burning down."

"Not Kyle. Archer."

"Archer's here?"

"Morning, sis," Archer said clearly. "How's my favorite little redhead?"

"Summer?" Honor yawned. "She's asleep in the next room. Must have inherited Kyle's genes, thank God."

"She sure got your temper."

"Ha. That temper is Jake's all the way."

Conversation faded into the indistinct, soft sounds of lovers saying good-bye. Archer tried not to think of Hannah and the warm pleasures of sleeping and waking with her in his arms.

"One hour," Honor said clearly. "Then we're coming to get you."

Hannah awoke, murmured sleepily, and searched for Archer's warmth. Then she remembered his icy, brutal instruction.

If you want protection or sex, punch number six.

Emotions shot through her, too many and too sharp to name. Nor did she want to name them. She didn't have to in

224

order to shove the unruly mass down and cage it in darkness. To survive. She had had a lifetime of practice at surviving emotion.

Angrily she told herself that there was nothing she could have or should have done differently last night. She wouldn't repeat the mistakes of the past. The purpose of pain was to teach you not to go there again. The greater the pain, the deeper the lesson.

Len had been a world-class teacher.

Hannah got up and went to the bathroom. It was clean, cool, done in a refreshing mix of navy blue, sunshine yellow, and white. The tub was big enough for two. She ignored it and headed for the shower.

She discovered that it was disconcerting to look out over the slowly thickening traffic while you showered, even when you knew the glass was one-way. Even more unsettling was the shampoo she lathered all over herself.

It smelled like Archer.

Trying not to think about him, she toweled herself dry with quick efficiency, raked her fingers through her hair by way of styling it, and climbed into the underwear she had rinsed out in the middle of the night when she hadn't been able to sleep.

The clothes she put on were the same ones she had worn in Broome—white slacks and a flowered shirt. The slacks had a tea stain on one knee. The blouse had stains, too, but they didn't show through the bright flowers. The sandals, at least, were her own. They looked as worn and ragged as she felt. She thought of makeup, then flinched at the memory of Archer applying it to her face, his eyes intent and his mouth smiling as he proved how waterproof the stuff was by kissing her deep and long.

She didn't bother to look in the mirror on her way out of the bedroom. She had done the best she could with what she had. Stomach growling, she set off down the hall in search of food. The smell of coffee led her to a big kitchen that managed to look cozy despite its size. A woman with gold-streaked chestnut hair and graceful hands was sitting at the breakfast bar, eyes closed, nursing a redheaded baby. Not wanting to intrude, Hannah began edging back out of the room.

Naturally, she bumped into something.

"Lianne, are you up, too?" the woman said, turning toward the sound. "Oh, hello. You must be Hannah McGarry."

"Um, yes."

"I'm Honor Mallory, Archer's sister. Kyle's, too, but I try to keep that a secret."

The mischief in Honor's voice and her striking, green-gold eyes put Hannah at ease instantly. "Good morning, Honor. Sorry to disturb you. I'll come back later."

"When Summer's nursing, you couldn't disturb her with a ten-ton bomb. She has her daddy's focus."

Hannah thought of Archer, the laser intensity of his eyes and mind when he wanted something. "Or her uncle's."

"You mean Archer?"

"Right."

The flavor of Australia made Honor smile. "She certainly has Archer's eyes."

Drawn by the contented baby, Hannah walked closer. As though sensing her presence, Summer opened her eyes and stared. An odd, silvery feeling went through Hannah, part pleasure and part pain. No matter what problems it might bring, the thought of holding Archer's baby called to her at a level too deep to deny.

"You're right," she whispered. "The baby has Archer's eyes."

"If Summer gets his discipline along with it, she'll be the first female president of the United States." Honor yawned. "If she gets my discipline, she'll be hell on wheels."

Summer released the nipple with a distinct pop and waved her little hands at her mother.

"All through, pumpkin?" Honor asked, laughing softly as she tucked herself back into her clothes. "Lord knows you ate enough cereal for both of us."

For the first time Hannah noticed the tiny gobs of cereal splattered here and there on the counter. And on Honor.

"The counter ate enough to be full, too," Hannah said, laughing. "Where's a rag?"

"There's a clean sponge in the sink, but you don't have to wipe up after my messy daughter."

"You can pay me back by letting me hold her. Unless she doesn't like strangers?"

"She's never met a stranger. They're all just big toys to her. Here, take the butterball and give me the sponge."

Though Honor's words were casual, her eyes were intent while she handed over the baby. When she saw Hannah's easy expertise as she supported and cuddled Summer, Honor relaxed and began mopping up after the arm-waving baby who was determined to feed herself and everything else within range.

"I can see Summer's in good hands," Honor said. "Do you have kids?"

The pain was accustomed, but still sharp. "No. At first my husband didn't want any. Then . . . it wasn't possible."

"I'm sorry. My tongue wakes up a lot sooner than my brain. Jake said something about you losing your husband recently."

The sympathy in Honor's eyes made Hannah feel like a fraud. She wondered how she could possibly explain her relationship with Len. Or more precisely, her lack of one.

"For the last seven years, Len and I shared a name and a place. That's all."

Honor looked at the other woman's dark indigo eyes, saw the lines of tension and unhappiness around her mouth, and felt even worse.

Summer waved her fists, caught one of Hannah's hands, and began gumming it enthusiastically. When she got to the big silver-blue diamond, she settled down to gnaw in earnest.

"Teething, aren't you?" Hannah murmured, smiling.

"Uh-oh, the drool factory is in full cry. Here, you don't have to put up with that."

"Don't worry. My hands are clean."

Honor blinked, then laughed. "I wasn't worried about that. She cut her first tooth on a fish cosh."

"What's that?"

"A blunt instrument used to put fish out of their misery as soon as we get them aboard." Honor smiled and looked hopefully at the other woman. "Do you like to fish? I can't get Faith out on our boat. Faith is my twin sister."

"The only thing I've ever 'fished' for are oysters, so I don't know if I like to fish." Hannah nuzzled Summer's fine, fiery hair and inhaled the paradoxical scent of a baby—fresh powder and wet diaper. She had skin that made a petal look like sandpaper. Eyes as wise and mischievous as a monkey's. "The Yanomami tribe we lived with were land people. Monkey hunting, slash-and-burn agriculture, that sort of thing. No fishing. Although some tribes hunted Amazon catfish that were bigger than men."

"Yanomami? Are we talking Brazilian rain forests?"

"Right." Hannah shifted Summer onto her hip, giving the baby a better grip on her hand, and herself a better grip on the baby. The motions were unconscious. Along with every village girl over the age of five, she had been a baby-sitter for the younger children while the mothers worked in the small, burned-over fields. "From the time I was five years old until I ran off to get married at nineteen, I lived with the Yanomami. My parents were missionaries at the time. My father still is."

"If anyone ever took me away from the sea, I'd miss it. Do you miss your rain forest?"

"No." The curt reply echoed, making Hannah wince. "I missed the place where I had spent my first five years—Maine and the kaleidoscope of seasons. But there were some good things about the rain forest. The scent of the air at dawn, the flash of butterflies bigger than my hand, the incredible liquid light after a rain, campfires at night, the laughter and mischief of the children . . ." She nuzzled Summer again. "But I never felt at home there. Not like my parents. I suspect that they loved the rain forest and the Yanomami even more than they loved God. I know that they loved their tribe more than they did me."

Honor laughed. Then she realized that the other woman had spoken the simple truth.

"Mother was forty-four when I was born," Hannah said calmly. "They had lived among the Yanomami for twenty years. They called me a gift from God, and accepted that they had to leave the rain forest for my first few years. The risk of childbirth and babyhood in Stone Age conditions is just too great. It must have been terribly hard on my parents to leave the land and people they loved. They gave me five years to grow strong before they went back. They were very dutiful parents."

"But not to be loved," Honor protested.

Hannah shrugged. "Their love and loyalty was unselfish, given to God and humanity rather than to a selfish personal concept of family." She rubbed her cheek against the sweet, soft baby. "I'm not that generous. I want to love and be loved, to have a family of my own."

Summer looked up at Hannah. Archer's eyes, clear and gray, hints of green, a whisper of blue; another layer of pain growing in Hannah like an oyster creating a pearl, layer after beautiful layer, growing in silence and darkness, waiting . . .

The shadows in Hannah's eyes made Honor wish she could go to her, hug her, tell her everything would be all right. Whatever everything was. But Honor was old enough to know that a lot of things didn't turn out all right. She looked at the clock and stood up quickly.

"Time to get Summer's daddy," she said. "Come with me and meet the monster's maker."

When Honor reached for Summer, the baby frowned, gnawed harder on Hannah's ring, and clung more tightly to her prize. Hannah laughed.

"I'll carry her," she said to Honor.

"She weighs a ton."

"That's the nice thing about healthy babies. They're an armload."

Honor coded their way into the elevator and out at a lower floor. The smell of a swimming pool greeted them as soon as they stepped out of the elevator. Along with chlorine came the musky odor of a well-used gym.

"Ah," Honor said, making a wry face, "the sweet scent of men."

"Women don't sweat?" Hannah asked, her dark eyebrows raised.

"Of course not. We glow like the delicate little flowers we are."

Hannah was still laughing when they rounded a corner. The double doors leading to the gym were wide open, giving a good view of the various instruments of torture that were the hall-mark of a well-equipped gym.

She barely looked at the collection of bars, barbells, pulleys, rowing machines, and the like. Her whole attention was fastened on the two big, physically well-matched men who looked like they were doing their best to kill one another. Hands, elbows, knees, and feet moved in blurs of speed as the men sparred—dodging, weaving, luring, trapping, and escaping in a deadly ballet. Blows landed, a man grunted and spun away, only to return with flashing speed.

Frozen, she stood and stared. She hadn't seen anything like it since Archer had fought their way through a riot. Then he had been burdened by Len. Today Archer was free. His speed and stamina were frightening.

"Whew," Honor said. "Archer's not wearing any padding. He must have really needed a full-adrenaline workout. Either that or Jake's getting fat and lazy."

"If Jake is the one fighting with Archer, he's not fat or lazy."

"Yeah." Honor smiled and silently saluted Jake as he ducked under a blow and flipped Archer over his back. "Looking good, honey. Looking *real* good."

Catlike, Archer landed fully balanced and ready to counterattack. Jake went down as his feet were scissored out from under him. More blows landed while the men scrambled to their feet and fought for position. Archer was protected only by his speed, his skill, and his partner's unwillingness to do real injury. Though padding protected Jake, Archer still pulled his punches; he wanted to keep the edge on his fighting skills, not to hurt the man who was his best friend and his sister's husband.

He threw Jake, followed him down, and set up for a killing blow. Jake could have dodged or counterattacked. Instead, one of his hands slapped the mat. "That's it, Archer. This old boy is ready for breakfast."

Instantly Archer stood, offered Jake a hand up, and then gave him a brief, rib-cracking hug. "Hell of a workout. Thanks."

Jake stretched his shoulders cautiously beneath the padding, and said, "My pleasure. Like hell."

Laughing, breathing hard and deep, sweat soaked from scalp to heels, the two men stood for a few moments longer on the mat, enjoying each other and the feeling of a good workout. When Jake began removing his padding, Archer turned toward the showers. The instant he saw Hannah, his smile vanished. So did his easy relaxation. Between one heartbeat and the next, he was fully on guard.

Honor saw the difference in him immediately. Archer's distant, ruthless side was one that he rarely showed to his family. Or needed to. She looked from her brother to Hannah's beautiful, shadowed eyes. Hannah, too, had lost her smile.

"I see you've met," Archer said, striding across the gym floor toward the two women. "Hi, sis. Want a hug?"

With a wary eye on her oldest brother's sweaty body, Honor blew him a kiss. "Consider yourself hugged."

"Huh. Is that what you're going to tell Jake?"

"Jake's sweaty body is different from any other sweaty male body on earth. He's sexy."

"Not to me."

"I'm soooo relieved."

Grinning, Archer turned to Hannah. But it wasn't her that he looked at. "Hey, Summer," he said gently. "How's the most beautiful angel in heaven?"

At the sound of her name, Summer lifted her head and looked around for one of her very favorite human beings. Archer held out his hands. She abandoned Hannah's well-chewed ring and waved her arms happily.

"She's teething again," Honor warned. "The drool factory is working around the clock."

"That's my girl," he said approvingly. "You need teeth in this world."

Despite Summer's eagerness, Hannah didn't want to hand the baby over to a man who just moments ago had been fully focused on turning himself into a deadly weapon.

Archer saw the hesitation and simply lifted Summer into his own arms. "Don't worry," he said to Hannah. "If it comes to visitation rights, I won't do any damage."

The icy flick of his voice made her flinch.

Honor's eyes widened. *Visitation?* She looked at Hannah speculatively.

Summer didn't notice any of the emotional undertones. She cooed and bounced and made a grab at Archer's nose. He could have ducked easily, but he didn't. He just turned and made gobbling noises against her fat little arm until she giggled and let go. Then she grabbed a handful of his chest hair and pulled. Wincing, he gently opened her fingers and growled against her neck, careful of her tender skin and his growing beard.

"Who taught you to fight dirty?" he asked the baby.

Drooling blissfully, Summer chewed on whatever part of her uncle she could reach. Archer grinned as though she was offering him the rarest of pearls rather than teething drool. Without even a token struggle, he surrendered his little finger, a willing sacrifice to the god of sore gums. As a reward, Summer leaned against him, sighed dreamily, and peed her diaper right through.

"Oops," Honor said, reaching for her daughter. "That warm stuff you feel running down your leg isn't sweat. Sorry about that."

"It's not the first time." Archer kissed Summer's nose. "Come on, beautiful. You and your uncle are taking a shower. How about you, Jake?" he asked, turning back toward the mat.

"Go ahead," Jake said. "I want to talk with Honor."

Carrying his niece, Archer headed off for the showers.

"You spoil her," Honor said to his broad, sweaty back.

"Yeah, ain't it grand?"

Carrying sweaty pads, Jake came up to Honor, kissed her thoroughly, and said, "Introduce me to the woman who can make Archer mad enough to kill."

Eighteen

S tanding in the entryway of the condo with cloud-filtered sun all around, Hannah tried to ignore the disapproval Jake hadn't bothered to conceal. All the way up in the elevator, his pale, cold gray eyes had measured her with a chill that reminded her of Archer at his worst. Dark hair, dark mustache, a height and strength to equal Archer's; and a ruthlessness, too.

But not toward Honor. For her, Jake's eyes went from ice to steamy mist. The passion and gentleness he felt for his wife were as clear as his dislike of Hannah.

Rubbing her arms as though to ward off cold, Hannah hurried into the living room, wanting to escape Jake's oppressive dislike.

"Not yet," Jake said, putting a hand on Hannah's arm.

She froze. Though his touch was light, it wasn't casual.

"Jake," Honor said, frowning at her husband. It was unlike him to treat a stranger so coldly. "What's going on?"

"That's what the merry widow is going to tell us."

Anger streaked through Hannah, burning away caution. She turned on him. "You're half right. I'm a widow."

"Are you in mourning?" Jake asked politely.

"Not since seven years ago."

"Care to explain that?"

"No."

"Okay. What did you do to Archer?"

"Nothing."

"Yeah? Then maybe you can tell me why he needed to whale the crap out of something this morning."

Honor winced. "Uh, Jake . . ."

"Yeah, I know. None of my business. Too bad I'm a nosy bastard." He looked at his wife. "She hurt him, honey. I want to know why."

"You're wrong," Hannah said, fighting to keep a grip on her temper. The contempt in Archer's glance earlier—and in Jake's now—raked over her. "I didn't hurt Archer. He's too ruthless to be hurt by anyone smaller or weaker than he is."

Jake said something blasphemous.

Honor was too stunned to say anything at all.

"You're blind, lady," he said coldly. "Deaf, dumb, and fucking *blind*."

"I'm sure you're a good friend to Archer now," Hannah shot back, "but you know nothing about Archer ten years ago. About what he did."

"You might be surprised. Archer and I were in the same business."

"I might not be surprised," Hannah said, furious. In her own way, she needed a fight as much as Archer had. "I married his half brother!"

"What?" Honor demanded. "What did you say?"

Abruptly Hannah realized where her temper had led her. Jake's dislike was uncomfortable, but she had lived with much worse. Yet none of it had gone as deep as Archer's withdrawal and the fear growing inside her that she might have been terribly, terribly wrong about a man.

Again.

If you wanted a child without complications, you should have gone to a sperm bank.

She rubbed her face with hands that were cold and told

herself that she hadn't been wrong in her assessment of Archer's ability to love.

Don't worry. If it comes to visitation rights, I won't do any damage.

Tears burned behind Hannah's eyes, tears she refused to permit. "I'm sorry," she said tightly to Honor. "I had no business telling you that. Whatever you do, don't mention it in front of your mother. She doesn't know."

"So it's The Donovan's son," Jake said.

Distantly Hannah noticed that he had taken Honor's hand and laced their fingers together tightly. The message was clear: whatever had to be faced, they would face it together. Envy stabbed through Hannah, surprising her with its cruel edge.

"Yes," she said, her voice much calmer than her eyes. "Before he met his wife. Long before."

"But Archer knew?" Jake asked.

"Yes."

"And this half brother . . . he's dead?"

"His name was Len, Len McGarry. And yes, he's dead."

"How?" Jake asked, but something in his tone told her he had already guessed.

"Murder."

Honor made a low sound.

Jake squeezed her hand and kept on talking, pinning Hannah with eyes that were like a cat's—pitiless and clear. "Are you a suspect?"

"I didn't kill him."

He looked at her a moment longer, then nodded. "Are you at risk?"

"I—" Her voice hitched, then steadied. "Yes. That's why I called Archer."

"You'll be safe here," Honor said.

"He told me the same thing," Hannah said in a low, husky voice. "But I can't stay."

"Why not?" Honor asked.

Hannah looked at Jake and shook her head.

"My husband is protective of the people he loves, but he'll be civilized about it in the future," Honor said. "Right, Jake?"

"Sure."

She turned toward Jake and gave her husband a level look. "I mean it."

"So do I."

Honor sighed, smiled, and went up on tiptoe to kiss him. "I love you."

His whole body changed, loosening, sliding away from battle readiness. He returned the kiss and the soft words. Then he looked back at Hannah.

"Tell us about it," he said. He managed to make it sound more like an invitation than a demand.

Just barely.

Kyle, Lianne, and Archer sat on the floor around Kyle's computer. She was wearing a pair of dark jeans and one of Kyle's sweatshirts. It stretched over the mound of her pregnancy with not much to spare. Her bare feet were small, narrow, and tucked neatly under her thighs. Kyle and Archer wore the preferred uniform of America—jeans faded nearly to white and sweatshirts that had been washed so often their colors were a memory. Like Lianne, the men had bare feet. Unlike her, their feet were big.

The thick Tibetan rug Lianne had added to Kyle's suite after they were married made a comfortable mat and a timeless, colorful background to the pewter-colored laptop computer Kyle sat cross-legged in front of. Lianne had her tired back braced against Archer's knees while her husband's fingers raced over the keyboard. They waited for the screen to settle.

"Okay," Kyle said, seeing the pattern instantly in the spreadsheet. "It's pretty clear that Len was laundering Chang's Tahitian pearls. He wasn't getting jack for it, though. Wonder why he did it."

"As a cover for his experimental shell," Archer said. "Go back two screens." He waited, then pointed to the bottom line on the screen. "See? Without those laundered pearls, he wouldn't have had anything to show for his investment. The government was already unhappy with his claim of forty percent experimental shell. If experiments on that scale didn't produce anything salable year after year, the government would have been more than unhappy. They would have been suspicious enough to come down on Pearl Cove like a hard rain to find out what the hell was going on. That was the last thing Len wanted."

"So he told the Aussies he was experimenting with producing Tahitian-style pearls from Australian shell, and he used Chang's laundered pearls to prove it?" Lianne asked.

"Right," Archer said absently.

"You sound like an Aussie," Kyle said, pronouncing it "Ozzie" in the Australian manner.

Archer thought of Hannah, who had adopted that particular linguistic mannerism. *Right.* Thinking of her made his whole body tighten in a combination of rage and hurt and need. *Get used to it,* he told himself savagely. *That's the way it is.*

After ten years he should have learned that fighting the inevitable only wore him out. He might as well fight gravity by pretending that someday he would flap his arms and fly just because he wanted it so bad.

But he still kept wanting, still kept trying to fly. Still kept crashing.

"Go forward again, Kyle." Lianne frowned at the screen. "That leaves forty percent of thousands upon thousands of oysters unaccounted for in terms of pearl production."

"Closer to seventy," Kyle said. "He was hiding more than he was admitting."

"Were the experimentals all opalescent black pearls like the one you showed us?" Lianne asked.

Archer forced himself to focus on his sister-in-law's clear, whiskey-colored eyes instead of on the indigo eyes that haunted and condemned him simply for being what he was. "From what Hannah has said, yes."

"Then where are the pearls? Surely all of them couldn't be as perfect as the ones in the necklace you described. Some of them had to be less valuable, even a noncommercial grade."

"Hannah told me Len ground those to dust."

Lianne's eyes widened. She shifted against Archer's knees, trying to balance against the freewheeling, agile twins she was carrying.

Absently Archer widened the space between his legs just

enough to reach through and rub Lianne's lower back, relieving the stress of pregnancy.

"Thanks." Sighing, she leaned into his long, soothing fingers. "They're in kick-boxing mode today."

Kyle looked up, grinned, and put one hand on his wife's stomach. He loved feeling the heat and urgency of life growing in her. "Want to go back up on the couch?"

"Archer and the floor are more comfortable. Your couches are too tall."

"Nope, you're just a Munchkin," Kyle said.

Lianne shot him a sideways look from under thick, black eyelashes. "This Munchkin dumped you on your butt the last time we got on the exercise mat together."

"You had just told me we were having twins!"

"Excuses, excuses. A little more down and to the left," she said to Archer. "Ahhhh . . ."

"Let me know if I push too hard."

As an answer, she made murmurous sounds of pleasure and leaned into the massage. But her mind was still working. "So Len launders pearls to keep the Australian government off his back. Chang gouges Len on the illegal goods to the point that Len barely has enough to survive on and keep Pearl Cove going. Sounds like Len had more reason to kill Chang than vice versa."

"That's not the way it happened," Archer said. "Chang wasn't even at Pearl Cove when the cyclone hit. As far as I can find out, neither were any imported surrogates."

"Surrogates?" Lianne asked.

"Hit men," Archer said succinctly.

"As in the Red Phoenix Triad?" she muttered. "God knows they have a full roster of killers."

Kyle remembered when Lianne had been the target of triad assassins. He ran his hand down her arm as though to assure himself that she was alive. "What about the Aussies?" he asked. "They have my vote as the guy on the ramming end of the knife that got Len."

The memory of Broome's impromptu morgue flashed in Archer's mind, Len's body so white, so still, so cold, the bruised mouth between his ribs grinning. . . .

"Why would the Aussies kill Len?" Lianne asked.

Archer shoved the memory down into the darkness along with other, similar memories. Too many of them. Bitterly he acknowledged that Hannah was right. He had seen and done too much. He wasn't fit for the tender intimacy of love.

"They're worried about the Chinese," Archer said. His voice was completely neutral despite the pain twisting through him.

Lianne rolled her eyes. Being half-Chinese, she had dealt with subtle racism and the more overt kind—from both Chinese and Caucasians. "The Yellow Horde garbage again?"

"That's part of it," Archer said. "The Australians don't have much tolerance for non-Caucasians. But bigotry isn't the only driving force in world politics. Often it isn't even the most important. Pull up that world map again, Kyle."

The screen changed to a map showing the continents on either side of the Pacific Ocean.

"See the lines and shadings Len added?" Archer asked.

Lianne leaned forward. "They don't overlap with political or geographic boundaries."

"Right. They're showing who controls what percentage of the various kinds of pearl farming."

Kyle looked at the screen, put the cursor on one of the icons, clicked, and waited. The information reappeared as a graph. He clicked again. The bar graph shifted. "Six years ago." Click. "Four years ago." Click. "Two years ago." He whistled musically. "The Chinese are coming on strong. They're going to own the pearl trade in the next decade."

"Exactly."

"Except," Lianne said, pointing to one column, "here."

"The luxury trade," Archer said. "The kind of gems Tahiti and Australia produce. Big. Very rare. Very expensive. The Chinese beat the Japanese at the freshwater pearl game and at the Akoya pearl game. Then they moved on to Tahiti for the high-end South Seas game. If you fish around in Len's hard drive long enough, I'm sure you'll find a projection for the future of pearl farming. It will be Chinese all the way."

"When you say the Chinese . . ." Kyle began.

"I mean the Chang family," Archer finished.

Discomfort forgotten, Lianne scooted around until she was

sitting between both brothers. "All right. The Aussies have damn few export products worth as much as pearls. They're worried about losing out to the Chinese. How would killing Len improve the Australian position in the pearl market?"

"If Len had a covert alliance with the Changs," Archer said, "the Aussies had good reason to fear that he would turn over the secret of the black rainbows to the Chinese."

"Which would give China a lock on all levels of the pearl trade," Lianne said. "Good-bye Aussie leverage. But Len had to know the Chang family was screwing him. Why would he give them anything as precious as the rainbow pearls?"

"He wouldn't," Archer said. "He would just let the Changs think he was going to. I'm sure he was dangling the same lure in front of the Aussies. Otherwise they would have driven him out of business years ago. Len was a big thorn in their jockstrap."

"Ouch," Kyle muttered. "What about the Japanese? They can't be happy either way."

Archer shrugged. "Japan doesn't have any warm oceans to grow South Seas pearls in or any chance of acquiring that kind of real estate, short of World War Three. They're hanging on to as much of their pearl sales monopoly as they can. Again, the high-end stuff is slipping away from them. Again, it's the Changs who are taking over. If the Japanese knew about Len's pearls, they'd want them."

"Who wouldn't?" Lianne asked. "I love jade, but that pearl you showed me was extraordinary."

She leaned against Kyle's shoulder and stared at the screen. The twins went into overdrive. She sighed and shifted again. This time she rested her round belly on Archer. Feeling the tattoo of life against his arm, he turned and smiled at Lianne.

"Isn't it time for their nap?" he teased.

"In my dreams." She grabbed his hand and put it on the most active twin. "Here, Uncle Archer. Soothe the savage beasts while Daddy slays the computer dragon."

Obediently Archer stroked over Lianne's big belly, pausing to savor the bump and seethe of hidden life before he stroked again soothingly.

Archer didn't know that he had a small, almost dreamy

smile on his face, but Hannah did. She stopped in the doorway to the suite and stared, frozen. The contrast between the hard planes of his stubble-shadowed face and the tenderness of his smile was shocking. The difference between his muscular body and the care of his hand soothing his petite and visibly pregnant sister-in-law was equally shocking.

The child will know his or her cousins, aunts, uncles, and grandparents. Most of all, the child will know me.

Archer's words echoed and reechoed in Hannah's mind, making her dizzy. She had assumed he was threatening her because he was angry. Now she realized that he had simply told the truth. Whether she liked it or not, whether she trusted him or not, he would be a part of their child's life.

If there was a child.

"Ah, see?" Lianne said, laughing softly. "The little devils are settling down. You're in for a lifetime of baby-sitting, Archer."

"Doesn't scare me a bit. When they get big and ornery, I'll give them back to you."

Kyle snickered. "I'm going to teach your kids how to make mud pies in the linen cupboard."

"Is that the worst thing you ever did?" Hannah asked from the doorway.

At her first word, Archer changed as he had in the gym, withdrawing into himself so completely that Hannah could almost hear the doors closing and bolts slamming home. He became again the man she feared, cool and ruthless, watching her with emotionless eyes.

"Sorry," she said, drawing back. "I didn't mean to intrude."

"No problem," Kyle said without looking up from the computer screen. "You must be Hannah. I'm Kyle, and the beautiful Munchkin draped against Archer is my wife, Lianne. I'd introduce you to the twins, but we haven't picked their names yet."

"Twins?" Hannah asked.

She didn't hear the wistfulness in her own voice, but Lianne did. "Two of them," she said. "At least, that's what my doctor is saying. At the rate I'm growing, I'm wondering about triplets."

"Bite your tongue," Kyle said.

She leaned over against him and whispered something that made her husband smile. He gave her a promising-remembering kind of look along with a grin. "I'll take a rain check on that," he said, "but not for long."

Archer didn't say anything. He simply watched Hannah standing in the door with the elegance of a dancer and the mouth of a siren calling to her man. The travel-wilted clothes she wore couldn't conceal the curves and hollows, the lure and the promise of her body. Distance couldn't conceal the deep wariness in her eyes, the tension that radiated from her when she looked at the man she didn't trust. The man she feared. The man who wanted her so much he had to remind himself to breathe every time he saw her unexpectedly.

Motionless, Archer waited, praying that none of the emotions seething beneath his calm showed through. But they must have, because Hannah took another step backward. At her retreat, his eyelids flinched in a reaction that was as involuntary as it was painful.

Deliberately he turned back to the computer, not wanting to look any longer at the woman he loved backing away from him.

"If control of the high-end pearl market wasn't motivation enough for Len's murder," Archer said neutrally, "our half brother had a talent for making enemies. Hannah could tell you more about that than I could. In the end, it doesn't really matter. Len is dead and the black rainbows are gone. Find them and you'll find Len's murderer."

With a smooth, powerful surge, Archer came to his feet. "That's why I brought Hannah here. She needs protection while I find the pearls."

"Protection? Why?" Lianne asked, turning to Hannah.

"Whoever killed Len thinks I have the secret of making the black rainbows," she said. The words came out tight, almost harsh, so curt that Lianne frowned. "I don't."

"Until Len's murderer is found," Archer said, "she's at risk." He looked at his watch. "I'll be back by dinner."

"You better be," Kyle said. "Dad will want to talk to you."

"Hannah knows more about Len than I do."

"What I know, your father doesn't want to hear." Abruptly Hannah fell silent, thinking of a graveyard in Broome, when Archer had asked her to remember the good things and let go of the bad.

"I've already answered Dad's questions about Len," Archer said as though she hadn't spoken. "There are more useful things for me to do than hash over a past neither one of us can change."

He walked toward the door as though Hannah wasn't blocking it.

"Where are you going?" she asked, watching Archer approach. Her voice was husky with memories and something she refused to recognize as hope.

He stopped very close to her, expecting her to back away. She didn't. "To see a man about some pearls."

"Len's pearls?" she asked.

"Possibly."

"Then I'm coming with you."

"No." The word was smooth and cold, leaving no room for argument or interpretation.

"You need me to—"

"No," he cut in. "Not now. Not ever. Not in any way."

Kyle and Lianne exchanged looks. They hadn't ever seen Archer like this, leaving ice burns with a few deadly calm words.

"Ah, Hannah," Kyle said, trying to defuse the explosion he sensed coming.

"If you think I'm letting you go after the Black Trinity on your own," Hannah said in a low, savage voice, "you're as crazy as Len was."

"Big as Len, cold as Len, and now as crazy as Len. Looks like your husband didn't die after all." Archer shrugged. "Too bad, Hannah. You'll just have to trust me not to take the Black Trinity and leave you flat broke."

The calm words infuriated Hannah as much as having Archer look at her like a stranger, as though they had never fused together in a naked tangle of limbs, hearts beating wildly, hands gripping, minds empty of all but urgency and ecstasy.

If you want protection or sex, punch number six.

"You wouldn't know the Black Trinity if it walked up and bit you on your bum," she said distinctly.

"It doesn't take a color-matching genius to recognize one of Len's experimental pearls."

"One of them, sure. Even a color-blind cat could do that. But how will you be sure any rainbows you find were once part of the Black Trinity?" she asked.

"Len didn't let any of his special pearls out."

"But some got out anyway. You bought one yourself. You know there must be others."

Archer did, and didn't want to admit it, so he kept his mouth shut.

Hannah's smile was all thin edges. "No one, not even a ruthless, clever man like Len, could prevent some of the black rainbows from leaking out. How will you know if you find pieces of the Black Trinity or just whatever was skimmed from the sorting shed or stolen from the experimental rafts?"

Silence stretched between them like a wire that kept getting tighter and tighter until it hummed with tension.

"You'll be safer here," Archer said finally.

"I'm coming with you."

"Not trusting me could cost your life."

"My life. My choice."

For just an instant something showed in Archer's eyes. He dropped his voice so that only she could hear. "Not quite, Hannah. There's the small matter of pregnancy."

"I could be as pregnant as Lianne and it wouldn't change the facts," she said in a voice as low as his. "You need me to find Len's killer. I need you to keep me alive while I'm doing it. End of discussion."

Silence stretched again. "You know," Archer said casually, "it's a bloody miracle Len didn't leave visible scars on you to go with the invisible ones."

"What are you talking about?"

"You. And Len. He never argued with anything but his fists."

"I didn't argue with Len. He knew too many ways to make me lose."

"But you don't mind going toe to toe with me at every opportunity."

"You won't hurt me. Not like Len."

"I know. I'm just surprised that you do. You have ten minutes to make yourself up like my mistress."

"Your *mistress?* Why?"

"Why else would you be hanging around with a rich, ruthless man you don't like?" Archer smiled without any warmth, just a row of hard white teeth.

Her chin came up and her shoulders squared for battle. "I'm no bloody good with makeup."

"I am. Remember?"

An involuntary shiver went over Hannah. She hadn't forgotten the horrid public toilet where Archer had stood close to her, so close, their breath mingling as he applied makeup to her with deft touches. And then she had turned to look in the mirror, and his hand had slid beneath her tiny skirt, touching her just once, slowly. It had been enough. She had turned to liquid and kissed his finger as gently as it kissed her.

"Yes," she whispered, shivering again. "I remember. Damn you, I remember."

But she was talking to Archer's back. He had already brushed past her and into the hall.

Nineteen

$\mathcal{S}$eattle's Pearl Exchange was an extraordinary mix of raw hustle and silky elegance. Unaffiliated traders, shop owners, luxury stores, people looking for a bargain, and salesmen looking for a mark all came together in a concrete hive six stories tall. Hannah hadn't seen anything like it, even the August Pearl Festival in Broome, when imported high-fashion models strolled down runways wearing European haute couture and millions of dollars worth of borrowed Australian pearls.

The lower floors of the Pearl Exchange were for tourists and people new to the allure of pearls. The sales outlets on those floors were little more than stalls placed around the perimeter of the building. The center was taken up with a maze of stalls. Strands of pearls dangled from every possible variety of hook, knob, rod, and handle.

". . . finest of Japanese pearls, fresh from the sea to you. Note the delicate blush of pink against the flawless . . ."

The woman's voice faded beneath others, but the sales patter made Hannah lift her skillfully darkened brows. Archer's skill, not hers. And if she had gotten light-headed standing so close to him, breathing his scent, all but tasting him, it was her problem. Obviously he didn't have one. His hand had been steady while he'd stroked cosmetics over her face.

Impatiently she tugged at the forest-green dress she had borrowed from Honor. The dress kept trying to creep up her hips. Hannah was an inch taller and at least two inches more around the bust and hips than Archer's sister. As a result, the silk sheath dress fit too well. She was certain her hips were stretching the seams across the butt. The bra she had borrowed made the most of her breasts, pressing them front and center so that they mounded above the scoop of the neckline.

Borrowed jewelry finished out the picture of a well-shaped, well-kept woman. To keep up with—or live down to—the new image, Hannah had switched the blue diamond wedding set to her right hand. The rest of her jewelry was also borrowed. She hoped that Susa truly wouldn't mind a stranger wearing her diamond-and-citrine rope and diamond stud earrings.

Impatiently Hannah ran her hands over her hips again, try-ing to coax the dress to lengthen by an inch or two. Then she made herself stop fussing. She was supposed to be for sale, wasn't she? Or at least up for a short-term lease.

Archer certainly looked the part of a man who could afford to keep her. Though he had dumped the Euro-silk and Kru-gerand, the handmade pearl-gray Egyptian cotton shirt he was wearing didn't look like a Kmart special. Nor did the black wool slacks and soft leather shoes. The thick black stubble on his face set off his pale eyes and the clean line of his mouth. A black Gore-Tex jacket with high-tech fleece lining was care-lessly folded over one arm. The jacket was Honor's, on loan to Hannah.

The stubble should have made Archer look badly groomed. Instead, he looked so sexy she was having trouble keeping her hands to herself.

When Hannah realized that she was staring at Archer's mouth, remembering what it felt like all over her, she forced herself to focus on the pearls and ignore the explosion of heat deep inside her, heat turning her bones and her body to warm honey. After a few moments she managed to see the booth in front of her. It was draped with pearl jewelry. The pearls were six to eight millimeters in size and of one dominant hue. Pink.

"Akoya rules here," she said. "They didn't stint on the pink dye, either."

"Americans like pink."

Hannah picked up a strand and ran it through her fingers. "Decent surface. Uneven drill holes. Poor depth of nacre. Adequate matching. Good graduation in size."

"Japan has tons of Akoya pearls," Archer said. "Literally. Size matching is rarely a problem."

Relieved to find something neutral to talk about, she dove into the discussion. "Color matching shouldn't be a problem either, if the stalls on this floor are any example. If the pearl doesn't look good, throw it back in the pink dye for a while longer. Or the black. How can they sell this?" she asked, holding up a steel-colored string of dyed pearls. "Ball bearings would have more character. If you want black, stick to the South Seas. The color comes from the oyster, not from a chemical bath."

He didn't pick up the conversational ball. Instead, he watched the room around them with eyes as clear and hard as diamonds. It beat watching Hannah fidget and wiggle in Honor's clothes—clothes that had never looked like that on his sister. It was all he could do to keep from lowering his head and running his tongue deep into the cleavage that was so nicely displayed.

Irritated by his body's relentless hunger for the woman who had no use for him beyond sex and protection, Archer turned his back and forced himself to focus on the room. The tail they had picked up as soon as they left the condominium was somewhere in the crowd behind them, fingering pearls as though she cared. The man who was with her didn't even pretend to care. He looked at everything but pearls.

Wistfully Hannah ran her fingertips over strands of gleaming dyed pearls. It had been nice to have a neutral conversation with Archer, if only for a few moments. Perhaps he could be lured back into it.

"Culturing pearls," she said, "inserting a bead, feeding and scrubbing the oyster for a year or two, then harvesting and grading the pearl—I understand that. Once the seed is in place, the oyster is responsible for the color and luster of the pearl. How can they call this kind of manufactured dyed stuff pearls?"

"No problem." Deciding their shadow was harmless, Archer turned back and faced the woman who could pierce his self-control with a word, a touch, a look. "Some folks are calling imitation pearls 'semicultured.' "

"That's deceptive."

"That's business. Let the buyer beware. Besides, pearl growers aren't eager to get into a public pissing contest over cultured versus manufactured. Then people might start asking at what point a cultured pearl becomes a manufactured one."

"When you add or subtract color," Hannah retorted.

"Not to the Japanese. Or the Chinese, for that matter. Then there are the Arabs. To them, cultured *is* manufactured. Imitation. And we're not even touching on Majorica 'pearls.'" He tipped his head toward the next booth.

"Glass beads dipped in fish scales and glue," she said, dismissing the legitimacy of the Majorica process.

"The people who produce Majoricas call the dip 'pearl essence,' " he said blandly.

"More like essence of bull dust."

"At least Majoricas have a brief history to recommend them. They've been made for a hundred years, they're heavier than plastic, cooler to the touch, and more expensive to buy."

"But still imitation. Not pearl."

He didn't argue the point. No part of a Majorica "pearl" had ever seen an oyster.

Hannah went to another booth. This one also featured Akoya pearls, but of a higher quality. Sighing, she fingered the cool, silky weight of several necklaces. They had the pale blue overtone that was common to Akoya pearls in their natural state. The weight of the necklaces suggested that the pearls had spent a year gathering nacre in the oyster shell rather than the six months she suspected was the maximum for the previous booth. This booth also had the pink Akoya as well, but they had been handled with care and dyed with discretion. The drill holes were smooth and uniform. Not surprisingly, the price reflected the higher standard of production.

Quietly Archer urged her on around the room, milling at random through the booths, trying to make sure that only the government was following him.

"Wait," she said suddenly. "Aren't these beautiful? Odd, but beautiful."

He looked at her hand on his arm. She didn't seem to be aware of having touched him. He wished he could say the same.

"Biwa," he said curtly.

"What?"

"Freshwater pearls from Lake Biwa in Japan."

"What a lovely, icy, iridescent white," she murmured, fingering a strand of the oddly shaped yet nearly identical pearls. "A necklace of little crosses. Natural or cultured?" she asked, turning to him.

"Natural, probably. But the ones in the next booth certainly aren't."

She looked at the next booth and laughed softly. "Little Buddhas. How on earth . . . ?"

"Same way mabe pearls are produced, on the shell itself rather than in the mantle of the oyster. Take a bead shaped like a flattened Buddha. Cement it on the inside of the shell. Cement lots of them, actually, like measles erupting all across the interior of the shell. The oyster just covers the intruders over. Six months later, the shell is harvested and the Buddhas are cut away. The Chinese have been doing it since the eleventh century."

"Like blister pearls."

Archer smiled slightly. "Nothing is like blister pearls. They're naturals all the way. I have one in my collection that's as big as Summer's fist."

"The pearl?" Hannah asked, startled.

"No, the blister. I haven't opened it up yet to see if there's a pearl inside the blister."

The rise and fall of conversations around Hannah faded as she concentrated only on Archer. "If there is a pearl, it would be natural. Priceless."

"And if there isn't, if the blister is full of organic goo, the shell is worthless."

"You won't know until you open it."

"I've opened other blisters and found nothing but tar."

"But you won't know about *this* one," she insisted.

"Would you open it?"

"Of course. Not knowing would drive me crazy."

"Even if you had opened other blisters?"

"Yes. That's what hope is all about. Knowing the odds are against you but going for it anyway."

His black eyebrows rose. "I should have been an oyster."

"What?"

"Then you wouldn't be afraid to open me and see what's inside. But you're sure it's tar and there's no point to this conversation. Let's go. The bureaucrats following us are getting impatient."

Touching her for the first time, he put his hand under her upper arm and led her toward a bank of elevators. Though the touch would look familiar to anyone watching, Hannah felt its lack of intimacy like a slap. There was no hidden circling of her skin, no tender caresses, no sweet feeling of connection, nothing but an impersonal pressure that directed her through the crowd.

"Where are we going?" she asked as the elevator doors closed.

They were alone in the cage that smelled of musty carpet, spilled espresso, and Chinese cigarettes. Asian nicotine addicts simply didn't get Seattle's no-smoking rule.

"To the next floor."

"And then?" she asked.

"To the next. Then the next."

"Do you really expect to find the Black Trinity in one of the retail stalls?"

"It isn't likely, but the Linskys aren't expecting me until eleven. If I'm lucky, I'll find a black rainbow in one of the wholesale booths. Then I'll trace it. If I'm not lucky, I'll have gotten a feel for what's new at all levels of the pearl market, and the two government bureaucrats following us will have learned more than they ever wanted to know about pearls."

Hannah smiled slightly. "What about the black pearl you already have? Why not trace it?"

"Dead end. Teddy bought it from a man who bought it from a woman who bought it from a man nobody can find, who supposedly got it in Tahiti. That's the reason Teddy showed me the pearl. He thought I might know where it came from."

"You did."

"He doesn't know that. That's why he sold it to me. He's been looking for over a year and found nothing more than rumors. He decided to take cash for a pearl curiosity rather than trying to assemble enough black rainbows to make a piece of jewelry."

The elevator door opened. The second floor was slightly better maintained than the lower one, but its atmosphere still was more carnival than restrained luxury. Despite not having the studied elegance of a high-end jewelry outlet, the goods on the second floor were obviously more expensive than those on the street level. Video cameras covered every angle of the area. The booths were more spacious, less jewelry was dangling within reach, and rent-a-cops watched everyone with bored eyes and big holsters.

It didn't take Hannah and Archer long to circle the second floor. The pearls were bigger and of better quality than on the first floor, but the emphasis was the same: finished jewelry. There was a very nice pair of Tahitian black earrings with violet overtones, and a tangerine South Seas parure consisting of brooch, necklace, bracelet, ring, and earrings. The latter made Hannah pause, but when the salesman came forward, she shook her head and moved on.

There were few loose pearls for sale. None of them was a black rainbow.

The elevator smelled the same on the way to the third floor. When Hannah and Archer stepped out, they were confronted by a desk and an armed guard who was even more bored than his buddies downstairs. Archer wrote his name, corporate identity, and wholesale number in the logbook on the desk, took two tags, and gave one to Hannah. He clipped his to his pocket. After several tries, she managed to clip hers on the neckline without wrinkling the material.

As he watched her smooth the borrowed dress beneath the tag, his hands itched to help her. Then he could savor again the creamy warmth and resilience of her breasts, feel their tips harden beneath his hands, his tongue.

Cursing silently, he turned away from the endless temptation of Hannah McGarry. A quick scan of the room told him that the same traders were in the same places. No new faces. In fact, he would have sworn that some of the same people were leaning across the same counters arguing the same prices as they had been six weeks ago, when he had strolled through the Pearl Exchange just for the pleasure of seeing so many varieties of loose pearls gathered under one roof.

Hannah scanned the various booths and almost smiled. This she understood: the people haggling over a tray of pearls, the other people watching as though placing side bets, the dramatic gestures of disdain on the part of buyer and seller, the handshakes, the voices rising and falling. Chinese, Japanese, Australian, American, European—the languages varied, but the focus didn't.

Pearls.

Everybody was buying, selling, trading, wishing, living, and dreaming pearls. Some people wanted only to match pearls for a pair of earrings. Others wanted to create triple-strand necklaces or parures with hundreds of pearls. A few people went from booth to booth, collecting for purposes only they knew.

"You like this, don't you?" Archer asked, watching Hannah because he couldn't make himself stop. Right now her eyes were a vivid indigo with flashes of violet. Her whole body was alert, quivering, like a cat closing in on pray.

"I love it," she said. "At first Len didn't let me do any of the selling or trading. For the last few years I've done all of it. I never went beyond Broome, but I always wanted to. Pearl Cove has some of the best-matched, highest-quality pearls in the world." Excitement faded as she remembered. "Or we had. Now . . ." She shrugged. "It depends on whether you want to resurrect the operation. Even if we find the Black Trinity, I don't have the money."

"Is that what you want? Pearl Cove up and running again?"

"It's what I know."

"That's not the same thing."

"It's as close as I can come."

"Why not do what you love?" Archer asked.

Eyebrows raised, she looked at him. "And what would that be?"

"This." He waved a hand at the room where pearls were changing hands. "Trading pearls."

She opened her mouth. No words came out.

He was right. What she loved most was weighing and balancing the merits of individual lots of pearls, pricing them, bargaining over them, coming away with a good deal because she had a better eye than anyone she had ever met when it came to matching pearls.

"All the professional traders I've known are men," she said.

"Yet it's a fact that most women's color vision is better than most men's."

"No argument here, mate," she said dryly. After a moment she smiled rather like a shark. "I'll just have to be the first, won't I? My color vision against theirs."

And she laughed.

Archer wished he could pick her up and whirl her around, laughing with her, sharing the heady feeling of a new world opening up. But that was the kind of thing you did with family or friends or a mate. Sex alone didn't qualify for the latter, sharing Len between them didn't qualify for the former, and she didn't like Archer well enough for them to qualify as friends.

"How do you go about becoming a trader?" Hannah asked.

"Get a reputation for knowing good pearls."

"I have one, but it's half a world away."

"Then we'll just have to work on it here."

"Not when I look like a tart."

The corner of his mouth kicked up. "What you look like is a sexy woman."

Unconsciously she smoothed the creeping skirt farther down her hips. "I feel awkward."

"Every time I've had my hands on you, you felt just fine."

She shot him a sideways look that glittered like blue-black sapphires. "That isn't what I meant."

He shrugged. "You walk around in three patches and a handful of string and never worry, but you're fidgety in a dress that covers you from collarbones to midthigh."

"That was the tropics. This is here. Honor's clothes just don't fit me."

"Then we'll go shopping after we're done here."

"We?"

"You're not getting out of my sight until all the players know that you're off the table."

"I was out of your sight last night," Hannah said before she stopped herself.

"That's different."

"Bull dust." She took a breath and a better grip on her too-quick tongue. "I can't afford clothes."

"I'll give you—"

"No," she cut in. "I owe you too much already."

"You don't owe me a cent."

"You've got that right, mate. I owe you a hell of a lot more than a penny."

"Wrong. You're family, and family doesn't owe family." Archer held up his hand, cutting off the hot words he saw ready to boil out of Hannah. "But I'll take whatever you spend on clothes out in work, if that will make you feel better."

"What about the airline tickets and the—"

"Right," Archer interrupted curtly. "You owe me a bundle. I'll tally it to the last cent. When this is over, I'll send you a goddamn bill, you'll pay it, and you'll be free of the Donovans." He gave her a look that had her backing up. "Unless you're pregnant. Are you pregnant, Hannah?"

"I—I don't know."

"I'll get a test kit."

She stiffened. "They're not reliable."

"Neither is life. We all get through it anyway."

"Stop looming over me!"

"I haven't moved an inch."

"You don't have to. You're just—just—"

"Cold, ruthless, incapable of love," he said neutrally. "I know, you've told me before."

"I never said anything about love."

"Then you think a cold, ruthless man like me is capable of love?"

She shut her mouth. "Why are you pushing me?"

"Because you're pushing me. Let's look at pearls. And forget the mistress bit. No one watching us would believe it. You stiffen every time I touch you."

Hannah wanted to deny it. She couldn't.

But it wasn't distaste that made her stiffen. It was desire. She didn't know how to handle it.

Or him.

"Right," she said through her teeth. "I'm not your hired playmate. Then what am I?"

"A woman who wants to break into the pearl game."

"What's my name?"

"Hannah McGarry. You're my partner in Pearl Cove."

She blinked.

"Lying got us out of Australia alive," Archer said. "Maybe the truth will get us to the pearls."

And maybe it would get them dead. Either way, hiding wasn't possible anymore.

Ian Chang stood fifteen feet away, staring at Hannah.

Twenty

he look on Chang's face said that he wasn't surprised to
find Hannah McGarry in the Pearl Exchange. His clothes said
he hadn't been off the airplane long enough to change. He
strolled forward, took her hands, and kissed her. If she hadn't
turned her head aside quickly, the kiss would have landed on
her mouth.

"Well, well," Chang said, looking Hannah over carefully. If
he was bothered by the fact that her heels made her six inches
taller than he was, it didn't show. "I almost didn't recognize
you."

Archer didn't like the gleam in Chang's eyes or the way he
was running his thumbs over the backs of Hannah's hands. But
she wasn't stepping away, even though the man's breath was
all over her low neckline.

"G'day, Ian," she said automatically. She hoped he didn't
sense how unhappy she was to see him. "What are you doing
in Seattle?"

The blunt question made Chang smile rather grimly. "I was
worried about you."

"Why?"

"Come now, Hannah." Chang's fingers tightened on hers. "Surely you realize that you're half owner of a very valuable commodity. People who own things of value are always at risk."

Sell Pearl Cove to the Changs. We're big enough to weather the coming storm. You aren't. Don't follow Len into the grave.

Hannah wished she could forget Ian's warning, and the threat implicit in it, but she couldn't. She could only put on a smile and pretend that this was a chance meeting half a world away from Pearl Cove.

"Archer Donovan," she said through stiff lips, "Ian Chang. Or have you met?"

"Indirectly," Ian said, releasing one of her hands and holding his right hand out to Archer. "A pleasure to meet directly."

"Mr. Chang," Archer said neutrally.

"Hannah told me you own half of Pearl Cove. Is that correct?"

Archer nodded, concealing his surprise at Chang's bald approach.

"The family of Chang is prepared to make you a very handsome offer for Pearl Cove," Ian said.

"I haven't considered selling."

"Do." Chang smiled. "It is worth considering, even for a man of your wealth and . . . connections."

Archer heard what Chang wasn't saying: Sell out or even Donovan International wouldn't keep him from being at risk.

"If I won't sell, you can always buy Hannah's share," Archer said mildly.

"My instructions don't include Mrs. McGarry."

Adrenaline slid through Archer's veins. *Not good. Not good at all. Someone has thrown Hannah to the wolves.* "I see."

Chang nodded curtly. "I hoped you would." He handed over a business card. "Please contact me as soon as you decide."

"You, the Australians, the Japanese." Archer smiled. "A lot of interest for a pearl farm that has been only marginally profitable."

"Under Chang leadership, Pearl Cove will be quite profitable." Chang looked back at Hannah. Desire, regret, echoes of anger; all were in his sad smile. "I wish you had chosen me, Sister McGarry. I would have kept you safe. Now it is too late. Stay very close to the man you did choose. Very, very close." With that, Chang released her hands and glanced at Archer. "Mr. Donovan, I look forward to doing business with you. Soon."

Silently Hannah and Archer watched Chang turn away and walk to the elevator.

"Why do I feel like he was saying good-bye?" Hannah asked.

"Because he was."

"He knew I would never be a married man's mistress," she said, and in her voice was the same mix of desire, regret, and anger as she had heard in Chang's. "I thought Ian was my friend. . . ."

"He is."

The sideways look she gave Archer was as sardonic as the curl of her lip.

"He just went against his family's business interests and warned you not to trust him when it comes to Pearl Cove," Archer said. "I call that an act of friendship."

"Ian warned me in Australia, when he was trying to buy me out."

Archer said nothing. He hoped she wouldn't follow that line of thought to its logical conclusion.

She did.

"Now he's not trying to buy me out," she said. "Why? Does he think you'll sell more quickly than I would?"

"What Ian thinks doesn't matter anymore. His daddy is calling the shots now."

"Right," she said impatiently. "I figured that out. But does his daddy think you'll sell?"

"Sam Chang thinks that I've got better protection in this game than you do. He'd rather buy me out than take me out."

Her eyes widened. "Take you out?"

"The way Len was taken out."

"Are you saying that Sam Chang . . . ?" she whispered.

Archer shrugged. "He could have, but the Chinese don't have a corner on doing business the jugular way. Whenever commerce slides over to become political leverage, things get dirty real quick all over the world."

She let out a breath in a rush of air. No matter how she felt about Ian Chang and his many mistresses, the thought of him being involved in Len's death made her sick.

"Anyway," Hannah said, swallowing hard, "nothing has changed. Not really. I knew I was in trouble when I called you." Yet even as she spoke, she was shaking her head in slow denial of her own words. "No, that's not quite true. I was *afraid* when I called you. Now I *know*. Thank you for—"

"Don't thank me," Archer cut in, watching the elevator again. "If I wasn't your partner, you would have sold out to Ian when he offered the first time. You would be out of the game."

"No."

Archer looked back at her. "Why not?"

"I wouldn't sell to anyone who might have benefited from Len's death. To anyone who might have practiced— What did you call it?"

"Jugular business."

"Right." Hannah smiled crookedly. "Every time I think I've escaped my childhood, it comes back to haunt me."

"What do you mean?"

"At my core I believe that personal honor matters and murder shouldn't go unpunished."

Archer agreed, but all he said was, "Acting on those kinds of beliefs could get you killed."

She closed her eyes for a moment. "I don't want to die. And I don't want to live if I can't look at myself in a mirror."

He wanted to hold her, to tell her that everything would be all right. He knew better. Yet it was like a knife turning in him.

"The Donovan family will do what it can about the first," he said evenly. "The rest is up to you."

The elevator doors opened. A man and a woman walked out. They were of average height, dressed in average business clothes, and had uncommonly alert eyes. They spotted Archer the same instant that he spotted them. Without pausing, they walked to the nearest booth and began looking at pearls.

"Is that them?" Hannah asked.

"Our government tails?"

"Yes."

He nodded.

"Why are they following us?" she muttered.

"Because America has a stake in the outcome of the pearl game."

"Who do they want to win?"

"Today? I don't know, but I suspect it's not us. Tomorrow?" He smiled thinly. "Who knows? Some diplomats could exchange cables, some new international business deals could be made, and *bingo*, today's hero is tomorrow's scum, and all bets are off."

"That's depressing."

"That's politics."

"I prefer pearls."

"So do I."

She took his arm. As she did, she tried not to notice his heat, his strength, everything about him that was male. "Show me some pearls, Archer."

The simple pressure of her fingers went through him like electricity. It brought a tingling awareness that heightened each of his senses. Taking a slow, hidden breath, he clamped down on his body's intense, unruly response to this one woman.

As though they had nothing more urgent than browsing on their minds, Hannah and Archer went from booth to booth, commenting on the rarities they saw. One booth specialized in South Seas baroque pearls. Some were the size of peas. Others were the size of marbles. A few magnificent ones were the size of a man's thumb.

Archer stopped at the booth. "Hello, Sun. How's the new granddaughter?"

The man with sparse silver hair and a face like a well-used map looked up from a table where he had been studying pearls. When he saw Archer, he leaped up with a grin. "Archer! I missed you the last time you were here." He reached into his pocket, brought out a worn black wallet, and pulled out a picture. "My new granddaughter is as bright as the sun and more beautiful than a spring moon."

Archer looked at the picture and couldn't help smiling back.

The newborn baby's black eyes were clear and very intent. Her little hands were fisted. "Look out, world. This one's a tiger."

Sun Seng laughed. "She will run her brothers ragged. High time, too. We had all but given up hope of a granddaughter."

"Congratulations," Archer said. "You're a very lucky man."

Seng grinned like a boy as he put the picture back in the wallet. When Archer introduced Hannah, Seng shook hands and watched her with barely concealed curiosity. Archer had never brought a woman to the Pearl Exchange before.

"Are you looking for anything special today?" Sun asked, glancing from one to the other.

"Do you have anything special?" Hannah countered easily, smiling.

Seng laughed approvingly. The first rule of trading was to keep your true desire to yourself. "My life is consumed by special pearls."

"Baroque pearls, from what I can see," Hannah said.

"Round pearls are so boring," Seng said, his voice bland and his eyes as intent as his granddaughter's. "I prefer pearls that call to my imagination rather than my greed. Faith understands that."

Archer smiled. "In this case," he explained to Hannah, "Faith isn't a belief. Faith is my other sister, Honor's twin. She makes incredible jewelry from baroque pearls. Seng is one of her best sources."

"It is my pleasure," Seng said simply. "Someday her jewelry will be as famous as Georges Foquet's or Rene Lalique's."

"Uh-oh," Archer said. "I hear prices going up. Yours, to be exact."

Seng smiled. "For Faith, only the best."

"Translation: most expensive," Archer said dryly. "Okay, show me what it's going to cost."

"It's her birthday," Seng said.

"Christmas is sooner."

"Whatever." Seng opened a drawer and pulled out a velvet-lined box. "This will make Faith smile. When I saw it, I thought of her eyes. That odd silver-blue . . ."

"Thank God it's not a diamond," Archer muttered.

Hannah looked at the ring on her finger and wondered

again how much it had cost. Certainly too much for her to buy, which was a pity. It was the first faceted stone she had seen that appealed to her as much as a fine pearl.

"Here we are." Seng came back to the glass counter that ran along the front of his booth. He set the box down and opened it carefully. Nestled in pale blue satin was a semicircle baroque pearl. It was nearly three quarters of an inch long and half an inch wide at its center.

"May I?" Hannah asked, reaching for the pearl.

"Of course." Seng lifted the pearl out and put it on Hannah's palm.

"Cool, smooth, heavy," she murmured. "Very heavy. It's either a natural or came from a seeded shell that got lost for a few years. Most likely a natural. It has the sheen of fresh water rather than salt."

"I should have known you were in the business," Seng said ruefully. "This came from a little creek in the deep South whose name is my secret. I've seen no other shade quite like it."

"Neither have I," Hannah said.

"The New World's freshwater pearls are famous for their regional variations in color," Archer said. "But you're right, Sun. I haven't seen one this shade."

"Considering its rarity, the price is quite reasonable. Two thousand dollars."

"Six hundred is reasonable," Archer said.

"Plus one thousand. That would be sixteen hundred."

"That would be bull dust."

"Excuse me?" Seng said.

"Ask Hannah. Seven hundred."

"But its rarity—"

"Will make it nearly impossible to match," Archer cut in. "As a solo in the hands of someone less skilled than Faith, the delicate shade of the pearl would be overwhelmed by the setting, and the result would look like chalk. Eight-fifty and I'm out of here."

"You're breaking me," Seng said, giving Archer a distressed look. "Think of my granddaughter's college fund!"

"Don't believe him," Archer said to Hannah.

"I don't. But I believe this pearl could be set against rose gold like an Arctic moon set against dawn."

Seng turned quickly toward her. "You're a designer, too, like Faith?"

"No. Just someone who loves pearls."

"Nine hundred," Seng said without looking away from Hannah.

Archer sighed. "Nine hundred."

They shook hands.

"I have something else to show you," Seng said to Archer. "It's not for sale, unfortunately."

"That's a relief."

Seng laughed and went back to the locked desk. He pulled out another ring box and opened it. The pearl was as big as a Georgia peanut, black as midnight.

Rainbows swirled just beneath its surface.

"Amazing, isn't it?" Seng asked.

"Not for sale?" Archer asked, his voice neutral.

"I sold it today. I would have shown it to you six weeks ago, but I missed you."

Hannah reminded herself to breathe. She didn't dare reach for the pearl because she knew her fingers would tremble.

"Then a few minutes ago this Hong Kong gentleman saw it and bought it on the spot," Seng continued. "As soon as his bank faxes confirmation, he'll take delivery of the pearl."

"Ian Chang," Archer said.

"Yes. Do you know him?"

"We met a few days ago. Do you have any other pearls like that one?"

"I wish I did. But no."

"Have you ever seen others?"

"I've heard rumors about such pearls for several years, but this is the first one I've seen."

"The person who sold it to you—do you know him or her well?"

Seng frowned. It was unlike Archer to pry into another trader's contacts. "Why?"

Archer hesitated, thought of the new granddaughter, and decided that secrets killed more people than knowledge did.

"The man who developed these pearls died recently. He never sold a single black rainbow. Not even the baroque ones."

"Are you saying that this was stolen?" Seng asked, looking unhappily at the beautiful gem.

"Very likely. The rightful owner won't pursue the issue, but it would help a great deal if you could give me the history of the pearl as you know it."

"Who is the owner?"

"We are," Archer said, indicating Hannah.

Seng's eyebrows shot up. "I don't doubt you, but I don't understand."

"The pearl is Australian," Hannah said. "My late husband developed the strain of oysters that produces these black rainbows. He kept it as secret as he could. Now that he's dead . . ."

"I was Len's partner," Archer said, picking up the thread. "Mrs. McGarry asked my help in tracing the stolen pearls."

Sighing, Seng closed the box and handed it to Hannah.

"No," she said, pushing the box back across the counter. "It's our gift to your granddaughter. But if anyone comes to you with pearls like these, please call us immediately."

"Don't tell anyone else what you know about rare black pearls," Archer added. "Gems like these—"

"—are to die for," Seng finished dryly. "I understand."

"If anyone comes to you with a handful of these pearls, or an unstrung necklace of matched spherical pearls, pay whatever you have to," Archer said. "Just get those pearls. Better yet, call me and let me take care of it. You'll get a generous finder's fee."

Seng measured both Archer's restraint and his intensity, and nodded.

"Whatever you do, Seng," Archer continued softly, "be careful. No pearl, however rare and beautiful, is worth dying for."

Again Seng sighed. "Tell me. Are the rumors true? Is there such a necklace as the Black Trinity?"

"Yes," Hannah said before Archer could decide. "Two people have seen it. One is dead. The other is on the run. Do you want to try your chances?"

Seng crossed himself and shook his head. "What I want is to see my granddaughter grow tall enough to look me in the eye."

"Then call me if you hear anything," Archer said. "If other people come to you with rumors, call me."

"I bought the black pearl from Jason Taylor," Seng said. "He had a bill of sale from a pearl farm I'd never heard of, owned by Angelique Dupres."

Hannah was glad Seng wasn't looking at her. She didn't think she had managed to conceal her shock very well. Angelique Dupres was Coco's half sister, who had stayed in Tahiti to have babies and run a tiny pearl farm for the family.

"What's the name?"

"Moonbeam Limited."

Archer almost smiled. "After the old legends?"

Seng smiled. "I hadn't thought of that." He saw another customer approaching. "Is there anything else?" he asked Archer politely.

"Nothing that we haven't already talked about."

"I will be in touch," Seng promised. Then he smiled at the elegantly dressed, very large woman who was looking into the display case. "Mrs. Janzen, thank you for taking time from your busy schedule to see me. Is your family well?"

Leaving Seng and his formidable customer to exchange greetings, Archer and Hannah drifted off to another booth.

"Unless there are two women named Angelique Dupres—" Hannah began.

"Later," Archer cut in softly.

She looked around. While no one was close enough to overhear what they were saying, that could change at any moment as people wandered from booth to booth.

"Okay. What's this about moonlight and legends?" she asked.

He took the change of subject without a pause. "Some folks—Pliny the Elder was among them—believed that pearls were formed when oysters swam up to the surface of the sea at the full of the moon, opened themselves, and were delicately impregnated by moonbeams."

The tension in Hannah's face dissolved into a smile. "Talk about the ridiculous and the sublime . . ."

"It gets better. In India, where pearls have been pursued for thousands of years, both Buddhists and Hindus have a category of god called nagas. They're snakes that have a human head."

"I think I've met them," Hannah said wryly.

A smile flickered over Archer's mouth. "Nagas are guardian gods. They guard pearls, drops of rain, and the elixir of immortality."

"Maybe Jung was right about all those archetypes running around in human brains," she said. "Not to mention Freud. He would have a lot to say about snaky phallic symbols and pearly drops and all."

This time Archer's smile stayed on his lips. "I can imagine."

So could she. And what she was imagining made heat slide into her blood. She wanted to hold Archer like that again, only this time she would taste as well as touch the liquid pearls that escaped his restraint.

He saw the small shiver that coursed through her. "Do you want Honor's jacket?"

"What?" she asked, dragging her mind away from the image of him naked and potent as she bent down to him.

"This," he said, holding up the jacket that had been folded over his arm. "You're shivering. You're used to temperatures a lot warmer than the open floors of the Pearl Exchange."

Rather than tell him that the goose bumps coursing over her came from thinking about getting him naked, Hannah let him settle the jacket over her shoulders like a cape. The casual touch set off another shiver.

"Why didn't you tell me you were cold?" he asked, rubbing her arms briskly, careful to keep the jacket as a barrier to direct touch.

"I didn't notice."

He gave her an odd look.

She looked straight ahead and wondered how other women dealt with being ambushed by passion in public places. Especially when they were with a man who was doing everything but walk on the ceiling to avoid touching her, skin to skin.

"Angelique Dupres is Coco's half sister," Hannah said in a low voice.

He simply nodded and filed the information away.

Side by side, not touching at all, Archer and Hannah went

to every booth in the room. They traded off asking about the special black pearls. Some people had heard of them. No one owned any. Or if they did, they were keeping it secret.

"Here they come again," Hannah said under her breath.

"Our shadows?"

"Um," she agreed. "What would they do if we walked up and introduced ourselves?"

"Chat with us until backup arrived. Then we'd have to go to the trouble of picking the new bureaucrats out of the crowd."

"Better the devil you know, is that it?"

"Sometimes."

"Is this one of those times?"

"So far."

"And when it changes?"

"We'll lose them." He looked at his watch.

"You're really angry underneath all that calm, aren't you?"

Archer looked at her with steel-colored eyes. The realization that she could see so well into him made him even more angry. "Yes."

"Why?"

"Someone told the Changs where we were. When I get my hands on her—"

"Her?" Hannah cut in.

Archer thought of April Joy: beautiful, intelligent, and above all, ruthless. "Her. Definitely."

Twenty-one

F red and Rebecca Linsky were in their eighty-first year of life and their sixty-second of marriage. Despite, or perhaps because of, that, they were known as the Battling Linskys. Lean, white-haired, childless, no taller than five and a half feet, they ruled their small pearl kingdom with a firm hand and an eye toward their employees' offspring. The lustrous pearls that had passed through the Linskys' hands had paid for many college educations. Their doctor, who lived next door in one of Seattle's many waterfront condominiums, made house calls at least once a week and never charged them a fee; her entire education had been paid for with Linsky pearls.

While Fred and Becky didn't live at the Pearl Exchange, it was their true home. They had built it, nurtured it, and continued to enhance it with the presence of their Third Planet Pearls collection. The huge collection was housed on the top floor of the Exchange.

Hannah barely acknowledged the introductions Archer performed when the Linskys greeted them. She was riveted by the cases of pearl objets d'art, the one-of-a-kind jewelry, and all the rest of the Linskys' eclectic collection, including the sorting tables just visible through a doorway at the end of the huge room.

"Excuse me," she said, turning back to Becky. "What was your question?"

Becky laughed and put her fragile but not frail hand on Hannah's. "I asked if you were interested in pearls. Your eyes tell me you are. Would you like to see the collection?"

"We both would," Archer said, "but I'm afraid we don't have time for the full tour."

Hannah made a soft sound of protest.

Becky smiled. "There are other days, dear."

Because she didn't know how to say she might not live to see those other days, Hannah simply smiled in return.

"A short tour, then," Becky said, pinning Archer with her faded blue eyes.

"A short tour," he agreed. Becky's eyes might be faded, but her will wasn't. Displaying their collection to an appreciative audience was one of the Linskys' greatest pleasures. He wouldn't deprive them of it.

Smiling, Becky walked eagerly toward a smooth cherry wood cabinet that was four feet high and divided into drawers that were wide and shallow. The top of the cabinet was clear, beveled glass, giving a view into the contents of the first drawer.

"Pearls were the first and most perfect of all the gems men used to make themselves and the things they prized more beautiful," Becky said to Hannah. "The oldest pearl fishery we know of started off in Sri Lanka more than two thousand years ago. Others contend that the honor belongs to Persians, who have been bringing up shell in an organized manner for at least that long."

Hannah looked down into the cabinet and saw what appeared to be irregular gold links forming a chain perhaps sixteen inches long. Small pearls, impaled on thin strands of gold, hung from some of the links.

"Forty-three hundred years ago," Becky said, "pearls are mentioned as tribute in China. Mother-of-pearl has been found in Babylonian ruins that are more than four thousand years old. Where there is mother-of-pearl, there is, inevitably, pearl itself."

"Is that how old this necklace is?" Hannah asked, startled. "Four thousand years?"

"No. Unfortunately, pearls are fragile. Buried in places that are either too damp or too dry, pearls die. The necklace you're looking at has the oldest pearls in our collection. It graced the neck of a Persian aristocrat—probably a priest or priestess—before Christ was born."

Archer had seen the necklace many times, but the history of it still fascinated him, as did the bottomless orient of the natural pearls themselves. White, ethereal, the luster of the pearls was like a sigh whispered through the ages.

"Why do you say a religious figure wore this necklace?" Hannah asked. It looked more decorative than symbolic to her.

"Odds," Fred said before his wife could answer. "Throughout recorded history, whether in this hemisphere or the next, pearls were objects of veneration. Priests of both sexes had first call on pearls, except for the supreme ruler—who was likely a priest as well. It doesn't take a great feat of imagination to see pearls and think of the moon, which was worshiped along with the sun. What is part of a god is also holy. If you own those pieces, you're holy, too."

"That's the fascinating thing about pearls," Archer said. "They're symbols of both chastity and carnality, depending on the time and place."

"A gem for all occasions," Hannah said with a sideways look at him.

"A gem for all cultures," Becky corrected. "Once pearl fisheries were established, pearls became the ultimate status symbol around the world. Whether in India, China, or Persia, the more pearls you wore, the higher you were in the pecking order. Romans wallowed in them. Caligula was mad for them."

"Caligula was mad, period," Archer said dryly.

"Just because he gave his horse a high appointment and hung a pearl necklace around the equine neck?" Fred asked. "Can't say I blame Caligula. Most men haven't the sense of a horse's butt, much less the whole horse."

"Cleopatra won a bet with pearls," Becky said.

"Who had enough nerve to bet against her?" Hannah asked.

"Marc Antony. To prove to him how powerful and wealthy Egypt was, Cleopatra bet him that she could serve a feast that was more expensive than any in history. She sat him down with an empty plate and a goblet of wine. She probably smiled like her pet cat to see him watching her skeptically. Then she took off one of her earrings—a single huge pearl—smashed it, dissolved it in wine, and drank it. When she was finished, she handed the other earring to Antony and dared him to do the same. He conceded on the spot, for the earring she had drunk was worth almost two *million* ounces of silver."

"Legend has it that he financed an entire military campaign with the proceeds of the second pearl," Fred said.

"That was the general Vitellius and it was his mother's pearl earring, not Cleopatra's."

"No, it was Antony, and it was Cleopatra's pearl!"

Squaring off face-to-face, Becky and Fred started quoting sources, talking louder and louder, and generally having a great time. The higher the volume of the argument rose, the brighter their eyes got and the quicker their minds.

"Which was it, Antony or Vitellius?" Hannah asked Archer quietly.

"Vitellius. Antony took his to Rome, cut it in half, and made earrings for a statue of Venus."

"Cut it in half . . ." Hannah repeated faintly. "For a statue."

"It was an act of piety as much as arrogance. Romans were completely in thrall to pearls. The more they got through conquest, the more they wanted. They were insatiable and quite happy to bankrupt themselves for pearls."

"You sound wistful."

"I am," Archer admitted, smiling a pirate's kind of smile. "It would have been a great time to be a pearl trader."

"Now isn't so bad," she said, looking around. "To see pearls like this at any other time, you would have to have been an emperor or a god."

A gleam from another display case caught her eye. She looked at the Battling Linskys—no sign of a truce—and sidled closer to the new case. Sealed within its glass walls was a rectangle perhaps eighteen inches by fourteen inches. Its surface was gold. Countless pearls set in the gold depicted the clothes of a saint: headdress, robes, girdle, all glowed with the ethereal inner light of pearls. Rubies, emeralds, and sapphires were scattered about, but it was pearls which dominated, pearls which were the true measure of piety and wealth.

"Where on earth . . . ?" she whispered.

"Either a monastery or the library of a very wealthy man," Archer said quietly. "It's medieval, Russian, and one of the finest manuscript covers ever made by man. It fairly vibrates with awe and reverence, with hope for immortal life laced with fear of hell everlasting."

For a moment all Hannah could think of was Len's fingers digging into her arm as he screamed at her that the Black Trinity wasn't finished, couldn't be finished, or he would be whole. The image of his rage and fear was so vivid that she said his name in a low, husky voice.

"Don't think about it," Archer said. "He wasn't the first man to go crazy and equate the temporal and temporary with the divine and eternal. There is something shimmering just beneath the surface of pearls that brings peace or madness, depending on the man."

"I know. It's just . . . sometimes it's so fresh, as though it happened two seconds ago and the screams are still backed up in my throat."

Archer reached for her before he remembered that all she wanted from him was protection and sex. Comfort wasn't part of their deal. He put his hands in his pockets and turned toward the next display case. "Give it time. It will get better."

He walked to a new case. "Here's another piece of pearl history. Strings of pearls that could have graced the royal treasury of India or Persia any time in the last two thousand years. Probably did, if I know Fred. The traders know that he'll pay more than anyone else for pearls with history attached to them."

Hannah turned and focused on the case. There was indeed a mound of natural pearl strands, enough to make a maharajah or a prince weep. "Beautiful," she said.

And they were, but not to her. Not at the moment. The ugliness of man still overwhelmed her.

"Iran has chests overflowing with strands like this. Priceless, even in the age of cultured pearls."

Without touching Hannah, Archer led her down a row of cabinets, pointing out some of the highlights within. Pearl-encrusted necklaces from medieval Russia and England. Persian slippers smaller than his hand that were completely covered with seed pearls. A necklace of pearls, diamonds, rubies, and amethysts that had once belonged to a Mogul princess. A tiny gold box completely framed with pearls; it was reputed to have belonged to a mistress of Henry VIII.

"Hardly a recommendation for exclusivity," Archer added. "He had mistresses the way some men had cups of wine."

Hannah didn't say a word. She was still working hard just to cope with the present.

"The interesting thing is that we only associate valuable pearls with salt water," he continued, pointing to another case, "but modern appraisers of centuries-old jewelry find freshwater pearls again and again. Even today, the best of the freshwater pearls are sold as saltwater gems. We have an enduring prejudice in favor of the sea's mystery."

"Exactly," Fred said as though he and his wife hadn't spent the past five minutes arguing with each other. "I've always said that freshwater pearls beat saltwater gems any day."

"Ha!" Becky said. "That's foolishness and you know it. No freshwater pearl on earth can stand against a good South Seas gold."

"Bull," Fred roared. "What about that natural pink pearl I bought last year from Tennessee?"

"What about it?"

Archer hid a smile. The Battling Linskys were off and running.

Hannah looked at the old couple and smiled despite the turmoil of her own emotions. Their enthusiasm for an argument was matched only by their enthusiasm for each other; their love was as transparent as tears.

"Becky handles the saltwater end of their business," Archer said.

"I never would have guessed," Hannah said dryly.

He looked at his watch, sighed, and knew it wasn't going to

be a short visit. Silently he followed Hannah down the first row of cabinets and display cases. They passed in front of a wall with photographs of the most famous pearls in history, from Western queens to Eastern potentates, all of whom were draped with huge, priceless ropes of natural pearls. There was a photo of the Hope pearl, a monster white baroque weighing in at eighteen hundred grams. There was a nod to Elizabeth Taylor's La Peregrina, bought for her by her lover and two-time husband, Richard Burton.

La Peregrina was a huge five-hundred-year-old pearl that had been owned by royalty. It was rumored to have been eaten by one of Taylor's lap dogs; the pearl had emerged from the canine digestive tract a shadow of its former sizable, lustrous self. The picture on the Linskys' wall was taken before the incident. Afterward, there probably hadn't been much left to photograph.

"Sad, sad story," Fred said, materializing at Hannah's elbow. "Pity she didn't feed him one of her whacking great diamonds. It would have emerged unscathed. Calcium carbonate is susceptible even to mild acids such as sweat, much less to the horrific acids in a mammalian gut."

"I heard it was only well chewed, not swallowed," Becky said.

"Either way, a legendary pearl was lost. I can't imagine anyone feeding pearls to a pet."

"I doubt that she fed La Peregrina to the dog." Archer looked at his wristwatch and added, "It probably scarfed the pearl off a bedside table."

"Barbara Hutton fed Marie Antoinette's pearls to a goose," Becky said.

"What?" Hannah said in disbelief.

"She heard that it was the best way to add luster to pearls."

"Good God." Hannah shook her head, appalled that anything so unique and valuable could have such an ignominious end. "So much history and beauty reduced to dog and goose droppings."

"Look at it this way," Archer said. "When Rome burned, the cream of the Persian pearls for the last millennium went up in smoke."

"Stop," she said. "I don't want to think about it."

"Then think about this." He gestured to a prayer rug whose elegant geometric designs were outlined in pearls. "A devout, and devoutly wealthy, Muslim said his prayers on this five times a day."

"Elegant and beautiful," Hannah said. "But it would be like kneeling on frozen peas."

Archer gave a crack of laughter. His hands reached to touch her, just for a few seconds, but he turned the automatic motion into one of looking at his watch.

"It's still there," Becky said tartly. "Is the buckle loose? You keep checking as though you expected your watch to be gone."

"Guilty," he said. "Hannah and I are on a tight schedule."

"Young people. Always rushing from one place to another. Never enough time to appreciate the place where they are."

"There isn't enough time on earth to appreciate your pearls," Archer said.

"Ha. Your collection—"

"Is just beginning," Archer cut in firmly.

"I still say that if you would trade that South Seas gold paragon for our—"

"Quit tormenting the boy, Becky," Fred interrupted. He tugged at the string tie he wore. His white shirt was so worn it gleamed like silk at the collar and elbows, but it was clean as a pearl. "He doesn't want to let go of that beauty, and I don't blame him. Instead of badgering him, let's show him the new stuff. I want his advice on one of the lots."

"I'm flattered," Archer said.

"You should be," Fred retorted. "I'm old, but I'm not a fool. I know my eyes aren't what they used to be, even with magnifying lenses. The boy we hired to color-sort isn't as good as he thinks he is. He sure as hell isn't as good as you are."

"Oh, all right," Becky grumbled. "We'll go to the sorting room."

Hannah didn't wait for a second invitation. She headed straight for the room that opened off the rows of display cases.

In some ways, walking through the wide door was like coming home. In one important way it wasn't: Len wasn't sitting in the corner, staring at her with eyes that weren't quite sane.

Nor was there the chatter and laughter of the Chinese workers who had slowly replaced the Japanese employees in Pearl Cove.

"What are you assembling here?" Archer asked.

He gestured to a sorting table where three groups of pearls were lined up on three different trays. The trays had channels of different sizes to hold the pearls in parallel, horizontal rows from top to bottom. Each tray held a separate color of South Seas pearls: black, gold, white. A nearby table held more pearls of each color, each in a separate tray. Small shipping boxes were stacked in the center. Each contained more pearls.

"That's the beginnings of a necklace, part of a parure for an old client." Fred sighed. "Or it will be if we ever get enough of the right pearls. Makes my eyes hurt just to think about it."

"How many do you need?"

"Fifty of each. Minimum. A hundred would be better. Spherical is preferred. The client can afford it and we have our eye on another acquisition for our museum."

Archer smiled in silent sympathy.

Hannah went to the table, looked at the pearls that were being sorted, and glanced over at the nearby table. "Is your first sort for color?"

"Yes," Becky said. "Since several pieces of jewelry are involved, color is more important than size variations. Luster is a very, very close second. So is shape."

"May I?" Hannah asked.

Becky looked at Archer.

"I'm told she's one of the best," he said simply.

"Go ahead," Becky said, gesturing.

Absently Hannah nodded. She was already focused entirely on the pearls. Switching on the overhead light, she began with the silver-white pearls. The gradations of color were both subtle and profound, enough for a roomful of philosophers to argue over. Yet she saw the differences as clearly as other people saw the gap between yellow, orange, and red.

Humming softly, enjoying the cool, silky weight of the pearls and the feeling of solving a fascinating puzzle, she sorted the gems. Like a Chinese merchant working an abacus, her fingers flew over the rows of pearls. Unlike an abacus, the pearls were free to jump up or down in the parallel rows.

When the sleeves of the jacket draped over her shoulders kept getting in the way, Archer removed it. She didn't even pause in her work. In fact, he doubted if she even noticed what he had done. She was wholly caught in the spell of the pearls and the challenge of matching them one by one.

When she was finished, she stepped back. Only seven of the hundred pearls had survived the sort. She had placed them side by side on the top row of the tray. The rest were lined up on the rows below in order of diminishing acceptability of the color match.

"My God," Fred said, staring.

"Incredible," Becky agreed. She stepped forward and bent over the tray. "You're very good, dear."

"The pearls in the next row are an acceptable match," Hannah said, "particularly if you're looking for a bracelet or a brooch to go with the necklace. But I sorted first for the necklace, because that's always the most difficult." Rather wistfully she looked at the table where other pearls waited to be sorted.

"Go ahead," Archer said quietly. "I don't think the Linskys will mind."

"Mind?" Becky laughed in disbelief. "You've accomplished more in a few minutes than any of us have in hours."

"You had already done the initial sort on that lot," Hannah pointed out.

"Don't bother to be modest," Becky retorted. "I'll bet you could have done the first sort buck naked and standing on your head."

"I've never tried it that way." Hannah smiled as she added, "Standing on my head, that is."

Fred laughed and his brown eyes glinted with a wicked male light.

Archer swallowed hard. The thought of watching her naked in a room full of pearls made heat settle heavily in the pit of his stomach. The smooth texture of her skin would rival that of the pearls. The flush of passion would be more beautiful than any pearly luster . . . and her sleek heat would be a delicious contrast to the cool heaviness of pearls.

"But it's too cold to work naked here," she added, "so I'll do it the hard way."

She turned to the next table, where groups of pearls were spread out flat. With amazing speed she moved pearls around in the first group, following clues only she could see. Very quickly she divided the group into two piles. The first she simply pushed aside and didn't look at again.

"Do you have more trays or should I use the one on the other table?" she asked without looking away from the pearls.

"We have more," Becky said.

"Coming up," Fred said.

Nodding vaguely, Hannah moved on to another unsorted pile. When the trays appeared at her elbow, she put them to use without a word. The only sound in the room was her soft humming. The tunes were a mixture of Australian folk songs and the hymns she had been raised with. Though the speed of the music varied, her concentration didn't.

Archer watched every move she made. He was fascinated by her skill, her quickness, her agile fingers. He considered himself a good pearl sorter, but she was better. Much better. Even in Mikimoto's huge sorting rooms, he had never seen anyone work with her speed and precision. No wonder Len had demanded that she match the Black Trinity for him.

Rows of pearls formed with dazzling speed on the sorting trays. Once the gems were lined up, the subtle color variations that separated one line from the next became more obvious. Sometimes it was simply a matter of surface perfection. Most often the differences lay in the orient, beyond man's ability to touch or change. Orient was the soul of the pearl, the mystery of it, and the primal magic; the god seed that mankind had worshiped for thousands of years.

Hannah looked at the finished trays, stepped back, swapped several pearls among the trays, and brooded over the result. One tray held only twelve pearls. Each one had the same silver-white, moon-goddess sheen. She turned back to the first tray she had sorted, picked up the seven gems from the top row, and mixed them in with the twelve other pearls.

The match was perfect.

Archer's skin prickled in primal response to the gift Hannah took for granted. It was one thing to color-match while looking at the pearls; it was quite another to have a visual memory so precise that you could match new pearls to remembered ones *without ever comparing them except in your mind.*

If he had any doubts about her statement that she would recognize individual pearls from the Black Trinity no matter where she found them, he had no doubts now.

"I wouldn't have believed it if I hadn't seen it," Fred said in a hushed voice. "She never even looked back at the first group."

"Dear, any time you want a job, come to us," Becky said. "We'd pay twice the going rate—three times—for someone with your skill."

Hannah made an absent sound. Her attention was on the unopened boxes of pearls. "I love matching them. It's like an endless, beautiful puzzle. The only thing I enjoy as much is carving wood, but all my tools are in Broome."

"Well, in that case," Becky said, heading for the unopened boxes, "why don't we dive into a few more of these lots?"

Archer started to object, but decided not to. The haunted look was gone from Hannah's eyes. For now she wasn't thinking of Len and death and the Black Trinity. If sorting pearls gave her that much pleasure, then the rest of the world could just stay on hold for a while longer.

"Wait," Fred said. "Do you remember all pearl colors that well, or just white?"

"My husband and I farmed South Seas pearls," Hannah said. "We had every color."

"Then maybe you can settle an argument my wife and I have been having. That's why we asked Archer to come here. I bought some pearls I think are abalone, even though they're big and round. She says they're from cultured saltwater oysters."

"I don't know if I could tell the difference," Hannah said. "I've only worked with saltwater oyster pearls."

"I might be able to," Archer said. "Let's see what you have."

Fred went to an electronic wall safe, entered the combination on a number pad whose keys were capped with mother-of-pearl, and pulled out a velvet jeweler's case.

"If they're abalone," he said, walking back to Hannah and

Archer, "then they're basically museum goods. The chance of finding enough for commercial use would be slim, because abalone pearls are nearly always baroque."

"But if they're cultured oyster pearls," Becky said, "there are more where they came from."

"These are too colorful to come from oysters," Fred objected as he opened the case.

Rainbows swirled and smoldered beneath clear black ice. The pearls were perhaps fourteen millimeters, spherical, and had superb orient.

"Oyster," Hannah said huskily. "Cultured. Australian."

"But—" Fred began.

"She's right," Archer said flatly. "If you cut one of them open, you'd find a bead of American pigtoe mussel. In fact, Hannah could have seeded the oyster that produced that pearl herself."

"Told you," Becky said. "If you would ever listen to me, you wouldn't have to bother other people with your problems."

Fred shot her a look. She smiled serenely.

"May I look at the pearls more closely?" Hannah asked.

Grumbling at having lost an argument to his wife, Fred handed the box to Hannah. Silently she turned toward better light and studied the pearls. After a time she carefully closed the box and gave it back to Fred.

"Hannah?" Archer asked softly.

She shook her head. However beautiful the pearls were, however valuable, they weren't from the Black Trinity. "A different group."

"Where can I get more of these?" Fred asked.

"Wherever you got those," Archer said before Hannah could answer.

"He said these were all he had."

"Who was he?" Archer asked.

Fred hesitated, then sighed. "They're stolen, aren't they." It wasn't really a question.

"Yes," Hannah said simply.

"From you?"

"Yes. And from Archer. We're partners in an Australian periculture operation."

Fred looked at Archer, who nodded.

"You've been sitting on pearls like this all these years and never told me?" Fred demanded, angry and more than a little hurt.

"My partner's husband was sitting on them," Archer said. "I saw one about seven years ago, then never saw another until last week. Who sold them to you?"

Fred opened the box and stared at the pearls, frowning. He wasn't happy about any of it, especially the knowledge that he had bought stolen goods from a long-standing source. He snapped the box closed. "Teddy Yamagata."

Twenty-two

*I*mpatiently Hannah stared at the café doorway as she tapped her short, buffed fingernails over the forest-green Formica of the table. Two tall double Americanos sent heat and fragrance up into the air. Archer was halfway through his. She had taken only a few sips. Espresso was a taste she hadn't yet acquired.

"Why don't we just invite them over to have coffee with us while we wait for Yamagata?" she asked irritably.

Archer didn't need to look over his shoulder to know who Hannah was talking about. The Feds were discreet but hardly invisible. They were parked just inside the front door of the small café, sucking up prime caffeine with the gratitude of stakeout cops who were more accustomed to muddy sludge than the kick-butt espresso of good Seattle coffee.

Outside the warm little café, wind blew clouds and rain sideways. Though it was only two o'clock, the streets were dark slices of autumn-to-winter gloom. The interior of the café was bright, colorful, and painfully retro. Neon light fixtures arced down the wall to end up in pots whose tall plants were made of welded junk. Vintage Rolling Stones pounded out of speakers the size of fists. Two espresso machines screamed and frothed, slamming steam through darkly aromatic coffee.

He glanced at his watch. If Teddy didn't put a hustle on, they would be late for the party that The Donovan had rescheduled when his oldest son left so abruptly for Australia.

"Do Feds always work in pairs?" Hannah asked.

"Except when they work in fours, sixes, eights, and more."

"Is that your government's answer to unemployment?"

"It's your government, too."

She blinked. "It's been so long that I forgot. Tell me again why my government is following me."

"To see where you go."

"Right. Why can't I remember that?"

When she saw the small smile tugging at Archer's mouth, she wanted to lean forward and brush her lips over his. Then the smile vanished, leaving behind a man with remote gray-green eyes and a midnight stubble accenting the hard lines of his face. That was the face he had showed her since last night: cold, hard, distant. If he touched her, it was as impersonal as rain. About as warm, too.

She told herself it was better that way.

And knew she lied.

She wanted his incandescent sensuality again. She wanted to feel her body ignite, to burn from the inside out, to be drawn on a rack of passion until she shattered into a million bright pieces of ecstasy . . . and then to sleep tangled with him, certain that he felt as she did. Complete.

She hadn't known that kind of pleasure existed between a man and a woman. Knowing, she couldn't forget, couldn't ignore, couldn't stop wanting more.

Tonight, she promised herself. Tonight I'll get past his pride. I know he wants me. His eyes are controlled, but his body isn't. Not always. I can raise his heart rate just by leaning against his arm. He can raise mine just as easily. We're adults who owe nothing to anyone. There's no reason not to be lovers.

Unbidden, memories of Summer flicked through Hannah's mind. The relaxed, satin weight of the child resting against her arm and her hip. The sweetly drooling smile. Clear gray-green eyes watching her, glinting with laughter and intelligence.

Archer's eyes.

If you wanted a child without complications, you should have gone to a sperm bank.

He and Len were alike in so many ways, it irritated Hannah that they couldn't have been alike when it came to children. Len hadn't worried when she miscarried. If anything, he was pleased; he didn't want children. Ever. After her miscarriage, she agreed with him. She would have no more children, not with a man who was too ruthless to be trusted with a child's fragile heart. She had taken great care not to become pregnant. After Len's accident, the question of children was answered. There would be none. Ever.

Then Len had died and she had fallen headlong into passion with another man who was too ruthless to be trusted with a child's heart; enjoying a niece wasn't the same as having the patience and generosity of spirit to raise a child.

Bitterly she wondered if there was something wrong in her, if unsuitable men would be the only kind she ever responded to sexually.

Beneath her bitterness was fear, the growing certainty that whatever man she finally chose as her mate, the passion she felt with Archer was unique to him. Even before Len's spine was severed, her husband had only skimmed the surface of her sensual possibilities. Other men hadn't managed even that. She had never looked at them and speculated how they might be as a lover; they simply didn't interest her sexually.

But Archer had and did. Instantly. Urgently.

Fear snaked through Hannah as she understood that she might marry and have children someday, but they wouldn't be conceived in blinding ecstasy. She would respond to no other man as she did to Archer Donovan.

The certainty made her both angry and bleak, like Archer's eyes watching her right now.

"Teddy's coming in the front door," Archer said. Then, reluctantly, "Are you all right?"

"Bloody wonderful. Why?"

"You look . . ." *Frightened. Exhausted. Hurt.* ". . . pale."

"Then I should fit right in with the natives." The emptiness in Hannah's voice was as unmistakable as the lines of tension and pain etching her face.

"You should have let me take you back to the condo," he said. "You need rest."

"Don't worry, boy-o. I'm not made of frigging French glass."

It had been one of Len's favorite sayings. Repeating it in Len's cadences gave Hannah a certain bitter pleasure. Seeing the narrowing of Archer's eyes gave her more.

"I'm with you every step of the way to the Black Trinity," she said in a low, savage tone, "so stop trying to dump me on your family while you run off and play without me."

Teddy dragged out a chair and sat down. Drops of water sparkled on his high forehead and his red pullover rain jacket. He unzipped the neck opening as far as it would go, revealing a startling pineapple-yellow shirt with a bright explosion of leaves strewn across the front. He nodded to Hannah before turning to the man who was watching him with an unsmiling face and eyes that were a lot colder than the rain outside.

"I'm supposed to be at SeaTac in an hour," Teddy said to Archer. "What's on your mind?"

"The pearls you sold to the Linskys."

"I've sold lots of—"

"You start bullshitting me and you'll miss your plane."

Teddy smiled slightly and leaned back, prepared to do what he was best at: bargaining. "Oh, *those* pearls."

A server appeared and looked at Teddy expectantly.

"He won't be here long enough for coffee," Archer said.

"I can make it to go," the server said, then took a good look at Archer. "Uh, never mind. Do you want your check, sir?"

"Not yet."

The server smiled brightly and got out of Archer's line of sight as fast as she could.

Archer never took his eyes off Teddy.

"I would have offered the pearls to you, but you were in Australia," Teddy said.

"Who sold them to you?"

"None of your business."

"Wrong answer."

Teddy shifted uncomfortably in his seat. "I have a connection."

"Who?"

"Damn it, that's—"

"Who sold you those pearls?" Archer cut in coldly.

Teddy had heard a few things about Archer's past. Right now he believed every one of them. There was no bargain to be struck here, only the kind of trouble a wise man avoided.

"A man from Broome."

"A man from Broome," Archer repeated neutrally, praying Hannah would stay out of it. "Name?"

"He didn't tell me."

"Keep it up and you'll miss that plane and every one after it until we're finished talking."

Unhappily Teddy took off his glasses, polished them, and put them back on. Cleaner lenses didn't help. Archer still looked like an executioner.

"Well, hell," Teddy muttered. His wife had been right: He shouldn't have bought the pearls from a man he didn't know. A nervous man, at that. Yet the pearls had been so extraordinary. And so cheap. "Qing Lu Yin."

Hannah stiffened.

"He was the original owner," Teddy said, glancing at her curiously. "He gave me a bill of sale. It was all done on the books and aboveboard."

"Where's the bill of sale?" Archer asked.

Sighing, Teddy pulled a breast wallet from his rain jacket's belly pocket. He had hoped he wouldn't need the bill of sale for this meeting, but he had been afraid he would. Something about those pearls had fairly shouted of trouble. Reluctantly he took out a sheet of paper.

"It's a copy," he said, passing the sheet over to Archer.

Ideographs marched down the right-hand side of the page. A smudged thumbprint sat crookedly on one corner. Letters and numbers were neatly written under the print.

"Keep it," Teddy said. "I have the original in my files."

"I didn't know you could read Chinese," Archer said.

"I can't. For all I know, it could be a laundry list. That's why I insisted on a thumbprint and a driver's license. Washington, state of. That's the number below the print."

"How did you meet him?" Archer asked.

"A cold phone call from an intermediary who saw my ad in the phone book."

"In Australia?"

"No. Seattle."

Adrenaline licked lightly beneath Archer's skin. A man who wrote only Chinese, yet had a Washington driver's license—probably a fake, or one that was borrowed/stolen from another Chinese. But all he said was, "He's here?"

"He was two days ago."

"Where is he staying?"

"I don't know."

"Where did you meet him?"

Unhappily Teddy tugged at one earlobe. "Some dump on Third Street called the Dragon Moon."

"Didn't we pass it on the way to the Pearl Exchange?" Hannah asked.

Archer nodded. Like any city, Seattle had some open civic sores despite persistent urban renewal. The land where Donovan International and the Donovan condo had been built was part of an urban renewal project. The Dragon Moon was one of the oozing pockets that had escaped razing and rebuilding. It was only three blocks away from the Donovan condo.

"You're a brave man," Archer said.

"Or a dumb one." Teddy sighed again. "Hell, it's hardly the first Asian dive I've been in."

"You're lucky it wasn't the last."

"Yeah, I got that impression. The customers were as tough a bunch as I've seen, and I've seen more than a few. I made real sure we conducted our business at the table closest to the front door and my back was to the wall."

One corner of Archer's mouth kicked up. Beneath the easy grin and loud shirt, Teddy was no fool.

"Cash?" Archer asked.

"What do you think?"

"Cash. How much?"

Teddy grimaced. "Five hundred each. Fifty-five hundred total."

With no change of expression, Archer filed the fact that the thief either didn't know what the pearls were worth or didn't have the contacts to get a better price. "You must have thought you'd died and gone to heaven."

"Not until I was out the door, in a cab, and across town," Teddy admitted. "Then I smiled a lot."

"Where are the rest of the pearls?"

"What pearls?"

"The ones you didn't buy until you were sure these were good."

Teddy's jaw dropped. "How did you know?"

Archer just smiled. It wasn't a friendly gesture. "How many pearls does he have?"

"He didn't say."

"What kind?"

"Black, mainly. The special kind of black."

"When are you meeting him again?"

"Who says I am?"

"I do. You're a good pearl man, Teddy, but you're greedy. The goods are stolen. You know it as well as I do."

"I don't know any such thing." He smiled an off-center smile. "So tell me—how is it better if you buy them than if I do?"

"They're already half mine by law."

Teddy shut his mouth, studied Archer, then slowly shook his head. "Nope. I'm not buying it."

Hannah flicked her nails against the tabletop, drawing Teddy's attention. "You'd better buy it, boy-o, or you'll go to jail for receiving stolen goods."

"Who's she?" Teddy asked.

"Hannah McGarry. She owns the other half of Pearl Cove, the Australian pearl farm that grew those black rainbows."

"Well . . . shit." Teddy leaned back in his chair and sighed hugely. "On the good-news side, I wasn't looking forward to seeing the Dragon Moon again."

Neither was Archer. But how he felt about it wasn't on the table. "When?"

"Tomorrow morning."

"You weren't flying very far today, were you?" Hannah asked idly, but her eyes were cold indigo.

"Just down to San Francisco."

She raised her dark eyebrows.

"Look," Teddy said defensively, "he gave me a bill of sale—"

"In Chinese, which you don't read," she cut in.

"—for those pearls. That's all the law requires."

For a moment she closed her eyes. Weariness rolled through her like a long, breaking wave. "The letter of the law. Lovely." Then, before Teddy could say any more, her eyes opened again. They were as bleak as Archer's. "I'm not judging you, Mr. Yamagata. If I did, I'd say that you're more honest than the law requires in the vast majority of your dealings. This deal, however, was the exception that proved your rule."

Teddy grimaced and didn't argue. "There's something about those pearls. . . ."

"They blunt a man's judgment," she said curtly. "I'm surprised you sold them."

"I'm a trader, not a collector. For me it's the deal, not the goods."

"What time tomorrow are you meeting Yin?" Hannah asked.

"Six A.M."

"I didn't think the Dragon Moon opened that early," Archer said.

Teddy shrugged. "They probably feed a lot of the invisible workers."

"Illegal immigrants," Archer explained to Hannah. "The ones who work for a few bucks a day in eight-by-ten sweatshops or fancy restaurants to pay off the smuggler who got them into the U.S. Obviously a Red Phoenix Triad smuggler, in this case."

Teddy winced. "C'mon, Archer. The place is a dump, but not that bad."

"The Dragon Moon is the Red Phoenix base in Seattle," Archer said matter-of-factly. "There are apartments above the restaurant for visitors from Hong Kong, Kowloon, Shanghai, the southern provinces of China, and anywhere else the triad has its tentacles. Everything the triad buys, sells, steals, or makes in illegal labs can be found inside the Dragon Moon's riot-proof metal doors."

"How do you know?" Teddy demanded.

"Does it matter?"

"Not to me," Teddy decided instantly, remembering again the rumors he had heard about Archer's past. "Anything else you need before I catch my plane?"

"How will I recognize Yin?"

"He's got a black eye the size of a pizza and a gash across his chin."

Archer's eyebrows rose, but all he said was, "Does Yin speak English?"

"No. He put out a pearl, I put out money, and when the amount was right, we exchanged. But there was a translator a few tables over. She was working with a bunch of guys in silk suits. She was pretty fancy herself. Sexy enough to make a man sixty feel like sixteen."

"Chinese?" Archer asked.

"ABC."

Hannah glanced at Archer.

"American-born Chinese," he said without looking away from Teddy. And probably her name was April Joy. The description certainly fit. So did the method. It wasn't the first time she had worked as a translator in order to penetrate a triad. "How many more pearls are we talking about?"

"Twenty times what I bought before. Two hundred pearls. Maybe more. Hand signals only go so far as a way of counting."

Another shot of adrenaline kicked into Archer's bloodstream. "Does he expect cash?"

"Yeah."

"Are you telling me you were going to walk into the Dragon Moon with a hundred thousand in cash?"

Teddy looked pained. "That's what he wanted. Besides, I got him down to one eighty-five."

"Did you see the pearls he wants to sell?"

"You bet I did."

"Describe them."

"Three sizes. Twelve, fourteen, and sixteen millimeters. Round as marbles. Same black opal orient."

Hannah felt as though her stomach had dropped through her shoes. She examined her fingernails and prayed that nothing showed on her face.

"Matched?" Archer asked.

"Hard to tell in that light. They looked good to me. No big surface flaws. Fine orient. And they rolled across the table without staggering. Round. Really round. Beautiful goods."

Deliberately Archer picked up his coffee and drank a swallow. "Drilled?"

"Nope. Virgin. Just like the others."

"Sounds like a steal at ten times the price," Archer said casually.

"Yeah." Teddy's voice was wistful. "I was going to put half of what I made in a school fund for my grandchildren. I've got eight of the little darlings and another on final approach."

"Look at it this way. Now you'll live to see them graduate."

"Oh, Yin didn't look like that tough a monkey."

"I wasn't talking about Yin." Archer stood up. "Have a nice trip. And if you see any more of those pearls, Teddy, call me. Just me."

The Donovan was an inch taller than his sons, and Susa was inches smaller than her daughters. Despite that, Susa wasn't as fragile as she looked. The steely discipline of an artist underlay her porcelain skin. The even tougher will of a mother lay beneath her warm smile. Because it was a party, she had dressed in a turquoise silk tunic top with slim black pants underneath. A necklace of baroque abalone pearls and handmade silver links circled her neck. Matching earrings and bracelet gleamed with each movement. The pearls had been a birthday present from her oldest son. The unusual design and workmanship were her twin daughters' present. The odd turquoise and gold of her eyes was a gift from a grandfather she had never met.

The door of the Donovan condo hadn't closed behind Susa before she recognized the approaching footsteps.

"Archer," she said, delighted. "I was afraid you wouldn't be able to make it. Don was maddeningly vague about your plans." As she spoke, she glanced over her shoulder at the man who filled the doorway. His thick black hair was streaked with silver, his body was straight and strong beneath the casual rust sweater and black slacks, and she smiled with pleasure just at being near him.

"Miss one of The Donovan's command performances?" Archer said, grinning as he crossed the living room to the entry. "Not likely. I feel guilty about everyone rescheduling the party just for me, though."

"Don't be silly," she said, holding out her arms. "Don said he could have a birthday whenever he damn well pleased."

Archer scooped his mother up in a big hug. Only Susa called The Donovan by his given name, just as only Susa was privileged to wind The Donovan around her little finger. The power flowed both ways, because she was wound just as tightly around his.

"More beautiful than ever," Archer said, kissing his mother soundly. "But still too skinny."

"Bite your tongue," she muttered, and gave him another kiss. "I'm just fashionable."

Though he smiled, he looked over his mother's honey-gold hair to his father. The Donovan nodded slightly, silently telling his son that Susa's health was good. Archer let out a long, silent breath. The thought of his mother hurting made him feel helpless. It wasn't a feeling he liked.

"Is she here?" Susa asked.

"She?"

"Len's widow."

Again Archer looked at his father.

The Donovan smiled rather sadly. "She knows. She knew before she married me. I just . . . wanted to spare her any . . ."

Susa's small fingers threaded through her husband's. She smiled up at him. "Silly goose." On tiptoe she kissed him. "Wonderful goose. I knew I wasn't your first."

"You were my last."

"Yes. And you were mine. That's all that matters."

He bent down and murmured something against her ear that made color rise in her cheeks and put a sparkle in her eyes. "Wicked, wicked man."

Archer grinned. "You wouldn't have him any other way, and you know it."

"Hush. I don't want *him* to know it."

"Too late, Mom. The cat got out of that bag before I was born."

Hannah walked into the living area and stopped cold, feeling like an intruder. The affection between the three Donovans was as clear and potent as sunlight. But that wasn't what made her go still. It was the change in Archer. Though he was dressed in black jeans and a black sweater, he looked . . . lighter. Nowhere did she see the remote, controlled man he had been to her since he had stalked out of the bedroom last night.

Tension deep inside her loosened and relief swept through her, leaving her with a feeling close to floating. Obviously he had gotten over his rage and was ready to be reasonable about their relationship. Two consenting adults, nothing more . . . and nothing less. The searing ecstasy she hungered for was once again close enough to touch, to taste.

He turned, sensing her. The instant he saw her, he changed. Doors slamming, bolts going home, shut down. Shutting her out. The fires that burned within him were out of her reach.

Emotions stabbed through her like dark lightning. She chose anger and ignored the rest, because admitting that she was hurt was something she refused to do. She lifted her chin, squared her shoulders, and walked up to Archer's parents.

"Mr. Donovan, Mrs. Donovan, I'm Hannah McGarry. It's kind of you to let me stay in your home. Since it's obvious you're going to have a full house tonight, I won't impose. Perhaps you could suggest a hotel where—"

"No." Archer's voice was cold. "You came to me for two things. It's easier to protect you here than in a hotel."

The tension crackling between Hannah and Archer made Susa's eyes narrow. Don looked from his son to the daughter-in-law he had never known. She was tall, nicely curved, with short sun-streaked brown hair and eyes so dark a blue he at first thought they were black. Their indigo gleam was repeated in a silk blouse whose open collar revealed a smooth throat, a large pearl choker of dubious quality, and just enough cleavage to tempt a man. The black jeans she wore fit her like a shadow and were so new they whispered when she walked.

From a man's point of view, it was a walk worth watching.

Susa glanced from her suddenly icy son to the tall woman with stunning eyes and a chip as big as a fist on her shoulder. "What's wrong?" Susa asked bluntly.

Archer looked at his father. "Unless you object, I'm telling her all of it."

His father shrugged. "Go ahead. She'd get it out of me before morning anyway."

In the neutral, concise manner of a man giving a report, Archer told Susa about Pearl Cove, Len, the Black Trinity, and the danger to Hannah until Len's murderer was found. Archer didn't mention the Red Phoenix Triad, April Joy, or the international pissing match over the luxury pearl trade.

Susa listened, but it was Hannah she watched, Hannah she weighed as though she was an incomplete canvas.

"I see," Susa said when Archer was finished. "You're welcome here as long as you want to stay, Ms. McGarry."

"I won't impose long. With luck, we'll find the Black Trinity tomorrow. Then we can ask Yin how a Pearl Cove employee came to have a fortune in stolen pearls."

"Yin is your employee?" Don asked sharply.

"He was," Archer said. "Obviously he's gone freelance."

Don grunted, gave his son a glance from wintry, cobalt blue eyes. He knew Archer was leaving out some important things; he didn't want Susa to know what those things were. "Are the girls here yet?"

"Jake and Summer are dressing," Archer said. "Honor and Kyle are frosting a cake in the kitchen, Lianne is on the phone with Hong Kong about some jade, and Faith is facedown in her room. She's been working eighty-hour weeks, and those are the short ones."

Susa smiled rather grimly. "She could work twice that and still be better off without that . . . without Tony."

"No argument here," Archer said. "One of the best days of my life was two weeks ago, when she showed up without that son of a bitch."

Kyle strode in from the kitchen area. "Hi, Mom and Dad. Are we speaking of the shit-eating insect?" he asked cheerfully between licks on a frosting-covered spoon.

"Do tell us how you feel about your sister's ex-fiancé," Susa said in a dry tone.

"I just did." He bent down and kissed the corner of his mother's mouth. "You're looking good enough to frost and eat."

Warily Susa licked her now sweet lips and watched the masculine hand waving a spoon heaped with icing. "Try it and I'll make you sit for a portrait."

"Oh, God, anything but that." Grinning, he kissed her again, gave his father a hard hug, and held the spoon out to Hannah. "Want some?"

She might have been an only child, but she knew a dare when it was waved under her nose. She took the spoon and gave it a good long lick. "Mmm, chocolate and what else?"

"Grand Marnier." Kyle laughed. "I didn't think you would do it."

"Luv, I've eaten stewed monkey parts from a communal pot."

"Yuck."

"Amen." Spoon in hand, she turned to Archer. "Want some?"

"Monkey parts? I'll pass."

"Icing."

He looked at the spoon, then at the dark frosting that clung to the indentation of her upper lip. At that instant he wanted nothing more than to grab her and lick her more thoroughly than any sweet and sticky spoon. His raw, relentless hunger for her infuriated him almost as much as her challenging smile.

"No, thanks," he said, looking right in her eyes.

The tone of his voice said it wasn't just the icing he was refusing.

Twenty-three

"Kyle, take Hannah and your mother into the kitchen and feed them some of that icing," The Donovan said. And it was The Donovan, not Don or Dad, who was speaking.

Susa gave him an approving look, hooked her arm through Hannah's, and pushed Kyle ahead of them. "Come along, children. I feel an urgent chocolate craving coming on."

As Archer watched the others walk away, he knew he was going to get the rough edge of his father's tongue. He didn't care. In fact, he was looking forward to it. One of the pleasures of being an adult was going toe to toe with The Donovan and coming out on the other side even closer to him than before.

"You were rude to a guest," The Donovan said. "Why?"

"She's not a guest. She's family."

"The question stands."

"I don't like chocolate icing."

The Donovan's V-shaped black eyebrows shot up. "Since when?"

"Since a minute ago. The lady and I rub each other the wrong way."

"Bullshit."

"Okay. We rub each other hot enough to set fire to plaster. That's not enough for me. It's enough for her. Life's a bitch and then you die."

His father sighed and raked his fingers through his hair in a gesture that was a mirror of his son's. Then he chuckled. "Giving you a run for your money, is she? Good for her."

"Thanks. Should I turn around so you can stab me in the back, too?"

His father gave a crack of laughter and hugged his oldest son with one arm. "I still think you should apologize to her for being rude, but I won't make an issue out of it. The course of true love never ran smooth, remember?"

Archer smiled thinly, hugged his father hard, and kept his mouth shut. Obviously The Donovan wasn't going to let go of his hope that his oldest son was finally going to know the joys of his own home and family.

"How's Faith doing?" Don asked.

Archer leaped on the change of subject with something close to relief. "Working too hard. Tony keeps dropping by the shop, telling her how he's learned his lesson and it will never happen again."

"It?"

"Whatever made her tell him to go to hell. Given his history, my guess is another woman."

Don said something scathing and profane under his breath. "She isn't weakening, is she?"

"I hope not. But I know it's tough on her, seeing her twin with a husband and a kid, and she doesn't have anyone at all."

"She could marry Tony and still not have anyone," Don said sardonically.

"She figured that out all by herself. That doesn't make being alone any easier."

"You ought to know."

Archer shrugged, but his eyes were the color of steel. "I've seen too much. Done too much. I'm not a good bet for hearth and home."

For a moment Don was too surprised to say anything. Then it was too late. Jake was coming down the hall carrying a happily crowing Summer. She was sitting on his broad shoulders with his hand braced behind her back. Her little fists were buried in his dark hair. She was holding on hard enough to make his eyes slant.

"Make way, make way," Jake said from down the hall. "Summer the Magnificent is coming through. Closely followed by Lianne the Gigantic."

Lianne gave Jake a swat on the butt as she walked past him. "Gigantic, huh? Watch it, big guy. I'll dump you on your pride and joy."

"Not for a few months you won't."

"I've got a long memory." She winked at Archer and smiled at The Donovan. "It's a shame how you got all the looks in the family, Dad."

He held out his arms and gave her a hug that lifted her right off the floor. "How's my favorite jade expert?"

"He's in the kitchen making icing, last I heard."

"I meant you, beautiful, not that tall blond ox you married."

"I'm fine. Eating for three."

"I hope they're girls. The world needs more women like you."

Lianne's whiskey-colored eyes darkened with emotion. The generous acceptance she had found in the Donovan family kept surprising her. Her in-laws truly loved her like a daughter. And she loved them right back. She kissed The Donovan on both cheeks, hugged him hard, and grinned up at him as he set her back on her feet with the easy precision of a man whose life-long love was fourteen inches and one hundred pounds smaller than he was.

Summer gurgled and bounced and held out her arms toward her grandfather. Don picked her off her father's shoulders and started making gobbling noises against her tummy. Squealing with laughter, Summer grabbed his thick, silver-streaked hair.

"How is Susa?" Lianne asked Archer as the others drifted off in the direction of the kitchen.

"Looking and moving like her old self."

The relief on Lianne's face sent warmth through Archer. He cupped her cheek in one hand. "Kyle is a lucky man."

She smiled, but the eyes searching his were intent. She sensed the turmoil beneath his outward calm. "What's wrong?"

"Nothing that you can cure." He bent and kissed her. "But thanks for caring."

"That's what families are for."

He thought of Len, who had never known a real family and had refused one when it was offered. And of Hannah, who had never known real love and had refused it when it was offered. Sex was all she wanted. Cold screwing. No emotion required or desired.

"How are my nieces?" Archer asked, putting his hand on Lianne's round, tightly stretched belly.

"Nieces," she said, rolling her eyes, but she guided his hand to the side, where one of the twins was doing backflips. "You and Dad. What if I have boys?"

This time Archer's smile reached his eyes as a tiny foot or elbow drummed against his palm. "Susa will lecture you on training them young, really young, because they're going to be big, really big trouble."

"Huh. Like your twin sisters never got in trouble."

"Of course they did. I led them down the primrose path every chance I got."

"Until they started wearing bras," Lianne said dryly. "Then you turned into a conservative monster."

"I knew how gullible they were. Somebody had to protect them."

She laughed. "That's not how they saw it."

"Sisters never appreciate their brothers."

"I appreciate you, even though you hated me on sight."

"I didn't hate you."

"Could have fooled me."

Archer bent and kissed her nose. "I was worried you were taking Kyle for the kind of ride that would break his heart—and the rest of him, too."

She patted Archer's hand where it lay on her restless belly. "I know. You're very protective of the people you love." She looked at him, measuring the changes. Tension where there had been relaxation. Ice where there had been laughter. Ruthlessness where there had been gentleness. She hadn't seen him like this since the night they sneaked onto an island and stolen a priceless jade burial shroud. There had been danger then, but there was no danger here and now, no reason for his fierce wariness. "I'm worried about you."

"I'm fine."

"No, you're not." She stood on tiptoe and kissed his bristly chin. "We love you anyway. C'mon, let's go get our share of chocolate icing before Kyle eats it all."

"Icing?" said Faith from the hallway leading to the suites. "Did I hear rumors of chocolate icing?"

"Rumors will be all that's left unless we hurry," Lianne muttered. "My husband can be trusted with a lot of things. Chocolate icing isn't one of them."

Faith's smile gave a gleam to her silver-blue eyes that hadn't been there when she woke up from her nap. She had had to nerve herself up to deal with the happy marriages of her sister and brother. It wasn't that she was jealous of her siblings. She simply ached to have that kind of partnership herself, to love a man and know that he loved her no matter what, to tickle her own baby and laugh when her baby laughed.

Simple things. Impossible things. At least for her. It had been a bitter admission to make, but it was better than continuing to live with Tony and kidding herself that it would all turn out okay in the end.

"When are Justin and Lawe coming in?" Faith asked.

"Not until the end of the week," Lianne answered. "They're still in Brazil."

"What happened? I thought Walker was flying down to bring them back."

"He was," Archer said. "When they went to take off, he didn't like the feel of the plane, so he aborted. Last I heard, the three of them were up to their ears in engine parts and bad language."

Faith worried her lower lip with her teeth.

"Don't fret," Archer said. "Walker is a careful man. They'll be fine." He drew Faith to his side in a one-armed hug. "You're looking good. I like that new haircut. Short and sassy."

"Tony didn't," she said absently, still thinking about her missing twin brothers. "He had a fit when I cut it."

"Tony's an anal orifice," Archer said.

"I know. Finally." She put her arm around Archer's lean waist and Lianne's swollen one. "Tell me, bro. How could a man as big as Tony be so small?"

"It's the nature of assholes to be small."

Lianne snorted. She hadn't liked Tony at all.

"Yeah." Faith tossed her head, making her short, sleek blond hair gleam. "So how could a smart woman like me be so dumb about a man?"

"A question for the ages," Archer said.

Lianne gave her sister-in-law a squeeze. "You're not the only one, Faith. A few years ago I was up to my lips in an affair with a man who didn't want me. He just wanted a back door into the Tang family."

Faith looked at her petite sister-in-law. "Seriously?"

"Seriously."

"How did you figure it out?"

"I didn't. He dumped me." She smiled thinly. "Being smart doesn't mean you don't make mistakes. It just means you learn from them."

As Archer gestured the women ahead of him into the kitchen, he wondered what he would learn from the mistake he had made with Hannah. Then he saw her standing next to his parents, listening intently to something Susa was saying, holding Summer while the baby gnawed on the big blue diamond Hannah still wore. He went still at the happy family portrait. When his mother glanced up and saw him, she nodded as though he had said, *What do you think, Mom? Is this one a keeper?*

If that wasn't bad enough, his father had the same gleam in his eye that he did whenever he glanced from Lianne to Kyle, silently saying, *Good job, son. This one will go the distance.*

But Hannah wouldn't. Not with him. The sooner his parents knew, the less it would hurt when they found out. Like yanking a bandage off—a gasp, a burn, and then it was over and healing could begin.

"There you are," Don said to Archer. "I was just telling Hannah about Len's mother. Figured she should know about us."

Archer barely managed not to say, *Why?* Instead, he gave his mother a sidelong glance.

Susa smiled at him. "I know it continually surprises you, but your father and I both had lives before we met each other. Not nearly as good as the lives we had after we met, but lives just the same. Don was explaining to Hannah—so tactfully that the point was all but buried—that even at sixteen he knew the difference between lust and love. Len's mother was cold and ruthless, but very sexy. Great material for a wild affair."

Archer reached for the bandage.

And yanked.

"Hannah doesn't have any trouble grasping that principle," he said neutrally. "She feels the same way about me. Great sex. No future, because I'm cold and ruthless. Like Len. So you can get that warm glow out of your eyes, Mom and Dad. She's not going to make an honest man of me."

Silence spread through the room.

Hannah flushed, then went pale except for a line of red high on both cheekbones. "Bastard."

"Notice she didn't call me a liar," he said to his parents.

"*Bloody* bastard."

Archer gave her an ironic bow. "At your service. Quite literally." He walked up to the icing bowl, ran his finger around the rim, and licked thoroughly. "Mmm. Your best yet, Kyle. Where's the cake?"

The condominium was so quiet that Hannah couldn't use city noise as a reason for her insomnia. She rolled over, punched the pillow into a new shape, and closed her eyes. The soft silk she wore—one of Archer's old shirts—slithered up her hips like a lover.

At your service. Quite literally.

Put that way, it sounded so cold. The fact that it was true made it worse. She would never forget the shock in Lianne's eyes, in Faith's eyes, and the way the two women had gone to stand on either side of Archer as though to defend him from an attack. He had smiled at them, the kind of tender smile he once had given to Hannah, and told them to relax, it was all right. *Just because Hannah doesn't want me as a husband is no reason to be hard on her. She's not the first person to think I'm a ruthless son of a bitch. She won't be the last.*

With that, Archer had led the conversation around to other topics—Faith's newest jewelry designs, Jake's negotiations for more Baltic amber, Lawe's surprising decision to come home for a time, Justin's unflagging love of wild country, and the end of the salmon-fishing season. Pearls hadn't been mentioned. Neither had Len.

By the end of the evening, it was as though Archer had never said anything about Hannah's opinion of him. The Donovans talked and laughed with her, washed dishes and tickled the baby with her, and generally made her feel at home.

Until she looked over and saw Archer watching her with icy eyes. No home there. No warmth. Just truth used against her like a sword.

At your service.

Heat snaked through her. She told herself it was anger. She had a right to it. He had embarrassed her in front of his family. He was exactly as she thought: cold and ruthless.

So why did she see him every time she closed her eyes, hear him whispering as his mouth moved over her, need him until she wanted to curl into a ball and cry?

There was no answer for her question but the twisting, gnawing ache that was both lust and something more dangerous, something she fled from even before she admitted to herself that it existed. Yet she kept circling around it like a wary moon orbiting a dark planet. Whatever Archer was or wasn't, he had come halfway across the world when she had asked, had put himself at risk for her, and had given her staggering pleasure.

In return, she had told him that he wasn't fit to be her husband or father to her children in any way but the most basic biological one. Truth wielded like a sword, wielded against a man whose only sin against her had been to help her.

Reluctantly Hannah admitted that they owed each other an apology. Not for the truth, but for the method of telling it.

She unclenched her fists, took a deep breath, and punched number six on the lighted pad.

His voice floated out of the intercom speaker. "Yes?"

"Archer, I—"

"I'll be right there."

The intercom went dead.

Glumly, slowly, she got out of bed. She was enough of a coward that she would rather have apologized via intercom, but she had too much pride to insist on it. She went to the hall door and opened it a crack.

Archer's hand pushed it the rest of the way. He was dressed in a pair of jeans he obviously had just pulled on. They were only half fastened. "Do you need protection?"

"No, I—"

She never finished the sentence. His mouth was over hers, breaking it open, taking it in a kiss as hot as it was deep. His hands kneaded her breasts and plucked at her nipples until her breathing fragmented into moans and her body went slack. His knee pushed apart her legs until she was riding his thigh. Holding her with one arm around her, he used his fingers to bring her to the shattering edge of orgasm. Writhing, breathing brokenly, she demanded that he take her.

He sent her over the edge alone.

While she was still shivering and crying, he put her on the bed, pushed her thighs apart, and opened his jeans the rest of the way. He was fully erect, already dressed for sex in a high-tech condom. Kneeling, he pulled her up his thighs and buried himself in her. Hips pumping, he drove her back to the edge. And held her there.

For Hannah it was like being caught in a wild, hot wave. She couldn't speak, couldn't think, couldn't breathe. She could only tumble out of control, darkness storming around her, blind ecstasy transforming her. Then came the lull between the waves, a lull that never quite let her catch her breath before another wave rolled over her, spinning her out toward the edge of consciousness, building and building and building until she could hold her breath no longer. Then she breathed in ecstasy and drowned.

Another wave came, rising, building, teaching her that she hadn't died. Not yet. She was still alive, still breathing, still feeling the next wave sweep up to her, lifting her, blinding her, ravishing her. This time she rode the sensual wave with primal abandon, turning and balancing, twisting and grappling, taking and demanding until all colors exploded into black and she screamed, drowning again.

And he was the seething, powerful wave she drowned in. He moved over her, inside her, around her. In the savage, glittering darkness that smelled and tasted of sex, her breath sobbed and shattered and re-formed again after each climax.

Finally she was boneless, weightless, spinning and falling, echoes of ecstasy beating in her like a runaway heart. With the last of her strength, she said his name.

"More?" Archer asked.

A shake of her head was all she could manage. Sighing, she reached out to curl up against him.

Her hands found only emptiness. He was already out of her bed, out of her reach, walking away. He didn't take time to dress because he had never taken time to undress.

With trembling hands, she pulled down the silk shirt that was wadded up beneath her armpits while understanding broke over her in a different, colder wave. He had played her like an instrument. No tenderness, no holding; just raw, hot sex, as much of it as she could take.

A stud at her service.

Eyes wide, staring at the ceiling, Hannah remembered the way it had been in Australia. Hot, yes. God yes. Yet there had been tenderness as well as fire, sweetness as well as rending ecstasy.

Archer had understood it before she had. He had told her. *Sex can wait until hell freezes over. Making love, now, that's different.* But then she hadn't understood the difference between having sex and making love with Archer.

She understood it now.

With swift motions she ripped off the borrowed wedding rings and dropped them on the bedside table. It was a long time before she fell asleep, holding on to herself because she had no one else to hold her.

Fire all around and screams echoing. Len dumping Archer's battered, bleeding body at Hannah's feet. The shabby room van-

ished in Len's laughter. She was in the center of a riot with blood all over her hands, her body.

Archer's blood.

It was everywhere. She couldn't carry him, couldn't drag him, couldn't get out of the violence that roared around her, black fire and red blood and screams like exploding glass. He had to get up, wake up, walk. Wake up! WakeupwakeupWAKEUP!

His eyes opened. He looked at her, through her, stripping her to her soul; but he didn't know. He was blind, living only in pain, blood everywhere.

"I'm sorry!" she cried. "I didn't think you would be hurt. I thought you were too hard to ever be hurt."

Then he died and she screamed and screamed, her voice rising and falling, her hand clenched around a broken oyster shell while Len's laughter rolled over her screams and midnight broke like thunder over her, destroying her.

Hannah awoke in a rush, all at once, her heart hammering frantically, her own words echoing in her mind. *I didn't think you would be hurt. I thought you were too hard to ever be hurt.* Cold sweat covered her. Tears blinded her. She couldn't breathe. She shuddered wrenchingly, rolled onto her side, and fought not to throw up.

"Just a d-dream," she whispered through clenched teeth. Holding herself, rocking. "Just a bloody dream. That's all. Len is dead and Archer's alive and the pain in his eyes . . ." Her mouth went dry. Pain like that only existed in dreams. Nightmares. "Archer is all right. Just a dream."

After a few minutes she pushed out of the tangle of sheets and stumbled into the shower, afraid that it wasn't a dream at all. Archer could hurt. Archer could bleed.

She ought to know. She had seen the pain in his eyes.

She had put it there.

Damn you, you're like Len! Great smile, great body, and underneath it all, as cold a bastard as ever walked the earth. It makes everything impossible, even the most simple affection.

Sex and protection, that's all you want from me?

Yes. That's all.

Clammy, shivering, she reached for the water faucet. After a few fumbles she got hot water to rain down over her, washing away the icy sweat. Blindly she reached for the soap that hung on a rope around the shower head. A familiar clean fragrance curled around her. The soap smelled like Archer.

She put her forehead against the cold tile and wept.

Twenty-four

*A*rcher sat in the cheerful breakfast nook and watched the view outside the window as the city slowly, slowly awakened. He was dressed casually—running shoes, jeans, dark blue flannel shirt, and a lightweight waterproof jacket with a zipper running down the front. The only thing not casual about him was the nine-millimeter pistol digging into the small of his back beneath the jacket. It was a cold gun in every sense of the word. No serial number, no history, a leftover from the days he couldn't seem to leave behind.

Damn you, you're like Len! Great smile, great body, and underneath it all, as cold a bastard as ever walked the earth.

He picked up his coffee cup and drained the potent liquid without feeling the heat. Not feeling was another hangover from working for Uncle. Knowing when to cut losses and get out of the game was another. With Hannah, it was too late to cut his losses; he had lost everything of importance already. That left getting out of the game.

Jake held up the coffeepot in silent question. As one, Kyle and Archer held out their cups. Kyle thought longingly of adding milk, but it went against his self-imposed rule: milk for the first cup, and if that didn't get it done, go back to bed or drink it straight and black as hell.

Lianne stared at the table as though it held a cage full of snakes instead of a sketch of the Dragon Moon's floor plan, the surveillance gear that would let the men communicate with each other, and the two cellular phones which would keep her in communication with Archer.

"Okay," she said. "I'll translate via cell if it's required. But Archer, if something goes wrong . . ." She just shook her head and looked at him with worry and love in her cognac eyes.

Archer's hand closed over her much smaller one. "You're right. I didn't think of that. Someone else can translate for me if it's necessary. It probably won't be." A gun cut across all cultural and linguistic barriers, but he didn't think Lianne wanted to hear about it right now. With quick motions he took what he needed from the table, put in the miniature earpiece, and adjusted the throat mike. "Testing."

The two earpieces remaining on the table whispered hoarsely, *"Testing."*

Satisfied, Archer switched off the mike by tapping his throat.

Lianne sighed and rubbed her back through the red silk robe whose ties kept getting shorter every month. "I'm happy to help any way I can. It's just that I'd rather be there so if something went wrong—"

"You're pregnant," Archer cut in.

Kyle and Jake said it just as fast.

Lianne listened to the male chorus and grimaced.

"But Lianne's right about one thing," Jake said, topping off his own cup. "You need some backup inside the building."

"No," Archer said.

"Bullshit," Kyle said flatly. He picked up his own electronic gear, stuffed in the earpiece, and put the throat mike in place. "If Jake or I tried to pull the stunt you've just outlined, you'd have our balls."

". . . balls," croaked the remaining earpiece. Despite Kyle's fine electronic touch, the tonal quality of the equipment sounded like the words were being pushed through gravel.

Archer didn't argue with his brother or the echo. What Kyle

said was the simple truth. Yet there were other simple truths. One of them was that he wasn't going to risk Kyle's or Jake's life to redeem the savage mistakes made by a man they had never met. So he agreed that they would cover the exits—and him—if he had to leave on the run. He didn't want them doing even that, but knew he couldn't keep them at home with Lianne.

"I'm wearing Kevlar underwear, just like Jake," Archer pointed out.

"Over your brain?" Kyle asked politely.

"What brain?" Jake retorted, coldly furious. He knew Archer's chances of going in alone and coming out alive were somewhere between lousy and awful. "Body armor is good, but not going up against the Red Phoenix Triad alone is even better."

"I'll keep my mike open," Archer said. "And the cell phone."

Jake hit his forehead with the heel of his hand. "Shit, why didn't I think of that? I'll be sure to tell Honor that you died before you fucking hung up."

Archer's smile was small but real. "You do that."

Kyle tried another tack. "What should Lianne tell Hannah when she wakes up and finds you gone?"

"I reset the clock in Hannah's room when I went in to get the gun out of the safe." Archer took another swallow of coffee. "If she wakes up at all, she'll think it's two hours ago. Before she knows different, I'll be back with the pearls."

"Pal, you're not coming back," Jake said, screwing the miniaturized transceiver in his ear. He hit the voice switch. "Take it from someone who used to be in the business."

Archer drank more coffee.

Kyle and Jake exchanged a look.

Archer said softly, "Jumping me won't work. I wouldn't pull my punches. You would."

"What if I call April Joy?" Kyle asked.

"You'd better pray I don't come back. Yin is the quickest way to Len's killer."

"So take more time," Jake retorted.

"No." Last night had pushed Archer right to the edge of his

self-control. Beyond it. He was afraid if Hannah asked him for sex again, he would give her what she didn't want from a ruthless bastard like him: love.

"Any particular reason you're in a hurry to die this morning?" Jake asked curiously.

"Hannah wants to get away from the man who reminds her of her husband." One of Archer's hands went to his key chain, where the cold weight of Len's odd ring clanged against keys. "I feel the same way. It's time to clean up the mess the past left and get on with our lives." He had walked away from her once before. He could do it again.

He had to be able to do it again.

"But—" Kyle began.

"No." Archer shoved to his feet with enough force to jolt the solid table. "I'm through talking. There's only going to be one life on the line, and that's mine. If you hear shots, call April Joy and tell her to bury the bodies where no one will find them."

When Kyle would have jumped to his feet, Jake clamped his hand over the other man's forearm. "Let it go, Kyle. You're not going to change his mind."

Kyle looked at his oldest brother, really looked at him, for the first time since Archer had dragged him out of bed and outlined his dangerous plan. Archer was controlled, deadly, balanced on a razor edge of adrenaline. Kyle had never seen his brother like this, even the night they pulled a commando raid on a modern pirate's private island.

"All right," Kyle said quietly. "We're with you, Archer. But I don't like it worth a damn."

Lianne let out a silent breath of relief. Though the brothers loved each other, both were hardheaded and stubborn. So was Jake, for that matter, but he had a longer fuse than Kyle.

"If you don't like it," Archer said, "stay home the way I asked you to."

"No." Kyle's expression was as hard as his brother's.

"Tell us again about that alley door," Jake said. "Is the lock electronic?"

"Yes."

Kyle's smile was like an unsheathed blade. "No worries. If it's electronic, it's mine."

"Leave it alone unless I tell you otherwise," Archer said.

"You sure? I was looking forward to a spot of breaking and entering."

"Good thing you're on the side of the angels," his brother muttered. "You have the soul of a B and E man."

"Speaks the man who can make mechanical locks fall open faster than a sex worker's thighs," Kyle retorted.

Lianne snickered.

"There aren't many mechanical locks left," Archer said. "The world is safe from me."

"Mechanicals, huh?" Jake said. "I always knew you were a retrograde SOB." He pulled the sketch of the Dragon Moon closer. "What about fire escapes, side doors, balconies, that sort of thing?"

"Fire escape in the alley, about here," Archer said, pointing with the same pencil he had used to make the sketch. "Interior balcony here, along the wall of the ground floor, and here, along the north side."

Jake frowned. "That sucks. No way you can sit up front with your back to the wall and still cover that rear balcony. This folding screen will block your view when you're sitting down. You need someone just inside, close to the front door."

"I'll have Kyle outside at the curb. Close enough."

Jake's jaw muscle flexed as he bit down hard on a sarcastic comment. There was no exterior glass in the Dragon Moon for Kyle to look through and warn Archer if someone was moving in on him from the balcony. The café was built like what it was: a gang headquarters. "How long has the triad used that building?"

"Ten years," Archer said. "Maybe fifteen."

"Then they've stripped the interior and rebuilt with all kinds of hidden passages and escape hatches."

"That kind of thing is usually limited to the back rooms."

"Usually isn't good enough when you go in alone." Jake looked at Kyle. "How does your gut feel about this?"

Frowning, Kyle rubbed the back of his neck where the skin tingled as if his body was trying to lift a nonexistent ruff. Though nobody talked about it much, they respected Kyle's hunches. He certainly had learned to—they had saved his life in Kaliningrad. "Damned unhappy, but not dead panicked."

"That's what Honor said when I got up this morning," Jake muttered. "A pity you two couldn't have gotten something useful from your mother's Druid ancestors. Reliable precognition would have my vote."

Archer disagreed. Knowing what would happen wasn't any use when nothing could be done about the outcome. He was going in alone, period. He looked at his watch. "You've got twenty minutes to get there and take up your positions."

Without a word Jake slid from the breakfast nook and picked up the hip length Gore-Tex jacket he had laid carefully on the kitchen counter. Beneath it was a short-barreled pump shotgun.

"What's that?" Lianne asked, spotting the odd shape.

"A cane. The alleys are slippery."

"Jake's covering the back entrance," Kyle explained. What he didn't say was that Jake was going to cover it from the inside, as soon as Kyle got him in past the locks.

Lianne closed her eyes and wished it was two hours from now. Kyle kissed her gently, then less gently, before he grabbed his own jacket and followed Jake to the front of the condo.

The elevator opened. They stepped inside. The doors closed behind them. Jake tapped his throat, turning off the mike. Then he tapped Kyle's.

"Fuck the alley door," Jake said. "He'll never make it that far. I'm going in the front. I'll sit between him and the most obvious source of danger. You're staying at the curb."

"Doing what?" Kyle shot back. "Playing with my dick?"

"Whatever turns your crank." Jake pulled out the shotgun and hooked it into a simple shoulder sling. When he put on his jacket, sling and gun vanished. "Five minutes after I go in, bring the car around. If you hear shots, open the car doors. We'll be in a hurry."

"I don't like it."

"You like Archer's plan better?"

"I'll take the shotgun," Kyle said. "You drive the car."

"You ever worked crowd control before?"

"No, but—"

"I have," Jake cut in. "That's why I'm wearing Kevlar and you aren't."

Kyle opened his mouth, but no sensible argument came to him. *"Shit."*

"Yeah, that about covers it. Let's get the car ready."

"Why bother with it? The Dragon Moon is only three blocks away."

"If you're trading bullets, three blocks is a long way."

The elevators opened. The two men walked out into the garage. Their footsteps echoed. Without a word Jake knelt down and started unscrewing the license plates on his car. When he was finished, he reached into the glove compartment and unrolled a piece of white paper that had big numbers on it and small print. It resembled the temporary registration that a new or used car carried instead of plates. With quick, almost angry motions, he taped the paper to the inside of the rear window.

"You carry that around all the time?" Kyle asked.

"Yeah."

"You're scary."

"Your brother's scary. I'm cautious." Jake pulled car keys from his pocket and threw them to Kyle. "Drive."

"Is that shotgun legal?" Kyle asked as he got behind the wheel of Jake's sport utility vehicle.

"Depends on how charitable the guy with the tape measure is feeling." Jake slammed the door. With quick, sure motions he pulled on surgical gloves.

Kyle didn't ask why. He knew. But he didn't know about the shotgun. "What's it loaded with? Birdshot?"

"Buckshot."

Kyle whistled musically. His gut was feeling better with every passing second. "Buckshot. That stuff will go through interior walls like shrapnel."

"I'm counting on it. That's why you're staying out on the sidewalk. Honor would never forgive me if I shot her favorite brother."

Archer walked out of the condo and into the cold darkness. Against the streetlights, rain flared like tiny comets before arc-ing down into black oblivion. Dawn, when it finally came, would be a dreary affair. He flipped up his jacket hood. Not only did it keep rain off his face, it concealed his features. He couldn't have been more anonymous if he tried.

Since it was downtown, there were a few people moving about. A jail bondsman or a stockbroker leaned against a bus stop, talking fast into a cell phone. A woman darted out of one doorway and into a waiting cab. Other than that, the streets were left to the gentle army of raindrops. The panhandlers who hadn't headed south for warmer turf were still at the local flophouses or missions, soaking up coffee, gospel, and heat before heading out to beg quarters for that first pint of fortified wine.

Archer checked his watch, pulled out his cell phone, and punched in the number he hated to call. He didn't scramble the transmission, because he didn't think the government had the right decoder at their command. Yet.

April Joy must have told her aides to put through anything from Archer Donovan whenever it came in. He was only halfway to the Dragon Moon when she got on the phone.

"This better be good," she said.

"Is Qing Lu Yin one of yours?"

"Son of a *bitch*."

"Did you twist him, or is he yours straight up?"

"Where are you?"

"If Yin is good for murder one, do you still want him?"

A half beat of hesitation, then she said, "Depends on who he did."

"My half brother."

Archer waited. He didn't have to wait long. April wasn't stupid or fainthearted.

"Yin's brother Ling sells us information from time to time, when it can be used against rival triads," she said, "but he isn't ours. Neither is Yin. Red Phoenix owns both of them body and soul. Don't trust Yin."

"Even if you told me he was yours, I wouldn't trust him. He's selling the kind of rainbow pearls men kill to own. Len's pearls."

April thought hard and fast. "What are you going to do?"

"Buy them. One way or another. Has Uncle decided which side of the pearl table you're on yet?"

Silence.

Archer hit the power button on the phone and mentally ran his probabilities again. Knowing that Yin wasn't a U.S. government agent improved the odds of getting out clean.

Uncle made a bad enemy.

A block away from the Dragon Moon, Archer pulled on a pair of surgical gloves, then tugged at his jacket to keep it out of the way of the pistol at the small of his back. The front of the jacket sagged. A spare magazine for the pistol was in one pocket. Cash was in the other. The wad of money was bulkier than the extra ammunition and weighed a lot less.

When Archer was a few buildings down from the Dragon Moon, he punched in the number of the cell phone he had left behind on the kitchen table. This time he turned on the scrambler.

Lianne answered on the first ring. "Archer?"

"Right here. How's the reception?"

"Fine. Or four-by-four or whatever I'm supposed to say."

" 'Loud and clear' works. Stay close."

"I'd like to be closer," she retorted.

"I hear you loud and clear." Archer pocketed the phone and glanced again at his watch. Five fifty-seven. Time to go. He tapped the throat mike to turn it on. "I'm moving."

"One is in place," Kyle said.

"Ditto two," Jake said. "But I'm on the front."

"What?" Archer snarled.

"Kyle's gut liked it that way. So does mine."

Anger whipped beneath Archer's control, but control won easily. It was too late in the game to lose it. "Just keep that damn street sweeper out of sight. You'd give the beat cop a heart attack if he saw that barrel poking out of your jacket."

"Roger."

Archer headed toward the Dragon Moon with the long strides of a wolf pursuing game.

"Who would call at this ungodly hour?" Hannah asked as she walked into the kitchen.

Lianne started so severely that she nearly dropped the cell phone on the table. "Hannah! You're supposed to be asleep."

"My body still doesn't know which way is up," she said, yawning. "Four A.M. or high noon, all the same to me. What are you doing up? Are the twins restless?"

"Not wildly. I'm just, um, a morning person."

"It's hardly morning," Hannah said. "Unless you think that four—" Her words stopped abruptly. She rubbed her eyes and looked again at the kitchen clock. "Six A.M.? The clock in my room said four."

"Want some coffee?" Lianne asked, changing the subject.

It didn't work.

"Six o'clock," Hannah said, appalled. "Ruddy hell! I'm supposed to be—"

"He's here. Ready?"

Both women jumped when the cell phone spoke.

"That's Ar—" Hannah began.

"Quiet!" Lianne interrupted in a fierce, low voice. She snatched up the phone. "Ready."

"Yin is alone at a table about fifteen feet from the street entrance. There's a box big enough to hold the pearls sitting in front of him."

"Thank God."

Archer decided not to mention the table of young toughs sitting between Yin and the front door. Despite their trendy Hong Kong clothes—heavy on colorful silk shirts and black leather jackets—the men might have been just day laborers sitting around drinking tea until it was time to go to work.

And Archer might have been Tinkerbell.

"Get ready to tell Yin a few things," Archer said into the cell phone. "One: I have one hundred and twenty-five thousand in cash for the pearls. Two: I'm not alone. Three: If his hands go under the table, he's a dead man. Four: If anyone else's hands go under the table, he's a dead man. Five: He should pass the word to anyone who might get twitchy. Got that?"

"Yes."

"Go."

When Lianne started speaking Chinese, Hannah knew where Archer was. Spinning around, she ran to her room.

There she dressed in a frenzy, yanking on her jeans, jamming her nightgown—Archer's silk shirt—inside the waistband of her jeans, kicking into her sandals. Still buttoning the jeans, she bolted for the front door. She didn't even notice the cold rain as she ran flat out toward the Dragon Moon. Fury and fear drove her flying feet. Even she couldn't have said which goaded her more—anger at being shut out or the memory of her dream, Archer bleeding and dying in horrible pain.

Poised for whatever might happen, Archer waited, watching Yin while Lianne spoke in rapid Chinese. Yin listened impassively, but he was looking around, trying to spot anyone who might be on Archer's side. No one was sitting in the dreary café but Red Phoenix men.

The front door to Archer's right opened, setting small bells to jingling. He spotted Jake immediately.

"Shit."

"You're welcome," Jake said.

He took a position that put him between Archer and the table where five gang members drank tea. It wasn't the seat that Jake would have preferred, for it didn't command a view of the whole cafe. But it was the best he could do when it came to getting between Archer and the obvious trouble waiting to happen.

Yin started explaining to the five men what was expected of them.

Without taking his eyes from the gang members, Jake worked the pump on the concealed shotgun. The distinctive *rack-rack* of a double-barreled pump shotgun being readied to fire was a lot more effective than any verbal warnings—or orders to attack—that Yin might be relaying.

Five pairs of hands came out onto the tabletop. Though the nails were too long for Western taste, they were clean and nicely buffed. Jake watched them, knowing that whatever the triad members might have on their mind, as long as their hands were still, they couldn't do anything but fume. At a gesture from him, the men scooted together until they sat in a semicircle, facing him across the circular table.

Archer beckoned Yin over to a table closer to the front door.

That seat still left part of the café in a blind spot that neither he nor Jake could cover, but there was nothing to be done for it.

Reluctantly Yin sat still, his hands in plain sight, the box between them. Archer sat down, keeping Yin between him and the table of men. Close up, Yin's black eye and the bruised, oozing gash on his chin looked painful, but Archer didn't waste any sympathy on the man. Triad life was almost as tough on its members as it was on the community of immigrants that were the triad's prey.

Watching Yin every moment, Archer picked up the cell phone and spoke into it. "Tell him if he answers my questions, I'll pay him another twenty thousand in cash, right now. If I find out later that he lied, I'll take it out on the Red Phoenix Triad and let them worry about evening the score with him. Then tell him to translate my message for his friends."

"Hannah got up early," Lianne said. "She—"

"Later," Archer interrupted curtly. "I've got the Red Phoenix boys on the front burner right now. Talk to Yin."

Archer didn't doubt that Lianne's translation would be accurate, but it was nice to see Yin's pallor increase and his glance flick nervously toward the table of men who were pretending to sit casually under Jake's unflinching eyes. Carefully Yin handed the phone back to Archer and nodded several times to indicate that he understood.

When Yin was finished speaking, so did the other men in the room. They looked at Yin speculatively, wondering how much bad luck he could bring down on the triad that was their livelihood, their brotherhood, and their home. One of the five men looked right at Archer and said, "Donovan."

He smiled like a wolf and nodded curtly. The Red Phoenix Triad and the Donovans had clashed before, indirectly. Archer had won.

Knowing that Yin would feel better if he saw money on the table, Archer rapidly counted out a stack of well-used one-hundred-dollar bills. Yin's dark eyes widened and his lips twitched as he kept his own tally. His eyes widened with simple avarice when the count went above one hundred thousand. Not until the stack of bills totaled one hundred twenty-five

thousand dollars did Archer put the much-reduced wad of cash
in his back jeans pocket. When his hand came into view again,
the nine-millimeter was in it. The safety was off. The muzzle
was pointed right at Yin's heart.

"Your turn," Archer said, gesturing to the cheap wooden
box and then to the table in front of him. "Open the box and
hand it over slow and easy."

Yin was working on the box before the translation came
through the cell phone. He took off the thick, dirty rubber band
and opened the lid wide on its hinges. Then he slowly pushed
the box toward Archer.

Without taking his eyes off Yin, Archer ran his fingertips
over the contents. Cool, smooth, round, heavy. He picked one
pearl at random and brought it into his line of sight.

Black rainbows gleamed.

"The pearls are right," Archer said into the phone. "Tell
him to put the rubberbands back around the box and give it
back to me."

While Yin worked, Archer pulled money out of his back
pocket. As soon as Yin pushed the securely wrapped box back
across the table, Archer pulled another thick stack of cash from
his jacket pocket.

Yin's eyes widened with simple greed. Archer fanned ten
hundred-dollar bills on the table. The wad in his hand said that
there was more where that came from. A lot more. Yin looked
at the money hungrily as Archer picked up the cell phone.

"Ask Yin where he got the pearls," he said to Lianne.

Then he held the phone so that the other man could hear.
As he listened, Yin's expression shifted, then shut down. He
shook his head.

Archer added ten more bills to the fan. Two thousand dollars. Three thousand. Ten thousand.

Twenty thousand.

Thirty.

Fifty.

Yin began to sweat.

"Now," Archer said to Lianne, "tell him he has a choice. He
can answer my question or I'll ask his buddies at the next table.
If they answer, they get the prize."

Sweat trickled down Yin's cheeks as he listened. He swallowed and said hoarsely, "Klistin Frin."

Before Archer could sort through the heavy accent, Kyle's voice was rasping in his ear. *"Christ, she's going in the front door!"*

Archer didn't have time to ask who "she" was. Breath sawing, Hannah yanked open the front door and glanced wildly around the room. When she saw Archer—and Jake off to the side, keeping a table full of thugs seated with their hands in sight—she sagged in relief. The nightmare hadn't come true.

"Get out," Archer said flatly.

The five men at the table shifted, but nothing had really changed for them. Jake was still watching them with eyes that gleamed like cut glass. Archer was still seated, his gun on Yin. Unhappily the men settled down.

Hannah squared her shoulders and turned toward Archer. "Not until I see if the pearls are what we're looking for."

"Take the pearls and *get out*," Archer said through his teeth, throwing the box at her.

She caught it and kept walking toward him, needing to be certain that he was all right. A flicker of movement along the wall behind his back caught her eye. Even as her brain registered the fact that there was a gun barrel glinting through a narrow slit, she screamed and launched herself at Archer's shoulders, knocking him over and out of harm's way. Hundred-dollar bills flew up like startled birds.

Though there was no sound of a shot, plaster exploded across the room before Archer hit the floor. Still falling, he pulled Hannah beneath him and brought his gun up, figuring angles on where the hidden shooter might be. It certainly wasn't Yin on the trigger—he had grabbed what cash he could and bolted toward the alley door.

Tile exploded as bullets whined across the floor. Archer grunted, then grunted again as lead thudded against Kevlar. He rolled over and over into the room, taking Hannah with him, trying to get beyond the shooting radius of the gun slit.

"He's in the wall behind you!" she screamed, her voice muffled by his chest.

Archer heard anyway. "Jake! Middle of the east wall, man-high."

Before Archer finished, Jake lifted his foot to the edge of the table and slammed it into the gathered triad members with a quick pump of his leg, scattering them like bowling pins. The instant Archer and Hannah scrambled out of the way, Jake pointed the shotgun toward the wall and triggered both barrels.

Buckshot-chewed wood exploded out in clumps of jack-straws, then fell in eerie silence, because the shotgun blasts had deafened everyone, leaving a violent ringing in their ears. Before the first bits of wood hit the floor, Jake racked two more rounds into place and searched for another target.

Archer yanked Hannah to her feet and all but threw her at the front door. *"Out."*

This time she didn't argue.

Quickly Archer took stock. A stunned silence followed the thunder of the shotgun, but he couldn't count on that lasting. Nothing moved along the ruined wall but a shred of dull red wallpaper. If the sniper had survived, he wasn't giving away his position. Off to one side, five of the Red Phoenix Triad's finest thrashed around on the floor, trying to suck in air through diaphragms that had been paralyzed by the flying edge of a table.

"You go next," Jake said, watching the wall and the struggling gang members.

Archer was already at the front door, his gun trained on the fallen men and his eyes alert for any motion along the walls. "You're covered. Pull out."

Jake shoved the shotgun under his jacket and went through the front door like a man who had nothing more on his mind than digesting a breakfast of dried fish and green tea. He got into the passenger seat of the vehicle that waited, doors open. Hannah was already in back. She clutched the box of pearls in her hands.

Archer slid in next to her and shut the door. "Go."

Then he watched out the back window while Kyle drove quickly into the rain.

Twenty-five

Streetlights whipped by, sending pulses of light over the faces in the car. Jake spoke into the cell phone, reassuring Lianne and Honor.

With fingers that shook, Hannah reached for Archer. He caught her wrists with one hand and held her where she was, across the seat from him. Blood oozed slowly down the collar of his jacket. Adrenaline was an icy fire in his veins. It fed an equally cold rage, a rage born of fear. Hannah could have died. So quickly. So easily.

So finally.

"You're bleeding," she said hoarsely.

"Cuts from flying tile." His voice was as hard as the fingers gripping her wrists.

"I heard bullets hitting you. *I felt them.*"

Kyle's head whipped around. "Archer?" The word was raw with the love of brother for brother.

"Drive. I'm fine." With his free hand, Archer yanked open both his jacket and his dark flannel shirt. Black Kevlar showed through like a wedge of midnight. "Body armor," he said curtly to Hannah. "Jake and I are covered from neck to knees."

"We'll have some bruises," Jake said. He rubbed his shoulder where a dull ache kept time with his heart. "But not to the bone. A silencer really slows down the bullets."

"I didn't know," she said, still shaken. "You could have told me."

"Why? You have less sense than a kid sucking on his thumb. You—"

"That's not—"

"—weren't wearing any armor, didn't have so much as a pocketknife, yet you walked into that triad den like it was a fucking Tupperware party. What in hell were you thinking of? Do you think they wouldn't kill a woman?"

"You!" she said in a low, harsh voice. "I was thinking of you!" Her voice broke as the nightmare bit into her again. "I saw you covered in blood. And the pain in your eyes . . . God, the unspeakable pain." She turned away as far as her captive wrists would let her. Then she stared out her window while shivers went through her like bullets, jerking her.

Archer made a rough sound. Knowing he would regret it, unable to stop himself, he pulled her close, then closer still, wrapping her in his arms. He took a deep, shuddering breath as he drew in the rain fragrance of her hair and let go of the bitter scent of gunfire. "It's all right, Hannah. All of us made it."

She burrowed deeper into his arms and hung on, just hung on, her fingers digging into the Kevlar that had kept her nightmare from coming true. The depth of her relief, of her caring for a man as hard as Archer, should have terrified her.

It didn't. The pulsing horror of the Dragon Moon was still too real to allow room for any other fear.

Lianne and Honor were waiting by the front door of the condo. They held their men for a long, urgent kiss, and only reluctantly released them. Then they stood even closer together than usual, needing the reassurance of physical touch.

"Next time," Honor announced baldly, "I'm going with you."

"We'll burn that bridge when we get to it," Jake said. The

downward slide off an adrenaline jag was no time to argue with a woman you loved. "Is Summer up?"

"She's sleeping like an angel."

He smiled down at his wife. "Help me take a shower, honey."

Honor looked at the grim weariness in Jake's eyes and wanted to cry. Instead, she smiled at him and put her arm around his waist. "Adrenaline overload?"

"Yeah." He hooked an arm around her shoulders. "Too much Seattle coffee will wire you every time."

"Jake," Archer said.

He looked away from Honor. "Yeah?"

"Thanks."

"What for? Hannah's the one who knocked you out of the line of fire."

Honor and Lianne both stiffened.

"I should have been the one with the shotgun," Archer said simply.

"Bullshit. Haven't you figured it out yet?"

"What?"

"No one's Superman. Not even you."

Archer's laugh was as grim and weary as Jake's eyes. He went and brushed a kiss over Honor's cheek. "I knew you had a good man, sis. I just didn't know how good. Take care of him."

Honor let go of Jake long enough to give Archer a hard hug. "I love you."

He ran the tip of his finger down her nose. "I love you, too. Now get out of here before Summer wakes up and spoils your shower."

Honor waited long enough to give Kyle a hard hug and get one in return. Then she and Jake walked away, arms around each other, talking in low voices.

Watching with something close to envy, Hannah leaned wearily against the entry wall. She wondered if the wild hum of adrenaline in her blood would let her sleep before she fell down.

Archer turned to Lianne. The sight of his petite, fierce sister-in-law brought a gentle smile to his lips. "I owe you a big one, Lianne. Thanks."

"As Jake put it so succinctly—bullshit." She stepped close and hugged Archer. "I wish I could have done more. I hated being here, waiting. Listening. Waiting."

"On any operation, communications is the hardest job of all. I was lousy at it."

She glanced up at Archer. The black stubble on his face made him look harder than ever. "I can't imagine you sitting back and relaying messages."

"Like I said, I was lousy at it." He looked at Kyle over Lianne's dark hair.

"Next time," Kyle said bluntly, "I'm wearing the Kevlar and one of you is sitting on his thumb in the car."

"There won't be a next time."

"Does that mean you aren't going after Len's killer anymore?" Kyle's voice was pleasant, but his gold-green eyes were as hard as stone.

Hannah straightened and pushed away from the wall. "That's exactly what it means," she said, but it wasn't Kyle she spoke to. It was Archer. She had come too close to watching him die, watching and knowing that she had put him in the path of the bullets that killed him. "Whatever you thought you owed Len died with him. Take off that armor and go back to your family. Be . . . safe."

"What about you?" Archer asked evenly.

"I'll sell my half of Pearl Cove to whoever wants it."

"Even if it's Ian Chang?"

"I don't care if it's Satan himself. It's over, Archer."

He almost laughed. It wasn't that easy to get out of the game. It never was. "I'll write a check for your half of Pearl Cove."

"No." Her response was instant and certain.

"Why not?"

"People would believe you know the secret of making black rainbows. You'd be a target. Like Len."

"I have more friends than Len did."

Her chin came up and her mouth flattened. "I want you out of this, Archer. All the way out. I have to know that I didn't lead you to your death."

"I don't lead worth a damn. Ask anyone. I'll pay you a million for Pearl Cove."

"I won't sell it to you at any price."

Archer's eyebrows rose. "Fine. Call Ian Chang. He'll buy your half."

"So he can kill you for your half? I'm stupid, Archer, but eventually I learn. I don't want you killed for a handful of bloody pearls."

"According to Yin, Chang isn't the problem."

"What?"

"Just before everything went from sugar to shit, Yin told me he got the pearls from Christian Flynn."

For a moment Hannah's ears rang as though someone had just fired a shotgun ten feet from her head. "Christian? I don't believe it."

Archer could. He had seen Flynn move, felt the calluses along the edge of his palm. "Let's have a look at the pearls."

She glanced down at the box she still clutched in her hands. For the first time she realized that her fingers ached from their death grip on the cheap wood. She stared at the box. At that instant she hated black pearls and everything they stood for.

"Even if you put it all down the garbage disposal, nothing would change," Archer said, reading her expression accurately.

Hannah shuddered. He was right. But if the garbage disposal would have solved the problem, she would have shoved everything down it and smiled while steel ground incomparable black rainbows to dust.

"I need nonincandescent light and a table," she said thinly. "The breakfast nook's light is wrong."

The tight, edgy quality of her voice made Archer ache. "Sell out. Get out. You're too gentle for the game."

"The name of this game is survival. If I'm too gentle for it, I'll bloody well die."

"Hannah." Just that. Her name. It was all he could think of to say.

The line of her shoulders told him it didn't matter what he said. She wasn't going to budge.

"There's a suitable table in my—your—suite," she said, striding down the hall. "I think the light on the night table is fluorescent."

Archer knew it was. Silently he followed her, ignoring the sting from the cuts on his face and the dull aches where bullets had slammed into Kevlar, bruising the much more fragile flesh beneath the high-tech fibers. It was far harder to ignore the rain-wet silk plastered to Hannah's body in a way that told him she wore nothing beneath but skin. He wondered if it was the same beneath her jeans: bare, beautiful skin.

The adrenaline of battle shifted into a different kind of readiness, his body humming with heat and life. While she set up the lamp on the coffee table in the sitting room, he had time to think about how quickly she had dressed, how much she might have left behind. He shifted uncomfortably, wishing that Kevlar shorts stretched like regular underwear.

When she bent over to spread out the pearls, the black silk clung to her breasts, outlining her erect nipples. A drop of water went from the ends of her dark hair to her neck, and from there to the soft, pale hollow of her throat.

Archer swallowed hard and looked away. He fought a brief, bitter battle for self-control. When he could no longer count his heartbeats in his crotch, he focused on the pearls Hannah had spread across the table. Without a sorting screen, he couldn't be certain, but they looked like they went from twelve to sixteen millimeters. There were at least two hundred of the iridescent black gems. Perhaps as many as three hundred.

Even if there had been only one third that number, he had made a hell of a buy.

Stretching the thumb and index fingers of both hands as wide as she could, she gathered the pearls into a group and nudged them along the table, watching how they moved. Her hands were too small to corral all the pearls.

"Here." Archer knelt across from her and helped her to form a bigger rectangle around the pearls with his hands. "Better?"

The huskiness of his voice sent a flick of fire over Hannah's nerve endings. Not trusting herself to look at him, not knowing what she would do if she saw desire in his eyes, she said, "Roll them." .

Together they eased their hands across the table, herding gleaming pearls within the rough rectangle their fingers created. She watched intently. There were no obvious culls, no pearls that lurched or staggered. She divided out one third of the gems.

"Roll those while I watch," she said.

Under Hannah's directions, Archer rolled and spun the pearls while she watched for any less-than-spherical gems. It would have been easier with the slanting table used in pearl-sorting rooms, but this way worked almost as well. Pearls had been sorted by hand long before slanted tables were used.

"Round," she said finally. "Not a wobbler in the lot. No obvious imperfections, but I'll check them individually. The orient is good. Excellent."

"So tell me. Did I buy the Black Trinity wrapped in a cheap rubber band?"

She bit her lip. She very much wanted these to be the Black Trinity, to have it over with. Finished.

She was very much afraid it wasn't.

"Do you want a loupe?" Archer asked.

"Do you have one?"

Instead of answering, he went in the bedroom. There he opened the belly drawer of his desk and pulled out the handy little magnifying glass jewelers used. Cleaning it on his flannel shirt, he went back to the living room.

Without looking away from the pearls, Hannah took the loupe. But she felt the casual touch of his fingers all the way to her toes. There was a fine trembling in her fingers when she opened the glass and put it to her eye.

Archer sat down to take off his wet shoes and socks. His jeans were also wet, but he didn't trust himself to take them off and not reach for her.

For a long time there was no sound but the soft click of pearls being picked up and returned to the table, one after the other. When Hannah was finally finished, she looked up. He was watching her with eyes that were patient and something more, something elemental. Hot. An answering heat snaked through her.

"Well?" he asked.

"No."

"You're certain?"

"Yes. These are the final culls, the ones that were replaced within the strands when more perfect color matches were discovered in each new harvest."

Archer looked down at the deeply iridescent, darkly mysterious pearls. He whistled softly. "These are *culls*?"

"Len's god was a demanding god. Perfection or hell."

"So we're back where we started from," he said.

"Not quite."

"What do you mean?"

"These pearls were kept with the Black Trinity."

Archer went still. "You're sure?"

"As sure as I can be without knowing Len's hiding place. But I can't think he had more than one."

"For all his special pearls?"

She nodded.

"How many does he have?"

"Rainbow pearls?"

"Yes."

"Even after he ground up the less-than-perfect ones, there must have been at least a thousand left, plus the Black Trinity."

"A small hiding place, then. One that is within reach of a wheelchair and proof against professional searches and natural disasters like cyclones."

"I never thought of it that way, but . . . yes."

"That's why you called me, Hannah. To think like Len." His voice was cool and remote.

She watched his long finger gently rolling a pearl back and forth, back and forth. A stark memory ripped through her: a gun barrel poking out of the wall, pointing at Archer and the table where money was stacked like poker chips in a deadly game. There had been no time for her to think, to reason, to plan. There had only been the certainty of his death and her scream tearing her throat as she threw herself at him and knocked him aside.

Then the bullets thudding home, making him jerk against her as they lay tangled on the floor.

Abruptly Hannah stood and combed back her damp hair with fingers that shook. She wouldn't think of what had happened. She couldn't or she would scream again. Somehow she had to force herself to be as calm as he was, to accept that murder was as much a part of life as safety.

Yet when she looked at him, she ached with the emotions that were buried inside her, clawing to be free. His face was shadowed by black stubble and something much darker. His hands were big, hard, and very careful with the fragile pearls. His shoulders were straight despite the weariness that she had seen in his eyes. She wanted to go to him, touch him, kiss him, sink into him even as he sank into her, to forget everything but the heat and vitality of him; and she wanted it so much she could barely stand.

And she feared wanting him. She feared showing vulnerability to a man as hard as Len had been.

The sound Hannah made was small, but it brought Archer's head up sharply. He saw the wet silk painted to her body, saw her tight nipples and soft mouth, her indigo eyes as wild as any storm.

"Don't think about it," he said quietly. "It's over. Everyone is safe."

She simply wrapped her arms around herself and shook her head. She was afraid if she opened her mouth, she would say that she wanted him. Then he would take her down to the floor and show her again the difference between making love and having sex. She didn't know if she was strong enough to survive another lesson.

Yet she needed him until she shook with it.

He stood, went into the bedroom, and came back with a towel as big as a sofa. "You're cold. Dry off and crawl into bed. Your body is still on Aussie time. You can't tell whether you're coming or going."

She tried to unwrap her arms and let go of herself, but it was too difficult. She simply shook her head instead.

"Hannah."

The word was whispered against her temple. The heat of Archer's breath made her tremble.

"You're shaking." He pulled the towel around her and

rubbed briskly. "You need a hot shower, warm clothes, and a long—"

"You," she interrupted. "I need you."

His hands paused. He looked at her eyes. They were wild and wary, hesitant and hungry, so beautiful his heart turned over. "Sex, Hannah?"

She closed her eyes. "If that's what you have, I'll take it."

"What if I have more?"

Tears slid from beneath her thick lashes. She wanted more. And she was terrified of it.

"Never mind," he whispered. "Never mind. It's all right. Just sex."

Even with her eyes closed, she knew Archer was bending down to her mouth. She could feel the shift of his body, the heat of his breath, the sliding pressure of his lips over hers as she opened for him. The taste of him was sweet lightning. The need of him was thunder shaking her.

She grabbed him and pulled him closer still. Her fingers raked down his jacket, only to be caught by holes in the cloth. She went still, remembering, reliving it all again.

"Change your mind?" Archer asked, lifting his mouth from hers.

"Holes," she said raggedly. "There are holes in your jacket. From the bullets."

He saw the stark memories in her eyes, felt fear turning her pliant flesh to stone. With a few swift movements he peeled off his jacket and tossed it aside. He was more careful removing the gun and holster, but no less quick. When he reached for his dark flannel shirt, her hands were already there, tearing away cloth that also carried neat, horrifying holes. Her strength surprised him. Her need stopped his breath.

The Kevlar defeated her. It had no buttons, no zippers, no surface to tear.

"Like this." Archer took her hand, showed her, watched her rip Velcro fastenings apart until he wore nothing but briefs.

Then he wore nothing at all.

The humming sound of approval she made as she cupped him stripped away his control as certainly as she had stripped away his clothing. He no longer tried to control the adrenaline, the need, the desperation for her. With swift, casual power he knelt and peeled her jeans down to her ankles. That was when he discovered that he had been right. She hadn't taken time to put on underwear.

He pulled her hard against his mouth, then made a deep sound in his throat. She tasted as hot and reckless as he felt. The twisting motions she made trying to kick out of her jeans opened her to him even more. He took it all, demanded more. Heedless, helpless, she gave it to him, too shocked by the searing demands of his mouth to do more than wonder that she had lived so long and never known this way to love.

Before her feet were free of her jeans, he drove her ruthlessly to the first climax. When her knees buckled he didn't release her. He followed her down to the floor, opening her even more while cries rippled and she writhed and he took, he gave, he demanded, he worshiped; and she came until she couldn't even draw breath to scream.

It wasn't enough.

Fighting to breathe, she reached for him, trying to draw him up her body, needing what he hadn't yet given to her.

He pinned her where she was, on her back, her legs over his shoulders. Her eyes opened wild and blind as he fitted himself to her and went in deep, hard. With quick, powerful motions he measured himself and her until his name came from her lips with each ragged breath and she convulsed around him, a slick satin fist demanding that he give everything he had to her. Body rigid, shaking, he bared his teeth and gave himself to the endless, pulsing violence of his own release.

Archer's sudden, slack weight on Hannah sent another shimmering wave of pleasure through her. With a hunger that she didn't understand, she stroked his back and shoulders and hips, memorizing the feel of him in her arms. When his breathing finally settled into a normal rhythm, he started to shift his weight off her. She wrapped herself around him and hung on.

"More?" he asked.

She shook her head and didn't loosen her grip at all.

"Not ready to be alone yet?" he guessed.

She nodded.

"I promised myself a nice long shower," he said. "Best thing for bruises. How about you?"

"Now that you mention it . . ." She winced. "I landed under you in that ruddy café."

"I put you there." He rolled over slowly, taking her with him. "It was the only way I could protect you."

Her breath stopped, then resumed with a husky sound. He was still buried deeply in her, filling her. "I don't want you to do that anymore."

"This?" he asked, deliberately stroking himself deep.

"No. Putting yourself in danger to protect me."

"Does that mean you're going to stop protecting me?" Archer asked.

"It's not the same thing."

"Wrong answer."

"It's the only one you're going to get."

"Same here."

"What does that mean?" she asked. Then she shivered when he lifted his hips against her with a slow, rolling motion. "You're trying to distract me."

"Is it working?"

She bit her lip against admitting it, but the kick of her heart against his mouth gave her away. He smiled, then groaned when she slipped through his arms and stood up.

"Let me take care of you, Archer," she said, holding out her hand. "Just this once. Let me."

Without a word he followed her into the shower. When the water was beating down hot enough to cook, he sighed and relaxed, letting the water take the worst of the aches from his body. Then her hands flowed over him, bringing a different kind of ache; not pain but something deeper, a pleasure whose piercing sweetness was like silver lightning stitching through his soul. She did no more than soap him, rinse him, sleek her hands down him to take off the excess water—and he felt as though he had walked into a bare electrical wire.

She turned away, shutting off the water. When she faced him again, he couldn't conceal the vital hardening of his body, the blunt physical need that made her eyes widen. Hunger poured through her like a firestorm. She took his hand and led him toward the bed. The coolness of the room after the steamy shower made her shiver. She didn't even notice it. At that moment, nothing existed for her but Archer.

"I didn't know if you still would—" she began, but her breath backed up before she could finish.

The smokiness of her voice and her eyes made him feel like he had been stroked from head to heels. "If I would what?"

"Want. Like me."

His smile was a razor acceptance of the pain that would come when she no longer wanted him. "When it's you, Hannah, I'll want until I can't. And then I'll still want."

"Then let me," she whispered.

"What?"

"Nothing. This. Everything."

She tasted his chin, his shoulders, his nipples, the median line of his body where water had gathered and slid down past his waist. And like water, she flowed down him. Her mouth was open, a heat that healed even as it burned. He gave an involuntary shudder when her tongue traced his erection.

"I'm told men like this. Do you?" Hannah asked.

"Yes. But it's not necessary unless you—" his breath ripped and his head spun as she sucked lightly on him "—like it, too," he finished hoarsely.

"I don't know." Her tongue swirled around him. "I've never done this before, just as I'd never had a man love me the way you did." She dipped her head again. Found him again. Murmured even as she circled him. "I think . . ." She closed her mouth fully over him, lingered, learned, memorized the heat and pulse of life in him, took him deeply and lost herself, tasted the salt of creation. Slowly, slowly, she released him. "Yes, I like it. A lot."

The pleasure on Hannah's face as she bent to caress him again made Archer fight for the control that she stripped from him so effortlessly. He lay on his back, fingers digging into the bedcovers. As the sultry tugging of her mouth consumed him, he wondered if she had any idea of what she was doing to him.

"You keep that up and you're going to make me come," he said finally, raggedly.

She looked up and his breath fragmented in a groan; her

eyes were heavy lidded, as sensual as her mouth caressing him, and her nipples were drawn into hard, hungry peaks. Clearly she liked arousing him, pleasuring him.

"I'd rather be inside you," he said thickly. "But it's your call, sweetheart."

"Would you mind?"

"Whatever you want," he said simply, closing his eyes, giving himself to her. "However you want it."

He felt her weight shift on the bed until she was astride him. She guided him home, taking him inside her with a slow, slow motion of her hips that made the world go a radiant kind of black all around him. Hot black. Deep and sweet and dangerous. Without knowing it, he groaned.

She heard. Need pricked her with exquisite claws. Shivering, she gave him what she couldn't hold back, took from him what she needed to survive. With every breath, every heartbeat, she kissed him, her mouth open and lazy. Forehead, eyelids, lips, neck, shoulders, everything she could reach without losing the slow, complete rhythm of giving and taking and needing and sharing.

And then she felt him change, sensed the rigid tension and the hot surge deep within her body, his strength given to her without hesitation, her name broken on his lips, and the elemental pulses that were both his and her own. She trembled with him, around him, in a long, shivering consummation that was all the more shattering for its tenderness. Boneless, spent, she sprawled the length of his body and waited to find out if she was still alive.

As the sweat cooled on their bodies, Archer shifted.

"No," Hannah whispered, wrapping her arms around him. "Don't leave me."

"Don't worry."

Leaving her was the last thing on his mind. That would come later, and with it would come the kind of pain he didn't want to think about. He grabbed the down comforter, wrapped them up in it like a sleeping bag, and drew her so close he couldn't take a breath without tasting her. It was the same for her, breathing him in, tasting him, holding him. With a long sigh, she slid into sleep.

She didn't fear her dreams now.

Twenty-six

The ringing phone dragged Archer out of deep sleep. After a moment of fumbling, he realized that he and Hannah were cocooned in a down comforter. He wriggled until he could free an arm and reach blindly for the phone. Hannah murmured and followed the heat of his body until she was covering him like a second blanket. As he lifted the receiver, he decided that he really liked the feel of her snuggled against him from his chin to his heels. The only thing that would have been better was being inside her at the same time.

"Yeah?" Archer said into the receiver.

"Slick, we need to talk."

Archer didn't need to ask who was calling. Only one person called him *slick* in just that impatient tone of voice: April Joy. His mind cleared instantly. "When and where?"

"What would you say to green tea at the Dragon Moon?"

"No, thanks."

"No shit." She laughed curtly. "My office. Now."

"My office," Archer corrected. "Thirty minutes."

"Your office. Fifteen minutes. Bring Hannah McGarry."

338

April hung up. Hard.

Archer put the receiver back in its cradle without disturbing Hannah, who was still lying on top of him like a cat on the hood of a warm car. And, catlike, she was watching him with big, curious eyes.

"Who was that?" she asked.

"The person who supplied us with passports and clothes in Australia."

Hannah blinked. "And now?"

"It's payback time." He kissed the corner of her mouth. "Much as I'd like to be ravished again, I'm afraid I'll have to go."

She smiled slowly, remembering just how much fun it had been to have him at her mercy. "I'm going with you."

"I want to keep you as far away from Ms. Joy as possible."

"You know what Len used to say?"

"No."

"Put your wishes in one hand and piss in the other and see which fills up first."

Archer smiled thinly. "Vintage Len. All right, Hannah. Get dressed. April Joy mentioned bringing you. She'll be in a better mood if I look like I'm cooperating."

Hannah started to slide off him, then stopped when his big hands fitted themselves to her buttocks. He gave a deep, slow squeeze that had her breath wedging and fire licking out from her core.

"Kiss me," he said. "Hard and fast. Then run like hell for the shower."

Even though Donovan International's headquarters in Seattle was the twin building across the courtyard from the residential condos, Hannah and Archer were late. She hadn't stopped with one kiss.

He hadn't stopped at all.

"Good morning, Mitchell," Archer said to his assistant. Mitchell Moore had worked for Donovan International for fifteen years. Ten of those years had been as a field supervisor on various mines around the world. After a mine caved in on him, he was given a choice between retirement at disability pay or using his organizational skills as Archer's assistant. Two years ago he had been offered a promotion to coordinator of overseas mining. He refused, saying that working with Archer was as close to exciting as desk jobs got. Archer had been so relieved that he gave Mitchell a 50 percent raise. "Did your wife like the opera?"

"Good afternoon, sir, and yes, thank you. Verdi is a favorite of hers." The emphasis on *hers* was just enough to tell everyone that Verdi wasn't Mitchell's favorite way to spend an evening.

"Is it afternoon?" Surprised, Archer looked at his watch. "So it is. Next time the tickets will be for a Sea Hawks game."

"There is a god," Mitchell said under his breath.

Hannah bit her lip to keep from laughing. Archer's secretary winked at her. The wink transformed him from a proper martinet into a rogue wearing a pale blue shirt, a conservative maroon tie, and a stainless steel watch with a mirror face.

The fax machine beeped a delivery warning. Mitchell spun his wheelchair and reached for the sheets that were piled up in the receiving tray.

"A Ms. April Joy is waiting for you downstairs," Mitchell said as he scanned the first page of the fax. "She claims she has an appointment. As you weren't expected to come in today, I told her I couldn't guarantee your presence. She wasn't happy." He dropped the page back into the tray. "The fax will wait until you're back from your emergency trip to Australia, whenever that might be."

"The emergency has moved to Seattle. Send April up in two minutes," Archer added, not answering his assistant's unspoken question about how long the emergency might last. "Coffee for three."

"She isn't alone."

Archer didn't move, but he changed. The easy humor was gone. In its place was cold readiness. "Who?"

"A man called Ian Chang."

That answered one question: Archer now knew who Uncle Sam was backing in the pearl sweepstakes. What he didn't know was why.

"Observations?" Archer asked quietly.

Mitchell wheeled back to face his boss. "If they're friends, it's not an easy relationship. Mr. Chang looked like he would rather have been somewhere else. Anywhere else. Ms. Joy could have etched glass with the edge of her tongue. Will you be needing the lawyers, or is Uncle Sam going to behave?"

"I'll buzz you if it gets sticky."

The phone rang. Mitchell picked it up. "Archer Donovan's office." He began reading the fax again. "I'm sorry, an emergency called him out of the office. Perhaps I could help you."

As Archer led Hannah through a door at the side of the office, she looked back over her shoulder at his assistant. Mitchell winked again. She winked back, drawing a wide smile from him.

Archer's office had a wall of windows overlooking Elliot Bay. A big green-and-white ferry was working its way across the wind-scoured water. Clouds revealed part of the Olympic Mountains and concealed the rest. The city gleamed white and shiny black in the aftermath of a cleansing rain.

The office itself contained all the standard executive appointments—large polished desk set at right angles to the view, big leather chair, a grouping of sofas around a low table, a wet bar. Some of the touches weren't standard. One of Susa's powerful, compelling landscapes hung on the wall opposite the desk, where Archer could enjoy the painting every time he looked up from work. The yellows, oranges, reds, and brooding purple of the sunset painting were repeated by a trio of free-form glass sculptures that graced the low table in front of the couches.

"Beautiful," Hannah said, running her fingertips over glass. "Hot to the eyes, cool to the touch."

"I like the sculpture in your house better. Couldn't stop touching it. Like you this morning."

Startled, she looked up at him. "Do you mean that?"

"About touching you?"

She smiled but shook her head. "No, the sculpture."

"Yes."

"Thank you. I threw away all the rest that I did, but I kept that one even though Len laughed at me."

"You created that?"

She shrugged. "*Created* is a big word for a bad carving."

"Created is the right word for that sculpture."

For a moment she looked at him, measuring the truth of his words. "You mean it."

"Of course. Why are you surprised?"

"Try shocked. Len couldn't say enough bad things about my carvings."

I'm not Len. But the savage thought went no further than Archer's mind. He accepted that Hannah saw Len every time she looked at his half brother. Nothing Archer did seemed to change that. Much of what he did made it worse. "Len was wrong about a lot of things."

Archer put his hand under her chin and kissed her slowly, thoroughly, trying not to think about how much longer she would want him. Lust was a hot, quick emotion. Love was hotter, and lasted as long as there was breath. That was how long he would want her. Thinking about the difference in their needs would only ruin whatever time they had together, so he put away that knowledge and concentrated on the woman in his arms.

"No wonder Susa looked daggers at me when I told her to forget having you as a daughter-in-law," he said, barely lifting his lips from Hannah's long enough to get out the words. "She had you pegged for a fellow artist."

"Ruddy hell," she muttered, embarrassed. "Your mother hangs in museums. I've nowhere near her talent."

"Bull dust."

She smiled, then laughed out loud and kissed him full on the mouth. "I don't believe a word of it, but thank you. It's nice to know I'm not the only one in the world who likes to pet wood."

"The only thing that feels as good beneath my hands as that sculpture is you."

Hannah's breath shortened. She remembered waking up, being pulled over him, and his long fingers sinking into her hips.

"Are you thinking about what I'm thinking about?" Archer asked huskily.

"I hope so."

He gave a crack of laughter and reached for her even as she came up to meet him.

When April Joy walked into the office she saw a long-limbed woman wrapped around Archer like a jungle vine. He was wrapped around her just as tight. April hadn't believed it when Ian Chang had told her Archer and Hannah McGarry were lovers.

She believed it now.

"Full points to you on that one, Ian," April said sardonically. "If they were any closer, it would take a surgical team to separate them. I didn't know he had it in him. Or should I say, in *her*?"

When Hannah stiffened, Archer broke the kiss and said very softly, "Follow my lead, okay?"

She hesitated, then nodded, watching April Joy uneasily. The woman was petite, beautifully formed, with raven hair and matching eyes, delicate Chinese features, and a way of moving that could set fire to brick. The crimson wool suit she wore was both elegant and severe. Though there was no badge in sight, she wore authority and ruthless intelligence the way other women wore perfume.

"What's on your mind?" Archer asked April.

"How to make the kind of pearls Yin's brother is dying for," she said coolly. "That would be the merry widow's department, I believe."

"You knew Len," Archer said, his voice hard. "You will apologize to Hannah for that crack."

"It's not necessary," Hannah said quickly.

April's smile was as hard as Archer's voice. She turned to Hannah. "I'm sorry your husband was a prick. If he had been mine, I would have put him under years ago and danced on his grave. Now, how do you make those damned black pearls?"

"I don't know."

"Bullshit."

"Wrong," Hannah retorted.

"Prove it," April said.

"How can she prove a negative?" Archer asked.

"Good question, slick. I'm waiting for an answer."

Chang looked at Hannah, who was even now flushed from Archer's arms. It galled Chang, but he didn't allow it to get in the way of business. "How do you think Len got his black rainbows?"

"I don't know. He never told me."

"Once I got past the lick-me lips and ball-breaking ass, I learned that you're a very bright lady," Chang said coolly. "I want your best guess."

Archer gave Chang a look that had April's hand sliding into her neat black purse.

"I suspect some kind of cloning of the mantle material," Hannah said. The neutral tone of her voice said it wasn't the first time Chang had talked about her body.

"Explain," April said.

"When we seed an oyster," Hannah said, "we carefully pry open the shell and make an incision in the living flesh. That's where the seed goes. With it we put in a bit of living mantle—the flesh that lines the shell and deposits nacre—from another oyster. It's the bit of introduced mantle that starts the process of pearl formation around the implanted seed."

"So you think the secret was in the bit of mantle he inserted, which told the oyster how to produce the rainbow blacks?" Chang asked.

"You told me to guess," Hannah said. "That's one of my two best guesses. The second possibility is that Len cloned the experimental oysters himself and used mantle from sacrificed experimental oysters for seeding."

Frowning, Chang absently shot the cuffs of his creamy linen shirt. The heavy wool and silk blend of his suit was an intense indigo that almost matched Hannah's eyes. The realization annoyed him.

"I know Len raised the experimental oysters himself," Hannah added. "They were never wild shell. That's why I lean toward the second possibility."

"Cloning?" April asked.

Hannah nodded. "It would explain the narrow color variation among all the experimentals."

"Coffee," Mitchell said from the door.

"Bring it in," Archer said.

Mitchell wheeled over, put the tray on the low table next to the unusual glass vases, and looked at his boss.

"I'll take it from here," Archer said. "Thanks. If anyone calls, I'm still in Australia."

"Is Ms. Joy here?" Mitchell asked.

"Ms. Joy," April said distinctly, "is not here. You've never heard of her."

"Mr. Ian Chang," Mitchell said, "is he here?"

"Who?" April retorted.

Mitchell nodded and rolled out, closing the door behind him.

While Archer poured coffee, April looked around the office. She tried not to stare at the vivid landscape, but couldn't help it. Outside of a museum, it was as close as she had ever come to a Susa Donovan painting.

"You can doctor your own coffee," Archer said, indicating the tray of sugar, cream, cinnamon, and various other spices.

April ignored coffee and additives alike. "What happened to the pearls you bought from Yin?"

"Did I buy pearls from him?" Archer asked, sipping coffee made the way he liked it—hot and very dark.

"Don't go sideways on me, slick. We both know where you and Hannah spent the morning."

"Since when is sleeping late a crime?" Hannah asked.

"Sleeping isn't. Neither is screwing. Sawed-off shotguns are." April flicked a black glance at Hannah. "You have guts, Ms. McGarry. Not much sense, but real guts. What's it like to love someone enough to die in his place?"

Hannah went pale. She didn't want to think about the dream she had had, or the instant early this morning when she had been certain that Archer would die if she didn't do something. She hadn't considered the implication of her action at the time, her reckless disregard for her own safety.

She didn't want to consider the implication now. It frightened her as nothing else had but the thought of Archer's death.

"She would have done the same for a stranger," Archer said curtly. "That's just the way she is."

"Saint Hannah?" April shrugged. "Whatever you say, slick. But I say you're wrong." She cocked her head slightly to the side, studying both Archer and Hannah for a long minute. "Okay, we'll try it your way. If that doesn't get to the bottom line in one hell of a hurry, we'll do it my way."

Archer waited, revealing nothing of his feelings. The thought that Hannah had chosen to put herself in the line of fire to save him both angered him and moved him as nothing ever had in his life.

"Two big white guys walked into the Dragon Moon shortly after six this morning," April said calmly. "Yin is drinking tea, counting money in his tiny little mind, and holding stolen black pearls. Five of his triad brothers are sitting around a nearby table scratching their balls. A few minutes later, a tall white woman walks in and throws herself at one of the white men's head. If she'd done the smart thing and jumped the other way, his head would have been blown off and we wouldn't be having this conversation. You hear me, slick?"

"I hear you." He glanced at Chang. "You look like you've heard it all before. Do you like green tea and dried fish for breakfast?"

Chang simply watched him with clear, clever black eyes.

"The man and the woman go down in a tangle while someone keeps firing a pistol," April said. "Jake Mallory—excuse me—the second white guy rams a table down the throats of the five triad goons and cuts loose with a sawed-off shotgun. It chews up a wall and a good chunk of Yin's brother, Ling, who was too stupid to know the difference between cheap paneling and body armor. The white folks leave, taking the pearls and leaving the money—unmarked, nonsequential hundred-dollar bills, by the way. The getaway car is driven by another big white guy. A blond. No plates on the car. No prints on anything at the café. No tracing the money. A clean job all around. You still with me, slick?"

He nodded casually, but he pulled Hannah closer. The fine trembling in her body made him angry. She had been through enough in the past week. She didn't need April's caustic summary of the few bloody moments in the Dragon Moon café.

"Okay," April said. "Uncle doesn't give a rat's fried green ass about what happened in some dirtbag triad cave. Even if Ling dies, he wasn't that useful. We wanted to have a show-and-tell with Yin, but he grabbed the first westbound plane he could and headed straight for Hong Kong. The Chang family is going to find him for us."

"I'm happy for you," Archer said blandly.

"I want those pearls."

"Why?"

"That's not on the table."

"What is?"

"Hand over the pearls and Uncle will be deaf, dumb, and blind on the subject of what happened in the Dragon Moon this morning."

"As you pointed out," Archer said, "it was a clean job. Put something more on the table."

April's eyes narrowed to fierce slits. "One of these days, big boy, you're going up to your lips in fresh shit."

"I've been there. That's why I'm here. If you want me to find those pearls for you, you'll have to pass the word that Hannah McGarry is off the table. No exceptions. Not even Uncle."

April raised sleek, black eyebrows. "The only way she's taken off the table is if she tells all she knows about making those damned pearls."

"I don't know anything," Hannah said curtly. "If you knew Len, you know how secretive he was."

"You were his wife."

"I was his color matcher. I wrote out the bills. I ordered supplies. That's it."

April started to say something cutting, then looked at Archer. He had the appearance of a man thinking hard and deep. "Think out loud, slick."

He shrugged. "I'm trying to imagine Len having the patience, the training, and the vision to breed and then clone a special strain of oysters."

"So?" April demanded.

Hannah was shaking her head. Patience and finicky techniques hadn't been Len's style.

"Not Len," Archer said simply. "As for cloning . . . no. He never even finished junior high. He wouldn't have had the first idea how to begin cloning anything. At least, he wouldn't have before the accident that put him on wheels for the rest of his life."

"He didn't develop patience, kindness, or a curious mind

after the accident," Hannah said. "If anything, it was the opposite. He shut down, not opened up."

April didn't argue the point. Len's file had been brutally clear on his limitations as an agent and human being. "Ian?" she asked.

"I didn't know Len before his accident. After, he was a very clever bastard with the devil's own genius for making trouble. He could play people off against each other better than any diplomat. People didn't like him, but they damn well paid attention to him. Including me."

Hannah made a weary gesture. "Len hadn't finished junior high, but that didn't mean he was stupid. Especially about what made people tick."

"Yeah," April agreed. "He had a hell of a jugular instinct."

"From you, that's quite a compliment," Archer said.

Her smile showed a lot of neat white teeth. "I could say the same of you."

He turned back to Hannah. "Beyond the usual machinery needed for running a cultured-pearl operation, did you have any lab equipment at Pearl Cove?"

"Nothing different from anyone else in the business."

"You're certain?" April asked.

"I did all the buying. I would have noticed if we had exotic equipment."

"How about the experimental oysters?" Chang asked. "Did you see any difference in them?"

"Just the pearls they produced. There were normal in every other way. In fact, it was a problem."

"What do you mean?" April demanded.

"When you breed your own shell—oysters—you have to keep breeding back to wild shell or the strain goes bad and dies out. But when Len bred back, he lost the mutation that made rainbow pearls. At least, he must have. It's the only explanation for the fact that he let the strain go weak when it should have been easy to fix by breeding back."

April looked at Chang, who nodded. "Every pearl farmer knows that strains of captive shell go bad after a few years," he said. "We're working on the problem in Tahiti and Australia, but we're not making much progress." He turned to Hannah.

"So, whether induced or natural, it was a mutation that made the rainbow shell?"

Hannah shivered at the intensity in Chang's eyes. Like Len. Obsessed. "That's my guess. There's a huge natural color variation in oyster nacre. The black rainbows are just one more color on the spectrum. It would be more surprising if the mutation *hadn't* occurred."

"Did Len ever say how he got onto the rainbows?" Chang asked.

"He was chasing them when I first found him ten years ago," Archer said. "He was the reason I became interested in pearls."

"Chasing them how?" April said.

"Following rumors. Twisting informants. Buying secrets when he couldn't get them any other way."

"Where?" Chang asked.

"From the Gulf of Siam to the Arafura Sea. The riot that injured Len started when he trashed a smuggler who operated outside of Kupang. The man was a raider, not a pearl farmer. He didn't want to tell Len where he got the special black pearls." Archer shrugged. "My guess is he finally told. By the time I got to Len, the smuggler was dead and Len was damned close to it. But he had a smile on his face and a black rainbow clenched in his fist."

"That fits," Hannah said. "Sometimes, when Len got really drunk, he would scream that the bloody black rainbows had put him in a chair and the bloody things would put him right again."

"How?" April asked.

"He believed in miracles," Archer said simply.

April muttered something under her breath.

Chang thought about miracles and Len, and nodded slowly. "Pearls have a long tradition of being used as medicine. Even today, in India, ground pearls are used to cure rickets. Quite effective, I'm told."

"Paraplegia is a long way from rickets," April said sardonically.

Archer looked at her. "What would it take to convince you that Hannah doesn't know how to grow black rainbows?"

April glanced at Chang.

Suddenly he appeared both weary and impatient. "I told you. I told my father. The more I looked at it, the less I thought that Hannah knew Len's secrets. Not before he died. Not after. He didn't trust her, and she isn't clever or devious enough to hide a secret that big."

Hannah wondered if she had been insulted or complimented. Both, probably.

Silence stretched while April considered and rejected various scenarios. It didn't take her long to choose one. "Okay, slick. Here's the deal. Chang will set a price and both of you will sign over everything you own at Pearl Cove to a person I'll name. Lock, stock, and barrel. Stuff you know about and stuff you don't. I'll put out the word that you and Hannah are off the table."

"You'll do more than that," Archer said evenly. "You'll make it clear that anyone who goes after Hannah goes after Uncle Sam."

April didn't like it, but she accepted it. "Agreed."

"Hannah?" Archer asked.

"I'll sign over everything except the Black Trinity."

"So it's real," Chang said eagerly. "I'll buy it from you. Top price."

"It's real," Hannah said. "I don't have it to sell."

"Why not?"

"Len hid it. We've found other rainbows, but we haven't found the Black Trinity."

"Did he bury it somewhere in Pearl Cove?" Chang asked her.

"If his murderer didn't take it, it's still in Pearl Cove. Except for one trip to Roti just after we bought Pearl Cove, Len never left home."

Silently Archer noted that neither Chang nor April appeared surprised by the statement that Len had been murdered. Nor were they interested. But both of them were quietly making plans for a trip to Roti, which wasn't that far from Kupang, which might, just might, hold the secret of the black rainbows.

"Buried treasure," April said, her voice ripe with irritation. She looked at her watch, mentally reshuffling demands for the rest of the day. One of her agents was about to get a rude awakening and a ticket to one of Indonesia's less delectable seaside villages. "Fine, whatever, keep the Black Trinity if you dig it up. The rest is Uncle Sam's. That includes Len's computer." She looked straight at Archer.

He nodded. "You'll get it after we sign the papers."

"I'll have them to you in an hour," April said.

"And you'll put out the word right now," Archer said.

"You're pushing, slick."

"It's what I'm best at."

She smiled in spite of herself. "True fact. I'll put out the word."

"Done," Archer said, holding out his hand.

April hesitated, then gripped his hand hard. "Don't disappoint me on this one. I'd hate to cut off your cock just when you're enjoying it again."

Twenty-seven

One does not learn the skills involved
At the drop of a hat.
It's the slow-learned skills in the depths of love
That I'm working at.
Lady Nakatomi
JAPAN, EIGHTH CENTURY

BROOME, AUSTRALIA

Though Hannah felt as if she had been away for months, Pearl Cove hadn't changed. The ocean was still a restless turquoise that was sculpted by wind. The sun still piled clouds upon clouds until the afternoon sky became a sullen quicksilver lid holding in the summer's tropical heat. Stripped down to shorts, tank top, and sandals, she and Archer looked very much at home on the sultry margin where salt water met land.

Hannah didn't feel at home. All the workers had left except Coco, who had stayed on to pack up some of the things in the main house. Hannah couldn't wait to leave Pearl Cove. Every time she looked at the beach, she saw Len there, his ruined legs drifting like pale ribbons on the water.

Shivering, she turned away from the sea.

Archer guessed her thoughts from the grim line of her mouth. "You should have stayed in Seattle. There's nothing in Pearl Cove for you but bad memories."

Then there was Christian Flynn, who had murdered Len. But Archer wasn't talking about that anymore. He was tired of arguing with Hannah. The time he had left with her could be measured in hours. He didn't want to spend them wrangling over the past that shadowed his present life like a curse echoing through time.

"I'm with you every step," Hannah said. "Until it's finished."

"Stubborn," he muttered.

"And you aren't?"

"I'm soft as the inside of an oyster."

"Soft?" She laughed and wanted to reach out to him, but she kept her hands clenched at her sides. If she asked, he would do . . . anything. If she didn't ask, he did nothing.

At your service.

She told herself that was what she wanted, all she could accept, that there was no future for her with Archer. Yet every time she repeated the words in her mind, time bent back on itself and *she was standing on a street corner in Rio with no money, no hope, nothing but night coming down on her like thunder.* The flashback was so intense she could smell the cooking fires and hear the liquid syllables of Portuguese as prostitutes called out to men. Staring out over the wild Australian land, she saw only cardboard shanties clawing up Rio's steep sides.

She wondered if she was finally going crazy. Smoke from city fires shimmered and twisted, and settled in a plume of red dust raised by Christian Flynn's car as he roared down Pearl Cove's road.

Savagely, futilely, Hannah wished that she had the power to change what would happen next. But she didn't. Like Len, Archer did what he pleased no matter what other people wanted.

With eyes the color of steel, Archer watched dust boil up as Flynn's car raced toward Pearl Cove.

"Did April say anything more when you sent Yin's pearls along with the computer?" Hannah asked. Her voice was like her body, tight, held against a blow that she couldn't see but knew was coming anyway.

"April was too busy trying to get a grip on the Red Phoenix Triad to make polite conversation."

"Is that why she helped us?"

"It sure as hell wasn't charity. That's also why she took the Chinese side in the trade. The Chang family doesn't know it, but they'll be her door into the triad. Or they may know it and figure they'll find out more from her than they'll give away. Either way, money is on Ms. Joy. Anyone who rides that tiger will get eaten alive."

Hannah almost smiled despite the chills that kept rippling over her skin. In her mind, bullets echoed and she woke up screaming that *Archer couldn't die, she couldn't bear it, she never meant to kill him.*

But in the dream he died, she had to bear it, and she had killed him.

Without really intending to, she went to Archer, put her arms around him, and just held on. Fearing him, fearing *for* him, needing him . . . she was being torn apart. Only when he held her did she feel anything like hope.

He stroked her hair and wished to the soles of his feet that he could take away the pain of the past. But he couldn't. All he could do was bring Len's killer to justice and then walk away, giving Hannah the peace she had earned at such cost. In time she would get over the nightmares that included both Len and himself.

In time, maybe he would even get over her. But he didn't believe it. He had spent years loving her without knowing it. Now he knew. Knowing didn't help the pain.

"It's almost over," he said softly.

She nodded against his chest, but she didn't let go until she heard a car door slam.

"If it turns nasty," Archer said, "remember your promise. Whatever you do, don't get between us."

"But—"

"Hannah."

She looked up at him with eyes that were full of fear and just as determined as his. "Let it go," she said harshly. "Just let it go. Len's dead. You can't bring him back."

"No. I can only live with myself. He was my brother and I

couldn't help him when he was alive. Now he's dead. Murdered. I can't walk away from that."

"And I can't live with knowing I was responsible for your death!"

"I don't plan on dying."

"Do you think Len did?"

"Whatever happens is my choice, my responsibility. Not yours. Go up to the house."

"Go to bloody hell," she said between her teeth. "Christian might be able to explain away your dead body, but not mine."

Archer's mouth thinned into a bleak line. He had hoped to get Hannah out of here. He didn't want to give her another nightmare, another close-up look at the part of him that reminded her of Len. But the time for arguing was over. Flynn was walking down the path toward them with the easy, ground-devouring stride of a strong, very fit male.

He wasn't alone. Tom Nakamori came along about thirty feet behind, losing ground with every step.

"All right, mate," Flynn said, walking up to Archer. "What's so bloody important that—"

Archer took him down with two blows that were as ruthless as they were measured.

Hannah made a muffled sound of shock. There had been no warning. Between one heartbeat and the next, Flynn was on his back, gasping, trying to figure out what had happened to him. The prick of a pocketknife in the tanned skin just over his jugular told him. His eyes cleared and his body tensed.

"Show me how bright you are," Archer said. "Don't try it. If you do, I'll cut your jugular so that no one will be able to stop the bleeding. You know just how it's done, don't you?"

Flynn's expression said that he knew the technique. He lay in the dirt without moving. But he watched, waiting for an opening.

"You're too close to his feet, Hannah," Archer said calmly. "Step back."

Without a word she retreated. "Far enough?"

"Yes." He never looked away from Flynn. "How did you kill Len?"

"What?" Automatically Flynn tried to sit up. A stiff shot to his diaphragm changed his mind.

Archer waited until the other man could breathe again before he repeated the question. "How did you kill Len?"

"Bugger you," Flynn said hoarsely.

"That was your free one. The next wrong answer will hurt." Without looking up, Archer said, "Don't come any closer, Nakamori."

"*Hai.* Okay." Nakamori stopped and looked from Flynn to Archer to the drops of blood that had started welling out beneath the knife point when Flynn tried to sit up. "He not kill McGarry."

"Qing Lu Yin says he did."

"He's lying," Flynn said flatly. "When I saw Len, he was already as dead as Kelsey's nuts."

"Convince me," Archer said.

Flynn looked at the flat, metallic eyes of the man above him and wondered what it would take. "Once I got word of the storm coming, I didn't go near the sorting shed. I was too busy."

"Doing what?"

"Working on the rafts."

"Cutting them loose?"

Flynn's eyelids flickered. He knew what lying would get him. He didn't know what telling the truth would bring. "Yes. We were cutting cables."

Though Hannah's breath came in sharply, she didn't say a word. She simply watched Archer and wondered if a man could be so merciless and still feel anything at all. Much less love. Len couldn't. He hadn't even wanted to.

"Who was with you?" Archer asked calmly.

Flynn let out a long breath. The truth hadn't set him free, but it hadn't killed him, either. "Tom."

Hannah looked at Nakamori. He didn't meet her eyes.

"Why?" Archer asked Flynn.

"Why do you think? I paid him. He was getting more crippled every day. He wanted to go home in style."

"Nakamori," Archer said. "Is it true?"

"*Hai.*"

"Who is paying you?" Archer asked Flynn.

"None of your sodding busi—" The last syllable was a gasp of pain.

Hannah's fingernails dug into her palms, but she didn't protest. She was still trying to absorb the fact that two men she considered trustworthy had been systematically sabotaging Pearl Cove.

"Who is paying you?" Archer asked calmly.

Flynn simply watched him with pale, glittering eyes. He wasn't going to talk about his employer until there was more pain. A lot more.

"I'll assume it's your government," Archer said. "If I find out I'm wrong—and I will find out—we'll talk again."

Flynn remembered what Maxmillian Barton had said about wanting to get a handle on Archer Donovan. He wished him luck. "We won't be talking again."

Archer nodded. "Why did your employer want Pearl Cove destroyed?"

"I've been sabotaging it a piece at a time since we decided that Len was selling out to the Chinese. The storm was a bonus. We could put paid to the whole business at once."

"Len didn't sell any part of Pearl Cove to the Chinese or to anyone else," Hannah said. "He didn't trust anyone."

"Then the Chinese were taking over without his permission," Flynn said bluntly. "Nobody but Chinese have been hired here for the past three years. Except for Coco and Nakamori, the whole sodding crew is Chinese."

Archer spoke without looking away from Flynn. "Hannah?"

"It's true. Len said he didn't trust the Japanese divers any longer, and the Aussies he knew would rather go on the dole than work hard."

"So your employer decided if they couldn't have Pearl Cove for themselves, they would ruin it," Archer said to Flynn.

"Yes." Moving only his eyes, Flynn looked at Hannah. "I'll give you a better price than anyone else. All you have to do is tell us how Len produced the pearls that look like Lightning Ridge opals."

"I don't know," she said flatly. "I've never known."

"It wouldn't matter if she did," Archer said to Flynn. "Didn't you get the word? She doesn't own Pearl Cove anymore. She's off the table."

The tone of Archer's voice made Flynn swallow reflexively. "I heard. No harm in trying, mate. Sometimes you hear things wrong."

"Not this time."

"Right. Anything else?"

"Who killed Len McGarry?"

"If I knew, I'd give the bloke a medal. He kept Pearl Cove from going to the Chinese."

Archer's hand moved too quickly to follow. Flynn's left arm went numb from shoulder to fingernails. Before he could react, Archer was on his feet and out of reach.

"By the time your arm thaws out, you and Nakamori should be halfway to Broome," Archer said. "While you drive, cool off and think. I could have broken both arms more easily than numbing one. If I see you again, I won't pull any punches."

Flynn came to his feet with a speed that told Hannah nothing had been dented but his pride. The icy coils that gripped her stomach let go so quickly she felt almost dizzy. She didn't understand her relief. She simply knew it was as real as Archer's restraint. He could have maimed Flynn. Len certainly would have.

The Aussie gave Archer a long, narrow look. Then Flynn laughed. "Bugger me, but I think I like you."

Archer smiled faintly. "You won't mind if we don't shake on it."

"Right. Let's go, Tom. Or do you want to hang around and see if Coco's willing to play?"

Nakamori turned and started for the car. Whistling musically, Flynn followed. Archer watched them until their car was no more than a dark spot against the brick-red road.

The wind lifted, bringing with it the smell of rain, the kind of monsoon downpour that would turn the land into an impassable mudhole.

"Are you going after Yin?" Hannah asked.

He didn't answer.

"When do we leave?" she asked simply. "And where do we go?"

"If you're serious about working as a pearl matcher, pick a city. Any city. Donovan Gems and Minerals will put you to work there. If you don't like that idea, the Linskys would jump at the chance to hire you."

"I'll worry about the future after this is settled."

"As far as you're concerned, it's settled."

"No," she said instantly. When it was all settled, Archer would leave. She wasn't ready for that yet. What terrified her was that she didn't know if she would ever be. "There's still one person to question."

"For now, Yin is out of reach."

"Coco isn't."

Archer hesitated, then shrugged. "I'd just as soon you were on a plane when I talked to Coco."

"Why?"

"You won't like my methods."

Hannah's smile was as thin as a knife blade. "I can't see you taking her down the way you did Flynn."

"Fear and pain work, but with Coco I'll try money first."

When they stepped onto the verandah, Coco was sitting in the hammock chair. The tension around her mouth said that she knew she was next on Archer's list.

"You are ver' quick for a big man," she said to him. "Like Len. Sssssss. *Snake.*" She made a striking motion with her hand.

Deliberately Hannah stepped in front of Archer. "Christian and Tom were too busy cutting apart rafts to kill Len," she said coolly to Coco. "You were the last one to see him alive. He closed the shed door in your face, I believe."

"*Oui.* But he searched me first, most carefully." The words were in French. The smile needed no translation.

Archer said something in swift, precise French that wiped the smile right off her face. Then in English he added, "English only, unless you can't answer in that language. Then I'll translate."

Without turning away from Coco's beautiful, sensual features, Hannah spoke to Archer. "Is she strong enough to chisel her way into the shed?"

He looked at Coco, measuring the supple muscle beneath the soft skin, remembering the easy, lithe walk. "Yes."

"I no kill Len!" Coco said, her eyes bright with what might have been tears or simple fear.

"But you saw who did," Hannah said. It wasn't a question. It was a summation of all the times she had turned around from any task in the pearl sheds or in the house and found Coco watching, watching. Always watching. "Who was it?"

Coco laughed bitterly. "I tell and die like Len, trapped and alone."

"You'll die the same way if you don't tell," Hannah said. "The Red Phoenix Triad isn't famous for its compassion."

Coco paled beneath her golden skin. "You know?"

Hannah's smile showed teeth and no mercy. "I know. We met Yin in a triad hangout in Seattle."

"Stupid."

"It had its moments," Hannah agreed dryly. "Who killed Len, Coco?"

She shook her head.

"Ten thousand dollars American," Archer said. "Even if you did it yourself."

Coco laughed, but it was a sad, bitter sound. "I? I love Len."

Hannah's eyes widened.

"Is shock to you," Coco said. Her full mouth turned down at the corners. "He is . . . fascination. Cold like snake. Danger like cyclone. Pain. Hate. He is all."

Hannah could only stare. The very things that had driven her away from Len had lured Coco. "He should have married you."

Coco's shrug was as fluid as the sea. "Then he no more have you. A cat with a bird, to play, you understand? He take one pretty feather at a time."

"Yes," Hannah said in a low voice. "I understand. He used my sense of honor to keep me within his reach. I knew it and I stayed anyway. I owed him my life. I thought I could change his for the better. I was wrong." She felt the heat of Archer's hands on her shoulders and wanted to lean against him. "The day Len died, Coco. What did you see?"

"Qing Lu Yin," she said simply. "He want the secret of the pearls. He hurt Len—fists, club, you understand?"

"Yes," Archer said. "Go on."

"Len smile. Make Yin crazy. Careless. Len move fast." She made a striking motion with her hand again. "Try to cut throat of Yin with oyster shell. Len strong, ver' ver' strong, but Yin not cripple. He kick the wheelchair upside down and put knife in Len's ribs."

Hannah went still but didn't interrupt. She believed Coco. Only Archer had ever mentioned the knife.

"Yin hammer shell in same place, hide knife wound. You understand?" Coco asked.

"Yes," Hannah said.

"Len still live. He try to pull shell away. Too weak. Yin take all pearls he dare and run."

"Yin is good at running," Hannah said, remembering the Dragon Moon café.

"What did you do?" Archer asked when Hannah was silent.

"I go to cottage, wait for big wind."

"You know the pearls that Len called the Black Trinity?" Archer asked."

"*Oui.*"

"You know that Hannah would recognize them if they ever came on the market?"

"*Oui,*" Coco said. "He hate her for that. Her eyes, better than his. Better than mine."

"You know what would happen if the Black Trinity was ever traced back to you?" Archer asked.

She looked in his eyes and she knew. "*Oui,*" she whispered.

"Tell me what happened to the Black Trinity," Archer said, "and I won't ask how Angelique Dupres's Tahitian pearl farm ended up with a fortune in Pearl Cove's new crop of pearls. The same pearls that went missing when Len died."

Hannah stiffened and tried to turn toward Archer. His hands tightened, holding her as she was.

"You didn't tell me," she said.

"I hoped I wouldn't have to."

"Why?"

"No one likes being betrayed by the people around them." His hands became subtly caressing. "You've had enough pain. I didn't want to be the one to bring you more. But that seems to be what I'm best at. Bringing you pain." He lifted his hands and pinned Coco with a cold look.

She spread her hands in an unconscious gesture of pleading. "I no see Black Trinity when Len die. I no see after. Pearls, they everywhere, you understand? Like—like sea-foam after storm. Yin take many. I take rest and send to sister to sell. Better Coco than the storm, yes?"

"Have you stolen enough from Hannah for your retirement yet?" Archer asked.

Coco simply smiled. "I work hard, monsieur. Ver' hard. Ask any man."

"Yeah, I'm sure you do. Say hello to Ian for us."

Surprise showed for an instant on Coco's face, then nothing showed at all.

"That's what I thought," Archer said.

"Good-bye, Coco." Hannah's voice was distant. "You'll understand if I don't give you severance pay."

"Oh, she'll get paid," Archer drawled. "But it will be Chang money, not ours."

With a lithe motion Coco came to her feet. "*Bonne chance* with your new cat, small bird."

His hands flexed at his sides. *A cat with a bird, to play, you understand? He take one pretty feather at a time.* Archer understood too well. He knew that every time Hannah looked at him, she saw Len. She saw the cruelties of the past rather than the possibilities of the present. Archer couldn't change that. He could only end the pain by getting out of her sight.

"I'll help you finish packing," he said neutrally.

Hannah watched him leave and wondered why it felt like he had said good-bye.

Standing on a street corner in Rio. No money. No hope. Nothing but night coming down on her like thunder.

And this time Archer was walking away from her.

Twenty-eight

There weren't many cartons stacked by the front door, because there wasn't much Hannah wanted to take except for clothes, a few household goods, and her wood-carving tools. Hannah was stuffing clothes, towels, and dive gear into a battered duffel bag. Her hands were clumsy, an accurate reflection of the turmoil in her mind. She didn't want Archer to leave.

And she knew he was going to.

You've had enough pain. I didn't want to be the one to bring you more. But that seems to be what I'm best at. Bringing you pain.

She closed her eyes and fought against the fear that was beating against her with black wings. She didn't know what mistake she had made. She only knew she had made one. A terrible one, every bit as bad as trusting her life to Len McGarry had been.

"I wish I had some bubble wrap for this," Archer said.

She turned away from the swim mask and fins she was blindly trying to cram into a space that was too small by half. He was standing across the room, holding the wood sculpture that was the only thing she had ever carved that she couldn't

363

bring herself to destroy. Too much of her was in that sculpture, the woman trapped in the very wave that would free her, but only if she survived the wild, dangerous ride.

Suddenly Hannah's hands itched to create the new form condensing in her mind, a woman who *was* the wave, driving force and consummation in one. No beginning. No ending. Just the timeless, infinite surge of life.

"Wrap it in this," Hannah said, throwing Archer one of the towels stacked within reach. "There's room in the duffel if I leave out some dive gear."

"Pack the dive gear. I'll carry this myself." As he spoke, Archer ran his fingertips over the haunting curves that suggested but never showed the woman within the wood.

Heat shimmered over Hannah as though she had been stroked.

Knowing he shouldn't, knowing he was going to anyway, Archer spoke without looking away from the sculpture. "Would you sell this to me?"

"No. I'll give it to you. It's the least I can do after all you've done for me."

"All I've done is remind you of the worst days of your life."

She was too shocked to do more than stare at him. "That's not true!"

"Not comfortable, maybe, but it sure as hell is true. You look at me and you see the past. Len. The miracle is that you didn't let Ling blow my head off."

The bitter acceptance beneath Archer's level voice made Hannah flinch. "In the beginning, yes, I saw Len every time I—"

"Quiet," he said across her words.

"No, let me fin—"

"*Quiet.*"

Belatedly, the change in him got through her. No bitterness now, no acceptance, simply the cool deadliness of a man trained to kill. He set aside the sculpture and turned toward the verandah door with a predator's focused grace.

Out front a car door slammed.

"Visitor coming," he said.

"Who?"

"No one I recognize. Come here, but stand to the side of the window."

Hannah went and stood close to Archer. Through the silvery porch screen she saw a balding man of middle years, medium height, and utter self-confidence walking up the front path. He wore tropical-weight slacks and shirt and carried a manila envelope in one hand. She had never seen him before in her life.

"Do you know him?" Archer asked.

"No."

The man knocked on the outer door.

"What do you want?" Archer called out.

"Message for Archer Donovan."

One of Archer's black eyebrows rose skeptically. The man didn't look like a messenger boy. "What's the return address?"

"April Joy."

He muttered something savage under his breath. Then, softly, he said to Hannah, "Stay here."

"Is the man dangerous?"

"Not to you. You're off the table."

"What about you?"

Without answering, Archer opened the door. He would have shut it behind him again, but Hannah's foot was in the way. Then all of her was. He allowed it only because it was too dangerous to divide his attention. He opened the outer door and gestured the man onto the porch.

"Ms. McGarry, I'm Max," Barton said, looking past Archer. "My condolences on your husband's death."

"Is that the message?" Hannah asked.

"My message is for Archer Donovan."

"You're looking at him," Hannah said, jerking her thumb toward Archer.

"The message is private."

"So am I," she said bitingly.

Barton looked at Archer, who was watching him with pale eyes that gave away nothing. Barton smiled coldly. "Has your number, does she, mate?"

"Yeah. I'm putty in Hannah's hands," Archer said. "She's solid brick in mine. What does April want now?"

"She wants you off the table. All the way off."

"Good idea," Hannah said instantly.

Archer and Barton ignored her.

"There's a problem with that," Archer said. Each word was clear, distinct. "April knows what it is."

The other man grunted. "I'm supposed to clear up that problem."

"I'm listening."

This time Barton's smile was genuine, if small. "I can see that. You sure you don't want back in the real game?"

"Dead sure."

"That's what she said you would say," Barton muttered.

Eyes narrowed, Hannah looked from one man to the other. She didn't like the direction of the conversation. The thought of Archer going back to the covert life made her stomach twist. Len had loved it, but Archer said he hadn't been strong enough to stay in the game. She hadn't believed him at the time. Now, suddenly, she did. Archer simply wasn't cold enough to play international chess with human pawns.

The memory of Summer teething blissfully on Archer's knuckles went through Hannah like lightning through darkness. Len would never have allowed anything that close to him, even his own child. Yet Archer had smiled at his niece with a tenderness that still amazed Hannah. But it hadn't amazed his family. They took his love for granted. And that was what it was. Love.

"Don't want to play again, huh?" Barton asked. "Not even to get your brother's killer?"

"I don't need April to get Len's killer," Archer said in a level voice. "All I need is time. I've got it."

"Right. Well, mate, I'm going to make your hunt easier."

Hannah's hand went over Archer's wrist as though to keep him from moving one inch toward Barton. Her nails dug in hard. She didn't want him hunting anything, especially a man dangerous enough to kill Len McGarry.

Archer ignored the pressure of Hannah's nails on his wrist. He was focused on Barton's shrewd, dark eyes.

"You're probably thinking that Sam Chang ordered McGarry's death," Barton said to Archer.

He didn't deny it.

"Sam's spies eventually figured out that Pearl Cove was being sabotaged by the Aussies," Barton continued. "The old bastard was beside himself. He had placed men everywhere but where he needed one most—in Len's confidence."

"I figured that out for myself."

"Did you figure that Chang offered a million dollars to the person who brought him the secret of the rainbows?" Barton retorted. "Qing Lu Yin decided he would be the one. The cyclone was his chance. He got Len alone and started questioning him." Barton shrugged. "Yin fucked up big time. McGarry died and took the secret of the rainbow pearls with him."

Hannah closed her eyes and saw again Len's body half beached, half floating, wholly dead.

"How did you find out?" Archer asked.

"Yin. Not directly," he added quickly, sensing the change in Archer. "The word was passed back up the line."

"By the Red Phoenix boys?"

The civilized voice didn't fool Barton. What he was seeing in Archer's eyes wasn't a bit civilized. "Right."

"Why should I believe them?"

Barton handed over the unsealed manila envelope. "They send you their apology on the death of your brother. They want you to understand it wasn't a triad matter."

Without looking away from Barton, Archer took the envelope and opened it. The cool, smooth surface of a glossy photograph met his fingertips. He pulled it out.

When Hannah gasped, he glanced down quickly. One look was enough. The color photo was Qing Lu Yin, right down to the black eye and oyster-shell gash on his chin. No possibility of a mistake, even though blood was everywhere and his severed head was tucked underneath his arm in the Red Phoenix Triad's trademark execution style.

Archer pushed the brutal photo back into the envelope. "Apology accepted."

The ruined shed sent thin, misshapen black fingers raking up into the late afternoon. Light the color of hammered bronze filled the air from the sea to the distant arch of the cloud-whipped sky. Wind swirled with just enough force to tug at the cloth of Archer's tank top and press his shorts against his body. The air was the temperature of blood, neither hot nor cool.

When he heard sound behind him, he didn't turn around. He knew it was Hannah. Everyone else was gone. He had made certain of it personally, searching every cottage, every shed, everywhere that was big enough to hide a human being. There was nothing but empty rooms, empty drawers, and bits of domestic debris that were already being blown away by the wind.

"Everything I'm taking is packed," she said quietly.

He nodded but made no move to leave. He wasn't ready to walk away from her. He never would be. But he would walk away just the same.

Soon.

Silently Hannah stared at the jackstraw ruins of the shed. Only the vault stood upright, and it gaped crookedly. There was nothing new for her here. Nothing old, either. Nothing that she wanted to take with her. Yet, like Archer, she found she couldn't simply turn away and leave. Hands on her hips, she looked at what had once been the center of her life and the soul of her husband's. She tried to find meaning in wreckage.

There wasn't any. It was simply a pearl shed that had been destroyed by a storm.

So she watched Archer instead, hunger in her eyes and a tension in her body that made it hard for her to breathe. He had walked away from her before. He would walk away again. She would be free of the past, of Pearl Cove, and of Archer, who reminded her of Len. She would be free of everything except the certainty that she had made another terrible mistake.

What's it like to love someone enough to die in his place?

Chills rippled over Hannah's skin in primal recognition of the truth. Like two pearls of the same size and color, Len and Archer were similar. And very, very different. The layers of Len's life that had accumulated in such pain and fury were uneven, pitted, flawed. The layers of Archer's life were different. Not perfect. Just . . . beautiful.

And she had hurt him as cruelly as Len ever hurt anyone. *You're like Len! Damn you, you're like Len! As cold a bastard as ever walked the earth.*

No wonder Archer wanted to get away from her. In surviving Len, she had become just as savage as he was.

Bile rose in Hannah's throat. Too late she understood the meaning of her dreams—Archer's pain and her screams of denial that he could be hurt. Because if he could hurt, he could love. If he loved, she had used his vulnerability like a weapon against him. The same way Len had used her own vulnerability against her, a cat with a bird.

Protection and sex. That's all?

Yes.

She had gotten her wish. Archer no longer threatened her with love. With vulnerability. Yet she was standing here, figuring it all out too late, vulnerable to her soul.

"Could Len get on any of the pearl boats by himself?" Archer asked, walking slowly toward the vault.

Swallowing past the constriction in her throat, Hannah forced herself to talk to the man who might have loved her, the man she had been too much a coward to love in return. "No. He had to be carried aboard."

"Could he dive alone?"

"He needed a mechanical lift to get in and out of the water. He couldn't reach the controls while he was on the lift."

Archer nodded and never looked away from the side of the vault. The thick outer door hung on its hinges like a broken jaw. The smaller locker doors inside were open, as though to prove that nothing of value lay beyond. "What about the car?"

"He couldn't handle it alone. Certainly not in the last two years. He was losing strength. It was slow, very slow, but it was real."

In the slanting light, Archer's eyes were almost gold. He measured the vault that had once held a king's ransom in pearls and the key to a man's dark soul. "Where would Len have hidden the Black Trinity?"

She shrugged. "Somewhere in this shed."

Silently he looked at the ruins.

"It's gone, Archer. Accept it. I have."

"If it had been anyone else but Len, I would," he replied evenly. "But Len always had one more layer than anybody expected, one more move, one more trick."

All of the lockers that were beyond the reach of a long-armed, seated man were closed. Even standing, the highest rank of lockers rose almost four feet above Archer's head. The slanting sunlight picked out every nick and scratch with unnatural clarity. Several lockers in particular showed scratches. All of them were on the right-hand side of the vault.

The image of Len's ugly, wicked ring flashed in Archer's mind. Maybe Len had used it for more than slicing up a man's face in a fight.

"You've opened all the drawers," he said.

Fighting for breath, Hannah forced herself to think of the present, not the corrosive past. She couldn't afford to make another mistake like Len. She simply wouldn't survive it. She knew it as certainly as she knew that it hurt too much to breathe right now. "Everything that was beyond Len's reach, I opened."

Remembering Len, Archer wondered just how much had truly been beyond his half brother's grasp. "The handles are too big for the lockers."

"Len's design, not mine."

"What about the locksmith? That many combination locks must have needed maintenance, especially in the tropics."

"Len did it."

"How did he reach the top locks?"

"He didn't. I did."

Archer turned toward Hannah. "How?"

"On a ladder."

"No, how did you open the locks?"

"He only had me work on one," Hannah said, pointing toward the vault. "The center one." Even as Archer spun toward it, she added, "But I already checked that locker. The Black Trinity wasn't in any of the trays."

Ignoring the closed lockers, he grabbed one of the lower trays at random and pulled it all the way out. The tray was almost as long as his arm. He measured the tray against the depth of the vault, then mentally added on the thickness of the open doors.

"Too short," he muttered. "But not by much." He pushed

the tray back in place and measured other drawers that were waist level or lower. They were all the same size.

Two inches too short.

He grabbed a flashlight and shined it into the hole where a tray had been. Nothing showed but the thick steel sheathing the vault. He pulled out more trays, put his arm between the multiple rails, and felt around. There was no hint of a hidden seam, a hinge, a panel, a button, a lever, anything that might open a compartment that held more pearls. No matter which rank of trays he tried, he didn't find anything but blood-temperature steel.

No sign of wires, either, which was a relief. Not that he had expected Len to risk a booby trap so close to his delicate Black Trinity. Len had hated explosives. He had learned the hard way that even C-4 degraded and became unreliable in the tropics.

One by one, Archer replaced trays and closed the locker doors. When everything but the outer door was sealed up, he simply stood and looked at the rank of lockers.

"What?" Hannah asked. The intensity in Archer was almost tangible.

"The vault has a false back."

"How do you know?"

"The drawers are about two inches too short for the depth of the vault, even when you figure in the shielding."

Silently she watched while he went over the exterior of the vault and then the interior locker doors with his fingertips.

"You're looking too high," she said finally. "Len couldn't get to the top two ranks of lockers."

"That's what he wanted everyone to believe."

"How would he get up there to unlock everything?"

Instead of answering, Archer reached into his pocket, took out his key chain, and removed Len's heavy ring. Ignoring Hannah's hoarse sound of surprise, he put the ring on his right index finger, where Len had worn it. Then he crouched down until he was about the height of a man in a wheelchair. Reaching above his head with his right hand, he grabbed a handle and did a one-armed chin-up. The locker handle creaked but held. He moved on to the next handle.

She simply stared at the naked strength of him as he

chinned himself again. "Do you really think Len could do that?"

"Easier than me," Archer said through his teeth. "He wasn't hauling as much weight—in his lower body. He would have smiled—every inch of the way at how—he was fooling the world."

Breathing hard with the effort, Archer grabbed another handle and kept on pulling himself up.

"But the top center locker was empty when I looked," she objected.

He didn't waste breath replying. Sweat gathered and ran down his spine as he dragged himself up the face of the vault until his eyes were level with the top rank of lockers. On the way up, he noted the marks on several of the lockers along the right side. He found out how the gouges were made when his right hand slipped and raked over the vault. Steel screeched over steel, leaving new marks.

"What's the—combination?" he asked.

"Ummm." Hannah gathered her wits. The sight of Archer pulling himself up the vault hand over hand was as unnerving as the sight of a dead man's ring on his hand. "Eight right, twenty left, thirty right, one left."

He started to work, lost his grip, swore, and went back to it.

"Brace yourself on your feet," she said.

"He—didn't."

The instant the last tumbler clicked, Archer let himself down the same way Len would have, hand over hand, fast, breathing hard. When he had his feet under him again, he looked at the wall of closed lockers and rubbed his shoulders until his breathing leveled.

"Right," he said after a minute. "By the time Len opened that locker, he wouldn't have been feeling up to much more in the way of monkey tricks." Sweaty hands closed around a handle that would have been within easy reach of Len. Then Archer stopped cold. "No good. I was pulling handles all the way down and nothing opened. *Shit.*"

"One at a time," Hannah said.

"What?"

"You were only pulling on one handle at a time. Try two."

Archer looked over his shoulder and gave her a smile. "Right. Now, let's pray that Len really wasn't feeling tricky when it came to this point. There's an infinite number of ways he could have mixed and matched open doors to make another combination."

"He wasn't really left- or right-handed. Not after the accident. He trained himself to do everything with both hands."

Archer knew that Len had trained himself to be lethally capable with hands, feet, and head long before he had met Hannah. But there was no need to remind her of that unhappy past. It would soon be gone. All the way gone. And Archer would be gone with it.

"Step back out of the shed," he said.

"But—"

"He could have booby-trapped this," Archer cut in, overriding her objections.

"Then you walk off and I'll open it."

He gave her a disbelieving look.

She gave it right back.

"All or nothing," he muttered.

He bent over and pulled two waist-level handles that would have been convenient to Len.

The lockers opened, revealing rows of trays. Empty trays. But Archer already knew about them. Breath held, he stood and listened, listened, listened for the sound of a hidden mechanism releasing. He wasn't worried about a booby trap anymore. If there had been one, he wouldn't have had to wait and listen. It would already have happened.

Silence.

He let out a soft, rushing curse and reached for two more waist-high locker doors. Before his fingers closed around them, he heard a faint sound. Then another.

Click. Click.

"Archer," Hannah said urgently.

"Yes."

Click.

Scraaaaaape.

Intently he watched the vault. But it was Hannah who spotted the faint line where a panel was trying to open. She jumped forward, stuck her fingers in the gap, and pried. Nothing budged.

"Here," Archer said, handing her a slender metal bar.

She jammed the bar into the opening and pulled back sharply. More metal scraped on metal. Shifting her grip, she yanked again.

A waist-high panel swung open, revealing several long, narrow drawers. There were no locks, no combinations, no handles, nothing but a perforated disk to indicate how the drawers might be opened.

Hannah looked at Archer. "Now what?"

"This, I hope."

After a few tries he fitted Len's odd ring to the disk on the middle drawer. The fit was tight enough to make a kind of handle. Gently he pulled back. A shallow drawer opened. Inside, resting on edge, was a long, flat jeweler's case.

Hannah made an odd sound. "Is it . . . ?"

"Go ahead. Find out."

With fingers that trembled, Hannah lifted out the box. Very carefully she pried up the lid. Archer watched her face rather than the box itself. Her look of relief, excitement, and wonder told him everything he needed to know. Wordlessly she turned and handed him the Black Trinity.

Silently he examined the gleaming, unearthly beauty of the unstrung necklace lying within the box's deep channels. He had expected the color match to be as good as humanly possible. He hadn't expected to be overwhelmed by the sheer beauty of the triple strands. It took his breath away.

Storm and rainbows. Excitement and serenity. Radiant midnight and suspended dawns. Secret dreams and impossible miracles. The Black Trinity had them all.

"No wonder Len expected this to heal him," Archer said in a low voice.

"If beauty could heal, he would have been whole," Hannah agreed.

"No." He closed the box and held it out to her. "He had beauty. It didn't heal him."

"What do you mean?"

"You, Hannah. He had you." Again Archer put the box in

her hands. Again she wouldn't take it. "This is the best of Pearl Cove. Of Len," he said. "Take it and leave the rest behind."

Hannah looked at Archer's eyes and saw all that he hadn't said. She put her hands behind her back, refusing the Black Trinity.

"Take it," he said. "It's yours."

"Half of it is yours."

"No. You earned this necklace in ways I can't even bear to think about. *Take it.*"

"Not if it means giving up you. That's what you're saying between the lines, isn't it? I get the Black Trinity and you get out of my life."

"You can't look at me without seeing Len. I won't do that to you, Hannah. I won't do it to myself. I can't bear seeing you flinch every time I do something that brings back the past. Take the necklace and build a new life. It's the least I can give you after leaving you to the mercy of a man who had none."

The weariness and acceptance in Archer's voice made Hannah's throat ache around a protest she didn't know how to speak. She hadn't meant to hurt him. She hadn't even believed that it was possible. Yet she had hurt him. She still was hurting him.

"I'll take the necklace on one condition," she said finally, her voice strained to breaking.

"What?"

"That it goes to our firstborn."

He went utterly still. "You're pregnant?"

"I don't know. I could be. I want to be. With your child. Only with yours. I want it all, Archer. The Black Trinity. The baby. You. You most of all."

He wanted to hold her so much it was like dying not to. But he had to be sure. He barely had the strength to walk away from her now. In a few days, it would be impossible. "Why?" he asked starkly. "I remind you of Len."

"Not anymore. That was fear and—and cowardice. I was so afraid to trust again, to—to—" Her voice fragmented.

Gently he cupped her chin with one hand and asked, "Is it so hard to say? Or is it that you can't love me after all?"

Tears spilled down her cheeks. "Hold me. I want you and I'm so ruddy *scared*."

Archer's eyes closed. He couldn't look at her and not take what she was offering. But what she was offering wasn't love. "You're afraid of me."

"I'm afraid of *losing* you. Every time I think about it, I'm back in Rio and night is coming down and—and I'm holding you to your promise. Protection and sex. And babies."

He looked into her eyes. Then he gathered her close, feeling her fit herself to him without hesitation. Her arms came around his waist and held on hard.

"Protection and sex, huh?" he said against her forehead. He wanted more.

He would take whatever she gave.

"And babies," she added.

"And babies. Does that cover it?"

"Um. Not quite."

He waited.

"Love," she whispered. "I want that most of all."

"What do I get in return?"

"Protection, sex, and babies."

He waited, hoping.

She fought against admitting her vulnerability. The hope in his beautiful eyes defeated her.

"Love," she said. "I love you."

His eyes closed for an instant. "Then it's a good deal all around. I've loved you for ten years. You're going to marry me, Hannah. Like you, I want it all."

She snuggled closer to him.

"Hannah? Will you marry me?"

She kissed the skin just above his tank top. Hair tickled her lips. She smiled and kissed him again. "Yes."

"Where do you want to honeymoon?"

"Here. Now."

He laughed softly against her hair. "Here it is."

It was now, too.